continued . . .

Also by Lisa Jackson

Sorceress
Temptress
Impostress

Dark
Emerald

Lisa Jackson

A SIGNET BOOK

SIGNET
Published by New American Library, a division of
Penguin Group (USA) Inc., 375 Hudson Street,
New York, New York 10014, USA
Penguin Group (Canada), 90 Eglinton Avenue East, Suite 700, Toronto,
Ontario M4P 2Y3, Canada (a division of Pearson Penguin Canada Inc.)
Penguin Books Ltd., 80 Strand, London WC2R 0RL, England
Penguin Ireland, 25 St. Stephen's Green, Dublin 2,
Ireland (a division of Penguin Books Ltd.)
Penguin Group (Australia), 250 Camberwell Road, Camberwell, Victoria 3124,
Australia (a division of Pearson Australia Group Pty. Ltd.)
Penguin Books India Pvt. Ltd., 11 Community Centre, Panchsheel Park,
New Delhi - 110 017, India
Penguin Group (NZ), 67 Apollo Drive, Rosedale, Auckland 0632,
New Zealand (a division of Pearson New Zealand Ltd.)
Penguin Books (South Africa) (Pty.) Ltd., 24 Sturdee Avenue,
Rosebank, Johannesburg 2196, South Africa

Penguin Books Ltd., Registered Offices:
80 Strand, London WC2R 0RL, England

Published by Signet, an imprint of New American Library, a division of Penguin
Group (USA) Inc. Previously published in a Topaz edition.

First Signet Printing, May 2004
10 9 8 7

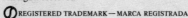
PUBLISHER'S NOTE
This is a work of fiction. Names, characters, places, and incidents either are the
product of the author's imagination or are used fictitiously, and any resemblance
to actual persons, living or dead, business establishments, events, or locales is
entirely coincidental.

The publisher does not have any control over and does not assume any responsibility for author or third-party Web sites or their content.

This book is dedicated with love to my parents, Jack and Betty Pederson, who gave me an enchanted childhood and who, through their own actions, taught me the value of family, loyalty, and laughter. They never doubted that I could do whatever I set out to do and gave me the tools and courage to try. Thanks a lot, Mom and Dad. You're the best!!!

ACKNOWLEDGMENTS

Thanks to all the people who helped me with this book. I couldn't have done it without you. Really. Special thanks to Ann Baumann, Nancy Bush, Sarah Dickey, Cecilia Oh, Tess O'Shaughnessy, Dave Painter, Sally Peters, Robin Rue, and John Scognamiglio.

Prologue

Wales
Gaeaf Forest
Winter 1271

Lodema's skin prickled, though she warmed herself by the fire. Something was wrong. She felt it in her bones and sensed it in the frigid winter air.

Cold as a demon's breath, the wind whistled through the worn thatches of her small hut, and the premonition that there was death in the forest clung to her as hungrily as leeches to a naked man. 'Twas a feeling she couldn't ignore, a sensation that time and time again had proved to be a warning of worse times yet to come.

Using the charred wooden spoon, she stirred the mutton stew that bubbled in a blackened pot suspended over glowing coals. Her young cat, a mottled creature with glassy eyes, was perched on the shelf where she kept her herbs, candles, and lengths of cord. "Ye feel it, too, don't ye, Luna? There be trouble and it's comin' our way."

Luna lifted a paw and, using her long tongue, washed her face.

Somewhere not too distant a baby cried. Soft. Muffled.

Lodema stiffened.

The cat froze.

Nay. Couldn't be. No babe would be out on as dark and cold a night as this.

Yet she heard it again. A pitiful, lonely wail.

"By the saints."

Lodema dropped the spoon. There was no babe. Couldn't be. Not this far into the forest in the dead of the coldest winter in years. 'Twas her tired mind playing tricks on her again. Had to be.

Again the muted cry, barely heard over the rush of · wind that swept through the timbers. Ears straining, she heard the plop of horse's hooves and the creak of cart wheels.

For the love of Cerridwen, who would be out in the middle of the night?

Spine arched, fur ruffled, Luna hissed, as if whoever it was outside was pure evil. Like a blaze of lightning, she leaped to the floor and streaked to her hiding spot in the shadows of the firewood stacked near the grate. Footsteps crunched in the snow outside the door.

"Lord, be merciful," Lodema whispered under her breath, but she had more faith in the tiny knife tucked deep in her pocket than in the Christian God's protection. She braced herself. Only fools and devils walked about in the middle of the night.

Bam! Bam! Bam! A fist pounded her door. Fingering the knife with one hand, she cinched the neckline of her wool tunic more tightly around her throat.

"Lodema!" A male voice boomed, and memories, not quite formed, tugged at the edges of her brain. " 'Tis I. Simon."

"Simon?" she whispered, disbelieving. Could it be— after so many years? Her throat tightened and her scarred heart galumphed in her chest as she threw the bolt and tugged the heavy door open. A gust of icy wind raced through her and into the cabin, causing the fire to glow more brightly.

And there he was.

Tall as ever. Pride stiffening his spine.

A priest for too many years to count, Simon wore fine robes and a harsh expression on a face that, Lodema suspected, smiled rarely. In one arm he carried a fancy basket covered in blankets. "Simon—?" How long had it been? A decade? Two? The wind tore through the woods, rattling the dry, naked branches and snatching at Lodema's brown curls. "Mother of God, what brings ye out this night?" Memories of a much younger man and stolen minutes of passion the like of which she'd never since known flitted seductively through her mind.

" 'Tis best if you ask no questions." His gaze touched hers for the briefest of moments, and she noticed that guilt still lingered in his eyes.

"I—I never do."

"Aye, that is why I came to you."

"Is it now?" she taunted, and his lips clamped together. She studied the man she'd adored in her youth, a man who had professed to love God more than a lowly peasant girl, a man who had seduced her and lain with her time and time again, only to leave her for his work in the church. Even now, it made her ache for the naive child she'd been.

"None of your tongue, woman. 'Tis a blessing I bring to you." He held the basket a little higher, and again she heard the pitiful, soulful wail.

"A babe?" Her throat went dry.

"Aye."

"Come in, come in, 'tis freezing." She stepped out of the doorway and for the first time saw Simon's wagon, little more than a cart pulled by a fine brown mare and driven by a lad who could not have been more than eight. The boy huddled against the night, his fingers poking out from tattered gloves, his head covered by the hood of his cloak, his face averted. "Bring the boy in for—"

"Nay. There is no time." Simon breezed past her, and she noticed the spatters of blood on his wool mantle, the worry etching his brow, the sense of haunted desperation in his eyes. A thin man, taller than most, with graying hair that touched his shoulders, he went quickly about his business. He set his basket on the single scarred table and folded back the lamb's-wool blanket. From beneath the soft covers a newborn baby with dark hair and a red face blinked against the sudden rush of light. Tiny fists curled and flailed by her head.

"Whose child is this?" Lodema asked.

"She is yours now."

Lodema's heart nearly stopped. She sucked in a whistling breath and didn't for a second believe him. *A child? For her?* Oh, by the saints, how she would love to have a newborn. But she didn't dare. From the corner of her eye she saw Luna, huddled behind the woodpile, feline eyes staring unblinkingly at Simon as if he were the embodiment of hell. "Surely the babe has a mother . . . or a father."

"None that can care for her."

Somewhere intricately entwined within his words there was a lie.

"There are many who would want a child." Lodema was cautious, for she smelled a trap—but oh, such a lovely trap. "Those who are more deserving of a child."

"Mayhap, but I offer her to you, Lodema."

"In exchange for what?"

"Silence."

She looked down on the child blinking up at her. Dark black curls topped the infant's head, sooty eyelashes curved over rosy cheeks, and tiny lips moved gently, as if she wished to suckle. The ice around Lodema's barren heart cracked and began to melt. "Ye and I, Simon, have not always seen eye to eye."

He glanced at her, then looked away, as if he, too, remembered the lost innocence of their youth.

" 'Tis true, but I forgive you," he said, warming his hands by the fire.

" 'Tis too kind ye be," she said sarcastically, stiffening, unable to soften the bite to her words.

"That is why I came to you, Lodema. There are those who would have had you hanged for a witch long ago were it not for my words on your behalf. 'Tis well known that you practice the dark arts."

"Nay—"

"Hush, woman," he snapped, turning swiftly, his eyes suddenly harsh as the winter wind that raced through the brittle branches of the trees and moaned in the chimney. "I have stilled their voices by reminding them that you have helped with the birthing of many a child and seen to the sick when physicians, apothecaries, and prayers seemed to fail." He cleared his throat. "I have not agreed with your ways, but you have a true soul, Lodema. I know this, though ofttimes it seems you be misguided."

She didn't answer. Oh, how she wanted this child. But the baby came with trouble; she could feel it deep in the marrow of her bones.

"I am offering you a chance to be a mother, a true woman. All I ask is that you raise her as a Christian, that you show her not the dark arts—that she learns not to chant spells, call the wind, speak to the beasts, or see into the future. You must agree to tell no one that she is not of your womb. You are a recluse and still young enough to have borne a child. No one sees you for weeks or months at a time. 'Twould raise nary an eyebrow if you were to appear next spring with a child and no husband. Oh, a few tongues would wag, of course, but 'tis of no consequence. You have never concerned yourself with what others say."

The baby gave off a quiet whimper.

"She is hungry," Lodema said.

"Aye." The priest's gaze held hers. " 'Tis up to you now." Slowly he took off his glove, exposing long, soft fingers—fingers that had once, oh, so many years ago, caressed her, working a wanton magic that even now at the memories caused her blood to heat and stirred a long-forgotten yearning deep in her center.

"I know I can trust you, Lodema," he said quietly, and his voice was like a feather against her skin. Just as it had always been.

"Aye, Simon, that ye can."

With his gloved hand he removed a ring, a gold band with a dark jewel that winked forest green in the firelight. "This will be yours. As payment."

"I need not—"

"Of course you do." The hard edges of his face eased a bit, and he looked like the lad she'd known in her youth, the boy she'd loved with all of her foolish heart. He set the ring on the table near the basket, then delved deep into the pockets of his mantle. Retrieving a small leather pouch, he withdrew a few coins and placed them near the ring.

The baby began to cry and Father Simon sighed heavily. His haughty demeanor evaporated, and for a second Lodema thought he would put his arms around her and kiss her as he had when they were young. Instead he slowly replaced his glove, working his fingers into the soft doeskin.

"Simon," she said, addressing him as she had so many years before, "who does this girl belong to?"

"You will know in time, and then you will understand why you must keep her identity to yourself. 'Tis for your safety and hers." His eyes were suddenly weary. "Please, Lodema, give me your word."

"You have it," she said without thinking, and he smiled, the lines of worry vanishing from his brow.

"Who else knows of this?"

"No one."

"You brought a driver with you."

Simon stroked one eyebrow thoughtfully. "He is but a lad and is paid to keep what he has seen to himself."

"Then he knows?"

"Only that I am delivering an orphan to a woman who would be her mother." He thought for a moment. "Worry not of him, Lodema."

"What is his name?"

Simon sighed. " 'Tis Henry. He is but a stableboy. He works for me because he was caught stealing and I offered him a chance to redeem himself by working for me rather than see him cast into the dungeon and lose his soul." Simon pulled his cowl over his head. "He will not betray me, Lodema."

"Nor will I," she said.

"I know." Gently he touched the side of her face with one gloved finger, and she, whom so many called tough as dried meat, felt the urge to weep for a love that had died so long ago.

"I knew I could trust you," he whispered.

Oh, Morrigu, save me.

"Always." Her throat clogged.

His eyes grew sad.

"Simon—"

"Say not a word, sweet Lodema." Then, as if he'd revealed far too much, he turned so swiftly his mantle billowed. He strode to the door, made a quick sign of the cross over his chest at the threshold, and disappeared into the night. The door closed behind him with a bone-jarring thud.

Rooted to the spot where she'd stood when he touched her, Lodema heard the sharp crack of a whip and the creak of wheels as the wagon rolled away.

The baby gave out a lusty wail.

Lodema snapped back to the here and now. "Shh. All will be well, little one," she murmured, hurriedly picking up the warm bundle and wishing she could believe her words. The baby needed a mother, aye, and, oh, by the gods, how Lodema needed a little one, but somehow this seemed wrong. So wrong. Rocking softly, she held the child close and kissed her downy curls.

From the corner of her eye she caught sight of the emerald ring, its stone dark and cold as it lay on the table. Firelight played on the many facets, but the emerald's reflection held no spark.

Pocketing the jewel, she stared down at the infant's perfect little face. "This will be yours, child, and from now on, you shall be known as Tara, daughter of Lodema. I will raise you as my own." Aye, as a Christian, but one who will know of the old gods as well, a girl who would love air, water, and fire as well as Father, Son, and Holy Ghost.

She brushed her lips across the baby's soft forehead and only hoped she hadn't cursed them both.

Chapter One

Wales
Gaeaf Forest
Winter 1290

"The devil take you, Abelard!"

Upon a horse he'd stolen not two days earlier, Rhys, known as the Bastard Outlaw, glared up at the ominous sky. His mood was as black as the clouds scudding across the heavens, his skin cold from the slap of the wind. Even the fine gray stallion mincing nervously beneath him gave him no satisfaction on this somber afternoon. Though the forest was usually a place of solace, it seemed malevolent today. The wind creeping through the woodland made him anxious. Mist rose from the earth, bare-branched trees lifted their scrawny, naked arms to the unforgiving sky, and the constant drip of moisture was unsettling.

Rhys yanked on the reins and swept his uncompromising gaze in a wide arc.

By the gods, where was Abelard?

The high-strung steed was edgy, and Rhys's own nerves stretched taut as bowstrings.

Abelard, the cur, had promised to meet him here in this narrow canyon between outcroppings of mossy rock, guarded by leafless oak trees. Yet he'd not appeared. Gryffyn pulled at the bit, shaking his great head, black mane damp, bridle jingling. "Son of a dog." Rhys squinted through the fog, surveying every inch of this rocky canyon.

Curse Abelard's sorry hide. 'Twas he who had chosen this spot for their rendezvous. He who had insisted upon a meeting outside the hallways of Broodmore, he who had intimated that he had secrets to share—secrets regarding Twyll that he didn't want overheard by others. At the thought of the tower from which he'd been cast—Twyll, a rugged castle perched high upon a cliff—Rhys's heart grew colder than this very forest. Injustice icily chilling his heart.

Vengeance, always lurking in the shadows of his soul, never rested. Hence his kinship with Abelard—thief, liar, and spy. The man to whom he owed his life.

So where was he?

Christ Jesus, the man was a thorn in his side!

Glowering into the shadows, Rhys let out the soft hoot of an owl, the signal he and Abelard had agreed upon. Then he listened, waiting, straining for an echo . . . hearing nothing but the steady drip from leafless branches and the rush of the creek slicing through the chasm. The wind picked up, dancing along his spine, reminding him that somewhere, deep in the great hall of Twyll, fires spat and crackled, candles glowed with warm, soul-penetrating light, meat sizzled and gave off a charred, spicy scent as it was brought to the lord's table where his half brother, baron of all Twyll, Lord Tremayne, feasted.

It had been ten years since Rhys had last been a freeman within the walls of Twyll, a decade since his half brother had sliced his face and broken his nose, but the pain, though dulled with the passing of years, still burned deep. And Abelard had promised him news this morn—news of Twyll.

Damn Abelard's black soul. Rhys's jaw clenched and he urged Gryffyn forward.

At a fork in the trail he slowed the horse again. A new sound carried over the rush of water—a woman's voice, soft and low, whispered through the leafless trees and bracken. He drew up by instinct and turned toward the chanting, pushing aside a branch that hindered his view of the creek and the woman kneeling upon its bank.

At first glance he thought she was a crone who had stopped at the stream for a drink. Her back was to him, her tattered cloak fanned around her small body as she dipped her hands into the brook. Over the gurgle of the water, her voice was muted but rhythmic as she chanted or prayed. To Rhys's mind it didn't much matter which. God no longer listened. Mayhap He never had. The woman was a fool.

Silently he urged his mount a little closer, and Gryffyn stepped softly through the dripping ferns and underbrush. The fog was dense here, rising upward from the forest like the spirits that some said inhabited this hollow, ghosts of those who had given their lives in defending Tower Twyll. Ghosts that Rhys had inadvertently hastened to their graves.

Rhys's jaw grew hard. He held the reins in clenched fingers and shoved his bloodstained memories aside.

"Cerridwen and Morrigu . . ." the woman murmured.

So she was a witch. Calling up pagan goddesses.

". . . protect me in my quest . . ."

His lips twisted irreverently. Poor old hag. Still believing in the magic of the ancient ones. He pulled on the reins, determined to leave the crone alone, when he saw her reach into a deep pocket and withdraw her treasure—a gold ring suspended from a length of silver chain. Rhys sucked in his breath. Mounted in the center of the ring was a sizable green gem, dark and mysterious as this forest, a jewel that winked in the fragile shafts of sunlight that were able to pierce this ungodly mist, a stone like no other. God in heaven, 'twas the Dark Emerald of Twyll—lost for nearly two decades. Worth a fortune. Said to possess powers beyond those of man.

Rhys's thieving fingers itched. In a split second he saw a new path home, a trail blazed by the light of the jewel in this woman's palm.

The crone held the necklace aloft as a gust of wind raced through the thicket, causing the stark branches of the trees to dance while tugging at her cloak. Her hood slid off, and the coarse fabric bunched around her neck to reveal a thick mass of ebony curls that caught in the breeze and glistened in the thick mist.

Rhys's gut tightened. His breath caught. This witch was far from old.

Prancing nervously, Gryffyn tossed his great head, muscles quivering beneath his mud-spattered coat, his bridle chinking softly.

She didn't seem to hear.

". . . be with me." Standing slowly, as if it were part of her ritual, she tied several knots in the chain. Then, in one deft movement, she removed her heavy wool cloak and draped it over the exposed roots of a willow tree. For but a second she stood in a russet-colored tunic; then it, too, was flung off, tossed over the cloak.

The spit in Rhys's mouth evaporated.

Nearly naked, she stood proudly, her back rigid as she shivered in the bare light of afternoon.

He should leave. Now. Something was wrong here, very wrong. Mayhap deadly. He smelled a trap as surely as if it were a carcass rotting in the sun, and yet he was drawn to her, unable to move.

Goose bumps rose on her flesh. With only a lacy chemise as protection against the damp cold, she turned her face to the sky.

Rhys's throat tightened as she lifted her arms over her head again and the hem of her undergarment raised, showing off well-shaped white legs that stretched out of her battered leather boots. In one defiantly raised fist she held the knotted chain with its glistening stone that winked a dark, seductive green. In the other her small fingers curled around a dagger—tiny and wicked as death.

Rhys's gut clenched. The ring. The stone. The rumors. He blinked, telling himself he was a fool.

"Please, Mother, be with me." Solemnly bowing her head, she slowly untied each little knot in the chain, then carefully looped the necklace over her head.

Crossing her arms in front of her, she gathered the folds of her chemise in her fingers and tugged the unwanted undergarment off. It landed in a pool atop the rest of her clothes and, aside from her boots and the chain, she stood naked on the shore of the creek, misty rain collecting on her bare skin, droplets sparkling in ebony hair that fell in unruly waves to the middle of her back.

By the gods, she was beautiful. Her body was lithe and young, the muscles of her back shifting beneath flawless skin, the dimple of her spine long and curving. With slim hips and a tight, round rump, she raised her empty arms upward as if to embrace the sky yet again.

And around her gorgeous neck, she wore the ring. With the cursed but legendary stone.

Gryffyn snorted and tossed his head, jangling his bridle loudly.

She stiffened. "Nay," she whispered in a voice
barely audible over the sigh of the wind and the gurgle
of the stream. She whirled swiftly, hands flying downward to cover her nakedness. Her gaze clashed with
his. "Sweet Jesus, nay." Her face drained of all color.
"Bastard," she muttered nearly inaudibly, and he
flinched inwardly. "Get away!" Her wide eyes, a deep
green, flashed in silent humiliation. "Who the devil—?
Oh, by the saints—"

The magic was broken. The ring dangling from the
chain at her neck glimmered between breasts as beautiful as any he'd ever seen—small, high, rounded perfectly, with rosy nipples that puckered in the chill
December air.

Inwardly Rhys groaned. It had been long since he'd
seen a woman—and never one like this. Never one
who wore the dark emerald of Twyll.

Scrabbling fiercely for her clothes, trying to cover
her nakedness with one arm while reaching for her
tunic with the other, she skewered him with one hate-
filled glance after another. " 'Tis enough you've seen!"
Heat flared in her cheeks. "Who be you to slink
through the forest like a serpent, spying upon—oh,
curse and rot you, just leave!" One pink nipple peeked
between her splayed fingers. He shifted his gaze lower,
past her flat abdomen and slit of a navel to the dark
nest of curls that was only partially hidden by her
other hand when she bent over to slide into her chemise and tunic.

"You . . . you have no right to look at me!" she
insisted as the rough cloth slipped over her nakedness.
She skewered him again with a stare of intense hatred.
"No right! If Baron Tremayne knew—"

Every muscle in his body clenched. In spite of the
fury burning in her gaze, he urged his horse past the

few scrawny trees that separated them. "What would the baron do?" he encouraged, inwardly angry that he didn't have the brains or the nobility to yank on the reins and ride off. Or at the very least to steal the stone nestled between those enticing breasts.

"He'd hang you! Or . . . or draw and quarter you! Then he'd spill your innards and feed them to his hogs!" She tugged her hair through the neck of her tunic and glared up at him, not giving an inch, her small chin jutting forward in self-righteous fury and her cheeks flaming bright pink. "Or mayhap he'd strip you of your clothes and that fine sword, then flay you within a whisper of your life, spit on your wounds, and throw you over the cliffs to bleed to death."

At that image he felt the rage that had smoldered deep in the dark recesses of his heart for a decade begin to ignite. "And what would he do to you if he found you practicing the dark arts in his forest?"

"I hurt no one—"

He lifted one eyebrow in mockery. "The priests at Twyll might disagree. They be a reverent and arrogant lot."

She swallowed hard, her courage flagging for a second. She licked her lips nervously and her eyes narrowed a bit. "Speak you of Father Simon?"

The old one. How did she know the old one? What would a witch want of men of God? "And Father Alden."

"You've met Father Simon?" she clarified, some of her ire seeming to fade, her gorgeous face turned upward.

"Has not everyone heard of the silent priest of Twyll?"

"Aye, aye, but you've spoken to him."

"Long ago." When he still confessed his sins.

"But he is at Twyll yet, is he not?"

"Aye." Or so Abelard said.

She was anxious, her face white, her embarrassment forgotten, but she glanced toward the other side of the creek where her horse, a bay mare, was tethered to a spindly sapling. The mare's ears were pricked forward, one back leg cocked lazily. "He speaks not?"

"Nary a word."

She bit her lower lip, as if worried or disappointed, then muttered something under her breath about rogues who spoke in circles as she tossed on her mantle.

"You know the baron?" he asked.

Her head snapped back, and she was staring up at him again with those damnable eyes. She hesitated but a second, her throat working. "Aye." She nodded vigorously, as if to convince herself. "And . . . and he's the very devil himself, he is."

"Is he?"

"Mean as a wounded bear. Banished his own brother." She snapped her fingers. "Just like that."

"Why?" he asked, curiosity getting the better of common sense. She was a liar. A beautiful, feisty liar. She knew not Tremayne, and yet she was determined to say otherwise. She was hiding something. Though Rhys knew he should leave well enough alone, be off before he was discovered this close to the gates of Twyll, he couldn't ride away. "Why would a brother banish his own kin?"

"Know you not?" she asked, suddenly wary again. "You who have spoken with Father Simon? Have you not heard of the bastard Rhys?"

"Once or twice," he said dryly, staring down at her raven-black curls. Who was this woman who chanted spells like a witch, had a tongue as sharp as a huntsman's blade, and was as beautiful as any lady he'd ever set eyes upon?

"Then you know that Rhys is an outlaw now. A murdering, thieving robber who . . ." She let her voice trail off as she eyed him more closely, taking in his worn tunic and breeches, scuffed boots and angry disposition.

"This outlaw—"

"Rhys," she whispered, swallowing hard.

"Yes. Rhys. You've met him?"

She hesitated slightly before she shook her head and apprehension appeared in her eyes.

"You fear him."

"I fear no one," she retorted.

"You've been to his brother's keep?" he prodded and watched her shift uncomfortably from one foot to the other. When she didn't respond, he swung down from his horse.

"Who be you?" she demanded, refusing to back up even one step.

" 'Tis the very question I was about to put to you." He motioned to the pile of her clothes still resting on the blackened roots. "And why call you up the spirits?"

"I was not—" She snapped her mouth shut, and he silently damned himself for staring down at her up-turned, innocent face. Though she played the witch, she was young and, he suspected, far from worldly. A light dusting of freckles bridged her straight nose, and sooty lashes curled around curious, intelligent eyes. A cunning expression crossed her features as she said, a trifle breathlessly, "Aye, sir, caught me, you have. Calling up the ghosts in these woods. If you be not careful they may arise and haunt you."

"Would they now?" He couldn't help but be

amused, even though Gryffyn was edgy, ears cocked,
nostrils snorting, as if he sensed an intruder. " 'Tis too
late to prevent it, witch. By the gods, there are demons
who plague me as if they were my shadow." He felt
a contemptuous smile twist his lips. "So chant if you
must. Tell your ghosts to rise up and bedevil me." He
leaned closer to her, so close that he saw the shifting
shades of green in her eyes. "Who be you?"

Stiffening, Tara bit her tongue. She couldn't trust
this man who seemed a strange cross between a knight
and a rogue. His clothes had once been fine, leather
stitched into the best black wool, his high-spirited
steed was cared for and appeared swift, and in his
expression a mixture of arrogance and anger shifted
upon a once handsome face that had seen more than
its share of battles. A thin white scar ran from his
temple to his chin, burying itself in the whiskers that
had not been scraped away in days. His nose was battered and not quite straight, one eyebrow had been
cleaved, and the eyes that glowered down at her were
the color of steel and twice as cold.

"Surely you have a name?" he asked again.

"Some . . . some call me Morgan Le Fay." 'Twasn't
a lie. Not really. Those who were frightened of her
often conjured up the names of the old goddesses
when speaking of her.

"Morgan Le Fay? The death goddess? So far from
Glamorgan?" His laugh was as bitter as the wind tear-
ing through the creek's chasm. He crossed the short
distance between them to stand close enough to her
that she could smell the scents of smoke and horses
that clung to him. "The one who can cast a destroying
curse on any man?" White teeth flashed in his dark
visage. "So 'tis you I should blame for all my ill fate?"

"Aye," she said, silently damning her quick and ofttimes too sharp tongue. "And who be you?" She'd seen no sign of his allegiance. He wore no colors, bore no shield with a standard emblazoned upon it.

His silver eyes twinkled wickedly. "If ye be Morgan Le Fay," he said so slowly that her gaze was drawn to his mouth, "then . . ." Stupidly, her silly heart began to pound, and she thought again how this man had seen her without a stitch upon her. "I must be Rhys, banished outlaw of Twyll."

Fool! Did he think she believed him? Fury tore through her. So he was taunting her. Arrogant spying cur! No honorable man would have watched her undress as he had, but then, there was not a hint of honor about this man. "I think, mayhap, that you be a bastard, sir, pure and simple."

Again the amused grin and bark of laughter. "Aye, witch, a bastard. But not so pure." His eyes gleamed in the frail light. "And never simple."

He was toying with her, he who had seen her naked in the woods, chanting spells, asking for help from any god who would speed her on her quest. Hot color infused her cheeks. "Curse you, then, outlaw."

"Ah, lady, I think mayhap you already have." In that moment she knew he would kiss her. His silvery eyes gleamed, and before she could take a step back his arms surrounded her and she was captured. Pulled close. She gasped, and his mouth bore down on hers. Her lips parted, and though she meant to utter a swift "no," no words passed. "Ahh, witch," he sighed, then his lips claimed hers. Hard, hot, demanding. She knew she should pull back, knee him hard, writhe away from him—but the wonder of the kiss, the sheer power of his lips molded to hers, kept her still.

Sweet Mary! Was this what it was like when a man and woman joined? Her blood heated in the cold winter air, and yearnings the like of which she'd never experienced stirred deep in her very core.

Her heart clamored in the cage of her ribs. *No, no, no!* She silently screamed while her muscles softened, and his tongue slipped easily between her teeth. His whiskers tickled her skin. Sensations, foreign and familiar all in one instant, caused her flesh to tingle, her blood to heat. The ivy-laced branches of the trees swam in her vision and she closed her eyes, losing herself to him.

Her knees went weak. Unwilling arms suddenly clung to him.

He groaned and an answering moan escaped her lips. Her breasts flattened against his chest and all the reasons not to kiss him scattered in the wind.

She kissed him back, unable to resist. Wanting more.

Somewhere in the distance an owl hooted. Once.

He raised his head and a touch of a smile lifted one side of his mouth. "Finally. He comes."

The hoot came again, sharper this time.

The outlaw froze. "Blast," he whispered.

Again the hoot. Harsh. Near.

"Bloody Christ," he growled in her ear. "Three hoots. God's teeth!"

"What?"

"Shh!" Still holding her prisoner, he glanced quickly around the mist-shrouded forest, his eyes scouring the canyon walls as if searching for a hidden enemy. "Don't say a word," he whispered in her ear, his breath teasing, his whiskers tickling her skin.

"But—"

" 'Twas a warning." He raised a finger and glared down at her with such fierce conviction that her question died on her recently plundered lips and she bit her tongue.

"Go," he mouthed. "Quickly."

Somewhere nearby a twig snapped and he, spinning, released her, his hand on the hilt of his sword. She didn't wait a second longer. The determination in the set of his jaw, the sense that he was about to do battle propelled her. She took a faltering step backward, nearly tripped on an exposed root, then grabbed the rest of her damp clothes and half ran across the stream to the spindly oak where her mare was tethered. Wild-eyed, the horse snorted as the sound of hoofbeats reached her ears. "Shh, Dobbyn!" Half-frozen fingers worked at the swollen knot in the reins. She glanced over her shoulder as she heard the hiss of a sword being unsheathed.

The outlaw was astride his warhorse and urging the gray through the stream. "Run!" he ordered, and she knew not if he was speaking to his own mount or to her. Swinging into the saddle, she gave the mare her head, leaning forward, digging her heels into the anxious horse's sides.

Dobbyn bolted.

From the corner of her eye she spied horsemen. Dark warriors riding eerily through the fog.

"Run, damn it!" the rogue whispered harshly, and she took heed, her heels kicking against the panicked mare's sides.

"Rhys of Twyll, show yourself!" The voice was huge and boomed through the fog.

Rhys? Her heart missed a beat. *The outlaw?*

Slap! Dobbyn doubled her effort as the outlaw smacked her rump with his hand. Tara clung to the reins, leaning lower, blinking against the branches and spiderwebs that stretched over the trail and slapped at her face. The shouts of their pursuers reached her ears.

"Rhys of Twyll! Halt!"

Dear Lord, help me!

Zzzt! An arrow whizzed past her head.

Thwack! Another lodged in a tree.

"I saw 'em, sure as 'ell," one man cried, his voice high-pitched as it carried on the wind. "Acrost the stream they was."

"They?"

"Aye, two of 'em."

"Then let's find them, shall we?" The ground shook as the search party spurred their horses on. Hooves pounded the mud of the trail and splashed noisily through the stream.

"This way," the outlaw ordered as his steed galloped past her and veered away from the path, taking a sharp turn into a copse of trees that provided little cover. Tara hesitated. Why had she thrown in her lot with his stranger? This criminal? As if he sensed that she might turn back, he slowed his horse, reached back and grabbed hold of Dobbyn's reins, jerking hard enough to strip the wet leather straps from Tara's fingers and force the mare to follow him.

"Wait—"

"Ssh! Do you want to get us both killed?" he demanded, his voice low, his eyes harsh as he sent her a glare that would have bent steel.

Any further protest died in her throat.

Behind them, on the trail, she heard the small army. Bridles jangled, men shouted, swords rattled, and hoofbeats echoed through the canyon as the pursuers urged their steeds ever upward.

Rhys doubled back, the gray warhorse running swiftly through the gloom while Dobbyn strained to keep up with the stallion's swift strides. Trees and bracken flashed by in a foggy blur. Tara's fingers wound into the mare's mane. Fear pumped in her heart. Mist collected on her skin and ran down her neck, and the horses, lathered now, ran with the speed of lightning. The outlaw's mantle billowed behind him. He couldn't be Rhys of Twyll. There had to be some mistake. Surely the fates would not have been so unkind. Yet as she stared at his back, the width of his shoulders, how easily he stayed astride though he held the reins of her mare in one hand and a sword in the other, she knew he was no ordinary man. An outlaw? A rogue? A blackheart? Aye, she would expect no more. But Rhys of Twyll. Nay!

If not Rhys, then who? And why were the soldiers after him? Were he not the blackhearted outlaw, then why did he run? And if he was . . . The thought curdled her blood.

Without slowing, he crossed the creek again. Icy water sprayed upward as the horses splashed through a pool and gamely scrambled up the opposite shore along the steep trail. The noise startled a bird; wings flapping, it flew wildly from its hiding spot, rising before them, only to disappear in the fog. Dobbyn sidestepped, nearly stumbled, but somehow kept her footing.

The sounds of pursuit faded as they sped deeper into the forest, and the mist gave way to a gentle rain that was as cold as death. A doe scurried out of their path, springing effortlessly over fallen logs and stumps before disappearing into the shadowy undergrowth. They were alone again. Somewhere. She had no idea how far they'd ridden, but the fog-shrouded sun was giving forth no more light and she could feel the darkness encroaching.

Tara's teeth chattered, her fingers were frozen, her vision blurred. For the first time since the beginning of her quest, she wondered at her stupidity. Even now she could be secure in the warmth of Lodema's cabin, mending clothes, drying herbs, gutting fish, making soap, and listening to her mother's off-key humming as she went about her daily tasks. Instead, because of her own impetuosity, she was cold to the bone and alone in the forest with a stranger who might well be the bastard of Twyll.

But only for a while.

She had held no thought of escape before now, had not even considered the fact that she was his prisoner. Just because he held the reins of her mount's bridle didn't mean that she could not find her own way back to Twyll. And find it she would. No one—not the woman who had raised her, the soldiers who had chased them, or this arrogant rogue—would keep her from her quest—her destiny.

"Where are you—?"

"Shhh!" His command was harsh, and over his shoulder he sent her a fierce glance.

Biting her tongue, she forced herself to keep her silence. They rode up a steep hill, and the trees became sparse. At the top of a rise, the forest gave way to a small clearing. He slowed the horses and, guiding his mount along the fringe of the woods, circumvented the open space until he found a wide trail that may once have been a road. Without a word he turned onto the rutted, overgrown path, which wound down to a river. A few blackened pilings were all that remained of the bridge that had rotted and partially washed away years ago.

He urged his horse straight into the torrent that cut through the land. Dobbyn tried to stop, to pull back, but the man was strong and he yanked hard on the reins, forcing her to follow. "Come on, you damned nag," he growled, as the muddy water swelled around his stirrups.

"Are you daft?" Tara cried. The river here was narrow but deep, its waters swollen and swirling.

" 'Twill be all right."

She had no choice but to cling to the saddle and horse's mane as the water crept up, over her heels, her calves, the tops of her boots. God in heaven, how had she managed to end up here with a dark stranger who had not a brain in his head? Ice-cold water eddied over her thighs and Dobbyn held her nose aloft.

By the gods, the poor animal was going to have to swim! They would surely drown! "Halt!" she cried just as she saw Gryffyn begin to climb upward, his wet gray coat slick and dark. Dobbyn, too, found her footing and a reserve of energy, bolting from the river as if she were on fire. Tara clung to the horse's mane and tried vainly to catch her breath. Only when the rushing waters were far behind them did either horse slow.

"Where the devil are you taking me?" Tara demanded. Her teeth were rattling in her head, her body shaking with the cold and covered with mud and wet leaves. He pulled up and sheathed his sword but didn't release Dobbyn's reins.

"Somewhere safe."

"Safe?" she repeated. "Safe? Naught you've done has been safe—the ravine, the creek, the cursed river." She was shivering uncontrollably, her bones feeling as if they were ice. Every inch of her tunic was dripping wet, and poor Dobbyn was breathing as if she might expire.

"Would you rather be left to Tremayne's men?"

"How know you they were soldiers of Twyll?"

The look he sent her was dark as night.

"Why are they after you?"

One side of his mouth lifted in a sardonic and heartless smile. "Mayhap they were after you, Morgan Le Fay."

" 'Twas not my name that was called. You . . . you be the outlaw Rhys."

His mouth twitched and a wicked gleam appeared in his eye. "As I said. Now, come—" He yanked the horse's reins again, and short of jumping off midstride and being left without her mount, she could do little more than accept her fate.

"We be far from Gaeaf," she said as darkness deepened through the trees.

"Aye."

"And Twyll."

"And the soldiers," he pointed out.

'Twas small comfort for Tara, frozen to her very marrow. She stared into the gloomy woods and the hairs on the back of her neck raised slowly, for as her mind cleared and old stories whispered through her head, she understood where she was. A tall tree, split clean through by an ancient fork of lightning, stood guard beside moss-covered boulders as tall as her mare. "Broodmore Castle," she whispered.

"You've heard of it."

"Who has not?" she asked, fear congealing in her heart as her horse continued, pulled by Rhys's strong arm. " 'Tis cursed," she said, and crossed herself deftly as they rounded a final bend and the old keep, now in ruin, loomed ahead—dark, dangerous, and haunted by spirits who had given up their lives to the fever and a fire that had killed everyone within the crumbling walls generations before.

"As well it should be." She heard the cry of a night warbler. A second later a man dressed in black leaped out from a hiding place and landed squarely in front of them. "Who goes there?"

" 'Tis I, Johnny," Rhys said with a sigh. "Did you not recognize me or my horse?"

The boy, for he was barely in his teens, sheathed his weapon but sent a suspicious glance in Tara's direction. "The horse is new."

"Aye." Rhys smiled wickedly. "A gift from my half brother."

"But I thought ye stole 'im."

Rhy laughed and winked at the boy. "Aye, Tremayne did not know he gave him to me, nor would he have done it willingly." He patted his mount's muscular shoulder. "A good steed he is. Take care of him for me."

"I will." Johnny's head bobbed emphatically. "Aye, I will, but who"—Johnny indicated Tara with a gloved finger—"is she?"

Rhys jumped to the ground and handed the boy the reins of both animals. "Well, son, as she tells it, she is Morgan Le Fay."

"Nay!" Even in the twilight, Tara saw his face pale in fear. His upper lip, barely sprouting the hint of a red moustache, quivered. "Morgan Le Fay—the . . . the . . ."

"And she is my guest." He reached up to help Tara climb off Dobbyn.

"I be not—"

"She'll be staying with me, Johnny. Tell Pigeon and Rose that we be hungry and cold."

"Nay," Tara said, her eyes locking with those of the man who so insolently gave her orders. She had her own reasons for being in the forest, and she was far from Twyll, far from her destiny. She glanced at the looming, blackened ruins of the castle. What was the old children's rhyme she'd heard years ago?

> *Broodmore, Broodmore,*
> *All that lived there died.*
> *Broodmore, Broodmore,*
> *All the children cried,*
> *Broodmore, Broodmore,*
> *The kiss of death be there,*
> *Broodmore, Broodmore,*
> *All visitors beware.*

She swallowed hard. Surely 'twas only superstition, but the menacing towers with their crumbling parapets and jagged wall walks did little to alleviate her case of nerves.

Clearing her throat, she told herself to take heart. Nothing sinister would happen to her. Nothing would deter her from her mission. There was naught to fear. Naught at all.

So why, then, as she reluctantly allowed this wickedly handsome man to put his hands around her waist and swing her down to the sodden ground, did she feel the footsteps of doom tread through her heart?

Chapter Two

"You broke the rules." Abelard's fist slammed down on the table. The candle jumped. Wax splattered. Mazers sloshed wine that spilled blood red across the heavy planks. Two men, a pickpocket and a poacher who had pledged their lives and skills to Rhys, backed away from the confrontation, as the fury of Abelard's temper was well recited.

"I had no choice."

"Bah! We make our choices!"

Rhys picked up his cup from the table and took a long swallow. He was tired and cold and had no use for Abelard's anger. Resting on the small of his back, he closed his eyes for a second and willed the aches from his body. This very chair had once held the lord of Broodmore, years ago, before the pestilence and death had struck. Broodmore had been teeming with life, a castle filled with bustling servants, hardworking peasants, knights and maids, heraldry and the laughter of children. Since the fire, no mason's trowel had helped rebuild the walls, no carpenter's hammer had pounded new nails into sagging timbers, no farrier's fire had burned bright, no potter's wheel had hummed, no weaver's loom had clucked. Nay, there had been more than a generation of silence in these blackened old walls.

Now Broodmore was an outlaws' lair. His hiding place. Charred and empty, filled with scarred men who hid their own secrets, none of which were shared. All that Rhys required was obedience—unwavering and true. What a man had done before he came to Broodmore was of no concern. What he did once he'd pledged his life to the others was carefully scrutinized. There was no room for dissent or any form of disloyalty. Not even from Abelard.

"No visitors. None." Abelard, an imposing man who stood at more than six feet, leaned across the table. His white hair fell around his face like a lion's mane, his amber eyes sparked with a seething fury—a rage born of injustice. "There can be no exceptions." He pointed the stub of his index finger—the one that Tremayne had lopped off years before—at Rhys. "This was your law."

"I could not leave the woman for Tremayne's men."

"Why not?" Abelard lifted both eyebrows. "What had she to fear from him?"

Rhys held his silence.

"If you ask me, you found a fetching maid in the forest and you brought her back here just to have your way with her!"

Rhys was on his feet in an instant, his broken nose so close to Abelard's that he could smell the wine on the older man's breath, see the web of tiny veins that had broken beneath the skin of his cheeks. His own mazer toppled, nearly falling to the floor, spilling a few drops. "There are reasons—"

"More than the simple fact that you'd like to lift her skirts?"

Rhys grabbed Abelard by his tunic. "I said there are reasons."

Abelard's mouth became a thin, impatient line. "What be they?"

With a glance at the two other men, Rhys jerked his chin toward the door. "Leave us."

Will and Benjamin, two sorry thieves without a set of teeth between them, were only too eager to make haste from the room. They hurried off, their worn boots scraping against the cold stones of the floor at a quick pace, before the animosity that was always simmering between the two prickly friends ignited.

Slowly Rhys uncurled his fingers. "Where were you?" he demanded. "You were to meet me at the canyon."

Abelard lifted a huge shoulder. "I was detained. Tremayne's soldiers were about. Heard you not my warning?"

"Too late," Rhys admitted, remembering the sharp hoots of an owl as he'd fallen into the seductive trap of kissing the witch. Even now he could feel her chilled lips against his, how she'd warmed at his touch. How she'd trembled.

"Because you've lost your edge, my friend," Abelard charged, spitting out the last word. "Because of the woman."

"You saw us?"

"Through the mist. Shadows only." He grabbed his wooden cup and gulped the last of his wine.

This was the way it was with Abelard, the way it had always been—a friendship that had survived all the hardships but had often worn thin with the difference of opinion and the struggle to dominate. Two men sharing the role of leader—'twas difficult.

"Why did you not show yourself?" Rhys demanded.

"Because of the soldiers from Twyll. Sent by Tremayne. They followed me from the castle and somehow knew that I was to meet you." His eyes narrowed as he slammed his empty cup onto the table. "Someone betrayed me."

"Know you who?"

"Nay . . . well, mayhap the lad." Abelard scowled and shook his head as if he didn't believe it himself. "Tremayne's boy—about nine he is and slides through the shadows like a cat on the hunt, silent and swift."

Rhys winced inwardly. The boy, Quinn, was Anna's son as well. His stomach knotted at the thought, and he was thankful for another swallow of wine.

"But . . . oh, bloody hell, anyone could be the traitor."

"You're losing your touch, old man," Rhys said, disturbed. He shoved his wayward hair off his forehead. "There was a time when you could sneak in and out of the gates of Twyll without a sentry suspecting."

"Aye." Abelard rubbed his chin in frustration. "Tremayne is ever more wary. I found out naught except that there was a search party looking for you. Apparently your brother is not pleased that you have seen fit to steal his favorite steed."

One side of Rhys's mouth lifted a bit and he took a swallow of wine. It warmed his throat and settled in his belly. "I claim him not as my brother."

"As he does not claim you."

Rhys lifted a shoulder. He'd never felt a kinship to Tremayne. Never. They'd been sired by the same father and that was the end of any family connection between them. No love. No admiration. No warmth. Just cold, hard anger and resentment. Now he walked to the fire and warmed the backs of his legs. He would not think of Tremayne. "So, if you were watching in the woods, you must have seen the ring."

"What ring?" Abelard asked, though from the gravity of his expression Rhys knew that he understood.

"The emerald ring."

"E—excuse me, sir," a soft voice intervened. The lass, Big Rosie's daughter, Peony, poked her head into the room. "Me mum, she asks if ye would like some more wine or ale."

"Come, come," Abelard invited, urging her into the room. She was a shy child with wide eyes and a budding womanhood. "Bring us drink and quickly, then be off."

She scuttled into the room, quick on her feet in her long brown dress. Her cheeks were flushed pink, and she glanced at Rhys as if frightened of him—or, worse, as if she found him intriguing. She offered him a shy smile, then she hurried about her task, pouring wine from a jug and biting her lower lip with slightly crooked upper teeth.

"See that the woman is cared for," Rhys said. "She'll need hot water and clean clothes."

"Aye, m'lord. Er, sir," she said, nodding as she lifted the jug, "me mum says as soon as she's finished tendin' the kitchen, she'll see to the lady." Embarrassed and gawky, she hastily exited the room, leaving the full mazers sitting near the solitary candle on the table.

The second she had disappeared, Abelard turned on Rhys. He drummed his fingers on his chin. "So now you tease me."

"About the stone? Nay." One corner of Rhys's mouth twitched. "I saw it, with my own eyes."

"The dark emerald of Twyll—this is the gem you've seen?" Skepticism tinged Abelard's words.

"Or one so like it as to be its twin."

Abelard licked his lips. " 'Tis sorcery."

"I think not."

"Did you not say that she was a witch—chanting spells?"

"The stone was real."

"Bah." And yet he rubbed the tips of his fingers with his thumbs as if he could feel the sharp facets of the stone. "If you be tellin' the truth—and I'll whip your sorry hide if you aren't—then your little witch either stole it or bought it from the true ruler of Twyll."

"Or she be the ruler herself," Rhys conjectured aloud, though a part of him wanted to hold this a secret close to his heart. Abelard had a twisted yet noble streak, aye, but when it came to money, his honor could be bought.

"She is a woman. The babe was a boy child." He shook his great head, loose strands of hair shimmering silver in the firelight. "It cannot be. Nay." He mumbled a curse under his breath and glanced into the grate, as if he could read his fate in the glowing coals and hot ashes.

"But who was there? Who saw the babe born?" Rhys had pondered this question so many times he couldn't count them. "All we have is rumor—hearsay from those who were in the midst of a war—some loyal to Baron Gilmore, others to my father." He rubbed his beard thoughtfully, his finger tracing the scar that ran down his face. "Since Baron Gilmore and his wife were killed, who would know if their child, born during the attack, was a male child or a female?"

"This witch is not the heir to Twyll. I believe it not."

Rhys lifted a challenging eyebrow. "You'll believe it when I show you the stone, Abelard. When that dark gem winks at you, even your skepticism will be vanquished."

"Fair enough, Rhys. I'll wait . . . though, understand, I be not a patient man."

"Nor am I, Abelard." Rhys crossed to the table, picked up his cup and raised it in mock salute, silently toasting his old friend, a man who had saved his life and yet a man he did not fully trust. "Nor am I."

Tara could not believe her bad luck. How could she have been so unwary as to let the outlaw capture her? For though he claimed that she was his guest, 'twas a lie—a lie spawned by the very devil. She was a prisoner here. Nothing more. Locked in a room on the main floor of the crumbling castle. She suspected the chamber had once been the chapel of Broodmore, for a few artifacts remained and an altar stood on a raised portion of the floor. Rubbing her arms, pacing in front of a fire that was blissfully warm, she plotted her escape. She would not spend a second longer than she had to in this jail. She knew from just a quick look around, however, that fleeing Broodmore would be near impossible.

Though the door of the room was unlocked, it opened to a guarded corridor that led to the great hall, where there seemed forever to be one or more of the thugs that inhabited this once proud castle. Years ago, pestilence and fire had destroyed a good portion of Broodmore, killing all of those who had walked these halls. In this room there was but one window. No shutters or panes of glass enclosed the room, and there was a view of the bailey, but if Tara hoped to use the window as an avenue of escape she was thwarted.

The sentry, a beast of a man, was positioned near

the gatehouse and from there had a clear view of the room. He was a burly man, with thick, meaty arms, stringy hair, a flat nose, and teeth far too small for his wide mouth. His eyes were set close together, but they focused with the intensity of a hawk hunting prey. They moved rapidly in his large head, ever scanning the grounds and the castle, sweeping the countryside, and, she suspected, missing nothing—even in the darkness.

Knowing that her ring wasn't safe on her body, that Rhys had already spied the emerald and as long as it was around her neck another one of the thieves might see it, she searched for a hiding place. The room was sparse, bare except for a bench, the pallet, and a table that must have once been used as an altar. Quickly Tara ran her fingers around the objects and, upon discovering a dark spot behind the altar with a tiny nail protruding from it, she slid the chain over her head and hung the necklace there. "Please, keep it safe," she prayed, crossing herself. If Rhys asked about the ring, she would say she lost it in the wild ride from the creek to Broodmore. Until she was certain that she wouldn't be searched and stripped of the treasure, she would keep it hidden.

Rap, rap, rap! "Here ye go, dearie," a woman called as she shoved open the door with her broad rump and carried in a large tub. A big woman, with arms that were strong from years of hard labor, she wore a friendly smile and a dress that was stained and dingy. A once white apron was tied around her body where her waist should have been.

Tara quickly made the sign of the cross again, as if she'd been praying, then watched the woman suspiciously. What would any decent female be doing with the ragged band of outlaws and cutthroats that lived within the run-down walls of Broodmore?

"Come on, Pigeon, hurry up with those pails."

A young girl of about twelve entered. Her thin body was just starting to bear signs of womanhood, and her smudged face was losing its baby fat. She would be pretty, Tara guessed, in time. She lugged two wooden buckets filled with steaming water.

"I be Rose," the heavy woman stated with a smile. Freckles spattered her face and graying, wiry red hair poked out from beneath a scarf tied over her head. "I tend to this sorry lot. And this be me daughter, Peony, but we all call her Pigeon, don't we?" She pinched her daughter's cheek rather roughly, but Pigeon, as if she were used to her mother's heavy-handed affection, didn't so much as wince. "Now, be a good girl and pour that hot water into the tub."

She eyed the tub and shook her head. "This ain't nothin' fancy, ye see, but ye can give yerself a good wash and we'll find something for ye to wear while yer clothes dry." As if the thought had suddenly struck her, she said, "As soon as ye finish here, Pigeon, go check the old trunks. There may be something of the lady's that . . ." Her voice faded. "What be yer name?"

Tara considered lying but decided there was no reason for that kind of deception. No one knew her. Her name meant nothing. "Tara."

"Of?" the older woman asked as her daughter poured first one bucket, then the second, into the wooden basin.

"Gaeaf. I was raised by Lodema, a midwife."

"Be ye not a lady?" Her brow wrinkled in wonder.

"Nay," Tara said, declining to give out any more information. 'Twas true enough, what she'd said, though Lodema had seen to it that she'd learned not only the dark arts but the fine ones as well. Her education had included learning to identify herbs—from Saint-John's-wort to foxglove—drawing runes in the sand, and chanting spells to the Great Mother, as well as kneeling for hours on the cold stones of a chapel and praying, seeking forgiveness from the Christian God. Lodema had taught her to speak well and learn the demeanor of a lady as well as the ability to skin rabbits or help with the birth of a new babe. Aye, Lodema had taught her much about life, and as Tara thought of her mother, she felt a pang of regret, for a part of her yearned to be with the woman who had claimed her as a daughter for all her life.

Rose fussed about, tending the fire, grumbling about the filth in the rushes, the cold and the "miserable bunch of thievin' curs that I have to tend to" as she swatted at cobwebs and motioned for Tara to undress. "Hurry now, you'll freeze to death in that tunic and I don't need to be carin' for ye along with the rest of 'em."

"I need not—"

"Ach, don't ye be arguin' with Big Rosie, dearie. Ye needs to chase away the chill from yer bones and get the mud from yer face and hands. Come now, hurry up, the water will be cold if ye don't step quick."

Though she hated the thought of being without her clothes for even a second, Tara yanked her tunic over her head. Wet boots and damp chemise followed and quickly, sucking in her breath as the hot water hit her chilled skin, she sank into the tub. It was cramped but heavenly. Rose found a chunk of soap and handed it to Tara.

Ignoring the woman, who was obviously curious about her, Tara washed herself quickly, the cold seeping out of her skin, the grit sliding from her hair, and though she could barely move in the tub, she felt her muscles relax. She washed her hair and wound it upon her head, then, with a cloth, scrubbed her skin until it tingled and the water started to cool. By the time Pigeon returned, carrying three dresses, Tara was refreshed, her stomach rumbling, her mind racing ahead to plans of escape. Rose offered Tara a towel that scratched her skin as she dried and ordered her daughter to clean "the lady's" wet tunic, mantle, and chemise.

Holding the towel around her, Tara reached into the pockets of her cloak and withdrew her most prized possessions, a small dagger with a curved blade and a pouch that held a few coins, some dried herbs, and a bit of candle. "There," she said and Pigeon mutely scooted out the door. Still clutching the towel at the cleft of her breasts, Tara studied the faded garments that had once been glorious—rose-colored silk, gray damask, and a lavender velvet that was embroidered with silver thread. She reached for the velvet gown. Footsteps sounded in the hallway outside.

The door swung open.

"Ahem." She froze, recognizing the deep timber of Rhys's voice, a sound, she was certain, that would follow her all the days of her life.

"Ah, Sir Rhys, 'tis not finished we are," Rose clucked purposefully, placing her broad body in front of Tara.

"Ahh." His gaze slid to the tub.

Holding the dress over her nakedness, Tara stepped from behind the woman who had positioned herself as a human shield. Rhys had already seen her without a stitch on, and this time she intended to give him the response he deserved.

"Is there something you wanted?"

He looked at her half-bare body as he had in the woods a few hours earlier. Tara's throat turned to sand as he viewed her bare neck, now devoid of her chain and ring. A spark of interest flared in his silvery gaze, and she felt her skin flush. The look that he gave her was not that of a man searching for a valuable stone; it was that of a man who saw her as a woman— a woman he wanted. The memory of his kiss, so fresh and breathtaking, caused her to blush, and she licked her lips before clearing her throat and looking away.

"Abelard wishes to speak to you."

"Aye, and she'll be ready in but a second. Tell Abelard he can well wait a minute or two more." Rose clucked her tongue. "Always impatient, that one!" She wagged her finger in his direction. "You, too, should rest easy. The lady will be out soon."

"The lady?" Rhys mocked and one corner of his mouth lifted sardonically. "Well, *lady,* do not tarry too long."

"Trust me," Tara said, swiftly stepping forward despite her nakedness. Staring up at him, she held his steely gaze with her own, the lavender dress a thin barrier between them. "I feel no need to linger here a second longer than I must. As soon as my horse is rested, I will be off."

"Will you now?"

Chin elevating, she clutched the folds of her dress more tightly to her. "Aye, Rhys of Twyll. 'Tis a promise."

"We'll see." With a glance at Rose, he said, "Hurry her along, will you?"

Then he was gone. Leaving her shivering, her hair dripping, crumpling a dead woman's dress in her fingers.

"Ahhh, Sir Rhys . . ." Rose clucked her tongue and shook her head sadly, as if the outlaw's destiny were a sorrowful twist of fate rather than a life of corruption of his own making. Pigeon, too, watched him leave, and in her wide, innocent eyes Tara saw a naively infatuated girl. Poor thing.

Tara felt not a breath of compassion for the blackheart who had forced her here against her will. Aye, she knew the story—that for some reason Rhys had been stripped bare, flogged until he couldn't stand, and banished from Twyll, left naked, bleeding, and raw. But there were rumors about how he'd betrayed his brother as well. Nay, any pain the outlaw felt was well deserved, in Tara's estimation.

" 'Tis a pity," Rose said. "But then love drives many a man to his own ruin."

"Love?" Tara repeated, stepping into the dress and feeling the softness of the old velvet caress her skin. Though musty, the garment smelled faintly of lavender and rose hips, as if it had been packed away with dried spices.

"Aye. True love. 'Tis a blessing and a curse and don't I know it?" She glanced at Pigeon and let out a long-suffering sigh. "Come, daughter. 'Tis time to check the fires. Ye know what a growling bear Abelard can be if he's hungry and kept waiting. Miserable man . . ." Muttering under her breath, she shepherded the love-besotted Pigeon out the door and left Tara to her own devices.

The gown was a little too large, for Tara was a small woman, and the hem dragged on the ground, but she used the extra room for her own purpose. She removed the chain and ring from their hiding spot, then, using a cord from another one of the dresses, she tied her necklace around her small waist, pulled the bodice of the gown over her breasts again and cinched the waist with another dark cord. Satisfied that her prize was well hidden, she filled her pockets with her remaining treasures and was warm at last.

Her stomach growled as the scent of sizzling venison and rich spices reached her nostrils, reminding her that she hadn't yet eaten this day.

Tara spent the next few minutes finger-combing her hair and silently plotting her escape. She had her own mission to fulfill at Twyll and she had no intention of spending a second longer than necessary in the charred, cavernous chambers of Broodmore.

Straightening and silently telling herself she was ready to face the outlaw again, she felt the stone, cold and hard, pressed against her bare skin. Why she needed to know the truth she didn't understand. And yet she was compelled to uncover the truth, to determine her identity.

So, her mind nagged, *what will you do if you find out you truly are the lost babe of Gilmore? So what if ye be the rightful heir?* She knew not; but ever since learning of her birthright she'd experienced an intensely burning need, a fire of curiosity that spurred her forward in her quest for the truth.

Tara had been disbelieving when Lodema first reluctantly gave her the news, but two days earlier. Tara had heard from an old gossip in the village, a woman who sold eggs and herbs, that Lodema planned to marry her daughter off to Adair, a lofty merchant who lived far to the south, an old man whose wife had died and left him childless.

"Tell me, Mother, that you did *not* promise me to that miserable old man," Tara had demanded, flying through the door of their little hut to find the woman who had raised her expertly plucking the feathers off a dead hen. Lodema's old hands pulled the quills from the chicken's flesh while the fire burned bright in the hearth. Her half-crippled old cat was curled in a ball near the warmth. At the intrusion, Luna lifted her head and yawned, showing off razor-sharp teeth and a rough pink tongue, totally unaffected by Tara's self-righteous indignation. "Tell me!"

"Oh, child, I s'pose 'tis time." Lodema's expression was sad, her usually smiling mouth a slice of unhappiness as she kept at her work, tossing the feathers into a cloth sack.

"Time for what? To get rid of me? To send me off to some . . . some vile liver-spotted old man's house and bed?" Tara raged, sick inside. Why would Mother do this? *Why?*

"Adair's a good man."

"I love him not. I *know* him not. And he's too old."

" 'Tis a good match."

"Have you gone daft? A *good* match? Mother, listen to you!"

Lodema's jaw, sprinkled with a few bristling hairs, was set. "He needs sons. You need . . . you need a husband."

"Nay!"

"Tara—"

"Sweet Mary, do not lie to me," Tara insisted, advancing upon the table where the half-naked, headless chicken lay. Her heart was pounding, fear pumping through her. Something was wrong. Terribly wrong. The old cat hobbled over to Tara and rubbed against her leg, but Tara had no use for Luna's fickle affection now.

"You needs not trouble yourself with—"

"With what? *My* life?" Angrily Tara swiped the dead hen aside and it landed on the floor with a thump. Brown and white feathers fluttered through the air. Luna scrambled to the safety of the woodpile. "What is this about? And do not lie to me, Mother— you have spent all of my life insisting that I tell you the truth, so, please . . . do me the same honor." Her throat was tight, her eyes hot with furious unshed tears. Never in all her life had she known Lodema to deceive her.

The older woman opened her mouth, stared into her daughter's face, then slowly bent to pick up the dirty chicken and put it back on the table. As if the dead carcass had never hit the dirt floor, she began removing quills again. "You must leave, daughter," she said, her old voice cracking. "Marry Adair and have children and forget everything else."

"Forget . . . ?" Tara repeated. "Forget what?"

"That you are my daughter."

"Nay!" Tara blinked back tears. "Mother . . . why?" She reached out, grabbed Lodema's tattered sleeve, and saw that the older woman's eyes were red-rimmed and watery.

" 'Tis for the best." Lodema twisted the bird and yanked out the longer feathers of one wing. "As I said, 'tis time."

"Time for what?"

"You are past the age most girls marry and have their own babes. I've taught you all you needs know— and mayhap more," she added, stuffing a handful of speckled feathers into the bag.

"I want not a husband."

"Oh, fiddle. All girls want husbands."

"Except for you."

A shadow of sadness passed in Lodema's gaze and she sniffed loudly. Her lips pulled together as if drawn by a purse string, the way they always did when she had made a decision and intended to stick with it. "Even I, once years ago, longed for a man, Tara." She cleared her throat and plucked the final feathers from the naked carcass. " 'Twas not to be."

"So this is why you are sending me off to a stranger?" Tara's eyes slitted suspiciously, and pain screamed through her soul.

"Aye."

"There be no other reason?" Tara asked.

"Nay." The hen was plucked clean. Lodema left it on the table and walked to the fire that burned brightly in the hearth, where she lit a thick taper. Holding the candle carefully so the flame would not burn out, she returned to the table and grabbed the carcass by its feet, then turned it slowly in the candle's flame, singeing off a few tiny hairs that clung to the bird's white skin. In the flickering light Lodema seemed older than she was, her skin more wrinkled, the lines near her eyes and mouth more pronounced. "You will marry the peddler and that is that."

"I would rather die."

Lodema jerked, burning herself. "Curse it all!" The flame sizzled against the hen's skin. "By the gods, Tara, do not taunt the devil."

"Something is amiss," Tara insisted, refusing to back down even though her mother's grimace silently told her to leave well enough alone. "I heard you leave last night and followed you to the river."

Lodema glanced up and frowned. "Why would ye follow me?"

"You've been troubled."

Resignation slackened Lodema's jaw. Tara's anger slowly ebbed into a deep, nameless fear.

"You went to the river, Mother, and there you began chanting, talking to Morrigu, begging the Great

Mother to watch over me and keep me safe. I looked on as you dusted mistletoe, Saint-John's-wort, and rosemary over a white candle, then you drew the rune for protection on the sand and placed a ring with a fine dark stone over your scratchings."

Lodema blew out the candle and set the smoldering taper on the table. She dropped the hen into a bucket of cold water and sighed as she sagged against the table. "Why must you ask so many questions?"

"Because you taught me to." Tara took hold of her mother's hand, twined her fingers through the older woman's. " 'Twas you who instructed me always to be wary but to seek the truth, never to accept a lie. And yet tonight all that is forgotten. What is it, Mother?" she demanded, her fingers tightening. "What worries you?"

Lodema glanced at her daughter, and Tara saw despair in the older woman's expression. She withdrew her old hand and wiped it on her skirt. " 'Tis better if ye do not know."

Tara shook her head vehemently. "Nay! You have always told me to follow the truth—that I should never lie. And yet you are keeping secrets from me. What is it that torments you?"

"Ahh, child." Lodema shook her head, stared for a minute into the pot where the chicken soaked, its blood congealing, and she sighed. " 'Tis complicated, I fear. And dangerous."

"What?"

She lifted her eyes and a small, sad smile toyed with her lips. "Who you are, Tara. 'Tis a question of your birthright. Years ago, when you were brought to me— hush, yes, brought here." She placed a staying hand on her daughter's shoulder when Tara tried to protest. "Carried into this house in a basket, oh, the finest I've

ever seen, and given me under the order of silence."
She leaned a hip on the edge of the table and worried
her hands.

"You—you are not my mother?" Tara was stunned,
her mind spinning in denial.

Lodema shook her head. "I was a mother to you in
every way except that I did not bear you, Tara."

"No—" A thousand memories flashed through
Tara's mind. She knew that she had no father, aye,
that he had been killed in a far-off war, or so she'd
been told, but she'd been raised believing that this
woman who had taught her to mend a hem, cast a
spell, shoot an arrow straight and true, as well as how
to eat properly as a lady would, was her own flesh
and blood. "Why do you lie?"

"You asked for the truth," Lodema reminded her.
"Now I give it to you."

Tara's mouth lost its spit and her stomach cramped.
Never had she guessed this horrifying, soul-rending
verity.

"You were motherless, I was told, and the man who
brought you to me, Father Simon of Twyll, swore me
to silence. It was only later that I heard the gossip
and pieced together the truth."

"Which is?" Tara asked, stunned. How could this
be? Lodema wasn't her natural-born mother? Nay!
Her heart felt as if it might crack.

"Methinks you be the daughter of Lord Gilmore
and Lady Farren of Twyll."

Tara's blood was ice. "Gilmore? Nay—the lord and
lady were murdered." She'd heard the stories, embel-
lished over the years, of the baron of Twyll and his
young bride, killed maliciously by the dark-hearted
Lord Merwynn of Gaeaf.

Lodema nodded. "Aye. Lord Gilmore and his wife

were slain in the uprising, and bloody it was." Lodema tucked a wiry strand of hair behind her ear. "Lady Farren was heavy with child at the time, but the babe was never found—not dead within her womb, not newborn and wailing." Her wizened gaze met the disbelief in Tara's. "Not a trace of the child was discovered."

Tara's skin crawled. "And you think I be this infant?"

"Aye." Lodema placed her hands on Tara's shoulders. "But ye be mine as if I spawned ye. I could not have loved ye more. Believe that."

"I—I do. But . . . how do you know I was not the daughter of a farmer's wife who had too many mouths to feed or—or the mistake of some girl ravaged by a soldier or—?"

"There be proof." As if she'd aged a hundred years, Lodema walked to the hearth, knelt before the flames, and used her knife to pry a stone free. From beneath the smooth rock she withdrew a small leather pouch, dusty and worn. "I have saved this for you," she said sadly. " 'Tis all that I have of your birthright." She tossed the tiny purse to Tara. The bag clinked as she caught it. Quickly Tara loosened the strings and poured the contents onto the table. A few gold coins and the ring—a gold band with the glittering dark emerald she'd seen the night before—rolled out.

"What is it?" Tara asked breathlessly as she picked up the gem and held it to the firelight.

"It came with you, daughter. A bribe for me to hold my tongue." Lodema straightened, her old back popping. She dusted her hands together. " 'Tis yours now."

"But—"

"Take it." Lodema was firm. She would not change

her mind. Tara knew this much as she held the green gem between her fingers, allowing the light from the fire to play upon its many facets.

" 'Tis beautiful."

"And dangerous."

"You say I be the true daughter of Gilmore?"

"Aye. 'Tis what I believe. This"—she pointed a crooked finger at the jewel—"be not a peasant's ring." Lodema's voice grew grave. "Why I was at the river last night, why I worry and fret and pray for your safety to any god who listens, is that Lord Tremayne, son of Merwynn, has started a search—not only for the emerald but for the child as well."

"But why? Why now?"

"One of his advisers has had a vision—which Tremayne believes—that the true ruler of Twyll will return, reclaim his castle, and destroy Tremayne. He knows not how he will identify the son of Gilmore, but he makes ready. And he knows of the stone—that it disappeared during the battle." Her old eyes held Tara's. "What he does not know is that the babe was a girl and that the cursed dark emerald, a stone that is rumored to have mystical powers, is with her."

Tara could barely breathe. Was it possible?

"Lord Tremayne is a ruthless man," Lodema said. "He would not flinch at killing ye. He beat his half brother nearly to death, not that the blackheart didn't deserve it, but after almost killing him, he banished him from the castle."

"What happened to the brother?"

"Rhys? Why, he became an outlaw—a thief, mayhap a murderer, a man with a heart as black as all of hell. Though only a half brother to Tremayne, Rhys is just as duplicitous and foul, a vile outlaw who would sell his own soul for a piece of gold. He has become his half brother's worst enemy." Lodema sighed. "A bad lot, they are."

Tara rubbed her arms. 'Twas hard to believe.

"Trust me, daughter, Rhys would rob ye blind and laugh at yer misfortune, and Lord Tremayne won't rest until he knows that no man, nor woman, will ever stop him from being baron of Twyll. If he believes the rumors to be true, that the babe of Lady Farron and Lord Gilmore yet lives, he will hunt him down mercilessly." Her voice had grown so soft it was hard to hear over the hiss of the fire and the breath of wind rushing against the thatching. "You are in danger, daughter. I can feel it in my bones."

"So you found a way to hide me by marrying me off to the peddler," Tara said aloud while she contemplated where her true destiny lay. With new conviction she clasped the ring tight in her fingers. A plan was forming in her mind, one her mother would protest. "I cannot marry a man I do not love."

"He is good and kind. Did not beat his wife. Owns a home in a village far off. You would be safe."

And I would die of boredom and live in fear. Nay, I will never. Never! But she stilled her thoughts. "Worry not, Mother," she said, as her scheme became more distinct in her mind. Though Lodema, clever and sly, was unconvinced that her daughter had changed her mind, Tara waited until long after the old woman was fast asleep, and snoring rhythmically.

Then, pocketing the ring and a few supplies, Tara stole out of the house that had been her home all of her nineteen years. She left two gold coins, took the horse, and determined to find the truth.

And what then? her mind now jeered as she stood in the dark halls of Broodmore. Outside, the wind cried mournfully in the night and Tara had no answer to her own question. She only knew that she had to find out the truth.

If I am not the daughter of Gilmore, then why was the ring with its dark stone left with me?

Lodema had always said that Tara's curiosity would be her undoing. Tonight it seemed the old woman was right.

Chapter Three

Tremayne stared into the night. Standing high on the watch turret, he scanned the surrounding countryside. Only a few stars dared to wink through thick clouds that had showered and misted for most of the day. Dark as pitch it was, and though he strained to see the hills and forests that made up the land surrounding the keep, he saw only blackness. The rain had stopped, but if there were a moon in the heavens, it was hiding tonight, casting not one solitary beam. The wind was still fierce, however, howling through the canyons, whipping across the turret and snapping the standard as it screamed through the crenels and pierced the arrow loops.

Tremayne scowled, and his hands, covered in soft leather gloves, curled into fists. There was something in the air tonight, something sinister. He felt it as certainly as if he'd just signed a pact with Satan himself.

"Sire?"

He jumped as old Percival, bent at the waist, his shoulders stooped, appeared from the stairway. Wearing a long, hooded mantle, the ancient man was wheezing from the climb. At first Tremayne was surprised the exertion hadn't killed him, but then he remembered that Percival was tougher than he first appeared.

"What is it?"

"The soldiers have returned."

With the outlaw?" Tremayne asked, knowing the answer before the near-cripple shook his head. He'd spied the search party as they rode through the gates a few minutes earlier—there had been no prisoner.

"Nay. The outlaw is not with them."

"Imbeciles! Why is it they cannot perform a simple task? I ask them to find Rhys and bring him back to me. How," he asked, his irritation causing a tic to jump beneath his eye, "can it be so difficult? He is but one thief! One!" He held up a solitary leather-encased finger. "They . . . they are an army! My best men." Tremayne kicked at a pebble, sent it slamming against the wall. At the thought of his snake of a half brother his blood boiled. For years Rhys had mocked him, made him appear a fool, when the truth of the matter was that Tremayne should have killed him years ago for his betrayal. He advanced on the bowed man who had been his father's strongest warrior but these days was little more than a pain in Tremayne's backside.

"There is other news," Percival said, clutching his hood so that the gusting wind up here did not blow it off and expose his bald head. " 'Tis not good, I fear."

"It never is." Recently all news seemed to be bad. "What is it?" Tremayne wasn't really interested. The old man was forever borrowing trouble.

"Innis of Marwood is dead."

Tremayne frowned into the darkness. For once old Percival was correct. If Innis of Marwood was dead, then all hell was sure to break loose. Not that it already hadn't. "How know you this?"

"Your spy returns with the news."

"Where is he now?"

"In the gatehouse downstairs—the constable's quarters—with the leader of the search party," the old man explained, but Tremayne didn't want to hear him out. Percival was still talking as Tremayne's boots rang on the curved steps down to the second floor. Flames of torches flickered as he passed, casting shadows against the opposing walls. As he paused at the door to the constable Regan's, chambers, he heard other footsteps hurrying downward, racing in front of him as if to scurry off before being discovered. Tremayne's skin prickled. Had someone been listening to his conversation with the old man—a spy in his midst? Rhys? His lip curled with the hatred he felt for his half brother, the only man he feared. This was not the first time Tremayne had sensed unseen eyes staring at him, not the only time he'd heard the soft pad of footsteps nearby in the shadows and then found no one. 'Twas unnerving.

Bah. 'Twas his mind playing folly with him, naught more. Rhys was brazen enough to hide in the shadows outside this keep, but 'twas unlikely that the coward had sneaked back through the guarded gates of Twyll and followed the old man to the turret. *Aye, but was the bastard not bold enough to enter the keep and steal your steed from under your very nose? Could he not do it again and this time slit your throat?*

Sweat broke out on his scalp, and he told himself he was a dozen kinds of fool. Rhys could not have scaled the thick walls, nor could he have passed the sentries, who since the stealing of Tremayne's prized stallion were in fear for their lives if ever his bastard of a half brother tried to enter again.

He considered chasing whoever was in front of him but knew he was too far away, for the footsteps were muffled and fading fast. Tremayne would double the guard. Whoever it was would be found out.

Without knocking, he burst through the door of the constable's chamber and discovered Regan seated at a small table where a solitary candle burned. Regan's hair was mussed, his expression as sour as if he'd sucked vinegar. He was only half dressed, with no shirt over his breeches. Two men stood on the far side of the room, one stiff-backed and impatient, the other slouched against the wall, chewing on a piece of straw and staring in amusement at a nearly naked kitchen maid, her red hair askew, struggling into what appeared to be hastily discarded clothes. Embarrassed, she hurried to the door, pausing long enough to bow to Tremayne, who recognized her as a lass who had warmed his bed on more than one occasion. "Be off with you, Mary," he ordered in a soft voice.

"Aye, m'lord."

She was a pretty thing in her given state, tousled and half dressed. Blue eyes, upturned nose, and small breasts, yet she would mount a man and ride him hard and fast, giving enjoyment with an abandon that was lacking in so many of the girls he called to his bed. "Wait for me. In my chambers," he said softly, not looking at her, his gaze connecting with the hot, angry eyes of Regan. Tremayne felt a moment's satisfaction. He was the lord of Twyll and no one could argue his orders.

Mary swallowed hard. "I—"

"Within the hour," he instructed and ran a gloved hand over the slope of her shoulder, still bare where her dress had slid to one side. Yes, bedding her would ease some of the strain in his muscles.

"A—aye, m'lord."

"Good. Be off," he said softly, and as she escaped

the room he slammed the door shut. Both of the soldiers came to attention when he turned toward them
again, and Regan, his mouth twisted in irritation,
stood.

"What's this I hear of Lord Innis?"

"He be dead, sire," said the former sloucher. "I
come from Marwood. Lord Innis died in his sleep and
his son, Cavan, is now the new baron."

Tremayne rubbed his chin. "Anything else?"

"Aye, the old man lingered on his deathbed for
days, and as he did he saw himself as a younger man.
He called his son to his side and told him that he was
brought to him as an infant, that he is the son of
Gilmore, that 'tis he, and not ye, who is the true ruler
of Twyll."

"And Cavan, he believes this?"

"With all his heart," the spy said. "He already
amasses an army."

Tremayne's headache thundered. "To be used
against us."

"Aye."

He closed his eyes for a second, then pinched the
bridge of his nose as he thought. "This day was coming. I've sensed it. Sooner or later the issue of Gilmore
would return and lay claim or siege to the castle.
'Twas just a matter of time. Now"—he opened his
eyes and stared at the informant, James, a cocky but
talented spy—"has he the stone?"

"The stone?"

"The dark emerald of Twyll. Does Cavan possess
it?"

"I know not." James's expression was puzzled.
"There was no talk of it."

" 'Tis said that the true issue of Gilmore has in his
possession the emerald."

Tremayne felt slightly better, though whether Cavan owned the gem or not was of only secondary importance. He was putting his army together, ready to strike at the gates of Twyll. A young pup full of piss and vinegar, ready—nay, determined—to prove to the world that he was ruler of all he chose. Tremayne had once felt that cocksure, self- righteous surge of power, of pure invincibility, that comes with youth. Before the first sword has sliced one's skin, or the first opponent has held a knife to one's throat, or the first sliver of understanding that death is an enemy one never escapes has entered a young whelp's mind.

'Twould come, though, that understanding, and Tremayne was only too eager to help Cavan on his road to enlightenment.

"So what of the outlaw? Why is Rhys not standing before me as I pass sentence upon his head for stealing my horse?"

"We caught him not," the stiff-backed one, Edwin, admitted. "Caught sight of him in the trees, but we could not catch him."

"He was astride Gryffyn," Tremayne guessed, his nostrils flared. His gray was the fleetest and strongest warhorse in the stables, mayhap the land.

"Aye . . . it appeared, and he was not alone. There was a woman with him."

"A woman?" Tremayne repeated, his mind spinning ahead to new territory. "But Rhys rides alone. Always has." There had been rumors, of course, that Rhys had a band of thugs loyal to him, but he was never spotted with any other men, and those who had been caught would not admit to knowing him, not even under pain of torture. Never had there been any mention of a woman. "You are sure that you spied Rhys?"

"Unless someone else rides your steed."

Tremayne's fist clenched and it was all he could do not to cuff the impudent soldier.

"Tell me of the woman."

" 'Twas thick fog, hard to see, but it seemed as if she and Rhys had been . . . embracing afore they heard us and made haste."

Tremayne advanced upon the sorry excuse for a warrior. "Are you telling me that both escaped? On *my* horse?"

"There were two horses, m'lord, but aye, we were unable to catch them." Edwin foolishly lifted his chin a notch. Tremayne balled his fist and slammed it into the upstart, sending him reeling. His head banged into the wall. Blood trickled from the corner of his mouth.

"Fool," Tremayne growled as he advanced on the smaller, younger man. "Now, hear you this. You are to pull together another search party, one with dogs and my best huntsmen. You are to find the bastard, this woman, *and* my horse, then bring them back to the castle. Alive. If you are successful, you will be rewarded handsomely, but if you fail, the consequences will be dire." He pushed his face near Edwin's. "Do you understand?"

"Aye, m'lord."

"Good." Tremayne, pain pounding through the base of his skull, whirled on the cocky son of a dog who had been spying on Marwood. "As for you, you are to leave Twyll this night and return to Marwood. You will take someone with you who will report back—aye, take Red." Though an unsavory sort whose love of coin would be his downfall, Red was one of the best spies in the castle—just less trustworthy than James or Edwin. "Track Cavan's movements, find out how many men he has called forth to help him with the attack, and uncover his intentions."

A corner of James's insolent mouth lifted. "And what is in it for me?"

Regan stiffened. Edwin rubbed his jaw, which had begun to discolor, and his gaze followed Tremayne's every movement. "What's in it for you?" Tremayne repeated. "Well, let us start with the most elemental—you shall live. If your reports are accurate and aid us in fending off—nay, in *defeating*—Cavan, you will be rewarded, mayhap with the recently vacated position of Sir Edwin here."

Edwin's hand, still rubbing his aching jaw, stilled.

"What if I want more?" James asked.

Tremayne's jaw tightened. "How much more?"

James's gaze slid to Regan. "Mayhap I could be constable."

Regan, who had been standing near the table, stepped forward. "You insolent, stupid fool—"

"Quiet. Just do your job," Tremayne said. "All of you." He leveled a stern look at each man in the room—and smelled deception. One of these men, mayhap more, was betraying him. He thought again of the footsteps scurrying away as he had descended the tower stairs. How many others were involved?

God's teeth, 'twas hell to be the baron.

"'Tis time." Rhys stood in the doorway, and Tara, still gazing out the window, started at the sound of his voice. Turning, she was surprised to see him in clean breeches and tunic—black decorated with brown leather and metal studs, the opening at his throat gaping where the leather cords held it together only loosely. Dark chest hair was visible, obscuring her view of the fine muscles beneath it. Not that she cared. He was an outlaw, a thief, her captor. Nothing more. Aye, he was tall, with a straight back and broad shoulders, and his silver eyes did hold her in a gaze so intense that she always felt the need to put some distance—breathing room—between his body and hers, but he was nothing to her. Nothing.

His gaze was once again centered on her face and slipped downward to the hollow of her throat and bare chest, where the tops of her breasts were visible.

"So tonight you are a lady," he said with that crooked half smile she found so irritating. "And earlier you were a witch."

"I be neither."

"So you say." He crossed the room and insolently lifted a still-damp curl from her shoulder. "You wear not your ring, nor the chain upon which it hung."

"I lost it."

He barked out a laugh. "I think not."

"Oh, but I did . . . on the ride here, mayhap in the river where both me and my horse nearly drowned, the chain snapped. When I took off my clothes here, 'twas gone."

Not a fraction of doubt entered his cursed gaze. Should I send out a search party?"

" 'Twould be of no use. By now the ring is probably a long, long way downstream . . . or mayhap lost in the forest."

So close was he that she smelled the leather upon him, noticed a few streaks of blue in his eyes. He pressed his face even closer, so that she smelled his breath, and her heart took flight, pounding so fast and hard she was certain he could sense it—hear it. He was going to kiss her again. She knew it. And though she willed herself to step backward, she couldn't. Her feet wouldn't move and her gaze was drawn to his mouth, which hovered so closely over hers. "Lost in the river? Forgotten in the forest?" His gaze centered on her lips. "Oh, lady, I think not. You would not give up your prize so easily. Methinks you've hidden the stone. Somewhere here."

"Nay, I—"

"Shh." He placed a warm finger on her lips and something deep inside her melted. "Worry not. Your secret—it be safe with me."

She didn't believe him for a second.

His gaze traveled slowly upward to rest at her eyes. It silently said things to her that were wicked and wanton. Her breath caught. She swallowed hard and glanced at his mouth, partially hidden in the dark bristles of a beard that needed to be shorn. She flushed. Her skin tingled at the thought of his lips pressed intimately against hers.

Oh, dear God, what was she thinking? Turning her head, she recoiled in disgust at the realization that she wanted to kiss him.

"Oh, woman," he said under his breath. "You vex me." Then, as if hearing his own words, he stiffened and drew back. "Come. As I said, 'tis time."

She managed a deep breath. "For?"

"You to meet the others."

"You mean outlaws and thugs?"

His smile was wicked—a devil's slash of white against his bearded chin. "To begin with. We'll move on to the murderers and kidnappers later."

"I be with a kidnapper," she shot back.

He clucked his tongue. "And I expected gratitude for saving you from Tremayne's men."

"What have I to fear of them?" she asked as his gaze slid down the length of her body.

He seemed bemused that she'd changed into the dead lady's finery. "They're not a trustworthy lot."

"And you . . . and your men are?"

He barked out a laugh. "Between ourselves, yea."

"But I be not a part of your clan."

"Not yet." He took her elbow and urged her toward the door.

"Never."

"Ah, but you might like the ritual of admittance."

"I daren't ask what that might be."

"Simple tasks," he assured her, and she guessed from the spark in his usually cold eyes that he was teasing her—flirting with her, this bold scoundrel of an outlaw.

"Such as?"

They passed into the dark corridor and walked toward the great hall, from which sounds of gossip and laughter emanated. Tara tried not to notice the possessive feel of Rhys's fingers through the velvet, half convincing herself that he was having no effect on her whatsoever. But when she tried to pull her arm from his grip, his fingers only tightened.

"Such as pleasing me."

Her heart thudded. "And how would I do that?"

"Use your imagination, witch."

Heat rose up her neck and she felt her cheeks stain with a blush she couldn't hide. She didn't risk a glance in his direction, for she was certain he would be laughing at her. "I dare not even think."

"Nay?"

He *was* mocking her.

She tried to wrench her elbow away from him, for even through the velvet she felt the hard pressure of his fingers.

"Mayhap, to join our group you might steal something of value from Tremayne of Twyll."

"Oh, yes, very easy," she mocked.

"Not only must you take a prized possession from him, but you must bring it here."

"And why would I endanger my life?"

"To join with us, of course."

"Of course," she replied dryly.

As they entered the great hall, the whispers and bawdy laugher that had been echoing down the hallway immediately ceased. A few men had collected around two tables, and the looks they sent her caused Tara's blood to chill. There were those without teeth, one was missing an eye, most looked as if they had lived in the clothes they were wearing for the better part of their lives. Straggly hair, beards in fierce need of trimming, and eyes that were shuttered, hiding whatever secrets they carried deep in their souls.

Rhys didn't bother with their names but made a general announcement. "This is Lady Tara. She is our guest and will be treated accordingly." He paused, looking each man in the eye for a split second, silently promising that were something unpleasant to happen to her the guilty party would have to answer to him. He didn't have to say a word; Tara and the others read it in the set of his jaw.

"She's joinin' with us?" one man asked, his pointed nose wrinkled in disapproval.

"For a while."

A few men whispered among themselves. Some leered at her, thinly veiled lust evident in their eyes; others ignored her, and still others seemed irritated that she had penetrated their private hideaway. "Wait a fool's minute," one, better dressed than the others, said when Rhys offered her a place at one of the tables. "I thought there be a rule. One that couldn't be broke."

"The lady hasn't decided how long she'll stay."

"But—"

"We'll discuss it later," Rhys said sharply, and the man, who had been pushing himself to his feet, sat down abruptly, his narrow little hips landing on the bench with a soft plop. "Now, let's eat."

"And it's about time," Rosie grumbled as she and Pigeon and a youth of about nine or ten carried in planks of food. Eel, venison, and pike—cooked simply and accompanied by hard bread and ale. The men ate hungrily, greedily, as if they doubted they would ever see food again. They surveyed her silently, with looks that turned her blood to ice and caused her skin to prickle in distaste.

She sat with Rhys on a short bench positioned at the end of one table, while the men around her ate with the worst manners possible. She was given a slice of bread topped with some of Rosie's salted eel. "Eat up," Rosie instructed, then ordered her daughter to fill the wooden mazers. "Hurry along with the wine, now, and you, boy, bring that venison here." She muttered something under her breath as Pigeon filled cups and blushed as Rhys offered her a kind thanks.

The girl was besotted with the man, sure as anything. She went about her tasks, filling cups before they emptied, but as the men talked and teased her, Pigeon managed only a weak smile. When she thought no one was looking, she stole longing glances at Rhys.

He didn't seem to notice, apparently intent on his joint of venison. There was talk of robberies planned, loot taken, and gossip that was heard about the villages, abbeys, and castles. Tara felt the emerald ring press against her skin and wondered which of these men would slit her throat for such a prize. From what she could gather, Lord Innis of Marwood had died, leaving his only son, Cavan, to rule. The general feeling at the tables was that Innis was a fair baron, his son a hotheaded, bloodthirsty tyrant.

" 'Twill be the end of picking off wagons going to and from Marwood," the man with only one eye insisted. "Cavan, 'e won't stand fer it."

"Ach. There wasn't much there, anyway," another man said around a mouthful of bread. He had a round face and a bulbous nose. His short fingers moved quickly as he talked. " 'Tis much better at Twyll."

"Aye, but Tremayne, he be gettin' more cautious as well."

Rhys's back stiffened slightly, but he didn't say a word until another man, taller than most, entered the hall. He took two long strides. Then, as his gaze landed full force on Tara, he nearly missed a step.

"Abelard," Rhys said without a smile. "Glad you could join us."

"Someone needed to check the perimeter. God only knows who might have been following you."

"Was it safe?" Rhys cocked a dark brow.

"So it seems."

Standing, Rhys gestured toward Tara. "This is the woman I spoke of earlier. Lady Tara."

"I be not a lady," Tara said swiftly. She felt the weight of Abelard's gaze and managed a stiff smile. He was a big man, larger than Rhys, with wild white hair in deep contrast to his black eyebrows. All of his features—eyes, nose, and mouth—were oversized, a mite large for a face that was clean and sculpted.

"What be you, then?"

"A . . . woman."

She heard a few snickers from the men, who kept their gazes downcast as they continued to feast.

"Not a witch? Rhys says you were chanting spells by the creek."

He pulled up a chair, squeezing next to her at one of the corners, and one of the men who had been close to her slid further down on the bench, grateful, it appeared, to put some distance between himself and the big white-haired one.

"I was praying."

"To whom?"

She managed a smile. "Whoever was listening."

"Well, ye best be on yer knees to the Holy Mother," Rosie said, entering the room through a side door and slapping a plank of sizzling meat onto the table in front of Abelard. "Pigeon, hurry up with that ale, would ye?" she called over her shoulder.

"I always pray to Mary," Tara said.

"And others as well," Rhys pointed out.

"Aye."

Rosie clucked her tongue and wiped her hands on the apron straining over her wide belly. "Well, remember, the Lord God is a jealous god, and ye'd be best puttin' no false gods before Him."

Tara caught the older woman's gaze and saw the fires of piety burning in her eyes. "I'll keep that in mind."

"We have no one 'ere practicin' the dark arts, do we?" the stubby-fingered thief demanded. "We all . . . we all be Christians here. Right?"

A few men nodded as they peered into the bottoms of their mazers and swilled more wine. "All Christians."

"Then you go to mass?" Tara asked and saw a few sheepish looks being exchanged among the men. "And you believe in the Ten Commandments . . . is there not one about stealing?"

The men grumbled among themselves, but no one

answered as they buried their noses even deeper into their cups.

"Aye, and I've mentioned it before," Rosie said, nodding her head like a stern mother.

"And what would ye do, Big Rose? If it weren't for what we get thievin', ye'd have no roof over yer head, no place fer you and yer little one. Ye'd have to start liftin' yer skirts fer a coin, methinks."

"That's the trouble, Samuel, ye don't think," she said, and she picked up a plank that still held a fat piece of eel and conked him on the head. " 'Twill be a cold day in hell before I'll be sellin' meself." She spun on her heel and looked hard at each man in turn. "And any of ye who thinks otherwise can take it up with me." She flounced out of the room, and not one of the motley crew of crooks, petty thieves, and kidnappers dared breathe a word.

Rhys didn't comment, but a smile danced in his eyes as he finished his meal and the talk circled back to Baron Innis and his death.

"There'll be trouble," Abelard thought aloud. He pierced a piece of venison with his knife and wagged it in front of Rhys's nose. "Some say he thinks he's the damned heir of Twyll." He bit the meat off the knife.

"Do they?" Rhys bristled. The emerald felt suddenly very heavy.

"He plans to make war."

"Why would he think he be baron?" the well-dressed thief asked.

"Good question, Kent." Abelard dropped his knife and rubbed his beard thoughtfully. "We all have heard the rumor—that Lady Farren was delivering a babe at the time of the attack on Twyll. Somehow both she and her husband, Lord Gilmore, were slain by Merwynn, who then declared himself the new lord."

The skin over Rhys's face grew tight and his jagged scar paled. Abelard's eyes, a shifting shade of amber in the firelight, focused steadily upon Tara, as if he were speaking directly to her. "Merwynn was Rhys's father as well, y'see. Anyway, the babe disappeared. Unborn or brought into this world, the infant vanished—no tiny body was ever discovered, alive or dead. 'Tis said that a servant ran off with the child and, as he did, managed to steal an emerald ring the likes of which no one has seen."

Tara wanted to wrap her fingers around the stone tied to her waist. Instead she lifted her chin and met Abelard's gaze. "And Cavan—this son of Innis—why would he think he be the ruler?"

"That's the interesting part. Aye, he was adopted by Innis, who fathered no sons of his own despite having two wives. Each died before she could provide Innis with any sons."

Abelard pulled off a hunk of bread and held it as he spoke. "Old Innis was a secretive man. He told no one of the circumstances of the child's birth. Many thought Cavan was the son of one of the women who warmed his bed. Who knows?" He lifted a broad shoulder. "There is no proof, of course, unless he somehow still owns the ring that was stolen with him." Tara's heart thundered and she was certain the cord around her waist would unravel and the jewel would drop to the floor at any second. She glanced nervously at Rhys, for he'd seen the stone, but his expression was calm.

Only when the others had left the room, upon Abelard's orders, did the white-haired man turn to her. "Now, Lady Tara, I think 'tis time we spoke the truth. Rhys told me about the emerald ring. If I be not mistaken, 'tis the jewel that was missing from Gilmore's castle when he and his wife were killed and their babe disappeared." Folding his arms over his chest, he said, "Where is it and how did it come to be in your possession?"

"I—I know not of what you speak," she protested, getting to her feet. "There is no—"

Rhys's reaction was swift. Grabbing her arm, he pulled her onto the bench, so close to him that their legs, separated by only a layer of velvet and his breeches, were pressed together. His fingers, tight around her wrist, were like manacles. "Tell him, Tara," Rhys said in a firm voice that brooked no argument, "for I, too, would like to know where the dark emerald of Twyll be and how you came to have it."

Chapter Four

Tara couldn't deny the truth. Rhys had seen her with the ring when she was chanting at the creek. Oh, she'd been such a fool, such an utter idiot to let him catch her. "My mother gave it to me."

"Your mother?" Abelard sneered, shaking his head and draining his cup. "The woman who once owned the ring has been dead for nearly twenty years."

"The ring was given me by Lodema, the woman I thought was my mother."

"Is she yet alive?"

"Aye." Tara experienced a pang of loneliness, for she missed Lodema, with her off-key humming, shuffling gait, and easy smile.

"Show it to me," Abelard ordered.

"The ring?"

"Is it not what we be discussing?"

"Oh, 'twas lost," she lied, knowing he wouldn't believe her but unable to admit the truth. "In the river where we crossed."

"I think not." Abelard's face had turned a rosy hue, either from the wine or from a quietly seething rage—mayhap a little of both. He snapped his fingers impatiently. "Show me."

"But I—"

"Do as he says," Rhys growled through clenched

teeth, "or I will search first the clothes that you wore at the creek, then the chamber where you were bathed, and then, if the ring still be missing, I will undress you myself and search your dress and whatever is underneath." His jaw was set, his eyes unabashedly demanding. "Where is it?"

She swallowed hard and fought the urge to run. She would get only a few steps before Rhys would catch up with her. Damn the man. Silently she cursed the second she'd met him. She should have run away when she heard the first jangle of his horse's bridle.

"The ring?"

Fire swept up her neck. Her mind raced with possible lies, all of which she quickly discarded.

"Where is it?"

"I have it. Beneath my dress."

"Good," Abelard said, some of his irritation seeming to disappear. "Let me see it."

"But . . . but . . . I cannot undress here . . ." Cheeks already flaming, she blushed to the roots of her dark hair and couldn't help notice the mockery—the damned amusement—in Rhys's expression. Her lips pursed, and pride lifted her chin a notch though she was dying of shame inside. Had he not already seen her without clothes—not once but twice?

"The ring," Abelard insisted, snapping his fingers yet again and holding out his calloused palm.

"But—"

"Oh, for the love of Saint Peter—" Rhys's grip tightened over her wrist.

"We will be but a second," he assured Abelard as he dragged her to her feet and hauled her out of the great hall to the darkened corridor. His legs were long, his strides swift, and Tara had to half run to keep up with him.

"Stop!" she cried, her boots scraping on the cold stone floor of Broodmore. "What do you think you're doing?"

He didn't answer, nor did he pause until he'd taken her into the chamber that had once been the chapel, the room where she'd bathed and he'd so recently seen her partially dressed.

"Get the bloody ring for Abelard," he ordered.

"But—"

"Now!"

He released her and stood in the doorway, feet planted shoulder-width apart, arms folded angrily across his broad chest.

"You would watch me?" she demanded.

"Aye. Gladly."

"But, but—" she stammered, then caught herself and glared at him. " 'Tis a beast you be, Rhys the outlaw. A blackhearted, cursed dog who—"

"No more arguments!" His eyes flashed fire and his back was stiff as newly forged steel. He posed a formidable jailer as he blocked her only avenue of escape. One long finger jabbed the air between them. "Get on with it."

Again she had no choice, and silently vowing to find a way to break out of this prison, a way to prove that she would not let any man, especially a criminal, tell her what to do, she spun on her heel, turning her back to him, and unlaced the quilted bodice of the velvet dress. Cold air caressed her bare skin as she lowered the soft fabric, and she felt his gaze, hot and burning, against her back. *Help me,* she prayed silently as her fingers fumbled with the cord tied around her waist. While unknotting the thin strap of leather with the fingers of one hand, she tried in vain to hold the dress over her naked breasts.

"Oh, bother," she muttered under her breath as the knot refused to give way.

"No spells to untie knots?"

"Nay, but I surely have one that will still your tongue," she snapped back.

"Do you?"

"Aye," she lied, "and another that will cause your eyes to dim and your brain to turn to gruel."

" 'Tis too late for that, I fear," he replied, amusement ringing in his voice.

Oh, the devil be with him! Arrogant son of a—

"Here"—she heard him approach—"let me help."

"Nay!" she spat, her spine stiffening. "Nay, I can do it—"

" 'Twill be faster, and we need not to keep Abelard waiting. He be not a patient man." She sensed him near, felt his breath against her skin, and yet she nearly jumped out of it when his warm fingers grazed the bare flesh of her waist. She sucked in her breath and held the dress tight to her chest. Heat started at the small of her back and climbed up her neck as he, growling about the knot, which had apparently swollen, worked with the cords. The touch of his fingers caused her to flinch a bit, not from pain but from anticipation. The knot gave way at last. She let out her breath as she slid the ring and necklace off the cord with fingers that shook.

"There. 'Tis done," Rhys said through clenched teeth. 'Twas all he could do as he'd fiddled with the knot not to move his hands up her rib cage, feel the weight of her breasts in his palms. He'd fought the urge to spin her in his arms, kiss her until the fight left her body, and then slide down to kiss her nipples and dig his fingers into the firm flesh of her buttocks. Instead

he'd released her and stepped back, forcing those
thoughts away.

He leaned a shoulder against the doorway and studied her without a trace of his earlier humor. Spying
her at the creek, he'd been fascinated by her beauty.
Earlier this evening while she was dripping from her
bath, he'd been amused at her fury. He'd found her
state of undress and ire erotic and, yea, amusing. Now
after touching her smooth skin with the tips of his
fingers, he was furious with himself for his attraction.
Worse yet as he felt compelled to bend her will to his,
he found no satisfaction in the flash of indignation he
saw in her eyes. He should never have told Abelard
about the stone—'twould only bring them grief. He
could feel it in his bones.

She slid her arms into the sleeves of the dress.

Rhys was not only aroused—his damnable manhood
springing to attention—he was furious with himself for
wanting her. She was a witch, or so she thought—a
woman who chanted on the banks of a stream in winter. She was a liar and mayhap a thief, not unlike
himself. How else would she have come into possession of a stone so valuable?

There was another possibility.

It could be that she was the rightful heir of Twyll,
the only issue of Lord Gilmore and Lady Farren, who
were murdered by Merwynn.

*Your father, Rhys. 'Tis possible this mite of a woman
is your sworn enemy.*

His teeth ground together and his jaw ached at the
thought. Was it possible? Could the rightful ruler of
Twyll be a woman—this beautiful sorceress whose
skin appeared flawless, her muscles sleek? He remembered the cleft of her spine slicing delicately down the

middle of her back to disappear invitingly beneath the gathered folds of velvet.

He caught himself up short and swore under his breath. "Curse it all!" For the love of Saint Jude, what had he been thinking?

"Pardon?" she asked, casting a look over her shoulder while struggling into the bodice and straightening the slender sleeves that tapered to points over the backs of her hands.

"Nothing." He cleared his throat and coughed. "You have the ring?"

Rotating swiftly, her hair and the skirt of her dress billowing, she held the chain aloft by one finger, the ring dangling seductively from her hand. "Right here." The gem sparkled in the dying firelight.

Striding quickly forward, Rhys reached for the priceless jewel, but Tara was faster. She swung the ring into her palm and captured it with eager fingers. "Let us be done with this," she said, starting for the door. Rhys was at her side in an instant. They returned to the great hall and once again, she dangled her prize from long, slim fingers, suspending the legendary stone before Abelard's greedy eyes.

For a second the older man was entranced with the glittering emerald as it swayed seductively in front of his nose. "Has it any power?" he asked. "Rumor has it that it brings good fortune."

"Since it has been in my possession, I've been kidnapped, chased by soldiers, and held prisoner in a crumbling keep where ghosts are said to walk and robbers and murderers hide." She gestured with her free hand to the empty, dark chamber lit only by a solitary candle and the weak light from a dying fire. Charred walls, cobwebs, faded tapestries, dust and a few battle-scarred tables, chairs, and benches were all that remained of the once fine and lively hall of Broodmore. "Nay, sir," she mocked, "I cannot say this stone brings any luck other than bad."

"Still, 'tis powerful." Abelard, his large features shadowed in the semidarkness, snatched the prize in midair, and this time Tara, with a lofty lift of an eyebrow in Rhys's direction, let it be taken from her. "By the gods," the white-haired man whispered, awestruck as he turned the ring over and over in his fingers, holding it in front of the candle's thin flame. "This is it. The damned dark emerald of Twyll."

"How know you this?" she asked.

"The size—the cut . . . what else? And all these years I thought mayhap it was idle gossip—only the wishful thinking of old women whose time has passed them by and now they enhance their own sorry lives by creating stories—braiding the truth with lies as easily as they weave scenes into a tapestry."

"So now we have it—proof that the stone and possibly an heir exist, that the rumors surrounding the siege of Twyll be true," Rhys said, taking the ring from Abelard's strong fingers and handing the treasure back to Tara. "Hide this. 'Tis not safe here."

Abelard seemed about to protest, but Rhys cut him off. "If you haven't noticed, my friend, there be a pickpocket or two here who, if given half a chance, would rob the lady blind."

"Would they now?" she asked insolently. Oh, she was a fearless wench.

"Aye, without the slightest bit of encouragement. Mayhap even slit your throat."

" 'Tis a pleasant place you've brought me to, Rhys of Twyll."

"Fear not, m'lady, for I will sleep at your door, keeping the vermin and thieves out."

"Or me in."

"Aye, that too," he admitted, unable to stay his lips from twisting into a grin that she appeared to find disquieting. Her mouth pursed in irritation, and if looks were to kill, he would certainly be ready for the grave, for she was glaring at him with all the hatred and disgust she could muster.

Abelard rubbed the silvery stubble that had the nerve to grow on the lower half of his face. "So," he said thoughtfully, his stub of a finger moving over his lip, "it seems Lord Tremayne has reason to fear an uprising from the issue of Gilmore, does it not?"

"Aye." Vengeance and satisfaction warmed the cold hatred buried deep in Rhys's heart. "So it does."

"But he knows not who that issue is." Gold eyes assessed Tara as if she, not the ring, were the true prize, and Rhys experienced his first unwelcome stab of jealousy.

Snapping his fingers noisily, Abelard called to the open doorway, "Rosie, girl, bring us more wine."

"And haven't ye had enough?" Rosie's voice was muffled.

"Now."

Tara stuffed the necklace into her pocket.

"Lord in heaven," Rosie grumbled. "Pigeon, the jug—nay, I'll do it meself. His lord and master be dyin' of thirst, it seems."

Abelard swallowed a smile, and his eyebrows rose in eager anticipation. "Let us celebrate, my friend," he said to Rhys, "for, soon, methinks, revenge will be ours."

"Mayhap." Rhys wasn't convinced.

" 'Twill be." Abelard motioned Rosie to quicken her step as she entered the room carrying a jug and wooden cups.

"I be not yer slave, Abelard," she reminded him. "I do this only from the goodness of me weak and foolish heart." She poured three mazers of wine and set them on the table near the candle, then tucked an errant wisp of hair under her scarf.

"And because you worship the ground I tread."

"In a pig's eye."

"Rosie, girl, won't you join us?" Abelard asked, and the heavy woman shook her head.

" 'Tis way past me bedtime, Abelard, and if I know ye, ye'll be yowlin' for a meal the minute ye wake up."

He picked up his mazer, held it aloft, and grinned wickedly, his golden eyes narrowing as he said, "To the defeat of Tremayne of Twyll. May I have the pleasure of sending his soul straight to hell."

Lodema closed her eyes and winced against a sudden jab of pain—the same piercing agony that fired her joints with each cold spell. Her knees creaked and her fingers were knotted and thick, aching more profoundly as the cold of winter seeped through the cracks in the walls of this old hut.

And there was more than the pain that bothered her. She was lonely, feeling more alone than she had ever in her life. Before she'd been given the baby, she was young and independent, and though many people in the village seemed to pity her, to think her odd for living alone in the forest, she'd cared not. Their eyes, filled with empathy, understanding, or even fear, had only amused her. She had reveled in her oddity and smiled inwardly to herself when they'd been desperate for her help. Oh, they shunned her in the village, women often crossing the muddy road quickly, dashing past wagons pulled by teams of oxen, or frightening high-strung horses as they scurried through the puddles just to avoid meeting her. She'd heard that many considered her a witch, a sorceress, or even a female emissary from Satan.

But when they were in trouble, when their loved ones were consumed with sickness, or when a babe was turned and unable to birth easily, they came running, their fears temporarily stowed away as they begged her to help. Then her spells and chants and prayers were welcome. Then the runes she scratched or the candles she lit were no longer distrusted. Then, instead of knowing, worried glances, she received pleas, fresh eggs, and all manner of livestock, along with empty promises of friendship eternal.

'Twas enough to make even the most cynical soul laugh.

And she had for years. Behind their stiff, self-righteous backs, she'd smiled smugly to herself, content in the knowledge of who she was and happy in her own life. With her daughter. But now, as she aged, when her little cottage seemed cold as death and oh, so empty, her happiness seemed only a bittersweet memory. "Think not on it," she told herself, blowing out the candle. Then she watched in horror as the smoke curled oddly toward the blackened crossbeams that supported the roof.

Her old heart stilled. 'Twas not a sign. Could not be. Tara was safe. And yet the wisps of smoke rose in a pattern that made her ancient skin prickle with the knowledge that there was evil lurking in the forest. Nervously, Lodema licked her dry lips and sent up a quiet prayer, one to the Christian God, that her daughter, wherever she be, was not in any jeopardy.

But the fear that was lodged in her heart could not be dismissed. Tara, light of her life, was in danger. Serious danger.

*   *   *

Seated on the floor of the old chapel, Rhys leaned against the door. One leg was stretched in front of him, the other bent so that his boot rested beneath the opposing knee. The fire was now merely coals that glowed an eerie red as once-hot embers turned to ash. Tara, if that be her true name, was asleep on the pallet near the old altar, her breathing regular, her chest rising and falling evenly, the stone presumably yet in her possession.

How could one tiny woman affect him so? From the moment he'd laid eyes upon her standing naked in the forest, raising her arms to the heavens, chanting pagan spells, he'd been captivated. The dark emerald ring of Twyll had only added to her allure.

And yet he was certain he was stepping into a trap, one carefully laid by the fates, a snare with sharp teeth of steel that were sure to rip out his soul.

As he gazed at her, he felt at a loss for words. Her hair parted and he caught a glimpse of her throat, still partially veiled by the thick black curls that spiraled past her shoulders. God in heaven, she was beautiful. 'Twas near impossible not to envision his mouth against her shoulder, his tongue sliding down that alluring cleft that led ever downward. He'd seen her naked backside at the creek and wondered what it would be like to touch each supple round cheek, to kiss that softness and smell the secret scent of her femininity.

Her coverlet had fallen away, and he stared unabashedly at her sleeping form. His damned crotch ached and yet he could not drag his gaze away from her, could not stop envisioning her bare body. Oh, to feel her naked against him. In his mind's eye he could see the two of them—unclothed, embracing, kissing in the most intimate of places. He imagined her lying beneath him, writhing in pure animal pleasure, twisting from back to front, her nipples erect and hard, her green eyes widening with passion and surprise as he kissed those perfectly formed breasts, tugged at them with his teeth, and then, when she was anxious and crying for the want of him, thrusting deep into the warm moistness of her most private hollow.

Again and again and again would he take her.

So innocent she was. So seductive.

His member grew thicker, and he forced his thoughts away from the sweet torment of his bitter-sweet fantasy. He plucked an old piece of straw from the floor and turned it in his fingers as he contemplated the mystery of her. How had she come upon the ring? Not that it mattered. The fact that the dark emerald of Twyll existed gave credence to the old rumors and created endless possibilities.

"Rhys," Abelard hissed from the other side of the door. A light tapping accompanied his voice.

Slowly Rhys got to his feet, then cast one final glance at the sleeping woman, resting so peacefully, as if she was not imprisoned in a thieves' lair, not held hostage in a burned-out castle that was rumored to be haunted, not sleeping in a dead woman's velvet gown.

Without making a sound, Rhys slipped through the doorway to the darkened hall.

"She is asleep?" Abelard asked.

"Aye."

"You're certain?"

"Look for yourself."

Abelard did just that. Shoving open the door a little further, he walked into the room without bothering to step softly. At the altar, he leaned over the pallet and watched for endless minutes. Rhys could almost feel the older man's fingers itch for want of the stone, could nearly read Abelard's galloping thoughts, running toward theft of the remarkable jewel.

Instead he gave off a satisfied grunt and strode to the door, shutting it softly behind him. He motioned Rhys down the passageway to the great hall. "You," he said to Kent. "Guard the woman."

Squatting near the fire, the toes of his polished boots nearly in the ash, Kent was cleaning his nails with the point of his knife. He managed an irritated frown. "I be not a jailer."

"Except for tonight. Go. Now." Abelard had no patience for insubordination.

"Is she our prisoner?" Kent, his blond hair gilded in the firelight, was finally interested. His knife quit flicking the dirt beneath his fingernails onto the floor.

"Nay," Rhys said.

"Then why needs she to be guarded?"

" 'Tis none of your business," Abelard grumbled. "Just do as I say."

"She is detained but for a while," Rhys interjected as Kent's nostrils flared slightly and the corners of his mouth drew into a tight, uncompromising grimace. Slowly he stood and shoved his dagger into the sheath he wore strapped to his hip.

"All you needs do is watch the door," Abelard added.

Kent scowled, then, without hurrying, made his way stiffly toward the dark corridor.

"I wonder about him," Abelard said under his breath. "He takes orders not well."

"None of us does. 'Tis why we are all here."

"Aye." Abelard sighed, then, assured that he and Rhys were alone, threw several thick chunks of oak onto the fire. Eager flames devoured the moss and pitch, popping and hissing hungrily. "Do you have any idea what that stone of the woman's is worth?" he asked, glancing over his shoulder to make certain no one was lurking in the shadowy corners of the vast room. The blackened chamber was empty, the single candle burning low and flickering in the wind that slid through the cracks in Broodmore's ancient walls.

"A fortune."

"Beyond that." Abelard dusted his hands as he straightened. "That gem is the very destruction of Tremayne of Twyll." His eyes glittered wickedly. "Not only does the emerald prove that there be a rightful heir to Lord Gilmore and that the story surrounding his death be not just the jabberings of some old women, but the ring itself is worth enough to buy an army of cutthroats and mercenaries, the likes of which all of Gaeaf and Twyll combined have not seen before." He bit the corner of his lip. "We all have reason to hate Tremayne—you for your banishment." Rhys winced inside. "Tara, if she be the true issue of Gilmore—and I be not certain that she is—because of the murder of her family, and me"—he held up his hand to show off his stub of an index finger—"For this. 'Tis lucky that my finger"—he wiggled the stump—"is all that Tremayne's blade found."

Rhys shook his head and stretched an arm upward, easing a knot of tension between his shoulder blades. " 'Twas not just your finger that he sliced, but your pride as well."

"Aye." Abelard had always believed himself to be the best swordsman in Twyll. Losing his finger and nearly his life in a battle against Tremayne had changed and embittered him. 'Twas the reason he'd taken Rhys under his wing years before when Tremayne's men had left him naked and nearly dead in the forest, believing that wolves would finish him off. When Rhys had wakened, his skin afire from the flogging he'd received, he'd prayed to a disinterested God that he die rather than suffer the torture of healing. Abelard, the brute, had tended to him, brought him back to life, and abetted his festering need for vengeance against his half brother. "Think on it, Rhys," Abelard said now, his face alive, his eyes brighter than the flames in the grate. "We now have the means to destroy Tremayne." His smile was pure evil. "The emerald has given us this opportunity. We cannot let it pass."

"The ring be not ours."

Abelard waved his hand as if he were dismissing a lazy servant. "That matters not."

" 'Tis Tara's."

"Do you believe her story? That it was given to her adoptive mother?"

Rhys scowled into the fire. "I know not."

" 'Tis far-fetched, think you not? Why would the old woman keep it all these years? Why would she not sell it? Did she get it by stealing the babe from the castle? How did she end up with the child? Who knows whether she only took the ring and the babe is elsewhere? Cavan of Marwood seems to think he be the true heir. Why?"

The same puzzlements plagued Rhys, though he had not yet voiced them.

"So. What the woman thinks matters not." Abelard was certain he'd made his point and that his logic was irrefutable.

Rhys eyed his old friend—a man he didn't trust and yet a man for whom he would lay down his sorry life. " 'Tis not ours."

"So? We are thieves, are we not?"

"Not this time."

"Oh, for the love of Saint Jude, why not? You're

not goin' soft on me now, are you? Since when did you care about booty, however it be gained?"

"This time 'tis different!"

"Aye! This time 'tis the damned dark emerald of Twyll we speak of!" Abelard sighed and shook his head. White strands of hair danced around his face. "We can use the ring."

Rhys shook his head. "Only if Tara agrees. No matter how she came upon the emerald, 'tis now in her possession, and our rule here is he who has it owns it."

"Until someone else takes it."

" 'Tis hers."

"Ah, Rhys." Abelard's eyes widened in sudden understanding. "Methinks you've fallen in love with her."

Rhys glowered at the older man.

"Aye, she's a comely lass. A beauty. All the men in this hall saw it. Dressed in finery, her chin held high, her hair tossed insolently behind her head as if she were a real lady. Did you not notice the lust in the others' eyes, feel the current in the air—the need to mate? Even old Ben was fairly quivering with lust.

"That woman brought the thought of coupling to mind for each and every man in this room tonight. There will be many of them who will have to find their own ways to ease their hunger, for they will go to sleep aching with the want of a woman—*that* woman. Any man here would have given whatever he had stolen in his lifetime to spend one night in her bed. However, none be fool enough to think he is in love with her."

"Nor do I." Rhys was tired of the argument, irritated that the older man thought him caught in the vise of love—with the witch. 'Twas lunacy.

"Then defend not her honor or her *right* to the ring that just happens to be in her possession."

Rhys's skin was suddenly too tight. His fist curled.

"She is playing with you."

"I brought her here against her will."

"And now all you can see is the need to please her so that she will welcome you into her bed."

Rhys sprang. Grabbing Abelard's tunic, he pulled roughly, catching some of the chest hairs beneath the fabric, but the older man only barked a laugh.

"So it's gone that far, has it? That now you are threatening me?"

"Curse you, old man."

" 'Tis not I who is lost. We need that stone, Rhys, if we are to accomplish all we have sought for years. With the dark emerald of Twyll we can bring Tremayne to his knees."

"Only if Tara agrees," he said through clenched teeth.

"Why would she not?"

Footsteps heralded Kent's arrival. He rounded the corner and for once his serene, arrogant face was lined with worry.

"Trouble?" Abelard's hand was on the hilt of his sword.

" 'Tis the woman. Tara."

Rhys's gut clenched and he silently called himself a dozen kinds of fool.

"Say it not," Abelard ordered.

"She's gone." Kent's Adam's apple bobbed with anxiety. "I opened the door and . . . and saw her not."

Rhys was already half running down the hall. Why had he left the door unguarded even for a second? The door to the old chapel was ajar. He shoved it open with his shoulder. *Bam!* It hit the wall, and even before his eyes swept the interior he knew that Kent wasn't lying. The chamber was empty. Tara the witch had most certainly escaped.

And she'd taken with her the jewel.

Chapter Five

Tara hardly dared breathe. Dagger in her hand and emerald ring again strapped to her waist, she hurried along the labyrinthine passageways of the blackened old castle. Her feet in the dead woman's boots were silent, and she sent up a quick prayer that she would find a way out of the tomb where so many before her had died.

Rhys, when he discovered her missing, would be furious. If he ever caught up with her . . . She shivered and decided she would make certain that she eluded him. Biting her lip, she hurried onward into the darkness. Mice and rats scurried out of her path, their tiny claws scraping on the cold stone floor of the keep. Cobwebs caught on her hair and face, and she imagined spiders and the dried, empty carcasses of dead insects collecting in her curls. Not that it mattered. Determined to find a path of escape, she forged onward, hands outstretched to feel her way through the inky hallways. She had so little time. 'Twould be only a matter of minutes before Rhys would discover her missing.

And then what?

She shuddered to think, but she knew there were even worse fates here in the shadowy corridors of Broodmore.

What if she stumbled upon one of those toothless, lusting crooks that inhabited this crypt of a keep? She'd seen the way some of the men had looked at her, their eyes narrowing on her breasts and hips when she walked into the great hall with Rhys. There had been an air of discontentment, a sense of desperation in their faces. Many, she suspected, had not been with a woman in years. Had it not been for the fact that she was with the leader of the pack of thieves, some of them might have tried to compromise her virtue.

Not that they could. Not without a fight. If she came upon any of those leering beasts, she was ready, dagger in hand.

If only she could escape this monster of a castle with its crumbling walls and ill-fated past.

> *Broodmore, Broodmore,*
> *All that lived there died.*
> *Broodmore, Broodmore,*
> *All the children cried.*

The old rhyme played over and over again in her head, and she felt goose bumps rise on her skin as she remembered how she had feigned sleep, how 'twas all she could do not to sit up and scream as Abelard stood over her, his gaze creeping across her skin while she lay still on the pallet, breathing softly, forcing her tense muscles to appear relaxed. Now her fingers, inching along the rough stone walls, encountered a corner. Taking a deep breath, she turned the bend and nearly fell into a hole—nay, a staircase leading ever downward. Swallowing her fear, she edged deeper into this tomb of a castle.

Broodmore, Broodmore,
The kiss of death be there,
Broodmore, Broodmore,
All visitors beware.

Her heart hammered, and though the stone walls
that scraped her fingers as she felt her way down the
stairs were like ice, a fine sheen of sweat broke out
beneath the gown she'd claimed as her own. Somewhere in the far reaches of the keep she heard the
muted sound of running footsteps and realized that
she'd been found out. Already Rhys knew that she'd
fled.

"Mother Mary, help me," she whispered as the tips of
her fingers began to bleed. She had a bit of candle in her
pocket, which, should she light it, would aid her in finding her way, but she had no means to start a flame, nor
would she risk it even if she had, for instead of helping
her in her escape, the flickering light would surely draw
her pursuers to her.

At the base of the stairs she stood in total darkness,
and her skin crawled at the thought that she might be in
a dungeon where the skeletons of dead prisoners were
scattered over the floor. The thought unnerved her, for
she'd never been in a true jail before, never witnessed
the torture of men who were locked away. Who knew
what lurked in these dark rooms?

A rank smell lingered, as if the few rushes lying
upon the floor had been soaked in urine. Cautiously,
her right hand tight around the hilt of her knife, she
stepped forward and resumed her slow progress
along the wall, following the bend where the stones
turned, losing all sense of where she was in the keep.
Yea, she was in a lower level, but the one above had
been raised, a set of steps leading to the great

hall. Was this dungeon underground or still above it? Her head began to ache and she reminded herself that she had only to turn around, run her fingers along the wall, and end up at the stairs.

And then what? Meet a furious Rhys and Abelard on the upper level? Face the consequences of their rage and retribution? Nay, she would continue onward. Her sense of direction was shattered, though, and she feared that she was only entrapping herself even further in the bowels of this monstrosity. The smells of dust, mold, and urine mingled in the stale air, and though she strained for any sound from the hallways above, she heard nothing now, not even the expected pounding of footsteps or shouts of men searching for her.

Biting her lip, she kept moving, wondering if she was only going in a huge rectangle and would eventually end up at the staircase again. Her heart thudded, her fingers were raw when she sensed the change, a subtle shift in the atmosphere.

She paused and realized that she was feeling the whispery touch of fresh air, a breath of wind gusting into the old chamber. But from where? Slowly she rotated until the breeze was against her face, then edged in the direction of the unseen and welcome current.

Thunk. The toe of one boot encountered a mound. She jumped and cried out. Hideous images of dead bodies, rotting carcasses, or skeletons devoid of flesh raced in ugly detail through her mind, but a soft *chink* as she moved told her that she had only encountered a coiled chain, long forgotten and used for heaven-only-knew-what.

Stay calm. Keep your wits. She moved forward slowly toward the breeze until she reached the wall, where an uncovered window was positioned at the height of her head. As far as she could tell, it was her only means of escape. With nothing to step on, she couldn't scale the wall. She leaped up and grabbed the sill but couldn't pull herself through. Her nails scraped as she tried to hold on. Slowly her own weight dragged her down and her palm scraped against a rough shard of metal—pieces of bars that had long ago rusted through. She dropped back to the floor and flung herself upward yet again, only to fall onto the cold stones of the floor once more. "You must," she told herself, grit and determination forcing her to leap upward again. This time she caught the far end of the smooth stone sill and felt the bits of bars press painfully into her belly. Nonetheless, she pulled herself into the opening and tried to get her bearings.

Blinking hard, she gazed into what had once presumably been the bailey. It was impossible to gauge how far beneath her the ground was, but it didn't matter. She couldn't return to the dungeon. She balanced and twisted carefully in the small space, moving cautiously so as not to jab herself with the remainders of the bars while forcing her feet outside. The voluminous folds of her skirt caught several times, and she had to strain to maneuver into the right position, but eventually she was able to lower her body slowly, her fingers holding tight to the sill. As much as she could guess, the drop to the ground was only a few feet. Bracing herself, she let go of the sill.

She landed on the wet grass and nearly sank into the mire to the tops of her boots. The rain had stopped, but the ground was soft beneath her feet and her skin exposed by the square neckline of the dress felt the chill in the air.

With difficulty she started walking, keeping to the

darkest shadows near the wall, needing to get some distance between herself and the dungeon. The walls of Broodmore encircled her. With its uneven blackened towers and decaying curtain, the castle was a perfect prison. She had no idea which way lay freedom, but she knew she would find it. She had no choice. Her destiny lay with Twyll and Father Simon. She only hoped that the priest who had brought her as a babe to Lodema's hut would know whether she was the daughter of Lady Farren and Lord Gilmore.

And what if you be their heir? What then? Would you confront Baron Tremayne with the truth, show him the stone, be so daft as to think he would lay down his right to rule to you? She could not look that far forward. First she would find out the truth; then she would decide what to do with it.

Her head cleared, she started toward the tallest tower. Mayhap beneath the watchtower would be a gate that had rotted through. She had taken but a few steps when she heard a soft nicker.

The horses!

Her heart leaped at her sudden turn of luck, for there, not fifty feet away, were several mares and stallions, tethered to an ancient wagon that was missing its wheels. Tara spied Dobbyn and nearly shouted at her good fortune, for she now had the means to ride away from this miserable castle with its crypts and secrets and darkly brooding men.

Or did she?

Would not Rhys expect her to escape on horseback?

Was there not a guard? Her gaze surveyed the curtain wall and the rectangular towers that rose above it. In the darkness she searched the confines of the bailey, wondering about the thickset guard who had been posted outside the window of the chapel. Was he asleep? Or if he had given up his post, would not another man, just as earnest in his job, take his place?

Convinced that someone must be about, she squinted into the darkness but spied no one. Rhys had to know that she had fled her room—would he not think she would take her horse? Or had all the men been alerted and even now were searching the inside of the castle?

Noiselessly she crossed the expanse of weeds and grass to the broken-down wagon. The horses stirred, snorting and pawing as she walked along the tether line until she reached her nervous jennet. Dobbyn snorted and pranced, pulling at her lead. "Shh." Gently Tara rubbed the mare's nose, feeling her warm breath and velvet-soft muzzle against her chilled, scratched fingers. "Aye, 'tis a good girl you be, Dobbyn," she whispered while untying the tether and preparing to use it as a single rein. As the horse minced in a tight circle, Tara managed to hoist herself up on the mare's sleek back, certain at any moment that she would hear a sentry's shout or spy a man leaping out of the dark shadows to accost her.

Morrigu and Rhiannon, guide me.

With her nerves strung tight as bowstrings, she urged Dobbyn across the bailey toward the main gate. She planned to ride the interior perimeter, searching for rotting timbers, an open door, a crack in the curtain wall, anything. Her dress bunched around her legs, bare from thigh to the tops of her boots, and she clung tightly to the single rein while winding her fingers in the mare's thick mane.

Please, God, let me find a way out.

Most of the bailey was overgrown with berry vines and bracken along with tall grass . . . it mattered not.

Past an old well and an eel pond that had long ago flooded its banks she rode.

Somewhere far away a wolf sent up a lonely cry, and for a second she thought she heard a man's shout. Her heart froze. She urged Dobbyn ever faster in the wide circle. *Come on, come on. There must be a way out. There has to be!*

The main gate was closed, a rusting portcullis blocking her exit. Her mount broke into a gentle lope. Searching every inch of stone and mortar—the collapsing towers, the once-regal fore buildings, the turrets—Tara saw no one and no way out of this tumbledown prison. 'Twas futile. 'Twas no wonder Rhys was not chasing her. He was probably watching from some hidden window, laughing at her thwarted attempts to find freedom.

Defeat entered her heart and she pulled back on the single tether, only to spy it—a dark crevice at the corner of one of the towers, a crack in the curtain wall. Her heart leaped for a second, then she told herself she was imagining things. But nay, it was truly there—a wide, jagged gap in the rough curtain wall.

Was it possible? Could there be so easy an escape route? Her heart pounded.

Tugging on the rein, forcing the little bay's head in the direction of the crumbling wall, Tara felt a small glimmer of hope. There was enough room for a horse to pass through the fissure in the chipped mortar and stone. "The fates be with us, Dobbyn," she said, though she hardly dared to believe her own words. Anticipating her first taste of freedom, Tara dug in her heels. The mare picked up speed, her hoofs no longer quiet as she raced toward the wide gap, the crevice yawning open. Tara's heart took flight. "Come on, come on," she encouraged. Then she saw him.

Tall and strapping, his shape even darker than the night as she approached, Rhys stepped out of the shadow of the tower.

So the outlaw was waiting for her.

At the very spot in the wall that she had thought was her means of deliverance.

No! No! No!

Despair tore at her soul.

For a second she thought about reining Dobbyn to a stop, but then she would have no chance to get away, no means to ride to Twyll, no way to find out for herself if she truly was the daughter of Gilmore.

All would be for naught.

Nay, she could not give up. This was her chance and take it she would. "Go!" she cried to her horse. "Run like the bloody wind!" Leaning forward, tangling the fingers of her free hand firmly into the mare's thick mane, she kneed Dobbyn hard in the ribs, intent on forcing her to fly past the cursed criminal. "Go! Run, damn you, run!"

Dobbyn's strides lengthened again. Galloping headlong toward the opening, she ran fearlessly—as bold as any warhorse. Tara clenched her legs tight around the horse. The wind tore at her hair. Her skirt billowed wildly behind her.

Rhys didn't budge.

Was he daft?

"Move!" Her heart was racing as fast as the horse's hooves. Sweet Mary, she didn't want to run him down.

But she would.

Dobbyn's hoofs flung mud, her neck extended, and she was running as if the devil himself were on her tail. The crevice was close, barely thirty yards.

"Halt." Rhys's order echoed throughout the bailey.

The game horse sailed onward.

Tara held on for dear life.

Rhys had to move. He had to! He had no choice—
and yet he stood his ground. Arrogant and imperious.
And a damned fool.

Faster and faster Dobbyn ran. *Go! Go! Go!*

The space between them was so small. Oh, merciful God—

He stepped aside at the last possible second, before
Dobbyn's steps faltered, before he was trampled.

Tara's spirits soared. She was free!

But, nay!

From the corner of her eye, she saw a flash. Rhys
coiled, then hurled himself at the bay. "Nay—" As
agilely as if he'd flung himself onto galloping horses
any day of the week, Rhys wrapped one arm around
Tara and managed to swing onto the jennet's back.
"Oh!" Startled, his weight slamming into her, Tara
screamed as she started to fall. The night swirled in
her vision as her head pitched forward. Strong arms
hauled her back onto the horse's shoulders, viselike
legs clamped around the racing mare's sides.

Dobbyn stumbled, caught herself, then as if
whipped, she soared over a pile of rocks and landed
on the soft loam outside the castle walls.

Shocked and shaking, Tara clung to the horse's
tether and mane. Rhys held her fast. Steely arms surrounded her, pulled her tight against him, so that her
back was molded to his chest, her legs shaped to his.
He moved with the horse, as if he'd ridden without a
saddle all his life. "Hang on!" he ordered as he
snatched the tether from her hand.

Tara shook her head. "Nay! You get off!"

He laughed then, unafraid as Dobbyn careened
around the massive exterior of the castle, hooves
flashing, eyes wild with fear.

Tara was doomed. Rhys would never let her escape. Short of throwing herself off the flying animal, she was trapped. Again.

Freedom, it seemed, was not to be hers.

Threading the tether through the fingers of one hand, Rhys took charge. His other hand was flattened tightly on her abdomen, his long fingers splayed possessively under her breast. She could barely breathe, didn't dare move. Oh, the Bastard Outlaw was a fiend! Letting her have a tiny taste of freedom, only to thwart her.

"Damn you!"

He laughed again. "I am."

"You have no right—"

"I know."

"Then let me go—"

" 'Tis too late, witch. Far too late." Rhys guided Dobbyn toward an old foot track that cut through the woods. He was breathing as hard as the horse. His chest was firm against Tara's back and his crotch was pressed hard against her buttocks. The only barrier between his body and hers was a few folds of velvet. Not that she cared. Not that it mattered. He was her jailer, nothing more. A man to be tricked.

Though she had failed.

"God's eyes," she swore, using a phrase that Lodema had always sputtered out when she was particularly disgusted. Rhys pulled gently back on the lead, slowing Dobbyn to a walk. "You were waiting for me."

"Aye. 'Twas only a matter of time before you found the only gate out of the bailey."

"Bastard!"

"Some say."

"You be the most irritating, arrogant, miserable blackheart . . . oh!"

He pulled her roughly to him and his lips were warm against her ear. "Careful, witch, or I just might prove to you how right you are." The hand on her abdomen was warm, the feel of him as seductive as the moonlight that pierced the thin veil of clouds.

'Twas impossible to escape the man! Fury pulsed through her blood as she tried again to devise a plan to rid herself of him, and failed. The arm around her was strong as steel.

Oh, cursed, cursed luck! She thought of the damned stone. 'Twas truly as if the ring were damned.

"Where did you think you were going?" he said in her ear as he guided Dobbyn into the darkness of the forest. The smell of rain still lingered.

"Anywhere," she replied, furious that he'd caught her, sick at herself for the tingle of her skin where his breath brushed the back of her neck and where his legs touched hers behind her knees.

"To Twyll?"

"Mayhap."

"To claim your birthright?"

"If it be mine."

She felt the horse begin to turn, and she realized that Rhys was drawing up on the makeshift rein, forcing Dobbyn to return to Broodmore. Sweat covered the bay's dark coat, and flecks of white lather showed in the moonlight.

" 'Tis dangerous at Twyll."

"More so than being trapped in a castle filled with the most vile of men?"

"No harm will come to you at Broodmore," he assured her, "Well—as long as you don't tell the men what you think of them."

"I should trust you?" she asked, unable to keep the sting of sarcasm from her words.

"You have no choice." His arm tightened a bit around her, and she tried not to notice the pressure of his chest against her spine, the way his thighs fit so perfectly against the back of hers. He was her captor, her sworn enemy, the reason she was not at this moment at Tower Twyll discovering the truth.

The moon, now low in the sky, cast a few weak rays through the trees to illuminate the decaying bastions of Broodmore. A prison. *Her* private dungeon. With a bastard outlaw as her jailer. Aye, the fates were cruel. Morrigu had abandoned her. As had God.

Rhys guided Dobbyn through the very crevice in the wall that she'd thought would be her portal to freedom. Ha! Freedom! 'Twas no more than a humorless joke.

"Halt! Who goes there?" A hearty voice ricocheted through the bailey.

Rhys turned his head upward and shouted, " 'Tis I, Peter."

So now the sentry made himself known. Had he been posted there in the turret all along? Hiding in the broken crenels? Ordered into silence so that Rhys could allow her false hope only to humiliate her?

"Oh. Sir Rhys."

"Sir?" she repeated, surprised at the title.

"No longer," he said curtly.

She saw movement near the broken wagon, and three men, dark shapes with sailing capes, ran toward them. As the trio of outlaws approached, Tara recognized their faces. Old beyond their years, with shifting eyes and scraggly beards, they were only a few of the men with whom she'd shared her last meal. Three pairs of eyes, shadowed by hoods, stared up at her without the slightest bit of warmth.

"So there ye be," the tallest man said. Though his features were shadowed, she recognized his shape and raspy voice. He was the one they called Benjamin. "And ye found the lady." Was there the hint of mockery in his words? Clucking his tongue—either to encourage the horse to step forward or to register the folly of Tara's attempted escape—he grabbed the rein as Rhys tossed it to him.

Finally releasing Tara, Rhys slid to the ground, then turned quickly and grabbed her waist again, forcing her off Dobbyn's back. The horse pulled at the tether and started to rear, but Benjamin held fast to the rein.

"Take care of the beast," Rhys instructed as Tara, slipping free of him at last, marched angrily over the bent grass to the damned castle. Though it was a prison, 'twas her fate. At least for a while. Her fists curled tightly, her nails biting into her already scratched palms. The wind picked up, racing across the bailey, toying with the hem of her dress, snatching at her hair. Tired, defeated, and feeling a fool, she forced her chin up and headed toward the once-great hall.

Within a heartbeat Rhys caught up with her. Steel fingers grabbed her elbow.

She tried to jerk away. "You need not lead me around like a hunting dog on a leash." His grip over her sleeve only tightened.

"A dog I would trust. You, m'lady, I do not."

"You are angry because I tried to escape?" She whirled on him, her temper exploding, every muscle in her body tense with rage. "And what would you do, eh, *Sir* Rhys? If you were forced to stay in a castle against your will, a place where you were watched every moment of the day and night, a disreputable stone keep where the servants and peasants are all outlaws— thieves, murderers, pickpockets, and the like? Would you sit idly by, twiddling your damned thumbs, and meekly accept your fate?" She angled her face upward to stare into the silvery depths of his eyes. "I think not!"

"I would do as I was told if it be for my own good—"

"Never!" she cut in, furious that he would lie so baldly. She jabbed a stiff, angry finger at his chest. "You would fight as I have, try to find a means of escape, a way to elude your captors. Do not lie to me, *Rhys of Twyll*. I know of you. Know what you're made of. 'Tis an insult to expect me to believe that you would accept your imprisonment and lie down, rolling over like a submissive hound. Nay, you would never."

With that she turned on her heel, and with her teeth clenched, her temper seething, she strode the final few yards to the center of the keep. Rhys, though silent, was with her every step of the way. His fingers never once relinquished their tight, uncompromising grip.

Fiend!

Criminal!

Bastard!

Her back as unbending as solid oak, she climbed the chipped stone steps to the great hall, and the night, moonlit but cold, closed around her. Who was this man, to treat her as if she were his own personal property? Again she tried to pull away from him and was rewarded by his fingers digging into her flesh.

"Careful," he warned, and she bit back a sharp retort as they matched stride for stride to the hall.

Inside the cavernous chamber, Abelard and a group of men waited. Two outlaws were wagering as they tossed dice on the floor; another, one with a huge belly, was half asleep by the fire, his feet near the embers; still another sipped wine from a cup.

Abelard looked up at the sound of their footsteps. He shot up from the table. His white hair was mussed, his skin suffused with color from anger or wine, his expression thunderous as storm clouds. So furious that he was shaking, he glared at Tara as if she were the embodiment of all evil. In the firelight his eyes gleamed a pale, malevolent gold. "No one," he said, rage causing his whispered words to quiver, "*no one* leaves Broodmore without permission."

"Is every man here a prisoner?" she demanded, refusing to be intimidated, refusing to back down.

"Each is here by choice."

"Then that is where I be different." She skewered each man in turn with her gaze. "I be not here of my own choosing. Nay. I was forced to join you and am held captive."

"And so you shall stay." Abelard's word appeared to be law.

Never, she thought, but she kept still. 'Twould do no good to anger this man any further. As it was, he seemed ready to wring her neck.

"She be a witch," one of the dice players said. He rattled the tiny blocks in his cup.

"Then she be evil." His friend sent a worried glance in Tara's direction.

"She wouldn't dare cast a spell here."

Tara's looked around the room and found the scrawny man, whose tunic was too large and tongue was too quick. Without a word she leveled her gaze at him and arched a brow.

"Sweet Jesus, she's casting a bloody spell, she is!" The worried outlaw gulped, his Adam's apple bobbing wildly, his eyes round, his lips trembling. "I've seen it before. Me da, he was struck down by a witch . . . his skin turned white as lamb's wool and his manhood, it shriveled." He couldn't help glancing down at his crotch.

" 'Tis a fool ye be to worry about the size of yer cock," his compatriot laughed. " 'Tis little more than a worm as it is."

"Enough!" Abelard thundered, his voice ringing against the ceiling. "Now"—he motioned to Rhys—"see that she doesn't leave again. And you"—he stepped closer to Tara—"do not bother the men with your tricks."

" 'Tis not tricks I practice."

"Bah! Take her away!" Abelard ordered Rhys, and Tara wondered who ran this thieves' lair. 'Twas as if each man was accountable to the other.

" 'Twill be my pleasure. Come, runaway, 'tis late." Rhys pulled her arm, forcing her to leave the room with him.

"Wait." Abelard caught up with them in the hallway. Whispering so that he wouldn't be overheard, he said, "I want to see the stone once more."

"Again?" Rhys asked.

" 'Tis with me," Tara said.

"Show me." Abelard blocked her path.

She glared at the older man.

"Enough." Rhys stepped between them. "If the lady says she has the ring, then we will trust her."

"She tried to leave."

"And she would not have done so without the emerald. Now, I will stay with her."

Abelard opened his mouth, snapped it shut again, and threw his hands into the air. " 'Tis on your head, Rhys. If the emerald is lost, 'twill be you I blame."

"So be it." Rhys's mood had blackened. Tugging on her arm yet again, he hurried her along the smooth stone floor of the corridor. His jaw was set, every muscle in his body strained, his strides long and swift.

Some of her bravado slipped.

Angering this man was dangerous.

He hauled her to the old chapel, where the glow of dying embers gave off a feeble scarlet light. "How you vex me," Rhys said, kicking the door shut.

Thud! Tara nearly leaped out of her own skin.

"Give me no more grief," he growled at her.

"And you give none to me."

His cleaved eyebrow lifted a fraction. One calloused hand raised, as if he were searching for something to grab. "Listen, woman, 'tis my throat that will be slit if you lie about the stone or if you try again to escape." He crossed to the grate and tossed a mossy chunk of oak into the hot ashes. Flames sputtered and snapped, consuming the new fuel, casting the dark chamber in shifting shades of gold.

Using a piece of kindling, Rhys bent to one knee and adjusted the charred logs. Tara watched his shoulders move beneath his tunic, noticed the stretch of his breeches across his muscular thighs. With a sinking feeling, she realized how utterly alone she was—alone with this blackheart, a man who with one look could turn her blood molten, though she dare not trust him. Not a bit. Never in her life had she met a man who with just one glance could cause her womanhood to pulse with lust that brought a blush to her cheeks and confusion to her mind.

Satisfied that the fire was blazing once again, he straightened and dusted his hands. The look he sent her made her silly heart skip a beat. "You . . . you lie," she said, as much to keep their conversation going, to avoid silence with him, as anything else.

"Do I?"

"Abelard would never slit your throat."

"Let us not test him," he said, and his eyes held hers. Dear God, why was she melting inside? "There are those who would rather see me dead."

Leaning down, she tugged at the wet leather of her muddy boots, finally kicking them both toward the fire.

"But not Abelard," she said.

Beneath the stubble on his jaw, his mouth twitched. "He is not known for his patience."

"Nor are you," she guessed as he approached. Surely he didn't mean to sleep so close to her. Certainly he intended to take up his post at the doorway again.

"All the more reason for you not to try me. Now, witch, 'tis time for bed."

Sweet Mary. She read the passion simmering in his eyes, knew that she'd pushed him far enough that any reluctance or nobility in his heart had now fled. "I—I be not tired."

"Well, I be. So, lie down, Tara."

Her throat turned to dust. His gaze slid to her mouth. Involuntarily she licked her lips.

He groaned and his hands reached out and captured her shoulders. She trembled slightly and knew in a second that this was a night that could change her life forever. "You are a witch," he whispered, and there was a new tone to his voice, as if he were disgusted with his own weakness.

"Nay." She shook her head.

"Then why do I feel that you've cast a spell on me?"

She opened her mouth to answer and he kissed her.

Hard, anxious lips pressed to hers. Warmth invaded her bloodstream. Sinewy arms dragged her even closer, forcing her body up against the hard length of his.

Tara's heart pounded. Her pulse raced. She knew she should stop this madness. Kissing him, touching him, trusting him was a mistake. Yet, her arms lifted, as if of their own will, wrapping around his neck. Deep inside, she began to ache, to yearn for that which she'd never felt. Tense male thighs pressed against her own. The breadth of his chest crushed her dress and flattened her breasts. Anxious and hot, desire sped through her bloodstream.

He lifted his head, his features seeming more sinister in the shifting light from the fire. His mouth twisted into a frown. "Now, woman, lie down and sleep."

She could barely breathe. Her heart was pumping wildly, thumping out a hard, irregular tattoo in her chest. "Nay—"

"Do it now," he ordered, his patience thin, passion still burning in his gaze. "Before I do something we will both regret come the morning."

His words were like cold water splashed upon her. She dropped onto the pallet, angry that she was obeying him and yet knowing she had no choice. Her skin was still hot with desire, her heart thundering, and her mind, while screaming at her to find a way to run from him, wasn't convincing. A part of her wanted to push him away for his boldness, to swear that she hated him, but another part was wickedly seduced and needed to feel him touching her in the most secret of places. Oh, vile, hideous desire. Why did she want him to kiss her and never stop? Her cheeks burned with despair, her heart ached for his touch, and her body, traitorous as it was, wanted him to lie with her.

To her horror he lay down on the bed beside her.

"Please, do not—"

"Then go to sleep," he growled. "Now. Before I change my mind."

" 'Tis a brute you be."

"So I've been told." Deep in his beard one side of his mouth lifted into a crooked, knowing smile. As if able to see into her mind, he pushed a wayward strand of hair off her cheek. "Worry not, little witch." His voice had softened a bit. " 'Tis weary I am. Your virtue is safe with me."

"You cannot sleep here."

"To argue is pointless."

"But—"

"Turn over and close your eyes."

"Nay."

"Oh, by the gods, do as I say, Tara."

Even in the darkness, she saw the spark of passion in his eyes, knew that if he kissed her again all would be lost. Furious with herself, with him, furious that she was still his prisoner, she turned over. She was determined to find a means of escape. Fleetingly she thought of Father Simon and Twyll, the fact that she could be the daughter of Gilmore, but when Rhys's arms encircled her and dragged her close, all images of her plans vanished. He pulled the fur coverlet over them, but even though her dress was slightly damp, she was already warm, her blood heating at his touch.

Determined to close her mind to him, she squeezed her eyes shut. But he was still with her. Holding her. Touching her. His warm breath ruffling her hair. Her gown was smooth, no folds bunched between her rump and the pressure of his loins. Stiff and hard, his manhood fit perfectly against her. She felt it twitch.

Her eyes flew open. *Morrigu, help me.*

Inside, she trembled and 'twas not from fear. She tried to shift away, but with each tiny move she made, he pulled her closer still. She could do nothing but stare at the wall, where the fire's shadows played in shifting golden hues against the cracks and cobwebs.

"Sleep," he whispered against her nape.

Swallowing with difficulty, she forced her eyes closed, but it was impossible to ignore the heat that pulsed through her blood. Though she silently swore that the bastard was the last man in Wales she would ever want, her body was on fire and wanton thoughts claimed her mind.

She even wondered what it would feel like to kiss him one more time. As if reading her thoughts, he brushed his lips across the back of her hair. Her skin tingled. "Rest, little one," he whispered. " 'Tis nearly morn."

Tara bit her lip and prayed for daylight, for she knew that she was doomed. This night, with the smell of Rhys teasing her nostrils and the feel of his manhood so boldly pressed against her backside, she knew she wouldn't sleep a wink.

"Leave me," Tremayne ordered after the wench had tried her best to satisfy him. Her hands had been gentle, her mouth exquisite, and yet his temperamental cock had refused to rise. He'd felt the need, the gut-burning want of her, and there had been a pulse or two as she'd kissed and licked and pretended to desire him, but even her wet, pliable lips were no substitute for what he really needed.

"Did I not please you?" she asked, nervously biting

her lip. Naked, her red hair tousled, she was a lovely thing.

But she wasn't Anna.

He'd never found another woman who could satisfy his lust as she had. Oh, there had been a few times in the past decade when he'd been able to discover temporary solace in a particularly apt wench, but 'twas only when he pictured himself mounting the one woman who had reached into his soul that he was able to spill his seed into another woman's body.

Anna.

Wife.

Lying whore.

He scowled and tossed off the covers. Deceit sliced through his heart and blackened his mind.

"Get out," he snarled at the confused kitchen maid.

"But, sire—"

"Now!" he ordered, and the girl scurried off the bed, scrambling for her clothes, her lovely body and slightly freckled skin gilded by the reflection of the fire. She was out of his chamber as quickly as a startled cat, and he was grateful to be alone. Only when she'd shut the door behind her did he reach down and touch himself. Closing his eyes, he envisioned his wife as she had been in the single year of their marriage. Her eyes had been as blue as a summer morn, her hair flaxen. Never happy, often petulant, sometimes outwardly defiant and oft-times scared to death, she'd never denied him. Her body had always been willing. 'Twas her mind that had not been his.

She had never loved him—he knew that sorry, bitter truth. But she'd warmed his bed with a fever born of fear. Night upon night he'd mounted her, taking her from every position, feeling the velvet softness of her body envelop him, sensing her tighten and draw away

because of her pride, then slowly give in to him as he
claimed her for his own. With pure animal force. He
had never felt the same sense of power with another
woman, never experienced the surge of omnipotence
that came with making her submit to him. She was
the one woman, the only woman, that he'd loved.

Even though she'd betrayed him.

With his own bastard of a half brother.

His vision was shattered and his cock again went
limp.

Rhys.

"Damn you," he snarled, his lips curling back. He
should have killed the bastard when he'd had the
chance.

Angrily he rolled off the bed, found a half-full
mazer of wine he'd forgotten the night before. He
gulped down the cool liquid but found the wine to be
as tasteless as his attempts at lovemaking.

"Hell." Walking naked to the window, the lord of
Twyll attempted to shut his mind to the demons that
were forever tormenting him—gnawing at his brain,
teasing his angry heart.

Rhys and Anna. What vile deception.

Staring out toward the bailey, he scowled at the
coming day. The first gray light of dawn washed over
the fortress to illuminate the inner grounds with pitiful
light. Twyll was coming to life. Girls had already been
sent to the roosts to gather eggs, and boys in wool
caps were dipping their nets into the eel pond. The
farrier's forge was giving off a soft red glow, and Father Simon, the silent old priest, was already taking
his solitary walk through the bailey, around the inner
perimeter, his eyes focused ahead, his hands folded in
prayer. Just as he did each morn. An odd one, Simon.

A pious man, but a man with demons that, if prodded, would rival Tremayne's own.

Twin towers still dim in the coming dawn surrounded the main gate, where sentries were changing guard. The portcullis clunked and clanged, gears grinding as it was winched upward.

A nervous bat flew past the window, and Tremayne flinched. He finished his wine in one swallow, wiped the back of his hand across his lips, and dropped his cup onto the floor. 'Twas time for him to get outside, into the fresh air, to ride like bloody hell into the forest to hunt. His need for vengeance was hot this morning. It burned through his blood and pounded with an ache in his skull.

Memories he'd locked away crept back into his mind—Anna running through the bailey as morning broke. Her pale hair had escaped her hood, and she had glanced nervously up at this very window. Her blue eyes had been filled with worry, her lips had trembled from the guilt of her whoring.

Damn it all! Why did he still think of her? His knees weakened a bit, then he braced himself. She'd lied. She'd given herself to another man. *Nay—the beast had raped her. Remember that! Above all else.* He would not forget that the loss of her virginity was not her fault but that of his bastard half brother.

Angry at the turn of his mind, he found a fresh tunic and breeches and dressed quickly. Drawing the string of his trousers, he contemplated the hunt yet again. This very morn he would track a stag and kill it swiftly, relieving some of his bloodthirst.

A bell pealed from the chapel, and the sound of muted voices reached him—voices of bondsmen and freemen who had sworn fealty to him, Baron Tremayne of Twyll. But he found no satisfaction in being lord over this domain. Not this day. Nay, he was empty and hollow—a poor husk of the man he'd once believed he was destined to become.

Angry with the fates, he flung on his mantle and reached for his sword. He fingered the blade as it reflected the blood-red embers of the fire. Oh, if only he were to run across the bastard Rhys this day! He would kill him without a second thought. And the woman. If Rhys had found a woman for whom he cared, Tremayne would take great satisfaction in raping her, just as Rhys had taken Anna. 'Twould be sweet, sweet justice.

Slamming his deadly weapon into its tooled scabbard, he picked up his quiver, saw that it was filled with new, sharp-tipped arrows, then stormed into the corridor. There he was unfortunate enough to run into Percival, who, he suspected, had been lurking in the shadow waiting to accost him. Old idiot!

"Sire—wait!"

Tremayne strode past the bent old man without so much as a glance in his direction. As Percival struggled to keep up, Tremayne's boot heels clicked down the stairs. Flames of freshly lit torches quivered as he passed.

The old man hobbled after him.

By the time they entered the great hall, Percival had nearly caught up with Tremayne. The castle dogs, always alert, jumped up from their sleeping spots near the fire and gave off disgruntled "woofs."

"Hush!" Tremayne ordered, slinging the strap of his quiver over one shoulder. "Stay!" The spotted hounds had the decency to look abashed as they circled before settling back down and resting their heads between their paws. "Mangy curs," Tremayne muttered under his breath.

"M'lord." Robert, the sentry at the main door of the keep, offered a smile. "Good day to ye."

"And to you." Shouldering open the door, he heard Percival's shuffling footsteps as he hurried along behind him.

Outside, the wind was fierce and cold, the sky a deep, shifting gray, the promise of sleet heavy in the air.

"Sire, listen to me—"

Irritated, Tremayne paused just long enough for the stubborn old man, hobbling and hitching across the muddy grass, to reach him at last.

"I needs speak to you. 'Tis about James."

"The spy?"

"Aye." Percival straightened his stooped back just as a gust of wind caught his hood and pulled it off his bald head. "He's missing."

"But I saw him just last night. He was to slip through the gates of Marwood and learn of Cavan's plans."

"Aye—I know. But his horse returned to the castle without a rider."

"When?"

"Just now."

"Damn it, man, can no one in this bloody castle perform a simple task?" Kicking at a clod of mud, Tremayne swore under his breath and ducked around the corner of the slaughterhouse. "What happened?" he tossed over his shoulder.

Percival, breathing hard, was right on his heels. "We know not."

"What about Red? Was he not with James?"

"Red and his horse did not return."

"Then he may still be on his way to Marwood."

"Or dead, or kidnapped. His horse stolen."

Pain pounded at the base of Tremayne's skull. Percival was forever borrowing trouble. "Let us not consider that possibility." Vexed beyond words, he strode two steps ahead of the old man. Geese honked noisily, flapping their wings and waddling out of his path, leaving a trail of feathers and droppings. A team of tired, muddy oxen strained against their yoke as they pulled a wagon loaded with casks of ale through the gate. Boys chopped firewood and women milked cows. A flock of sheep, pellets of dung caught in their fleece, bleated raucously from a pen, but Tremayne was caught up in his own private thoughts, too angry to notice.

"Send out a search party," he ordered, remembering the cocky informant who had bartered with him for Regan's job as constable. James had been so bold as to ask for Regan's position in front of the man. 'Twas odd that so brazen and deft a spy would be caught so quickly. Was there a reason? A traitor, mayhap, who within the castle listened at doorways and reported back to Marwood—or to the outlaw.

'Twas not the first time this thought had crossed Tremayne's mind. Too many incidents had occurred. Too many times the walls of Twyll had been infiltrated. Too often he'd felt that he was being spied upon within his own keep. That James could have been caught so quickly was unsettling—as worrisome as the fact that his outlaw brother had managed to slip into the castle past the sentries, avoid waking the dogs, and steal his prized steed.

His gut still burned at the treachery, the bold arrogance of Rhys.

By the gods, was there no one he could trust? To the old man he said, "Find James and Red. Both of them. Send out search parties with spies and thugs and the dogs as well."

Percival nodded, following as Tremayne, caught in his own dark musings, made his way to the stables. A striped cat scurried out of his path and two kitchen maids laughing and talking as they walked to the bakery fell into silence at the sight of him. No doubt his expression was as dark and threatening as the clouds gathering over the western hills.

Something was wrong within the walls of Twyll.

Insidiously wrong.

He rounded a corner and the stables came into view.

His mount, deep brown with white markings, was saddled and tethered to a post. "He's anxious to run, m'lord." Timothy, a gangly boy with a ruddy complexion and tufts of wiry, burnished hair that stuck out at all angles, handed Tremayne the reins. The lad's teeth were crooked and too big for his mouth, but oddly they seemed to balance the wild disarray of his hair.

Tremayne eyed the steed and his lips twisted in disapproval. A fine animal, but nothing compared to Gryffyn, a stallion he'd raised from a colt, a horse like none other in all of Wales.

And now ridden by the outlaw.

Bile rose in Tremayne's throat.

If only Rhys had died when he was supposed to have, ten years past.

"Take you not a guard?" Percival asked, breathing hard as he once more struggled to catch up with Tremayne's swift, angry strides.

The lord of Twyll swung into his saddle and adjusted his quiver upon his back.

"Nay."

"But there is unrest in the land—rumors that the

haunted of Broodmore arise, and Cavan is mounting an attack and the outlaw Rhys—"

"I fear him not!" Tremayne growled, rage pounding through his head. He pulled hard on the reins, and the stallion, shaking his head against the pain of the bit, danced in a tight circle. "In truth, if I find the bastard in the forest today, 'twill be the end of him." The thought of hunting down Rhys was a pleasant one. Wounding the bastard first, spilling his blood a little at a time, then slitting his traitorous throat was a fantasy Tremayne had dreamed of often enough. The image brought an evil smile to his lips. The demons that tore at his soul were hungry for blood.

"Send out the dogs," he yelled, and Henry, the stable master, nodded, passing the word along to the kennels. Within minutes the keeper of the hounds arrived with three of the finest dogs in the castle. The animals strained against their leashes, eager for the hunt.

"Release them," Tremayne ordered, and the burly man untied each of the shaggy beasts.

"At least ye might consider takin' yer boy with ye," Percival suggested.

Tremayne's back stiffened. "Quinn?"

"Aye. Would it not be good for him?"

"Nay. 'Tis dangerous," Tremayne replied. "Too dangerous for the lad." In truth, the boy could handle the danger, was quick with a quiver and bow. A fearless, brash sort, Quinn was a defiant, clever lad, but the thought of being alone with him, even for a few hours, curdled Tremayne's insides.

"But—"

"Another time, mayhap. When 'tis more safe."

"As ye wish," Percival reluctantly agreed. "Godspeed."

Tremayne barely heard him as he reined his steed

toward the main gate and cast a glance at the threatening sky. 'Twould rain or sleet soon. Not that it mattered. In his current foul mood Tremayne welcomed the bad weather. 'Twas fitting.

He kicked his destrier. The horse launched into a smooth gallop, running across the outer bailey, turning up sod as he sped across the winter grass. The portcullis was open, the drawbridge down as the baron of Twyll tucked his head lower and urged the horse ever faster. Soon the smells and sounds of the keep were behind him.

Yet he experienced an odd feeling, one that had cursed him for the past few weeks, that someone was watching his every move. As he glanced over his shoulder to the high walls of Twyll he thought he caught a glimpse of a hooded figure, dark and blurry, hiding in the crenels of the west tower.

His horse missed a stride as the dogs zigzagged in front of him, and Tremayne ordered the baying hounds to follow. By the time he looked over his shoulder again, the figure had disappeared.

" 'Tis only your mind playing tricks on you," he told himself sternly, but the sense that someone thought to be loyal to him was betraying him burned like fire in his gut.

Chapter Six

"Do not let her out of your sight," Rhys commanded, motioning toward the door of the chamber where Tara was sleeping. The glare he sent Kent was strong enough to wither the boldest of souls.

"She'll not escape again," Kent promised, apparently determined to keep Tara under lock and key. Rhys felt a second's guilt for imprisoning her, then reminded himself 'twas for her own good. A lone woman riding to Twyll was at risk—a lone woman with the dark emerald in her pocket was an invitation to murder.

"Good. See to it."

Rhys hurried out of the castle and forced his thoughts away from the witch and the way her body had felt nestled next to his. For three days and nights he hadn't left her side, and the tension of being with her as well as waiting for news from Twyll had finally caused his temper to snap.

He'd been sharp with Abelard, barked orders at the men, and tried to convince himself that he could not make love to her. But as the long hours of the nights had ticked by, he had begun to change his mind. He'd endured the torture of holding her close, of smelling the scent of lavender in her hair, of hearing her soft sighs as she slept, and of bearing the pressure of his manhood, strong and throbbing as it pulsed with a need that he'd tried vainly to ignore. The hours had been sweet torment as he lay with her, desire warring with common sense. Bedding her would only spell trouble of the highest degree.

Outside, the night was cold as all December, and the needle-sharp wind slapped his face. Yet the moon was high, an opalescent sliver, and bright stars spangled the sky.

Abelard waited for him by the horses, two of which were saddled and prancing nervously. His wild white hair shone silver, stark against his dark expression. He held both sets of reins in one gloved hand and growled, "Let us not tarry," as Rhys approached. He, too, had been testy these past few days. Ever since seeing and touching the damned ring, Abelard had been anxious for battle, his caution thrown to the wind, his patience nearly spent.

He'd waited years to exact his revenge against Twyll, and now that it was at hand, he would not be deterred.

He slapped Gryffyn's reins into Rhys's hands. "Hurry." Climbing onto his mount, a striking sorrel, he nodded his head toward the main gate. Rhys swung onto Gryffyn's broad back. "Let us ride!" Abelard slapped his steed with the reins. Both horses bolted, flinging mud as they galloped through the sagging gates of Broodmore. Down the steep cliffs and into the forest the horses ran, faster than 'twas safe, as if they, too, needed the raw energy of the run.

As the path narrowed, they slowed, following a trail that was as familiar to Rhys as the corridors and secrets of Twyll. Through the forest, where thick stands of pine were interspersed with rolling hills of grassland, over a river and south past a village near Gaeaf.

Rhys and Abelard rode in mute tandem, the only sounds the steady plop of the horses' hooves as they climbed an old mining trail, the rustle of a bat's wings, the solitary hoot of an owl. Abelard was deep in his own thoughts, and Rhys knew him well enough not to say a word. From the first time they'd met, nearly ten years past, Abelard had always been moody, and ofttimes after periods of brooding silence his barely restrained temper would explode.

Through the foothills, where the dank smells of the forest filled their nostrils and the trees were thick again, they rode. Finally, as if he could stand his silent musings not a second longer, Abelard spoke. "We need the ring."

Of course. Rhys had expected as much. Yet he didn't budge. " 'Tis not ours. We already spoke of this."

"Aye, but that was days ago."

"Naught has changed. The ring and the emerald belong to Tara."

"What says she?"

"We speak not of it."

"Bah!" Abelard glowered into the night, staring at the space between the sorrel's ears. "She is our prisoner. Whatever she owns is now ours. 'Tis our rule." Twisting in his saddle so as to stare hard at the younger man, he asked, "Do you not remember?"

"You needs not remind me." Rhys shifted uncomfortably upon his mount.

" 'Twas our bargain—yours and mine. You agreed."

How could he argue with the man who had saved his life? Were it not for Abelard, who had found him naked and bleeding in the forest, he would have died of the cold or been killed by marauding beasts. Wolves were howling in the forest that night, wild boars grunting, bears hiding in their lairs. As he'd shivered and drifted in and out of consciousness, he'd felt icy rain pound against the raw wounds in his bare, flayed flesh, and through the fog in his brain, he heard the creatures of the night stirring, smelling blood.

His skin was on fire, the sleet painful as it struck his body, balming as it melted. He was too weak to rise, unable to walk or crawl to shelter. Left for dead, he lay on the forest floor, wet leaves, worms, and insects beneath him, a dark, cloud-covered sky above.

As he closed his eyes and succumbed to unconsciousness, he envisioned her image. Anna. Beautiful. Playful. Blue eyes dancing with mischief, pale hair falling around her face in long, damp strands. Her warm, lithe body had eagerly curled up to meet his as they joined at a fever pitch, only to tumble into each other's arms spent and sated. Pine needles were their mattress, lacy, entwined branches their canopy.

He'd told himself that the lovemaking was worth the risk, that intimately caressing his hated half brother's betrothed was a joy he would carry with him to his grave. But they'd been caught the day before the wedding.

He'd spent the night in the forest with her and they'd returned to the castle at dawn. Despair and hopelessness weighed heavily upon him. He drank a tankard of ale, dropped onto his bed, and didn't hear the bolt of his door slide out of place, had no chance to open his eye and catch a glimpse of the strong hand that forced a rough sack over his head and beat him until his nose cracked and blood smeared his face, until he lost consciousness.

Hours later, deep in the dungeon of Twyll, he awakened. He was strapped to two iron posts, not wearing a stitch of clothes, his arms and legs spread as far as they would stretch. When he tried to break free, the leather around his wrists tightened painfully. Blood crusted his nose. His face was swollen, his eyes nearly shut from the beating he'd received.

"So, the bastard awakes."

Tremayne's voice was behind him, and though he tried to twist his head, he couldn't see anything in the smoky torchlight but the dripping, dank walls and rusting chains. Several cells, barred doors locked, faced him, and the prisoners, who were not much more than agitated skeletons with hollow eyes and stringy hair, glowered at him, reminding him of cornered hungry beasts.

Fear congealed Rhys's blood.

Tremayne, dressed in a fine linen shirt and dark breeches, rounded one post. His lips were curled in disgust, his gaze aglow with unmasked hatred. Slowly, as if he had all the time in the world, he plucked a long, thick-handled whip off one wall. Without a word, he strolled behind Rhys once again, and Rhys braced himself. There was a long silence, then Tremayne's swift intake of breath.

The whip cracked.

Like a snake, it bit into Rhys's flesh.

Pain shot up his spine. His body jerked.

Crack!

Again.

Pain burst between his shoulders.

Crack!

Again. His entire body convulsed.

Crack!

Another spasm. And a sting that roared through his senses.

Rhys closed his eyes. Bit down on his lip. Tasted blood.

Blackness hovered around the edge of his vision.
Crack!
His body tensed.
The whip flailed.
Again and again and again.
Ten times. Twenty. He lost count. *Oh, God save me.* Losing consciousness would be heaven. His knees buckled.
Crack!
Blinding pain.
This time he sagged, the welcoming blackness swirling over him like soothing waters. Blissfully, he succumbed.

Water, near the temperature of ice, splashed over his face, ran down his body. Sputtering, coughing, gasping for breath, he awoke, his swollen, slitted eyes barely able to focus.

His back throbbed, his leg muscles cramped, his hands were numb. Pain pounded through his brain. Oh, God, he was still here.

" 'E's comin' 'round, m'lord." A toothless goon who reeked of these foul dungeons smiled evilly as he threw another pail of water over Rhys's head.

Cold water cleared his brain, fired his hatred. Coughing, Rhys sagged against his bindings.

"Good." Tremayne, striding in front of his victim, slowly removed his shirt. Sweat sheened beneath the swirls of graying chest hair. "Now, we'll see how strong you are." His eyes gleamed fiercely and he walked behind Rhys again, the length of whip dragging behind him. Slowly he coiled it and Rhys, half dead, steeled himself yet again, refusing to bend or beg for pity.

He heard a shuffling on the stairs, a horrified woman's cry. "Nay, oh, nay, do not take me—"

Anna. Sweet, sweet lady.

Propelled down the stairs and into the dank cellar by a guard with arms as big as hams and a bland, spiritless expression, Anna was flung into the dungeon. She stumbled on the hem of her silk gown, and spying Rhys staked between pillars, she gasped. "Oh, God, no!" She recoiled in sheer horror and tried to return to the stairs, but the guard grabbed her arms, turned her around, and forced her to stare at the man with whom she'd so recently been intimate.

Despair clawed his soul.

"I take it you do not want to watch," Tremayne said from somewhere behind Rhys.

Anna, her face ashen, shook her head vehemently and stared past Rhys's bare, bleeding shoulder. She was quivering with fear, the shiny blue silk shimmering in the dim, smoky light. Tears streamed from her eyes. "Nay, oh, please do not. Leave him be . . . he . . . he . . . sweet Jesus, he is half dead as it is." Her voice cracked, and one lovely hand covered her mouth, as if the very sight of him made her stomach roil.

Rhys sagged in his chains, his shoulders screaming in pain, his back burning.

"He is only getting the punishment he deserves for betraying me," Tremayne said calmly. Rhys, his head pounding, barely heard the words.

She couldn't stop shaking.

"This is what happens to those who deceive me."

"Dear God," she whispered hoarsely as Tremayne, still dragging his whip, approached the woman doomed to be his wife.

"You see, *love,* I know of your trysts."

"Nay—"

"Oh, yea, my bride. I've seen you with him. You've made me a laughingstock with your whoring."

"Nay, I did not . . . we did not . . ." She was trembling so violently she could barely stand. Through his blurry vision, Rhys saw her quake. He tried to break free from his bonds but could not. "Stop this . . . this torture," she pleaded. "Tremayne, please, you must!"

"Shh!" He raised his hand, ready to slap her hard, and she, sobbing, cowered. "You, Anna, must promise never—do you understand, *never*—to betray me again. From tomorrow morn until forever you will remain faithful to me."

She glanced at Rhys's battered face. Her throat worked and her lips moved, but no words could be heard.

"Say it."

"I—I—"

"So be it." He dropped the whip, slid his dagger from its sheath, and strode purposefully up to Rhys.

"Nay!" she cried as Tremayne grabbed his half brother's hair, snapped his head back, and brought the knife up to eye level. "Nay, do not, please, I beg you—anything— For the love of God! I will do anything!"

His neck bowed back so far it felt as if it would snap, Rhys watched the blade with one eye. "Shh!" he yelled at Anna. " 'Twill be all right."

"Never, you filthy bastard. Never will it be all right." Tremayne set his jaw. Raised his hand. The dagger flashed downward, the curved blade gleaming hellish orange in the light of the burning rushes.

A thin line of pain scorched down the side of Rhys's face. Blood spurted and blinded him as it washed over his eyes.

Anna screamed as though she herself had been sliced. "Stop, oh, sweet Mary, please stop, Tremayne," she begged, her voice so low Rhys could barely hear the words. "I will . . . I will be yours forever."

"Then we start now. Here."

Rhys could see nothing through the curtain of blood, but he sensed that Tremayne crossed the small space, his boot heels ringing like a death knell.

"Please, m'lord, not here, not now . . ." Anna protested weakly. Rhys again tried to free himself of his bonds as he heard the soft rending of silk, of cloth being torn.

"Nay!"

"Why not?"

"We be not married yet."

"Nor were you married to the bastard, and yet you rutted with him like the whore you are."

"Please . . . nay, nay . . . oh, God, no."

There was the sound of fiendishly jubilant laughter from one of the cells.

Anna protested, crying and sobbing. "Oh, please, not here. The guards . . . the prisoners . . . they all . . . oh!"

"Hush, woman!" With guttural noises that scratched at Rhys's brain like talons, the lord of Twyll claimed his wife.

Over the snickers and cheers of the guard, a wild, pained bellow echoed through the dungeon. Only much later, after once again he'd lost consciousness and awakened in the frigid forest, his throat as raw as his flogged skin, did Rhys realize that it had been his own scream.

He'd never seen Anna again.

'Twas only by chance that Abelard, a thief who had himself felt the humiliation of Tremayne's sword, had found Rhys in the steep ravine and brought him back from the edge of death.

Their bond ran deep.

Each had reasons to seek vengeance against the man who still ruled Twyll.

Now, as they rode through the silent, night-shrouded forest, Rhys glanced at the other man.

"We need the ring," Abelard said again over the rush of the wind. " 'Tis time. The fact that you're besotted with the witch is of no consequence."

"Besotted?" Rhys spat out the word. The horses were straining, plodding upward along a steep, forested slope. Ears flattened, they climbed.

"I've seen it before," Abelard insisted. " 'Tis the reason you be in such a foul mood."

Rhys's jaw clenched so hard it ached. Abelard was an idiot. There was no other explanation. Aye, he wanted to lie with Tara, to kiss her again, to feel the sweet promise of her body wrapped around him, but 'twas not as if his thinking was addled. Nor would he allow himself to feel the pain of love ever again.

"The ring belongs to everyone at Broodmore. 'Tis how we've always shared the spoils." Abelard turned in his saddle and pinned Rhys with his glare. "This be the opportunity we've been waiting for these past ten years. Do not let love blind you."

"I am not in love."

Again Abelard snorted in disdain. "So be it, then. And good it is, for if Tara be the true heiress of Twyll she will be your sworn enemy. Forget not that your father slew Gilmore and his wife. Any issue of theirs would seek not only his or her birthright but a fair measure of revenge as well."

"As we seek ours."

They reached the summit of the hillside and rode along the ridge, guided by the sparse moonlight.

Rhys was lost in his own grim thoughts. Abelard,

damn him, was right about the dark emerald of Twyll. The stone, with its legacy of fortune and mystery, could buy an army that would bring Tremayne to his knees. However, 'twas one thing to consider bedding Tara, yet another to steal from her. She would not give up her ring easily, and though he'd lifted many a fine bauble from any number of ladies, this time 'twas different. Why, he didn't know, and he didn't want to examine his hesitancy too closely. He could not think, would not deign to believe that the old man was right and he was falling in love with the sorceress—if that was what she truly be.

He glowered at himself and hiked his mantle closer around his neck as the wind blasted and keened over the hills.

Tara was everything Anna hadn't been.

Anna had been a lady, a pious, soft-spoken woman who flirted and smiled and touched his heart with her kindness. She'd come to him willingly, unhappily betrothed to Tremayne against her will. Tara, though beautiful, was raised a peasant, a sharp-tongued woman who was as hardheaded as any mule, an independent sort who thought she could do whatever she pleased, a rebellious soul intent on her own purposes.

Aye, she had a softer side, a bit of vulnerability that he'd only caught a glimpse of now and again, but outside she was bristly, tough as leather, and prideful to the point of not bending, even when 'twas to her benefit.

She was not the kind of woman he would ever love.

The path curved downward and the horses picked their way cautiously through the brush. At the bottom of the ravine, Abelard took the lead, maneuvering his mount along a stream where swift water rushed and splashed loudly, carving a crooked path through the narrow canyon. On the far side the way continued through dense woods.

Eventually they came upon a wide, pebble-strewn path that had once been a road leading to a rock quarry, now abandoned.

They rounded a bend, and the trees gave way to a broad expanse of stone that had been hacked away years before. Rhys pulled up short and whistled sharply. The noise echoed and bounced off a sheer rock wall. Another whistle answered, and a minute later a lone man jumped down from his hiding spot on the ridge to land in the middle of the open space.

"James?" Abelard asked.

"At your service," was the cocksure reply.

Always irreverent. Always one step away from an enemy's blade.

"I'm surprised you be here," Abelard said.

"Did I not promise it?"

"But 'tis sometimes difficult."

James lifted a shoulder, dismissing the older man's concerns. "Then 'tis up to me to be more clever."

Rhys climbed off Gryffyn and embraced the bold spy who had the nerve to betray the lord of Twyll.

"What happened to your horse?" Abelard asked as he dismounted. His boots crunched on the gravelly ground.

"It seems, if my story is to be believed, that I lost the beast when I was captured by Cavan's men." James brash smile, a white slash upon his dark jaw, showed in amusement.

"Was not another spy with you?"

"Aye," James said, nodding as he spun his tale, "but at the sound of Cavan's men we were split, riding off in different directions to avoid being caught." He hooked a thumb to his chest. "I, unfortunately, was captured."

"And what if the other man was captured as well?"

"Red?" James thought for but a second. "It matters not; I will claim I escaped my mindless and drunk captors, then spent days walking back to Twyll."

Abelard snorted. "You have more balls than brains."

"Sometimes 'tis best." James rolled up his sleeve and tightened a leather band around his wrist, pulling the laces with his teeth, wincing as the leather gouged his skin.

"What is that?"

James laughed wickedly. "Know you not my bonds? If I am to have been held prisoner, would it not be best if there be marks and bruises around my wrists?"

"Have you also flogged yourself?" Abelard asked.

"Nay, I thought I'd leave that to you."

Abelard snorted again. "Be careful, James. Tremayne is not a fool."

"Is he not?" James spat on the ground. "That, my friend, is where you are mistaken."

Rhys clapped the spy upon his shoulder. "Take heed. Abelard is right. 'Tis best if you use caution."

"As you did?" James asked, feigning innocence. "When you stole the lord's horse from under his nose?"

"Bah! You both be without minds!" Abelard dismounted and threw up his hands in disgust.

"I take care. Always," James said, but Rhys knew he was lying, brushing aside their fears and heeding not Abelard's advice.

"Tremayne is treacherous."

"Worry not. I can fool him. I can fool anyone."

"For the love of Saint Peter, lad, you'll get yourself hanged, you will."

"You worry too much." He glanced expectantly at the horses. "Did you not bring some ale? Or mead?"

"Nay. This night we need clear heads," Abelard insisted as they huddled together and the first clouds floated across the moon. "What have you learned?"

"Tremayne is worried. Not only because his prized stallion was stolen from the keep"—James rubbed the hard spot between Gryffyn's eyes and the gray lowered his head, silently asking for more—"but because Cavan is on the march."

" 'Tis time to strike, I tell you," Abelard insisted.

"Aye. He has sent troops looking for you—troops led by Edwin." James studied Rhys carefully. "And there is more. Some of the men claimed to have seen you with a woman."

"Did they?" Rhys asked, and he sensed Abelard tense.

"Aye. Tremayne has instructed that she be brought to the castle as well. Any man who brings you and the woman in will be rewarded."

"Damn!" Abelard growled, kicking angrily at a stone and sending it flying.

"So there is a woman?" James asked.

"Nay," Rhys said, before Abelard could speak. James frowned.

"If ye say."

Rhys moved on. The thought of Tremayne's knowing anything about Tara caused his gut to tighten and his fists to curl. "Edwin—" he said through suddenly clenched teeth. "He is loyal to Tremayne?"

The spy shook his head. "He can be bought. For the right price."

Abelard cleared his throat, and Rhys knew what he

was thinking. The dark emerald of Twyll could buy many allies. Mercenaries, thugs, and those who cared not who ruled but how they could profit from it, along with those who still felt the sting of injustice for Gilmore's death and the others who hated the current baron. Aye, a sizable army could be led against Tremayne.

James patted Gryffyn's sleek neck. "But Abelard is right. Never again will there be the same opportunity to overthrow Lord Tremayne. While he is distracted, not only worried about your criminal deeds but also concerned that Cavan be the rightful ruler of Twyll and is ready for war." He paused for a second, as if wondering how much to divulge, then said, "There is talk that Cavan can prove he is the true issue of Gilmore, that he has the stone in his possession, the dark emerald." James frowned and looked from one man to the other.

"Does he?" Rhys asked, though he knew the answer.

"Nay." James was thoughtful, his eyebrows drawing together as if pulled by an invisible string. "No one knows if the cursed ring really does exist." He rubbed his jaw, scratching the stubble on his chin. " 'Tis a myth. Nothing more."

Abelard and Rhys exchanged glances, for as much as they believed in this man who lived as one of Tremayne's most trusted soldiers, they kept their thoughts to themselves. 'Twas not the time to disclose that they had seen the true gem, that the dark emerald of Twyll belonged to a woman who at this moment was being held prisoner in Broodmore.

" 'Tis a sorry excuse for a woman you be," Tara chastised herself as she drew the gray dress over her head. 'Twas the color of a dove's underbelly and trimmed with forest-green velvet upon the bodice and sleeves. Again, it was a little too large, but she cared not.

For the past three days she'd tried to find a way out of this keep, but never had a means of escape revealed itself to her. Everyone from Big Rosie to that pimply-faced Johnny appeared to be watching her, and the only time she was alone was when she claimed a need to relieve herself.

She was tired and restless, and she needed to put distance between herself and the outlaw. He'd been forever at her side day and night, and always when she thought she'd found a minute to herself, she would discover that he was not far away, observing her through slitted eyes, studying her as if she were some strange creature he could not fathom.

And all the while she should be off to Twyll. 'Twas time to discard the fine, worn clothes that had once belonged to the lady of Broodmore, time to put her dagger in her pocket, sneak off to find Dobbyn, and leave this creepy old castle far behind.

This morn when she awakened Rhys had not been in the chamber with her. The pallet had seemed empty and cold. She felt a shaft of disappointment, then told herself that she was being silly—a ninny of a girl. Aye, they had shared the same bed. Aye, she'd grown used to cuddling up to the strength of him and had slept well in his arms. And aye, she felt a curling want deep in the middle of her whenever his finger grazed her bare skin or his breath, in slumber, stirred her hair, but 'twas all for naught. He was a thief. An outlaw. Her captor. Nothing more.

Padding on feet that didn't make a sound, she listened at the door but heard nothing. Crossing herself for luck, she edged the door open and started to creep through, only to find Kent leaning against a corridor wall.

As he often did, he was using the tip of his dagger to clean his fingernails. "You be awake. Good. Big Rosie asks for you."

"Why?" Something was amiss. "Where is Rhys?"

Kent's eyes, a pale, icy blue, were shuttered. "Away."

"When will he return?"

"When he chooses."

"And Abelard?"

"Who knows?"

The man was forever sour. He sheathed his knife and the corners of his mouth pinched, as if he were in pain. 'Twas easy to see that he didn't like his position as her keeper, and Tara intended to make his job miserable. For when Rhys was not within the imprisoning walls of Broodmore, she intended to find a way to make good her escape.

Tension in the keep was as thick as Rosie's greasy rabbit stew. The men were restless. They grumbled and snarled at each other as if they were expecting a fight, and with each passing night new faces had appeared, joining the ranks of the criminals, anxious for some kind of battle, a battle that was spurred by the coming war between Twyll and Marwood.

"Ah, there ye be!" Rosie waddled down the hall carrying Tara's clothes in her arms. "Here, just let me put these inside, and then I've got some work for ye." She pushed open the door to the old chapel and laid the folded clothes on the pallet where Rhys and Tara had spent three nights. Glancing at the four walls of the old room, she frowned. "Come along, now, ye've spent far too many hours here as it is." As if she didn't notice that Kent took note of Tara's every movement, Rosie escorted Tara outside to what had once been the inner bailey.

The sun was out, streaming pale winter light past a few filmy clouds. The ground was soggy, long-bladed grass bent, an overgrown herb garden hardly recognizable with its dead plants.

Water could be drawn from a well in the center of the bailey, and fish swam in what had once been the pond, but no ducks or geese scattered feathers over the ground, no chickens clucked, no children laughed, and the mill wheel no longer turned. The mill itself was crumbling, and most of the huts that had once housed potters, bakers, candlemakers, armorers, and the like were burned and tumbled, their thatched roofs missing, their timbers rotting. Aye, Broodmore, once so full of life, was little more than a tomb now. A sentry stood guard in the old watchtower and the horses were tethered near the remains of the old stables. Gryffyn and another stallion were no longer part of the small herd.

Tara wondered where Rhys had gone and was surprised to feel a pang of loneliness, as if she truly missed him.

'Tis a ninny ye be, she told herself for the dozenth time. Why would she miss a man who bullied her, shamed her, even laughed at her? A few stolen kisses did not wash away all his sins, and she guessed that he had amassed enough transgressions that were he to ever confess, he would certainly be on his knees for years.

"Abelard and Rhys. How know they each other?"

"Ah. 'Tis a long tale, that," Rosie said as they walked along an overgrown path to a hut that still stood. Though the thatching on the roof was rotting through and the wattle-and-daub walls had eroded

over the years, inside a fire burned hot. A large kettle
of lamb stew simmered over the flames, and Pigeon
sat on a stool near the grate. She was peeling onions
and fighting tears. She glanced up, spotted Tara, and
quickly looked away. Her small mouth flattened into
a line of dislike, and she sniffed loudly, using a slim
shoulder to wipe her nose.

"Here, ye can help by kneadin' this dough," Rosie
suggested to Tara. Measuring flour from a sack, she
dusted a tabletop, then reached for three pans that sat
near the fire. Dumping the rising dough from each
onto the table, she punched down each grainy lump.
"These be yours," she said, gesturing to Tara. "We'll
be needin' five loaves and as many trenchers. Get
what you can out of 'em."

Leaving Tara to the bread, she tasted the stew and
added handfuls of cut onions to the pot. After ordering Pigeon to find more firewood and water, she began
greasing pans with lard. Alone with the woman who
seemed to know so much about everyone at Broodmore, Tara asked a question that had been plaguing her
since the first time Rhys had spoken to her.

"Why was Rhys banished?"

"Do ye not know that story?" Rosie elevated a
bushy brow, then sniffed.

"Only that he was beaten and left for dead."

"Aye, that he was." Rosie paused a moment to
gather her thoughts. "So ye know that Rhys, he be
the bastard brother of Tremayne."

Tara nodded as she worked the dough.

"For that Tremayne never forgave him, though
what happened was not his fault." Sighing, she wiped
her hands on her apron. "Nay, the bad blood started
before Rhys was born. Merwynn was lord of Gaeaf
and Helen, Tremayne's mother, was his wife. When

Tremayne was but a lad, Baron Merwynn took up with another woman—a peasant who sold lace. So besotted with the woman was he that for a while he turned his back on his wife and child, ignoring them for the comfort of the other woman. Belinda was her name, methinks, though I be not sure."

Rosie's broad forehead puckered with deep lines as she tried to recall the details of decades-old gossip. "As I remember, Lady Helen was riding back from Rhydd, or maybe 'twas Syth, I cannot say. But she was not with her husband that day. On the way back to the keep she was attacked, her guard killed, and . . . well . . ." Rosie's lips pursed in distaste. "They all took turns with her. Drunk they were and 'tis said they were soldiers from Twyll, though that was never proved." She sighed heavily and crossed her ample bosom. "The lady, she died of shame or wounds, I know not which. But Merwynn laid the blame at the lord of Twyll's feet."

"Lord Gilmore," Tara said, kneading the bread by rote, her mind filled with horrid images.

"Aye," Rosie continued. "Merwynn swore his revenge and had it by laying siege to Twyll and killing Lord Gilmore and his wife. She was with child, ye know, about to deliver, or had . . . just had the babe when the attack took place. But the poor infant was never found and so there always be talk of 'the true ruler of Twyll,' as if the babe, now grown, will take back what is his." She smiled sadly and tucked a stray wisp of hair under the edge of her scarf. " 'Tis all foolish whimsy, if ye ask me.

"Though he was now a widower, Merwynn never married Rhys's mother, but he doted upon Rhys and let the woman and her bastard son live in the castle.

"Tremayne never liked the situation."

She wiped her hands on her apron, then stirred her stew slowly. She scooped up a spoonful of the boiling soup and touched it to her lips. "Hmm." Tapping the spoon on the edge of the pot, she said, "Nor did Tremayne ever trust Rhys." Sighing, she pulled a small jar from its shelf, then reached in for a pinch of pepper and dropped the grains into the stew.

"There's always been bad blood between those half brothers. 'Twas only made worse when Rhys decided to bed Tremayne's wife."

"Did he?" Tara asked, and she saw Pigeon enter through the doorway.

"He wouldn't do that!" the girl argued. She lifted her pointed chin proudly. " 'Tis a noble man Sir Rhys be."

Rosie chortled. "Noble? Nay, I think not. No more noble than his father, who slew the lord and lady of Twyll. Aye, they be a sorry lot, always fightin' fer a castle and worryin' about a stone that don't exist. Y'know the one I mean, don'tcha?" she asked.

"The dark emerald of Twyll."

"Aye. So now Cavan of Marwood, he thinks he's the son of Gilmore, but no one has seen that damned stone, have they?"

Pigeon shook her head violently and shot a petulant look in Tara's direction.

"And ye never will. I'll bet my soul it never existed, no more than those gods and goddesses ye pray to do."

Tara didn't argue. Her stomach was in knots, her mind running in circles over the treachery and deceit that had occurred in the very castle she thought might be her home. She turned her attention to the bread and tried to ignore the emerald ring, which seemed somehow heavier as it rested deep within her pocket.

Chapter Seven

"The plan be simple," Abelard repeated as he pulled his horse to a stop at the crossroads—two deer trails that wound through the hills. One led east toward the forest surrounding Broodmore, the other angled north and would bisect the road leading to Marwood.

Rhys held his nervous horse in check, though Gryffyn pulled at the bit. Somewhere in the underbrush a startled bird squawked. Dew and a thin mist sparkled under a pale winter sun that held little warmth but dappled the ground.

Abelard lowered his voice, as if he were afraid he might be overheard by someone spying in the thickets. "You steal the ring from the witch, and I will approach Cavan. We will align with him and attack Twyll together. Marwood's troops will lay siege with his army after our men have slipped into the castle. James and those who have secretly vowed to rid themselves of Lord Tremayne will help us enter as we always do—at night—and by dawn Cavan's army will surround the fortress. After we have quieted any rebellion from the soldiers guarding the gates, we will open them for Cavan's army. What could be easier?"

Rhys snorted. "Aye, what?"

"Do not mock me."

"Never," Rhys said dryly as a morning wind rustled the trees.

"Allying with Cavan and stealing Twyll from Tremayne. Will that not be sweet justice?" Abelard's grin was a leer.

Rhys rubbed the stubble on his chin with his free hand. "Why would Cavan throw in with a band of thieves? Why not use his own spies to gain entrance?"

"Mayhap he has none. Aside from which, he will need all the allies he can get, as many men who would lay down their lives for him as he can muster—and," Abelard added knowingly, "we have the stone. With the emerald we can prove that he be the true ruler of Twyll. With the emerald in his pocket, Cavan would convince even the most doubting that he is the true issue of Gilmore."

" 'Twould be a lie."

"A small one. A necessary one. To convince and unite those who live in Twyll."

"So you would give the ring to Cavan of Marwood?" Rhys's fingers tightened on the reins.

"Nay. 'Tis not a gift. Oh, no." Abelard's lips protruded and he shook his head. "For our allegiance and the emerald, Cavan would pay and pay dearly. He is a rich man, ruler of Marwood and soon Twyll, which also includes Gaeaf, does it not?" Abelard's face grew thoughtful. "We will strike a deal with his lordship. We will offer the ring, our men, and our allegiance. In return, Cavan will promise us Gaeaf."

"A barony?"

"A *small* barony with a run-down castle."

"And what of Tara?"

"The witch?" Abelard snorted. "She can conjure up her own damned castle!"

"Nay. She, too, must profit."

"Bloody Christ, she's but a woman."

Rhys's jaw clenched. For the first time since he and Abelard had vowed allegiance to each other and made a pact to defy the law, he had a twinge of conscience. "She is in danger. Because of me. Tremayne knows of her."

"All the better that she does not have the stone, elsewise she would be his enemy."

"I fear she already is."

"Because she was seen with you." Abelard let out a sigh. "She's in this whether she likes it or not. We need the stone."

"I will talk to her."

"Nay! 'Tis far past words. She has no choice. Remember that, Rhys. 'Twas your decision when you brought her to us." Abelard's horse minced backward, and he reined the beast in further. Both animals were tired and nervous, their ears flicking. "We dare not tarry. 'Tis now we strike, while Tremayne's head is turned and his belly exposed. Should we wait any longer, or should Cavan fail, there will be not five men searching for us but twenty or fifty." His whispered voice rang with conviction, and his gloved fist shook in the air beside his head.

Dogs bayed in the distance.

Abelard froze.

Gryffyn gave off a soft, nervous neigh and pawed the ground.

Rhys strained to listen. Again came the howl of dogs—not wolves. Without a word, Rhys and Abelard exchanged glances. Dismounting and tethering their horses to the low-hanging branches of trees, they slipped through a thick copse of oak and pine and climbed a few feet to the crest of the ridge. Lying on their stomachs, they peered over the edge.

Far below, through the thickets, bright colors clashed with the gloom of the forest. Horsemen wearing the emblem of Twyll—a blue dragon on a gold field—searched the woods. Rhys's eyes narrowed on the soldiers as they rode, dogs swarming around the steeds only to bay noisily, dart through the underbrush, and flush out game. As James had warned, a party of five men with a pack of dogs was searching the forest. For Rhys.

Searching for the outlaws who taunted their lord.

For the first time in ten years, Rhys felt a frisson of fear slide down his spine. Not for his own life, nay, nor for Abelard's sorry skin. Even the men who had banded with them knew the risks of their chosen profession

But not Tara. She was being held against her will.

Nor should Big Rosie and Pigeon be punished. They had joined when Rosie's husband, Tom, was killed by Tremayne's men. He'd been caught poaching in Tremayne's forest, and the penalty for killing the boar was his own quick death. Tom's act of treason, for that's what the lord of Twyll had called it, was punished swiftly and publicly to keep any other men within the villages surrounding the castle from making the same mistake. Rosie had met Abelard in an alehouse, and he'd offered her a chance for retribution.

So she and Pigeon had become a part of the band.

She had known the danger, of course, but decided it was worth the risk. "I'll not be livin' me life under that bastard's thumb—oh, excuse me," she apologized to Rhys on the first night she and her daughter came to the camp, which at the time was only a wagon and two tents pitched near the river. She blushed to the roots of her hair. "Me tongue is me downfall, I fear. I dinna mean to—"

"Worry not," Rhys cut in quickly. "I wear the title with pride."

Rosie's eyebrows raised, and Pigeon, hiding behind her, dared peek around her mother's leg.

"Aye," Abelard clapped Rhys on the back. "This way his blood is only half the same as Tremayne's."

"Lucky ye be, then," Rosie said. "For the baron of Twyll be the very spawn of Satan, that one, and 'twould be me pleasure—me and little Pigeon's here—ta join up with ya."

Rhys eyed the woman skeptically. " 'Tis not an easy life."

"Easier than livin' in fear." She stuck out her fleshy chin and said, "I could help ye—all of ye." She motioned with one arm to the few men who were part of their small band. "I can cook and clean, ride a horse and shoot an arrow straight as any man. I work hard and I'll be no trouble—except if any of ye be takin' the Lord's name in vain—and I'm not speakin' of that bastard lord of Twyll, but of Our Father and His Son. I'll hear nothing but praise for the saints and the Holy Mother." She crossed her big arms firmly over a bosom that was rising and falling with conviction.

"This be a hard, lonely life," Rhys said, not certain he wanted the responsibility of a woman and her child.

"No more hard or lonely than livin' where ye be afraid to say what ye think."

Rhys glanced at Abelard, who only shrugged. "She wants to be a part of it?"

"Aye. 'Tis a chance I can have to avenge me poor Tom."

Rhys wasn't convinced, she sensed it.

"I know what yer thinkin', I do. A woman and her daughter would only be a burden to a group the likes of you. Cutthroats, pickpockets—a mangy lot ye are, but I can help ye, I swear it. I can make an eel pie that'll make yer mouth water, or jelly eggs as quick as that." She snapped her thick fingers. "I can sew a seam and mend a boot as well as chop firewood and wring a chicken's neck. I'll tend to wounds, whether ye get 'em from that devil's spawn Tremayne or by yer own hands. I take care of meself and me daughter, and any man who thinks not had better think again, as I could gut him as easily as I could carve out the innards of a stag in the forest."

Rhys was certain that letting her stay would be a huge mistake, but the others were more lenient. She talked her way into cooking that night and prepared a feast of jugged hare and salmon pie with the most rudimentary of utensils and little else. From the moment the men tasted something other than charred pigeon and venison, they all agreed that Rosie could join. She'd never left.

Now, as Rhys, lying on his stomach and looking over the edge of the bluff, spied upon Tremayne's handpicked group of soldiers, he thought of Tara and what would happen to her if she were captured. His eyes narrowed as the soldiers fanned out through the trees and brush, sending the dogs ahead. 'Twas only a matter of time before these men, or the next group, would find them.

Abelard was right. 'Twas the time to strike.

The search party disappeared, following the course of the creek that slashed through the canyon floor, the very creek Rhys and Abelard had crossed not two hours before.

"So be it," Rhys agreed when they'd inched their way back to their horses.

"You will steal the ring?"

Rhys's gut clenched, but he nodded and his gaze clashed with that of the man who had once, long ago, saved his miserable life. "Aye, Abelard," he agreed. "Consider it done."

"I'm tellin' ye, I would na trust James." Red's lips protruded, and he shook his head slowly as he stood in the constable's quarters. The beard for which he was named was showing a few signs of silver and he worried a wool cap in his dirty fingers. "Him and me was near to Marwood when we split up, him taking the north, me goin' south. I tied me horse to a tree in the woods and walked in totin' a load of firewood, says to the guard that I be bringin' it fer old Matilda in payment fer a pair of boots she fixed fer me. Then I goes about me business and keep expectin' to meet up with James. But he never returns and so I, after seein' what I had to see, came back here."

"You don't think he was taken prisoner?" Tremayne said, rubbing his chin in one hand and cradling a cup of wine in the other. Warming his back in front of the fire, Tremayne shifted his gaze to the constable, whose frown was as dark and unreadable as the stars on a cloud-covered night.

Red scratched his head. "Nay. I was in Marwood. If any of Cavan's troops had found a spy, I would've heard of it."

"His horse returned riderless. Mayhap an accident."

Red snorted. "James be an excellent horseman."

"And a good fighter?"

"The best. Quick with a dagger, swift at dodging a blow, fierce with a sword."

Tremayne sipped his wine, but his teeth were beginning to grind in frustration. Something was amiss and badly so. He smelled the treachery and deceit that had invaded Twyll. He lifted a finger from his cup and pointed at the constable, Regan. "What think you?"

"I trust no one."

"Aside from that."

"James is a cocky bastard, to be sure." Regan crossed the room, placed a polished boot on a bench near the table, and leaned closer to Tremayne. "Can his loyalty be bought? Nay, I think not. Would he turn against you for the thrill of it? Mayhap. Does he have the balls to defy you? Aye, he's an irreverent son of a bitch. But why? Would he throw in his lot with Cavan?"

Tremayne's thoughts ran down the same crooked, gloomy path of questions, and as always he found no answers. "Would he?" Tremayne pushed himself to his feet and crossed the short distance separating himself from the spy. "Would you?"

Red's Adam's apple bobbed. Sweat beaded his brow, though it was a cold afternoon and the heat from the fire wasn't enough to take the chill off the stone walls and floor. "Would I throw in my lot with Lord Cavan and . . . and take up arms against ye? Oh, never, m'lord," he said, shaking his head so vehemently that his floppy red hair swung low and covered his eyes. As if to prove his loyalty, he dropped to one knee and hung his head. " 'Tis. at your service I be." The man was nearly licking the pointed toes of Tremayne's polished boots.

Still, Tremayne didn't trust the groveling spy. No more than he trusted James or any of the other spies who came and went from castle to castle, reporting back to him what they'd seen . . . or what they wanted him to hear. The baron's muscles tightened with the treachery that was afoot in the cavernous halls of Twyll. The same worrisome thought that had nagged at him ever since James's horse had arrived at the castle without a rider burned through his mind now. "Is it possible," he asked no one in particular, "that the outlaw be a part of this?"

Red's head snapped up, and he gazed upward from his kneeling position. His ruddy brow furrowed beneath his shag of hair and Tremayne squinted down at this rumpled spy who smelled of smoke, dirt, and sweat. "I saw him not," Red said. "No trace of the bastard anywhere near Marwood, but a farmer, he came to the keep and he was spouting some nonsense of riders, mayhap a pack of thieves, near Broodmore."

"I have heard this not before. Broodmore?" *Was it possible? Could the traitor be near the haunted castle? Broodmore?*

The bitter taste of betrayal climbed up Tremayne's throat and though it could not be proved, he would bet his barony, every last fertile acre of it, that Rhys was behind this. He knew it in the darkest places of his heart.

"Get up," he snarled to the sniveling spy. He downed the rest of his wine but felt no warm glow start in the pit of his stomach or heat his blood. "Tell me, what did you see at Marwood?"

Red scrambled to his feet, and some of his insolent manner returned. No longer did he squeeze his cap between his fingers. He was a man used to bartering, and Tremayne was certain he would as easily carve out Tremayne's heart if offered the right price as lay down his life for Twyll. Oh, he was surrounded by ingrates without one fiber of loyalty in their bodies.

"There be mercenaries and thugs arriving at Marwood daily—'twas the reason I entered so easily and unnoticed. Inside, the men, eager to do battle, quickly pledged their fealty to Lord Cavan and swore to join him on his quest."

"So he amasses an army." Tremayne wasn't surprised, but he was irritated just the same. His blood boiled when he considered Cavan, a young whelp, a boy who had no knowledge of war, no fear of death, one who took his wealth and station for granted. Cavan would have to learn a very painful and expensive lesson, and Tremayne would be only too glad to teach it.

Settling back in his chair, he rested a boot heel on one of the scarred benches positioned around the table.

"What else did you hear?"

" 'Twas on everyone's tongue that Cavan and his soldiers will march within the fortnight. Mayhap sooner. They say the baron has a bloodlust. He wants revenge for the murder of his family."

"So he really believes he be Gilmore's issue—the infant heir that was never found."

"Aye. He is certain of it, as Lord Innis, upon his deathbed, said it to be true."

"And he wants his vengeance, when 'twas Gilmore's soldiers who defiled my mother." Tremayne turned his thoughts away from that painful time, when his own mother had lost a mind that was fragile to begin with. "Then we must counter." Tremayne tried to rein in his temper, for Cavan's intent to wage war against Twyll was as infuriating as the outlaw's attempts to humiliate him. Tenting his hands beneath his chin, he touched his fingertips lightly to his lips and mentally counted to ten. When that didn't work, he went on to twenty. Finally, deciding he could run numbers in his head forever, he forced his voice to hold a thread of patience he didn't feel. "Know you anything else?"

"Nay. I feared I was about to be found out and made haste to return."

"We know enough, I suppose." He focused on Regan. "Call up all our soldiers. Any man of age will be expected to defend Twyll. See that the stores are filled and that the armorer has enough weapons to fend off a siege."

"Should we not attack first?" Regan asked.

" 'Tis too late." Tremayne drummed his fingers on the table and motioned to the spy.

Footsteps accompanied by shouts rang through the tower.

Bam! Bam! Bam!

"M'lord?" Percival's voice pierced the thick oak of the door. " 'Tis Sir James. He's returned!"

Tremayne was on his feet in a second, and Regan threw the bolt. The door swung open and James, his face bruised and scratched, his clothes tattered, dirty rags, stood with the old man and a sentry whose fist was raised to beat against the door again.

From the corner of his eye Tremayne saw Red gulp. His ruddy complexion darkened a hue. "Well, well, well," Tremayne said. "Sir James. How is it that you lost your horse?"

"I was attacked." James lifted his chin a fraction and had the impudence to stare at Tremayne through an eye that was swollen near shut.

"By Cavan's men?" Tremayne asked.

"No, m'lord." James's gaze shifted away for a second. " 'Tis not proud to admit it I am, but I was ambushed by the outlaw. The rogue who managed to take *your* steed." His lips curled in disgust.

For a second Tremayne didn't move. His fingers itched to strangle the upstart, but he couldn't, not when there was information to be gleaned. "My brother did this to you?"

"Aye. He and the white-haired one."

"Abelard?" Tremayne's gut clenched. He'd heard this before. Though Rhys was known to ride alone, there had been rumors about Abelard, a knight loyal to Merwynn and Twyll until once, after a night of too much ale, Tremayne had separated him from a finger. Some said that 'twas Abelard who saved Rhys's life and had taught him the ways of being a thief. There had been times when they had been rumored to have been spotted together, but none that had proved true. Another thought struck him, and he asked, "What about the woman?" His hand moved in a tight circle in the air near his head as he tried to recall. "Did not Sir Edwin say that the last time he chased Rhys, the bastard had been with a woman—embracing her, I believe."

"There was no woman with them."

"And they spoke not of her?"

"Nay." James was certain.

"Odd." For years Rhys had been a loner—or so Tremayne had been led to believe—but not only a woman without a name but also Abelard had been linked with him. Closely. 'Twas trouble. Thick and deep.

"Why were you spared?" he asked again, just to see if James strayed from his story.

"They would've kilt me, too, but I managed to escape."

"What did they want from you?"

"My purse."

"Is that all?"

"Nay. They were seeking information about Cavan of Marwood."

"And they thought you would have it?" Tremayne's suspicious eyes bored into the spy. Was it his imagination or did the man seem to be enjoying this—as if it were part of an intricate game of chess?

"Aye. I had just parted from Red. Was circling Marwood, when I was set upon. They knew that I had visited Cavan's keep before."

"How?" Tremayne demanded. "How did they know?"

James thought for a second, studied the floor. "The only way is if they had someone on the inside."

"At Marwood?"

"Nay," James said in a serious voice. "The spy would have to come from here. In Twyll."

A sensation cold as death stole up Tremayne's spine. How many times had he heard the scrape of boot heels chasing after him when no one was there? How often had he felt the heat of someone's gaze, only to find no one watching him?

But all those puzzling occurrences were about to end. Finally the fates had not smiled on Rhys. The outlaw had tripped himself up at last. Or had he? Mayhap Sir James was a traitor and this a well-planned trap. "So you know where the outlaw's lair be?"

"Nay," James said and rubbed his wrists, where the skin had turned an ugly greenish hue.

"You were not taken there?"

He shook his head.

Tremayne, his interest piqued, folded his arms over his chest. "Tell me what you know of the outlaw's lair."

James hesitated but a moment. "What price would you pay?"

So the cocky soldier had the nerve to barter with

him. Good. Tremayne leaned down until his face was nearly touching that of the spy. "If you tell the truth, Sir James, you will live . . . and be paid well for your trouble." Tremayne gestured to the bruises and cuts upon James's body. "But if you lie . . . you'll be hung until you be half dead, then drawn and quartered, for 'twill be treason."

The man didn't flinch. " 'Tis the truth I speak," he said, as if he believed it to the very depths of his soul. "I was taken to a quarry, far from their camp."

"Yet you escaped."

"Aye, when they slept. The older one, on his shift to stand guard, nodded off and I slipped my bonds."

Tremayne nodded. "And their camp?"

"As I said, I know nothing."

"What of Broodmore? Could the outlaw hide there?"

" 'Tis the castle of the damned," Red whispered and crossed himself with his stained fingers. Regan snorted his disbelief.

Tremayne raised a hand, cutting off any further comment. "What say you?" he asked James.

A haughty eyebrow lifted over James's blackened eye. "As Our Father judges me, no one would stay in Broodmore. Not even the bastard."

Tremayne felt a lie in the air. He snapped his fingers. "We shall see. I will send my men, but you, Sir James, will wait here, under guard."

James stiffened. "You trust me not?"

Tremayne paused. "My trust must be earned." Motioning to Regan, he strode to the door. "Lock him up and assemble the rest of the men. We ride to Broodmore at dawn." For the first time in a long while, Tremayne smiled. Finally he sensed that he had a chance at getting even with the outlaw.

*   *   *

"For the love of the Virgin Mother, girl, what d'ya think ye be doin'?" Rosie's voice, a pitch higher in her excitement, echoed through the small space that had once been an herb garden of Broodmore. She threw up her hands, looked to the sky, and whined, "'Tis a hard lesson ye be teachin' me, Father."

Tara scrambled quickly to her feet. She'd escaped Rosie's watchful eye and managed to draw a small rune for her protection in a spot of soil she'd exposed. Though she stepped over her scratchings, Rosie wasn't fooled. Beneath the edge of her scarf, Rosie's eyebrows pulled into a tight knot of frustration.

"Don't ye know that all this is the very work of Satan?" She flapped a fleshy arm at Tara's work as she strode across the weeds and grass.

"Nay, 'tis only to the Great Mother that I pray, as well as to God."

"'Tis a sin, I tell ye! Blasphemy. I should be rinsin' yer mouth out with soap and sendin' you to the priest for confession." Rosie's face was flushed with conviction, and she wagged a fat finger under Tara's nose. "Oh, by the saints, 'tis a sorry lot I live here with, only thieves and outlaws and no man of God to keep this flock on the right path to heaven."

"They're robbers," Tara said. "Criminals. They threaten people with weapons, perhaps maim and murder them. No priest could possibly wash their sins away—"

"Shh. If a man repent his sins to a priest and God, mind ye, he has every chance of salvation. This I know because my own past ain't so pure." With her hefty body, she shoved Tara aside, glared down at the scratchings in the mud, and shook her head, using her boots to scrape dirt over the rune. "But what if Pigeon

were to see this? 'Tis trouble enough that she doesn't
go to mass . . . oh, mercy, Lord, have I not been a fit
servant?" Again she rolled her eyes toward the darkening sky and crossed herself with deft, well-practiced
fingers. " 'Tis being punished I am."

There was no talking to the woman when she was
in one of her frenzies of piety, so Tara wisely closed
her mouth.

"I only hope that this"—Rosie motioned toward the
destroyed symbol in the mud—"will not anger the
Father."

"I don't see how—"

"Oh, He's a vengeful God, He is." Rosie's head
nodded quickly. "He'll take His wrath out on ye—and
the rest of us here as well, mark my words. Oh, sweet
Mary . . . mayhap it's already happened."

"What?" Tara didn't like the sound of this.

"Mayhap all your black arts are the reason Rhys
has not yet returned."

"Nay—"

"Nor Abelard as well." She sighed as if suddenly
weary and played with the frayed edge of her apron.
"They be late. Both. Oh, Tara-girl, I hope with all this
chantin' and callin' up spells, ye haven't cursed us all."
She looked around the ruined walls of Broodmore and
bit one side of her lip. "If anythin' has happened to
Rhys, 'twill be yer fault."

Tara didn't believe it for a minute.

"Now, come along, 'tis time for ye to go to the
chamber. I can't . . . I won't be responsible for ye if
yer intent on talkin' with the dark one. Come along."

Tara wanted to argue but couldn't. Not only did
Rosie grab her arm in a grip that pinched her flesh
but Kent, ever-present and unnerving, had been hov-
ering in the doorway of a broken-down hut. Tara, busy

with her sketch, hadn't seen him hiding in the shadows, but now, as Rosie was hauling her into the keep, she caught a glimpse of movement. He stepped out of the burned-out shell and into the fading light of sunset.

"I'll take her," he offered, and Tara's skin crawled. 'Twas time to leave this place. And she would have no better opportunity than now, while Rhys was away. At the thought of him, her stupid heart felt a pang of regret. Aye, she would miss sleeping in his arms and looking into those damnably erotic eyes, miss his touch and rare smile, miss the dream of sometime lying naked with him. Her throat was suddenly thick, and she swallowed with difficulty. What was wrong with her? Never before had she been such a goose. And certainly not because of a man—nay, a criminal— set upon holding her hostage.

Rosie refused to give up her grip. "I'll take her back to her room, Kent. You just sit yer skinny arse by her door and don't let her escape." She slid a glance at Tara. "Sorry, dearie, but I can't trust ye, now can I? And if I lost ye, oh, Sir Rhys, he'd near to tar and feather me."

Her anger seemed to diminish a bit as they walked through a doorway where no door hung. She shook her head and breathed loudly. "Now, listen. Fer the sake of yer soul, and the safety of all of us, you get down on yer knees tonight and pray for forgiveness. The Father . . . He be understanding."

And vengeful, and wrathful, and jealous, Tara thought unkindly, but seeing the true worry in the heavy woman's eyes, she nodded. "I will pray. For all of us."

A bit of a smile spread across Rosie's broad face.

" 'Tis good ye be, Tara. No wonder Rhys is in love with ye."

Tara stopped short. Her heart jumped. "In love?" she repeated, stunned. "Nay, I think not."

"Do ye now? Well, it only takes one look at the man to see his soul. Do ye not feel it?" Rosie chuckled as they rounded a corner and Pigeon, lugging a pail, nearly ran into them. Her face was white as parchment, her eyes round. Dirty water sloshed onto the floor and she flushed bright red. Tears threatened her eyes. "Oh! . . . Mum . . . sorry."

"Be watchin' where yer goin'," Rosie ordered tartly. "Saints be with us. Come along," she insisted, and Tara was forced down the hallway.

"You don't have to treat me like a child," Tara complained, pulling her arm out of the older woman's strong grasp. Though she didn't look over her shoulder, she felt Pigeon's gaze following her as they stopped at the chamber door.

"I know, I know." Rosie seemed suddenly contrite. " 'Tis worried I am about Rhys and Abelard. Never have the two of them been gone this long before, and it has me nerves strung tight as the laces of Kent's breeches." She smiled to herself. "An unbending one, he is." She threw open the door and Tara's heart dropped. Being held prisoner at Broodmore was bad enough, but being confined to this room where she'd been with Rhys was even worse.

As if reading her thoughts, the older woman patted her lightly on the shoulder. " 'Tis sorry I am about this, ye know, but"—she sighed—" 'tis how it must be."

Tara's spine grew as stiff as if it had been pressed. Who were these people, this group of thugs who thought they could keep her locked away? The days were moving swiftly by, and she badly needed to be away, to ride to Twyll, to face Father Simon and demand the truth. "So be it," she said without a smile and determined that this night, this very evening, she would make her escape.

And never see Rhys again. Her heart felt suddenly heavy in her chest. Poor Rosie was mistaken. What she saw in Rhys's eyes was not love for Tara but lust for the stone that was hidden in her pocket.

"I'll send Pigeon down with a trencher of brawn," Rosie said and crossed herself again. "Now, as I said, ye . . . ye talk to the Father. Promise to practice not the dark arts and ask forgiveness."

Tara forced a smile. "I will do what I have to," she said and touched the bit of candle and the herbs in her pocket. Her fingers grazed the smooth surface of her ring, and she knew she would leave this night. If she set eyes upon Rhys again, she might change her mind, fool that she was. But the longer she stayed with these men, the more likely it was that someone would steal the ring—the very link to her destiny.

Lodema shivered as she sat on the edge of the pallet in her empty hut. Luna rubbed up against her arm, trying to wheedle a pet or a scratch behind the ears, but 'twas for naught. Tonight her mistress's thoughts were far away, to Twyll, for that was where Tara had gone.

Nearly a week had passed since she'd last seen her daughter. Not too long a time, and yet it seemed an eternity. A peddler had passed by today; humming he'd been as he'd tried to sell her spoons and thread and all manner of things she didn't need. While he showed her his wares, he talked of trouble brewing at Marwood Castle.

Old Lord Innis had died and his son, Cavan, claiming to be the missing heir of Gilmore, was gathering an army, plotting his vengeance against the very keep where Tara herself was searching for her own heritage. Lodema was troubled. Why would Cavan think he was the son of Gilmore? He had no ring as proof, just the word of a dying man who knew not what he said. Oh, 'twas troubling, to be sure.

As the timbers in her little home creaked and the fire burned low, Lodema stared into her cup of now cool water and herbs, a drink she always sipped before slipping under the covers. She picked up the candle and noticed that her hands were shaking and more spotted than they had been. When had she grown so old?

Luna folded her paws beneath her and settled against Lodema's leg. Purring softly, the cat let her eyes close. Carefully Lodema dropped a few drips of wax into her cup. Barely daring to breathe, she saw the swirl, watched as the wax hardened into the shape that she feared.

"Nay," she whispered, but her eyes did not deceive her. The wax, as well as the smoke the other day, were omens—dire and certain.

By the gods, Tara was in trouble—serious trouble. And there was naught she could do but pray.

For the first time in twenty years, Lodema sank to her knees. The cat, disturbed from her nap, stretched and yawned as the old woman bowed her head and fervently hoped that God was listening.

Chapter Eight

"Me mum, she sent you something to eat." Balancing a platter of brawn and bread, Pigeon slid through the open door of Tara's chamber. With a nervous glance cast over her shoulder, she bit her lip and nearly tripped over her own two feet. "Damn." The platter wobbled and gravy sloshed onto her hands. She sucked in her breath and managed to set the tray on the altar. "Oh . . . I'm sorry. Me mum, she says I always be a fumble-de-dum." Sniffing as if she might cry, Pigeon wiped her hands on her apron.

"Worry not." Tara pushed herself to her feet. She had been sitting on the edge of the pallet, plotting her escape and trying desperately not to think of Rhys and how it felt to have him hold her. Curse him and rot his soul, he muddled her thoughts in a manner that made her want to scream, or kick at the floor, or punch a hole in one of these thick walls. She would not think of the way his hands held her or the warmth of his body curled so close to hers. She would not! Half the time she wanted to kiss him until her lips were bruised, the other half she wanted nothing more than to slap the arrogant smile off his face. " 'Tis fine," she told the anxious girl.

Swallowing hard, Pigeon stole across the room and quietly closed the door so they would be entirely alone. "Please. Now, listen." Pigeon's eyes were round, and she swallowed as if there were a lump the size of an apple lodged in her throat. She walked to the fire and warmed her hands. " 'Tis here to help ye I am," she whispered, clearing her throat.

Tara doubted it. The girl had done nothing but send her daggerlike glances for days. "Help me?"

"Aye. Do ye na wanna leave Broodmore?" There was a note of excitement in Pigeon's voice, a tremor of anticipation.

Tara's eyes narrowed. This could all be part of a trick, for Pigeon was much more clever than anyone here at Broodmore, including her own mother, suspected. "Aye, Pigeon," she said carefully. " 'Tis no secret I feel a prisoner."

"Then ye must go now, before Rhys and Abelard return."

Tara didn't answer—she didn't trust the girl and she didn't want to give herself away. If she agreed to whatever foolish plan Pigeon had concocted, she was certain the girl would use it against her to gain favor with Rhys.

When Tara hesitated, Pigeon threw up her hands and shook them, as if silently asking God to help her make Tara understand. "Do ye not hear me? This . . . this be your chance!" Her eyes were bright with eagerness, and there was more than mischief in her expression, much more—a dark need that was fueled by girlhood fantasies. She wanted Tara to leave as much as Tara desired to go—but for very different reasons. "We have not much time." Digging deep in her pocket, she withdrew a small, decidedly deadly knife, one not unlike her own. Along with the dagger was a strong piece of cord, and a tiny bit of flint. "Take these with you." When Tara didn't move, the girl grabbed her hand and slapped the items into her palm, then curled Tara's fingers over the treasures. "Take them." So close to her that Tara could see the thread-like veins in the whites of her eyes, Pigeon said, "I know ye are plannin' yer escape. Do not deny it. I will help ye by lurin' the guards away."

"How will you do that?" Tara asked, her fist closed tightly over Pigeon's gifts.

"Do not worry. You will know." Pigeon winked at her, and Tara felt more than a shiver of mistrust, for there was thinly disguised hatred in the girl's eyes. "I must go now, but this I vow, you will know when the time is right."

With that, Pigeon scurried out of the room, her head bent, her demeanor poor and self-serving, as it usually was. As she swept through the door, she did not once look back and Tara, knowing she was making a mistake, decided to trust the flighty, love-besotted girl.

Shadows lengthened in the room as night blanketed the keep. She glanced at the pallet where she had slept with Rhys, smelled him, felt his body pressed so tightly to hers. Damn the blackheart! She'd felt womanly stirrings deep within her and a hollow aching that had never completely left her. Whenever she thought of him, as she did now, the yearning swept over her, and she remembered the taste of his lips and the feel of his hands on her bare skin.

"Stop it," she muttered to herself and changed out of the dead woman's clothes into her own simple tunic and mantle.

As she tucked the cord and flint into her pocket, Tara told herself not to worry about Pigeon and her plot, whatever it might be. 'Twas probably nothing more than a girlish fantasy of being a part of something daring. An adventure. Though Pigeon's home was with the outlaw band, she was considered nothing more than a servant, a silly goose of a girl who had to do the most menial of tasks. Her mother, albeit loving, barked orders at her. The men thought her without brains, but Rhys offered her shreds of kindness, which she transformed into a young girl's dreams of romantic love. Pigeon was hopelessly in love with him, but he didn't seem to notice or care.

And what about you, Tara? Are you not falling in love with him as well? That horrid, nagging voice in her mind asked the question.

Nay! Never! He was a rogue. An outlaw. A man who had boldly diverted her from her purpose, a man who had shamed her by insisting that he share a pallet with her, a once-upon-a-time knight turned to lawlessness. She would not ever fall in love with the likes of him.

Angry at the wayward turn of her thoughts, she slid the knife into her boot, examined the platter of food, ate a few bites of cooling brawn and wastel bread, then ignored the congealing mass. Her stomach was already tied in knots, her palms were damp though it was cold, and her heart beat wildly in anticipation of this night. Skulking in the shadows, she would locate her mare, then leave through the crack in the wall as she had before.

If it was still unguarded.

It had to be. Surely the fates would not be against her. *Oh, Morrigu, watch over me. Make Dobbyn swift as a bolt of lightning, keep the sentries dull-witted and slow, and, please, please, I beg you, help me escape these oppressive walls. Let not Rhys return to stop me.*

Surely this time Rhys would not be around to thwart her.

So where was he?

Attempting to rid herself of any thoughts of him, assuring herself that she would not heed Rosie's worries about him and Abelard, Tara tried and failed to ignore the gnawing sense of anxiety that had been with her for hours—that something dire had happened to him and that whatever misfortune had befallen him was somehow her fault.

"You're as big a worrier as Rosie," she chastised herself.

The emerald ring was already tied to her waist. She reached into her pocket, her fingers grazing her own knife, cord, candle, herbs, flint, and a few precious coins, all that she owned in the world aside from her horse. Aye, she was ready to make good her escape.

If only she had a chance.

If not, she would have to create one.

She didn't dare close her eyes while she waited for the fire to die down, needing as much darkness as possible. It felt like an eternity passed while she lay there counting her heartbeats in those frozen moments before she put her plan into action. Without firelight behind her, she would be less visible, less likely to be discovered.

She inched closer to the window. The smell of smoke drifted through the air. From the bailey a horse gave out a worried neigh. Someone coughed. Muted conversation was audible over a gently whistling wind.

Tara spotted the sentry, Rupert, leaning against a post that supported a sagging roof. Arms folded over his massive chest, he observed the grounds with a lazy eye and spoke to some of the men passing by. They joked and laughed, but he never gave up his vigil. Even while talking to Bertrand, an outlaw with a crooked leer, stringy beard, and thin hair that didn't hide his scalp, Rupert continued his watch on the keep.

Finally Bertrand, who limped slightly, ambled off, and Rupert yawned. If only he would fall asleep, Tara thought. As long as he was awake, it would be more difficult to execute her plan. Somehow she would need to crawl quickly out the window, drop to the ground, scurry silently past him when he turned his back mayhap when he had to relieve himself—then run like the very devil across the bailey to the spot where the horses were tied, and . . .

The sentry suddenly snapped to attention, his mouth dropping in horror. He took off at a dead run to the far side of the bailey.

From the corner of her eye Tara recognized a treacherous glow. Bright orange shadows played upon the rough surface of the castle's outer wall, and smoke drifted across the bailey.

Fire!

"Nay," she whispered. "Oh, nay!"

Frightened, she stuck her head through the window and, craning her neck, looked toward the rough shed that housed the kitchen. Her heart dropped. Thick black smoke rose in ghastly billows above the hut. "Dear God in heaven." Her heart hammered. Fear spurted through her blood.

"Fire!" someone in the hallway yelled. "Fire in the bailey! Fire!"

Men shouted. Heavy, panicked footsteps thundered down the hallway, racing past her door. "Come on, you lout! You, Leland, get off yer sorry arse! Have ye not heard? Fire! There's fire—bloody goddamned fire in the keep!"

Tara climbed onto the windowsill and stretched to see

past the kitchen. Above the roof, behind Rosie's domain, angry flames crackled, lengthening ever upward in sinister orange, licking hungrily at old timbers and remaining bits of thatching. Smoke clogged the air, teased Tara's nostrils, and drifted into her lungs.

"Christ Jesus," a man yelled, "the damned place is blazin'. Run! Run!"

"Move! Kent, over here!"

"Ben! Tom! Get the buckets!"

Tara jumped to the floor of her chamber and sprinted to the door.

"Leland! For the love of Christ, wet down some damned sacks. Get 'em from Rosie."

"God almighty, how did this start!"

"Pigeon! Find yer ma! Oh, for the love of Mary . . ."

Just as Tara reached the door, it swung open, thudding against the wall. Pigeon, red-faced and breathless, her chin trembling a bit, raced into the room. "Go," she ordered in a harsh whisper. "Now! You must leave—"

"But the fire. I cannot—"

" 'Tis nothing! A small fire in the old apothecary's quarters near the eel pond. 'Twill be out in no time."

"How do you know?"

"Hurry!" the girl screamed. "Go now! You have but a few minutes before I will tell everyone I cannot find you, so run—*now*."

Tara hesitated.

" 'Tis now or never. The fire will be out soon!"

She raced through the door and down toward the decaying great hall, hoping she could slip out unnoticed in all the confusion.

Pigeon was right behind her. "Hurry. We must make haste!" she insisted, and followed after Tara to the bailey and the old wagon where the horses were neighing and rearing at the smell of smoke. With wild, white-rimmed eyes, flashing legs, straining muscles under coats lathered from nervousness, they struggled to break free.

Tara reached her mare and patted the horse on her nose. "Shh, Dobbyn, 'tis a good girl you be," she whispered, though she was as terrified as the animals. Acrid smoke filled her lungs, and the fire raged on, sending bright sparks into the black, smoke-riddled heavens. Tara's fingers fumbled, and she began to sweat as she untied the tether and pulled hard, separating Dobbyn from the other horses. A dappled gray reared, his haunches tight, his front legs flailing. Pigeon untied his lead and he took off, propelled by fright, streaking across the bailey. "Hurry!" she whispered to Tara.

Holding the single rein tight in one hand, Tara swung onto the mare's smooth back. Other horses whinnied. One reared. Another lashed out with a swift hind leg.

Tara paid little attention. Already, from atop the horse, she saw more than twenty men slogging water and throwing dirt onto the fire that burned within the shell of a hut. The flames slowly recoiled, hissing like angry snakes as water drenched them.

Tara pulled on Dobbyn's reins and with a prayer to any deity inclined to listen, kicked the mare hard. "Save us!" Like the shot of an arrow, the bay sprang forward, galloping full tilt around the perimeter of the bailey. Hooves pounding in fear, the mare raced over the soft loam. Another horse, eyes wide with hysteria, sped past.

From the corner of her eye, Tara saw Pigeon releasing the horses and slapping them hard on their rumps. One by one they ran, terrified, neighing, zigzagging and galloping in all directions. The orange glow receded. As Pigeon had foretold, the fire was dying.

Tara steered her horse toward the crevice in the wall. It loomed large and dark, a craggy portal to freedom. "Run, Dobbyn!" she yelled into the smoke-laden air. "Faster! Faster!"

"Hey!" a man yelled. "The horses! Hey! Oh, bloody hell, now what? The damned horses! How in the name of—"

More shouts and terrified neighs punctuated the night.

Dobbyn didn't falter. She gathered speed and raced headlong to the jagged opening. Through the black cleft. Without missing a stride, the mare sailed over a pile of rubble to land with a bone-jarring thud outside the chipped curtain wall.

Tara clung tight. With the ring tied securely to her waist and a taste of freedom in her heart, she rode into the gloom of the night-shrouded forest, determined to put the imprisoning walls of Broodmore and any thoughts of the Bastard Outlaw behind her forever.

"What do you mean 'she's gone'?" Rhys thundered as he stood in front of the smoldering pile of ash that had once been a part of Broodmore. Charred timbers still glowed fiery red in a few spots, and all of the men in the robber band stood on the wet, trampled grass, surveying the damage to what had long ago been an apothecary's hut. Pieces of chipped pottery, remnants of jars, and a smoke-stained jug poked out of the ash. 'Twas a miracle that the kitchen itself hadn't burned.

Rage boiled through Rhys's bloodstream. Tara! She was behind this. The witch had brazenly defied him. Deceived him. Outsmarted his men. His fists clenched in frustration. Had the men not been so tired and defeated, he would have taken them on—each and every one of them.

"What I meant was that Tara escaped. In the confusion." Kent, clearly annoyed at himself, stared Rhys squarely in the eye. His usually clean and well-kept clothes were a shambles—ripped mantle, breeches split in the knee, mud and soot covering not only the fabric but his face as well. In the poor illumination of the single torch that Rhys held aloft, Kent looked gaunt and haggard, a criminal who had no home or loved ones of his own. A man such as himself.

"I don't understand how that could happen." A pulse throbbed at Rhys's temple, and his fingers, encased in leather gloves, dug painfully into his palms. "How did she escape? Was she not guarded?" He leveled a hard, uncompromising glare at each man and most of them looked away, or to the ground, shuffled their blackened, muddy boots, or cleared their smoke-singed throats.

Kent coughed, then squared his shoulders. "Somehow she started the fire, then as everyone was trying to put out the blaze, she set the horses free and took off." Kent's lips pursed into a blade-thin line of disgust. His eyes became slits. "She put the castle and everyone's life at high risk. 'Tis evil she be."

"Is this true?" Rhys asked, turning to the other men.

They nodded and shrugged, grunted their agreement and stared disconsolately at the remains of the fire. Soot streaked their faces, smoke clung to their clothes. Benjamin's eyebrows had been singed and Oliver's arm bled from the fall he'd taken when he ran for a bucket of water.

" 'Tis just how it happened," Pigeon offered, her

lips trembling in a nervous little smile. She looked up at him with shining eyes. "I saw it meself. She went from the apothecary's hut to the wagon where the horses were. She let 'em all go, slapped them on their behinds she did. I . . . I tried to gather the horses together, to stop her . . . but . . ." She turned her palms upward and glanced at the ground as if ashamed. " 'Twas too late. The animals, they scattered when she released them. Scared they were. As . . . as we all were." She swallowed hard, and her little chin quivered. " 'Twas horrid."

"Shh," Rosie said, surrounding the girl's thin shoulders with a fleshy arm. "Never would I have believed this of the lady. We were good to her and . . . ah, well, we survived. All. The Lord was with us this night."

Rhys wasn't so certain.

"We should all pray that—"

"Later!" There was not time for kneeling and talking to God. Not just yet. Rubbing his jaw, Rhys glared at the remaining walls of the keep. Had any passerby seen the glow of the fire through the trees? Had the safety of their lair been compromised by the witch? Hell! Soon they would have to move. Very soon. His thoughts darkened at the thought of the sabotage.

"Dinna ye say she be a witch?" one man asked.

"Aye," another agreed. "I seen her meself, drawin' in the ground, talkin' to the evil ones. Rosie, here, she had to put a stop to it. And a good thing she did, or maybe Satan himself would've been here."

"He was. Bloody hell, Lucifer was here!" Rupert said with a nod. He spat on the ground in conviction.

"Enough!" Rhys said sharply, irritated at the gossip and angry that Tara had eluded him. His head pounded, his fury was as forbidding as the night. "How did she get out of her room?"

"Through the window," Pigeon offered.

"She did not go through the door," Kent agreed. "I was at my post until the alarm."

"So was I!" Rupert hoisted his chin. He folded his beefy arms indignantly over his chest and refused to be intimidated. As if fearing he would be blamed for the conflagration, he said, "She came not through the window."

"It matters not," Rhys thought aloud. "Somehow she got away. We only be lucky that no one lost his life." He scanned the rubble, the smoldering timbers and ash that littered the bailey floor. Kicking at a piece of charred limestone, he fought the demons clawing at his soul. He didn't wonder where she had gone—he knew that she would ride to Twyll if she could get there.

The thought burned hot in his gut. "You," he said, singling out Kent, "will have the first post. Stand guard here and watch that this fire doesn't flare again. The rest of you will take turns as well. I will fetch our prisoner back to us."

Pigeon's smile fell and her lower lip protruded a bit. "Why would ye want to do that?" she demanded and received a cuff on the shoulder from her mother.

" 'Tis sorry I am," Rosie said, grabbing Pigeon's arm. She growled in her daughter's ear, "Never question Rhys or Abelard. They be our lords. Ye best be rememberin' that."

"Hey, the girl's got a point, don't she?" Bertrand demanded. "Lady Tara's been nothin' but trouble— and a witch to boot. I don't know about ye, but I don't like takin' me chances with the dark arts."

A few others grumbled their agreement, but Rhys cut them off. "Argue not. She will return with me." He pointed a finger at each man in turn. "And you will obey Kent while I'm away." To Kent he added, "If there be any more trouble, the blame will fall on your shoulders."

"Aye." Kent's back straightened. He gave a stiff nod.

"Good. Wait for me. When I return, we break camp." Spurred by anger and the thought that Tara was riding alone into the gates of Twyll to face Tremayne, Rhys strode swiftly to the spot where Gryffyn was tethered. He saddled the big stallion, swung onto his back, then rode like fury through the main gate.

He would ride until he found the witch and when he did—he would either shake the living hell out of her or make love to her and never quit. He wasn't sure which.

"Run, damn you, run!" Tara leaned low over her Dobbyn's neck, her knees tight against the mare's heaving sides, her eyes squinting against the icy wind that tore at her face and clawed at her hair.

She'd ridden most of the night before, slept a few hours, and stopped at an inn at the outskirts of a village where she'd eaten, fed Dobbyn, and asked for directions to Twyll.

A sense of urgency claimed her, as she'd been unfamiliar with the forest surrounding Broodmore and had lost much time finding a path that led to a rutted trail wide enough for a single cart. For most of her journey she'd avoided the main roads, hoping not to attract attention, for she wanted to enter Twyll unnoticed and unaccosted as she searched out Father Simon. She didn't want to have to explain herself to other travelers, soldiers, any of the criminals of Broodmore, or Rhys, should she have the misfortune of meeting him.

Rhys. Dear Lord, is he still alive? It had been but

a few days since she'd seen him, and yet it felt like an eternity. The thought that he may have come upon the soldiers, a sheriff's search party, or another thug sent chills down her spine. *He's an outlaw, Tara. He lives in defiance of the law, is a sworn enemy of his half brother, the lord of Twyll. Sooner or later he will be caught and imprisoned or hanged.* She set her jaw against that unavoidable thought, but the painful images whirled through her mind and the prospect that she might not see him again caused a stone to settle deep in her heart.

Where the trail met a river, she slowed Dobbyn, so the mare could catch her breath. Fir and pine trees gave way to mossy rocks that banked the water. A partridge fluttered through the cold, shimmering air, and the mists of evening began to rise, thin wisps of fog that crawled across the ground and slowly ascended to the darkening heavens.

Good. Nightfall and fog would soon give her the cover she needed.

She kneed Dobbyn forward, through the river. 'Twas the only way to Twyll. The mare balked at the icy current, but Tara prodded the beast, and Dobbyn nervously splashed into the rush of freezing water that swirled swiftly around her legs and belly.

"You can do it," she assured her horse, though fear gnawed at her insides when Dobbyn slipped. The mare tried to catch herself but stumbled, pitching Tara forward. The horse floundered again, neighing in fright. Her legs thrashed. Water as cold as death splashed upward, showering Tara.

Madly she clung to the sodden rein and the horse's heavy mane. "Come on, come on," she whispered, her teeth chattering. Dobbyn lunged forward toward the shore. The bay's hooves scrambled on the slick stones, her legs flailed desperately.

"You can do it!" Her heart pumping madly, Tara hung on for dear life as the little mare finally found her footing again. Tara held her breath. *Please, Father in heaven, help us.*

Rocks and gravel shifted under the horse's hooves, but she slogged onward, the deadly river giving up its grip unwillingly. With a snort, Dobbyn found solid ground beneath her hooves and flung herself up the bank, then sprinted madly along the shore.

With numb fingers Tara pulled on the reins, slowing the frightened horse and turning her into the woods again, north toward Tower Twyll. Her teeth rattled, her skin was turning blue, and she knew she must find a place to rest and build a fire. She hoped it wouldn't catch anyone's attention, but she hadn't eaten for hours, her stomach grumbled, and she shook from the cold. Come the morning, she would enter the gates of Twyll and search out Father Simon.

And what then, Tara? What if you find out you are the true daughter of Gilmore? Clenching her jaw to keep her teeth from chattering, she rode until she found a clearing with a pit where an old campfire had burned. " 'Tis here we be, Dobbyn," she said on a sigh. The mare, too, was hungry and tired. "In the morning I'll see that you're fed and fed well." She patted the horse's soft neck and was rewarded with a soft nicker, snort, and nudge of Dobbyn's forehead against her chest. "Yea, 'tis a good mount ye be." Tara's fingernails scratched between the mare's eyes and ears, and she felt an incredible sense of connection to the animal.

As she gathered dry sticks from beneath the surrounding trees and used her dagger to strike the flint over and over again until a spark ignited, she tried not to think about how alone she was. Images of Lodema, old now, her joints aching as she crushed herbs or tended the fire or made candles, flitted through her tired mind. *Oh, Mother, how I miss you.*

Bending low, she leaned over the ring of rocks and blew on the start of her fire, watching as the embers glowed brighter, tiny flames exploding to eat hungrily at the twigs. Images of Rhys came to mind, and as she tried to heat her chilled body and dry out her mantle, she remembered how warm and safe she'd felt in his arms, how right it had seemed to sleep cuddled together with him, the current of desire passing between them.

He is an outlaw, Tara. A man who held you captive. An arrogant thief who will stop at nothing to serve his own purpose.

The fire burned brighter and she rested, her drying mantle wrapped around her torso, her eyes growing heavy. She would sleep for a few hours, then awaken and ride the few miles that separated her from Twyll . . . from her destiny.

Yawning, exhaustion finally taking its toll, she closed her eyes, and as she drifted off to sleep she imagined that Rhys was with her, touching her, pushing her hair away from her face as he kissed the hollow of her throat . . .

So there she was.

Finally.

Damn the witch! Morgan Le Fey? Tara of Gaeaf? Missing daughter of Gilmore?

Bah!

Lying on the forest floor, her face turned toward a

fire that burned low in a ring of stones, Tara was as beautiful and as cursedly bewitching as ever.

Rhys's gut clenched and his heart pumped hard. He'd been searching for her for too many long hours, had just about given up after a full day, believing that she was already inside the massive gates of Twyll, a prisoner of Tremayne. Bloody Christ, what a mess! At least she was safe and not a captive in Twyll.

Bone-weary, every muscle aching from nearly three days in the saddle, he climbed down from Gryffyn's broad back and, pulling off his gloves, quietly walked up to the pit where the embers of the dying campfire glowed a deep scarlet. Tara's small, beautiful face was illuminated in the dancing red shadows. Her black hair was burnished with crimson light, and as she sighed, the anger surging through his veins cooled a bit. Dear God, she was lovely. As lovely a woman as he'd ever set eyes upon. His heart thudded and he gritted his teeth in a combination of fury and lust. Why did he want this woman? Why? Aye, she was exquisite, but she was a thorn in his backside, a fiery-tempered upstart who had the stubborn streak of an ass and the ability to make him think of nothing other than taking her to his bed and taming her.

But he hadn't. The nights he'd spent with her he'd kept a tight leash on his lust, closed his eyes to an ache that had been with him since the first moment he saw her at the shore of the creek, chanting her spells and holding the damned stone high in the air.

So what was he going to do with her? Haul her to her feet, force her back onto her horse, and ride all the way to Broodmore? He hesitated but a second. He had no choice. He'd promised Abelard that he would take the stone from her, and Rhys's word was his law. She would have to return to Broodmore; the forest of Twyll wasn't safe.

Kneeling, he stretched out a hand. She started. Before he could touch her shoulder, she turned swiftly, a dagger in her hand, her eyes wide. "Stand back!" she yelled, scrambling to her feet and facing him. Wild black hair fell around her face, her body was tense and ready to attack, her wicked little knife pointed directly at him. "Oh . . . Rhys." Some of the fear in her eyes disappeared, but she didn't drop the weapon. Her chin inched upward a notch. "You've come to take me back."

"Aye, to Broodmore. What's left of it."

"What?" she whispered.

"From the fire."

"Oh, no! It did not burn down!" Wariness turned to despair. Regret showed in her beautiful eyes, and in that moment's hesitation he lunged. His fingers surrounded her small wrists and forcefully he yanked her arms over her head. "Nay, witch, your plan did not work. Broodmore still stands and everyone was saved."

"Thank the saints."

"What? No thanks to Morrigu? Or Myrddin? What about Rhiannon?" he growled, anger beating a pulse in his temple as he considered the danger she'd brought to those who had pledged their lives to him. "How would you have felt if anyone had died?" He shook her wrists. "How?"

"But—but I did not start the fire."

He snorted. "Lie not, Tara."

" 'Tis not a lie." She glared up at him, some of her rebellious nature surfacing in her expression.

"Others say differently."

"Then they are the ones who speak not the truth."

"Why did I know this is what you would say?"

She looked about to argue but held her tongue. Staring down at her upturned face, he could barely stop himself from giving in to the urge to kiss her.

"I make no apologies," she said, and he noticed the rapid rise and fall of her chest, as if she'd been running. "I harmed no one. You held me captive."

"For your own protection."

"And because I have the stone," she shot back. "I saw the greed in Abelard's eyes as he gazed upon it, heard him whisper that he wanted it." She tossed her hair back from her face. "I wonder if it is me you are after, outlaw. Did you chase me down for my safety or because of the ring?"

"Mayhap both." His hands around her arms were sweating, his fingertips feeling the wild beating of her pulse on the soft inside of her wrists. In the darkness, with only a bit of moonlight and the shadows of the fire for illumination, she seemed more ethereal than ever. Her eyes were luminous, her skin a pearly white, her lips dark and lush.

"Let me go," she whispered.

"Never."

"Unhand, me, Rhys, or I swear, I'll . . . I'll . . ."

"Cut out my heart with your dagger?" he mocked, his gaze flicking to the useless weapon still curled in her fingers.

She shifted just slightly, lifting her foot, but before she could kick him, he widened his stance, still holding her fast. "Careful, witch. Do not provoke me."

"As you provoke me?" she taunted, and his temper snapped. In one swift movement he yanked her closer. She tumbled against him, the knife falling from her fingers, and he kissed her. Hard. Punishing. Demanding. Still holding her arms imprisoned over her

head he slanted his eager lips to hers and felt her
stiffen in resistance.

"Nay—" she began, but the word died in her throat
as his tongue pressed against the seal of her lips. With
a sigh she yielded, her mouth opening to him, her eyes
fluttering shut.

A thousand reasons to stop raced through his mind.
She is your enemy, mayhap the daughter of Gilmore.
The tip of his tongue touched hers.

*She is a witch, a woman who has cast a spell over
you.*

She moaned low in her throat.

*She is heartless, a person who would burn down a
castle for her own means.*

His heart thudded, his blood raced hot, and he
began to ache as his member grew hard.

*She is like poisoned water, innocent-looking but
death to you.*

Her lips moved anxiously, her body quivered, and
all the reasons not to claim her as his own quickly
fled. He wanted her. All of her. Had from the first
time he'd seen her. He ached to feel the touch of her
skin on his, the heat of her naked body against his
own. All the nights of holding her close and yearning
for her, needing her and forcing himself not to do
what was only natural burned through his mind.

His tongue probed deeper, flicked against the end
of hers, mated, and clung as if created for this. Rhys,
Bastard Outlaw, a man who knew no master, was suddenly lost. His weight dragged them onto a carpet of
needles and leaves, and she didn't fight him. They
tumbled together, the forest seeming to draw close as
he kissed her again and again and again.

Tara's blood thundered through her veins. Her
heart raced and she could barely breathe. *Stop,* she

thought in a moment of sanity, but she could not. Too long had she wanted this. His mouth was warm and demanding, his hands possessive as they stroked her back.

Remember who he is—an outlaw who wants only to bend your will to his.

He kissed her cheeks, her eyes, the corner of her mouth. When his lips brushed lower, across the sensitive skin of her throat, her head lolled back, and she felt the tingle of his mouth caressing her.

Her breasts ached, and deep inside she experienced a longing so intense it throbbed with need. More. She wanted more. Her arms encircled his neck, her fingers twining through his hair.

The wind moaned softly through the trees, the firelight faded to the faintest of scarlet glows, and Tara opened her eyes to stare into his. "This is madness," he whispered, and she thought with a sense of disappointment that he might stop.

And yet she knew in her own heart that he was speaking the truth.

Darkly shadowed, his face hovered over hers for the barest of moments before he growled, "Oh, bloody hell." Lightning blazed in his eyes and he kissed her again, his lips firm, his tongue demanding.

Tara barely caught her breath.

Rolling her onto her back, he began unlacing her mantle, his hands searching beneath the layers to find her skin. Quickly he pulled the cloak over her head. Still kissing her, he managed to rid himself of his own cloak, then he went to work on her tunic.

His hands were everywhere, unlacing bindings, pushing wayward locks of hair off her face, splaying possessively over her back. Throughout it all, his lips locked with hers, his breath mingled with her own, and the night seemed to fade around them.

Alone in the universe with pine needles as their mattress and the branches of leafless trees as their canopy, he removed her tunic. Moonlight caressed the forest and caught in his gaze. He kicked at her boots as well as his own, and somehow the soft doeskin fell from her feet.

She shivered as he stared down at her, and though she was wearing her chemise, she felt naked to him. To God. To the universe. Her heart beat wildly, and her body heated from the inside out.

Through the thin fabric of her chemise, he touched her breast, his palm at her nipple, his fingers five warm pressure points as he squeezed gently.

She gasped. Her nipple hardened and he lowered his head. The tip of his tongue teased her through her chemise and a dam of aching need burst deep within her. Her back arched and he nipped at her, his teeth playing, one hand open against the small of her back as he dragged her even closer.

Liquid warmth seeped through the darkest, most intimate places of her body and her soul. She couldn't breathe, couldn't think, could only feel the hard, sinewy strength of him. His heart beat counterpoint to her own, his eyes shone with a smoldering lust that was a reflection of all the emotions raging through her.

Refusing him was impossible, denying herself even more so. Of their own accord her arms surrounded him, her fingers searching beyond the folds of his tunic to the steely muscles beneath.

Straddling her, he yanked the garment off, and she saw him above her in the moonlight, the silhouette of muscular shoulders and torso, his dark hair wild, his eyes gleaming like a wolf regarding its prey.

His fingers found the hem of her chemise and he

slowly bunched the fabric, crawling it upward, over her calves, her thighs, her hips and waist. Finally he pulled the sheer garment over her head and she was naked in the night.

Though the air was cold, bringing goose bumps to her skin, the womanly fires deep inside burned hot, and he stoked the blaze by dragging a solitary finger up her ribs.

Her breath caught.

He leaned forward. Kissed her breast. Lifted his head and let the wet nipple pucker in the night air.

Her throat turned to sand, and her hands explored the sinewy muscles of his arms and shoulders and back. The tips of her fingers discovered old welts—scars upon his skin, and her heart ached for all the pain he had borne.

Again he leaned forward. He kissed her breasts, his tongue lapping, his teeth teasing. She arched upward and he caught her, one big hand on her back, forcing her upward, her lower abdomen pressed hard against the coarse fabric of his breeches. She felt his manhood, hard, thick, and pulsing. Deep in her mind she knew that she should stop, that she was near the edge, that if there was any way to end this madness, she had little time before 'twould be too late.

"You be the most bewitching woman in all of Wales," he admitted as his mouth moved anxiously against hers. His lips were hard, his tongue wet and teasing, the stubble of his beard rough. Tara met his passion eagerly. His hands slid over her body, the fingers trailing heat. Her blood thundered, and she sensed that he removed the last barrier between them. He kicked off his breeches and spread her knees with his own.

Deep inside she throbbed.

He gazed down at her.

Desire pulsed hot, wild. He was so close to her, the shaft of his manhood only inches from her most intimate of places.

With one hand he reached up and molded her breast, then slowly pulled his fingers down the ladder of her ribs to her waist. " 'Tis beautiful you are," he said, fingering the cord that held the ring against her. "So damnably beautiful."

She quivered. Swallowed hard. He played with the ring and the cold stone grazed her flushed skin. She thought for a second that he might try to remove her treasure, but he kissed her lips and his hand moved to the nest of curls between her legs. Her hips lifted in response and he cupped her buttocks in his hands. Tingling sensations swept upward. The cold air blew across her bare skin.

His fingers dug into her flesh.

Her heart jolted.

"Ahh, sweet witch Tara," he said, her name torn from his throat. " 'Tis a sin to be with you."

"Aye." She didn't want to think about right or wrong.

His eyes found hers. "Then willingly I condemn myself to hell."

He thrust into her.

Hard.

Pain burned through her.

She cried out.

Hot, blinding, a rending deep within. Her maidenhead gave way.

She gasped. Tears came to her eyes. Her muscles tensed and for a moment she thought it was over. Then he kissed her. More gently. Again and again and again. He began to move within her and slowly the pain became pleasure, the ache within her sweet torment. Her skin flushed, her fingers delved into the hair of his chest. Faster and faster he moved. Her body found his rhythm with an answering beat of its own.

"Tara, sweet, sweet . . ." His voice was rough. Her fingers dug into his chest. She felt as if she were riding a dozen horses all at once, that they were galloping wildly toward the edge of a wide abyss. Her breath was lost somewhere in her lungs. Her thoughts had vanished. Closer to the brink. Faster and faster. The edge loomed before them, and in her mind's eye the horses soared into the air. Took flight. Into the stars.

She bucked upward. Cried out and heard his own primal cry ringing through the trees. Head thrown back, teeth bared in ecstatic pain, Rhys spilled himself into her. His muscles flexed. His voice rang through the trees. Tara convulsed again and he held her tight.

"Ah, witch," he moaned, as he fell against her, heaving. His weight flattened her chest, his neck and torso were wet with sweat.

Her arms surrounded him, clinging to his slick muscles, holding him against her as if afraid he would vanish into the rising mist. She basked in the wonder of joining with him, of becoming one, of learning the secrets of womanhood.

The forest was dark, the fire long since dead, and she sighed in contentment. At last. At last. *Oh, Rhys.*

Slowly he stirred, his heartbeat quieted, and his breathing became regular and even once more.

"Son of the devil," he whispered raggedly, his words edged in torment as he lifted his head and stared down at her. His eyes were grave, his voice raw, his expression a mask of regret. "Curse the fates, woman. Curse them all to hell." He lifted a strand of hair off her face, and the corners of his mouth turned down in self-derision. "Now what have I done?"

Chapter Nine

Tremayne's skin crawled as he looked upon the deserted and eerie walls of Broodmore. Blackened by fire, overgrown with weeds and vines, splitting apart where the battlements crumbled—'twas a sinister castle, a fortress fit for Satan himself. As the moon rose behind the ruins, the lord of Twyll reminded himself that he was a Christian, that pagan rites were foolish and curses didn't exist. Yet he knew deep in his heart that he was a liar. In the darkest reaches of his soul, he feared all that he didn't understand. Astride his mount at the edge of the forest, Tremayne stared at the foreboding keep and felt more than a small frisson of fear skitter down his spine and settle like lead in his gut.

As if a dark spirit were reading his thoughts, the wind picked up, lifting his hair in cool, damp gusts that smelled of the dank forest floor and brushed the back of his neck.

" 'Tis haunted," Red whispered as he halted his broad-chested steed alongside Tremayne's and stared, transfixed, at the charred behemoth resting on the cliff.

"Cursed," Sir Lawrence agreed. A big man with thinning blond hair and eyes that missed nothing, Lawrence, riding high upon his white destrier, eyed the wreckage that had once been a thriving castle teeming with freemen and villeins, pulsing with a life-blood all its own. His fingers worked nervously in his mount's reins. "No one survived the pestilence."

" 'Tis said ghosts lurk in the dungeons and stand guard in the tower," still another chimed in.

"Foolishness!" Tremayne didn't need any of his men to add to his own silly trepidation.

"Nay, look!" Red's hushed voice quivered, and he pointed a wavering finger at one of the square towers rising above the decaying stone wall. "There be one now."

Tremayne froze, then fixated on the silhouette of a guard standing watch. His fear gave way slowly and he swallowed a smile. " 'Tis no ghost," he said, as even in the pale moonlight he recognized a thug who had eluded his own sheriff for far too long. " 'Tis old Bertrand, the pickpocket. See how he walks, dragging one leg. I gave him that wound." Tremayne nearly laughed out loud. He looked at each man in turn—loyal every one of them. Or so he hoped. Sir James's theory that there was a spy hidden in the circle of the most trusted men in Twyll worried him. Could one of these soldiers—all of whom had pledged their fealty to him, be a traitor? A Judas who had been watching him, following him throughout his days? Each man met his gaze evenly. "Spread out," Tremayne ordered. "Do as we planned. Just before dawn we strike."

Red gulped but yanked on his destrier's reins.

Sir Lawrence's jaw became solid steel. "Aye," he whispered, one hand on the hilt of his sword.

Tremayne could almost taste his victory. Rhys, damn him, was about to learn a valuable lesson. "Kill as few as possible. The rest we'll bring to Twyll and if anyone"—he let his gaze wander from one loyal

man to the next—"discovers the bastard or this
woman he be with, you are to bring them to me immediately."

'Twould be sweet revenge to see the expression on his
irreverent half brother's face when Rhys realized he was
to be taken prisoner and tried for his crimes in the very
castle from which he'd been banished so many years before.

"Is there anything else?" Sir Lawrence asked.

"Yes." Tremayne's horse danced, and he gripped the
reins more tightly. "When we have the prisoners, set fire
to the castle."

"But, m'lord, 'tis already burned it is."

"Not completely." Tremayne scowled at the blackened spires of Broodmore's towers and thought of all
the myths surrounding the ancient keep—myths of
ghosts and omens and curses. "Destroy it. All of it."

Sir Lawrence hesitated but a moment. "'Twill be
done."

"See to it. As soon as Rhys is captured." The cockles
of Tremayne's icy heart warmed a bit. *Aye, Rhys . . .
brother, now 'tis the time for our reckoning.*

Tara stirred, her eyes opening and adjusting to the
dark sky above. She was in the forest and a strong
arm sprinkled with dark hair held her fast. *Rhys!* So,
'twas not just a wanton, wild dream. Her heart
thumped madly in her chest. The throbbing between
her legs reminded her of their joining, the passion of
their bodies, the feel of his manhood driving deep
into the most intimate part of her. Even now, hours
later, the memory brought with it yearnings that
came from her very core. Yearnings to which she
couldn't fall victim. Ever again. She had to leave now,

while he slept. Once he was awake he would not release her.

Biting her lip, she decided to slip away this very second. Painstakingly, she inched out of his grasp, sliding her naked body away from his, disentangling legs and arms, ignoring the heady male scent that clung to him and the earthy odor of sex, so recent. Holding her breath, she cringed with each rustle of the leaves beneath her, freezing at the sound of a wolf's lonely howl far in the distance.

Rhys snorted and turned over. Tara was certain he was reaching for her, his fingers searching the area around him, but he sighed deep in his sleep, his broad back white in the moonlight, the web of scars visible across the muscles.

Naked save for the emerald ring bound to her waist, Tara fumbled for her clothes. Locating her boots, chemise, and tunic, she inwardly prayed that the stone truly was magical, that it held some power that would let her escape her seductive captor without waking him.

Her mantle lay crushed beneath Rhys's body and she couldn't risk retrieving it. Nay, she would go without.

Shivering, she dressed without making a sound. Her gaze never left Rhys. What would he do when he woke up and found her gone? She shuddered at the image of him in her mind's eye when he realized that she'd duped him. Never would she want to be the target of his wrath; he was too volatile, too dangerous. And yet her silly heart was filled with regret at leaving him. She started for the horses, stepping soundlessly, slinking behind a tree so that, for just a second or two, he was out of her line of vision.

Only a few more feet.

"Where do you think you're going?" A big hand grabbed her ankle.

"Oh!"

She screamed before she realized the fingers gripping her leg so possessively belonged to Rhys, who, stark-naked, had stretched his arm as far as it would reach to capture her.

"I—I—" So astounded that no words would form in her mouth, she could only stare at him. The fingers around her boot tightened for a second, then he released her and sprang lithely to his feet—directly between her and the horses.

She forced her eyes to remain on his face. Though she'd lain with him, even felt his coarse chest hairs rub against her breasts as he fell against her, spent, after spilling his seed into her, she averted her eyes from the thick mat of hair, dark and curling, that arrowed down past his navel to the thatch where his legs joined and his manhood, as she could see even in her peripheral vision, seemed intent upon making itself known.

Her throat tightened.

Her heart was beating like a drum. Surely he could hear it. Surely all of Twyll could hear it.

"I asked you a question," he said, advancing upon her. She backed up one step. Two. She didn't fear him—nay, 'twas herself she didn't trust, the emotions she couldn't control when close to him.

A third step backward. Her buttocks slammed into the rough bark of a giant oak tree.

"I know . . . and I . . . I was trying . . ." Oh, Lord, she couldn't think. She focused on his eyes again. Luminous and silver, they gleamed with satisfaction.

"You were trying to escape."

"Yes!"

"And trying to get to Twyll. By the gods, woman, will you never learn?" He stepped closer to her, so near that her tunic brushed against his bare skin and the scent of him enveloped her. Her skin tingled and she told herself she had to ignore him, to get away, to run as fast as her legs would carry her and pray that she could lose him in the thickets.

She glanced past him to the horses and knew there was no way she could reach them before he caught her.

"Do not even think it," he warned. "Whether you like it or nay, you are staying with me, little witch, and you can curse, claw, chant spells, draw runes, flee, and plot your escape from now until forever, but until I decide 'tis safe you will stay with me."

"Until *you* decide?" she repeated, seeing red. "Until 'tis *safe*?" She glared at him and considered shooting her knee upward and connecting hard with his manhood. "'Tis not for you to choose my fate."

"No? 'Tis wrong you be." With both hands he grabbed her shoulders, and for the first time she heard a sense of regret in his words.

"Why? What care you?" she said, but a needle of understanding pricked her mind. "Oh, God's eyes, this be about the stone."

His fingers gripped tighter through her clothes. "I need the ring."

"Why?"

"To use against Tremayne."

"'Tis mine," she said, disappointed to think that his attention had been because of the damned emerald. 'Twas why she was kept captive. Why he kept her close. Why he'd lain with her. "So you were not talking of my safety but of the ring's." Sick inside, she tried to pull away, but his hands were strong, his fingers digging into her muscles like the jaws of a gentle trap. When she thought of what she'd done, how wantonly she'd lain with him, the way his tongue and lips had explored the most intimate reaches within her, she felt nothing but shame—though no regret. Oh, vile, vile heart, to be so betrayed.

"Aye, we need the ring, but I be concerned about your safety as well."

Don't believe him, Tara. Trust him not. He cares for you not one little mite. Had you not the ring, he would not have chased you down, found you, and bedded you.

Her cheeks flushed scarlet in the darkness, and she stiffened when he pulled her close, his arms surrounding her, his lips slanting urgently, anxiously, over hers. She forced herself not to respond. Though inside she was aching, her breasts tightening, the newfound fires of passion sweeping through her blood, she refused to fall victim to them. To him, again. Rhys was using her, wanting her only for the hard stone bound to her waist. She willed herself not to give in to him.

Yet the sweet, slick pressure of his tongue against her mouth, the movement of his hands upon her back, and the pressure of his hips molded to hers weakened her resolve.

His lips were warm, the smell of him enticing. With one hand he twined his fingers in her hair, gripping and pulling gently, forcing her head back. She stared up at him. "Trust me, Tara," he said, drawing his face away from hers in order to look at her.

"Never."

"I do what is best for us both."

"Nay, I do not think—"

His mouth crashed down on hers and he kissed her

hard, roughly, his tongue insistent as it pressed against her teeth. Her mind screamed at her to stop. *This is madness. He wants you not. Tara, don't do this again. He has robbed you of your maidenhood, now will you let him steal the ring from you as well?*

Her mouth opened to him.

Her body quivered at his touch.

Nay, nay, nay! Do this not. Run! For the love of all that is holy, Tara, run!

But she couldn't. And when she felt his fingers find the hem of her tunic and draw it over her head, she allowed the garment to be stripped from her. His hands surrounded her breasts and the heat, that glorious, wondrous rush of warmth, invaded every part of her.

Her nipples hardened as calloused fingers expertly rubbed them, her skin was on fire, and deep within her she began to ache, the pain of the night before fading with a new, throbbing need that she knew he could satisfy.

His lips traveled slowly from her mouth and down the column of her throat to a small place between her neck and shoulder, a sensitive spot that caused her heart to beat as rapidly as a hummingbird's wings. All thoughts of denial faded and she gave herself to him. Willingly. Eagerly. Anxious for the moment of elation when their bodies became one.

"Oh, lady," he whispered into the night. His voice was rough as his hands caressed her naked breasts, pearly white with the faintest webbing of blue veins barely visible through her translucent skin in the shimmering light from the stars.

Kissing her, he lowered himself and lifted a breast in his trembling fingers. Eagerly he took her nipple into his mouth.

Her breathing stopped and her brain thundered
with the want of him. Teasing, toying, nipping, he
suckled hungrily and slipped one hand around her
waist, his fingers stretched over her spine, dangerously
close to the cleft of her buttocks.

Tara could barely stand, her knees went weak. He
slipped lower still, leaving her nipples wet for the winter air to blow across them. He kissed her abdomen
and licked the slit of her navel.

Inside she was quaking and tears sprang to her eyes.
Need, a throbbing, pulsing ache, burned within her.
Her back pressed to the tree, she tried to writhe away
as, kneeling, he parted her legs with his face. She
jerked backward, but his hands had slid to her buttocks and he held her close. As he kissed the insides
of her thighs she gave herself up, leaning against the
trunk and moaning softly, anxiously. Cold air caressed
her for a second before his warm breath stirred the
curls at the tops of her legs, and then he found her.

She convulsed at the feel of his mouth and tongue,
tried to back away, but he held her fast. Gasping, she
sensed him probing and kissing and . . . and . . . oh,
sweet ecstasy! She closed her eyes, gave herself up,
and sagged against the mossy bark as he created a
maelstrom of desire, a wild, rushing whirlpool of need
that pulsed through her. Hotter. Hotter still. Faster
and faster. She couldn't breathe. Couldn't think. Her
mind spun in wild, sensual circles. She tossed her head
back and cried out, her hair caught on the bark and
her rump pressed hard into the tree. She felt a wild,
reckless abandon as something deep inside broke and
she jolted.

The fingers digging into her buttocks held fast.

Rhys didn't stop. He lifted her slightly and leaned

forward, kissing her again in the most intimate of places.

Breathing hard, she tried to pull away, but he held her fast, his tongue and teeth and lips exploring, his breath causing sweet, sweet ecstasy to race through her blood again. The stubble of his beard was rough against the inside of her legs.

Her world began to tilt. A long, low moan escaped her throat, and heat poured from her.

Again she convulsed.

Oh, God! She was going to die. Right here, naked in the woods with Rhys . . . sweet, horrible Rhys kneeling before her, kissing her, touching her, plying his sweet, sweet magic. The heat built yet again, the pressure so intense she thought she would burst. She squirmed against the tree, trying to get away and closer all in one instant.

He touched her—finger and tongue.

Her body slammed against the hard bark. The stars in the sky streaked through her brain, colliding, spinning, shooting tails of incredible color as she collapsed, spent, into his waiting arms.

" . . . so I am to understand that you be willing to give up the ring—as valuable as it be—and pledge your loyalty as well as that of all the criminals who are part of your band to join up with me and do battle against Twyll?" Lord Cavan was seated in his ornately carved chair in the great hall of Castle Marwood. His beringed fingers tapped together under his chin as he stared at Abelard with suspicious eyes.

"I would want to be compensated."

"Ahh." A benign smile pulled at the corners of the baron's wide mouth. A huge fire burned bright in the grate, illuminating the whitewashed walls, the intricate tapestries, and the high dais upon which the lord of Marwood posed. Black curls framed a face on which the barest of beards tried to sprout, and his purple tunic, trimmed in gray velvet and fur, made him appear all the more like a monarch. "So now we discuss the true nature of your business," he said, snapping his fingers at a comely maid who was hurrying toward the stairs.

She stopped midstride. "M'lord?" Her rosy cheeks flushed a more vibrant hue, and she glanced nervously from the baron to Abelard and the other men, two burly soldiers who stood in attendance near the door.

"More wine," he ordered, pointing to the floor where his empty silver cup sat. "For me and Sir Abelard here."

Abelard cringed a bit. It had been years since his title had preceded his name, and being within the walls of Marwood, where soldiers were teeming and preparations for war were visible in the bailey, made him anxious. Upon his arrival, he'd been searched by the sentries before he was allowed to pass through the outer bailey, where carts and wagons were being loaded with supplies. Destriers, jennets, palfreys, and sumpter horses had neighed and tugged at their leads as they'd been herded together by dozens of soldiers. Abelard had seen crates of weapons—longbows, crossbows, knives, and swords, as well as hammers, saws, picks, shovels, and other tools—casks of food and wine, crates of torches, flint, and all manner of supplies that had been hauled from the castle stores and were waiting to be carried to battle. A skeletal trebuchet had been partially assembled in preparation for hurling missiles over Twyll's vast walls. The battering ram was ready to roll on its sturdy wheels toward

Twyll, where it would be used to bash the heavy gates of the castle.

Cavan's attack would be vicious, the siege arduous and prolonged.

The serving girl nodded curtly at Cavan's request. "Aye, m'lord," she said, scurrying off, her blue skirt swirling around her ankles.

"A fair lass, Meghan," Lord Cavan thought aloud, his eyes following the girl, one ringed finger tapping the arm of his chair thoughtfully.

"Aye."

"Now, tell me." The baron crossed his long legs and focused his distrustful eyes upon Abelard. "What is it you want in exchange for all that you offer?"

"A keep."

"Aaah," Cavan said, nodding and raising one hand. "A keep. Such a small request." Sarcasm flavored his words as he glanced at the men standing by the grate, where huge andirons in the shape of wolves' heads held a massive log that burned hot.

"The emerald ring will prove that you were the true issue of Gilmore. Many who have been secretly loyal to the old baron would easily change their allegiance from Tremayne and accept you as the rightful baron of Twyll." Abelard nodded to himself. " 'Twould undermine Lord Tremayne from the inside, from the heart of the castle. His people would rise against him."

"Some of them," Cavan agreed, tapping a finger against front teeth that overlapped a bit. The girl returned with an empty cup and a full jug. She filled both mazers and Cavan's gaze wandered to her bodice and the sway of her hips. As she disappeared from sight he sighed, then brought his thoughts back to matters at hand. "So who does the ring belong to?"

"Pardon?"

Cavan leaned forward, elbows resting on knees, eyebrows elevated. "Well, Sir Abelard, if I am to follow
your reasoning, the ring belongs to the true ruler of
Twyll, given to him at birth, when, as the myth indi-
cates, the son of Gilmore was stolen from his keep
just before his father's death. My own father, Innis,
claimed 'twas me. That I was the missing babe. Yet
you have come up with the ring . . . this is what you
are leading me to believe?"

"Aye."

"So either it was given you or you stole it." He
took a sip from his cup, and firelight played upon the
shining silver surface. Though he appeared outwardly
calm, there was a restlessness burning within him, a
hunger. Before Abelard could answer, Cavan added,
"And where is the ring now?"

"Safely stowed away."

"Not on you?" His fingers rubbed nervously against
the mazer.

"Nay."

"So I am to take your word as truth, though there
is nothing to prove it?"

"My men are willing to join with you."

"So you say. But your men are cutthroats, murderers, rapists, and robbers. Their loyalty could be bought
with a single coin or the promise of a wench lifting
her skirts."

"They are willing to go before you, to open the
castle doors of Twyll and offer up Lord Tremayne
to you."

"Or leave us open for slaughter as we pass through.
How know I that this is not a trap, that you are not
sent from Tremayne? His spies have been here before." He shook his head. "Why should I trust you?"

"Because I hate Tremayne of Twyll as I hate no

other." Abelard lifted his hand, showing his stump of a finger. "I have him to thank for this."

" 'Twas not his fault that you are slow with a weapon." Cavan took a huge swallow of wine, draining his mazer, and wiped his mouth with the back of his sleeve. "Nay, 'tis no reason to trust you."

"I ride with Rhys."

Cavan's head snapped around. Every muscle within his long body tensed. "The Bastard Outlaw?"

"Aye."

"Yet he is not here with you, is he? I have heard of this, that you and he are sometimes seen together. Why is he not here now?"

"Because he is the keeper of the dark emerald." Abelard smiled inwardly. This meeting had gone just as he'd expected. "Were I to bring the stone to you, what would stop you from taking it from me?"

"What would stop me from taking you hostage and trading your life for the emerald?"

"Nothing." Abelard tossed back the last of his wine.

Cavan waited, his smile disappearing.

"Nothing except that you would gain the wrath of the Bastard Outlaw and all the men who ride with him. The emerald would never be yours, and for the rest of your miserable life, you would never be able to sleep without the knowledge that at any moment Rhys of Twyll could slit your pathetic, scrawny throat."

Cavan shot to his feet, and from the height of his dais he glared arrogantly down at Abelard. "With one word, I could have the rest of your fingers cleaved off at the knuckles!"

"Aye, 'tis powerful you be, Lord Cavan, but if you make that mistake, you will regret it for the rest of your life." Abelard's voice lowered. "This I promise."

"And then I could start with your toes."

"And you would never see the emerald. Also, you would lose a good advantage in your battle. Want you not revenge against Merwynn's son?"

Lord Cavan settled back into his thronelike chair. His eyes snapped with the fire of bloodthirst, for Cavan, though spoiled by an aging Lord Innis, had never known his mother or the love that only she could have given him. The old man had been heartless and cold.

Abelard had the audacity to smile. He worried not about having his fingers or toes severed. This whelp of a lord didn't intimidate him. He knew that when the new baron thought about his choices, he would throw in with the outlaws. 'Twas lunacy to do otherwise, and Cavan of Marwood seemed very sane, extremely vengeful, and exceedingly greedy.

In the silence of the still afternoon, Rhys stared at the rubble that had been Broodmore. Smoke still drifted from the blackened timbers, and even the walls that had not been charred before were now stained by soot and smoke, many reduced to ash.

"No one is here," he said as he walked through what had once been the bailey. The grass was singed and dry, the old wagon where the horses had been tied was but a scorched skeleton.

Tara's face had drained of color. She stood on a small rise near the eel pond, one hand to her mouth, tears filling her eyes. The wind tore at the folds of her mantle, swiping off her hood, and causing her loose black curls to fall over her face.

"You did this." The condemning words were out of his mouth before he thought. Pain, raw and blinding, cut to his very soul. Rosie. Leland. Kent. Pigeon.

Johnny. Benjamin. And so many others. Holy Christ, were they all dead? His skull ached, despair pierced his heart.

"Nay."

"Aye—'twas your own self-serving purposes that killed them."

"Nay, oh, nay!" She wobbled unsteadily for a second, then forced some steel into her spine. Her small shoulders straightened. "I set not the fire."

"No?" Turning swiftly on his heel, guilt propelling him across the bent, dead grass, he strode up to her. "Then who did?"

"I—I know not. But I saw the flames, the guards ran to douse the fire, and I . . . I slipped through the window. I could not have set the fire had I wanted to. I was locked in my room, guarded day and night. And . . . and you were here, were you not? Was not the blaze extinguished?"

He snorted. Blast the woman, he wanted to believe her, wanted to trust the innocence he saw reflected in her eyes. "Not quite."

"Mayhap they are not dead," she said, her voice trembling with the need to believe her own words. "We have yet to find any bodies, or . . . or . . . skeletons," she added in a whisper. "The horses are missing and . . . could it not be that they escaped?"

"And went where? Why did we not meet up with any of them?"

"Because we were hiding, as were they. Or . . . or mayhap they traveled in another direction."

"All of them?" he sneered.

"Why not?"

Aye, why not? He shoved the hair out of his eyes and experienced an overwhelming sense of guilt. Never had his band stayed in one camp so long, but he'd been lulled into believing that living here in a supposedly cursed castle was safe.

He'd been wrong.

He hadn't moved fast enough. Though he'd sensed that there was danger, he'd ignored it and chased after the witch, believing that fate would be with him for a few more days.

And now those who had trusted in him had paid, perhaps with their lives.

"Did you not see them—all alive, the fire only embers?"

"Aye." He remembered the smoldering piles of rubble, which had been far less than this, and the damage had been contained to the old apothecary's hut. "But a spark must have ignited again and . . ." His heart was heavy when he thought of those who had trusted him. Relied upon him. Thought him their savior of sorts. Deep inside he ached. " . . . and no one saw the fire restarting."

"Did you not leave someone to watch it?"

"Aye. An overburdened, weary man." He closed his eyes, disgusted that he had put finding Tara and the damned stone above the safety of his men. All the members of his band had been far too tired from battling the blaze earlier and rounding up the horses and searching for Tara to do justice to tending the smoldering timbers.

Rhys fought the urge to shake his fist in the air and rage at the heavens.

Kicking a piece of mortar into a pile of rubble, he told himself that what was done was done. He would bury this pain in the darkest places of his heart. He hoped that Rose, Kent, Pigeon, and the others had escaped, but he didn't believe it. People had died.

Because of Tara.

Because of him.

And because of the damned dark emerald.

Well, now 'twas time for the stone to pay them back.

"Come," he said, grabbing her hand and tugging her back toward the portcullis, where their two horses were prancing nervously from the smell of smoke. " 'Tis time to set things right."

"Set them right?" she repeated, half running to keep up as he strode across the bailey.

"Aye. You are about to give up your prize, witch."

"I—I don't understand." But he saw in her eyes that she was lying. She knew full well what he was suggesting.

"The stone." He reached for Dobbyn's reins and smacked them into her hand. He was furious with her, with himself, and he dared not think of their lovemaking, so wild and hot, so overwhelming. When he kissed her, he lost his mind, and therefore he knew he could never take her into his arms again. "Your damned emerald." He put a foot into Gryffyn's stirrup and hoisted himself into the saddle. " 'Tis time for you to give it up."

She hauled herself onto Dobbyn's back and tugged lightly on the reins. "Give it up? Why?"

"Abelard is striking a deal with Lord Cavan of Marwood. The stone and our allegiance to join up with him in the defeat of Tremayne."

"Nay, I will not surrender what is mine."

Rhys felt a cruel smile creep over his lips. "You have no choice, I fear—because, *m'lady,* others have surrendered far more." He swept the ground with his angry gaze. "These men and women have died, Tara. Died. Because of you. Now, 'tis your turn to sacrifice a little of yourself." He wheeled Gryffyn around and glared down at her from the back of the rearing horse. Refusing to give in to the overpowering urge to forgive her, to climb down from his steed, drag her off her mare, take her into his arms, and kiss her until they both could no longer think, he hardened his heart. She had caused all this misery by escaping from Broodmore.

And were you not to blame for bringing her here? his conscience insisted, but he ignored it. Before he changed his mind, he said, "You will give up the emerald."

"Nay—I—"

"There will be no more arguments."

"But—"

"Listen, woman, either you will remove it yourself when we get to the village where I am to meet Abelard or I will strip you of your clothes, unknot the cursed cord myself, and take it from you." He scowled down at her, and she met his gaze with bristling defiance. Rather than cower and shiver and swear that she would do his bidding, she offered him a haughty, frigid smile as she held the reins tight and her little mare pranced backward, shaking her head against the bit.

"Know you this, Rhys. I will never—do you hear me, I will *never*—let you or anyone else tell me what I shall do." She released her tight hold on the horse's reins, kicked her sides, and the bay sprang forward as if shot from a catapult. Her head tucked low, Tara rode as if all the furies of hell were chasing her.

And they were. Rhys kicked Gryffyn hard in the flanks. The gray bolted, racing across the bailey in swift ground-eating strides that brought him closer by the minute to the escaping mare and her rider. Tara's hood fell away from her face, her black curls streamed, and her mantle billowed behind her as her mount disappeared through the open gate. But it didn't matter. 'Twas a futile effort.

In a matter of minutes Rhys would catch her and then, by the gods, would show her what it meant to cross him.

His jaw clenched so hard it ached, and his lips were twisted into an evil smile. Oh, yes, the witch was going to learn a lesson. A sensual, erotic, but oh, so difficult lesson. One she needed and needed badly.

He couldn't wait to give it to her.

Chapter Ten

He caught up with her at the creek.

"Do you never learn?" he demanded, the two horses running neck and neck as they splashed wildly, legs churning, through the racing brook. Cold water sprayed Dobbyn's belly and Tara's boots.

Rhys and Gryffyn were within inches of her.

She saw the fury in his eyes, read the consternation in the flattening of his lips.

"Leave me be!" she warned, yanking on the reins.

He laughed out loud, a brittle bark that rang through the trees and held no mirth. "Never."

"Hi-*ya*!" She kicked Dobbyn and the bay scrambled up the opposite bank, but Rhys anticipated her attempt at escape. He stayed right with her. As one, the two horses scrambled up the bank, leaping exposed roots of the trees guarding the creek and rocks that jutted out of the mud. Rhys leaned over, dangerously close to her—to her horse. With one hand he held to the saddle and reins; with the other, he reached out—

"Watch out!" she cried, hoping that he would straighten up in the saddle, but he didn't. He was daft! At any second he might topple to the heather- and rock-strewn ground. Tara jerked on the reins, trying to angle off through the bracken.

Rhys grabbed the reins. With one sharp tug, he

threw his weight back into the saddle and stripped the leather straps from her unwilling fingers.

"No—don't you—"

Dobbyn skittered, wrenching her head away from Rhys, but he held fast, his fingers strong as steel.

"You're addled! You're going to kill us both!" Tara screamed. "Let her go."

From the taller horse, he threw her a look that pierced to her core, a sizzling, intimidating glance that drove deep into the most feminine part of her. She clung to the saddle. Her throat went dry and she knew the despair of those who were cursed. Rhys, damn his irreverent smile, would seek his own justice from her. 'Twas only a matter of time.

She didn't know whether to anticipate his sweet torture or fear it.

She reached for the reins again, but he held fast, standing in his saddle and leaning back, forcing both horses to slow to a quick walk.

Breathless and embarrassed, Tara avoided his eyes, staring straight ahead to a point in the path between Dobbyn's ears.

"So this is the way it must always be with you," he said, and she thought she heard just a touch of sadness over the steady plop of the horses' hooves and the hammering of her heart.

Remaining shards of late-afternoon sunlight penetrated the clouds and branches overhead, dappling the ground in spangles of yellow light, but the winter air was cold and high above, clouds were already gathering, threatening rain before nightfall. A few birds and squirrels rustled in the undergrowth, and the earthy smell of the forest surrounded them, ferns and fungi mixing with the odor of loam and horses.

As the path narrowed, Dobbyn followed docilely

after Gryffyn and Tara was forced to watch Rhys's back, his broad shoulders, the set of his spine, the way his buttocks molded to the saddle and swayed with his mount's gait, the strength of his legs as he clamped them tight over Gryffyn's sides.

She remembered all too vividly the strident muscles of his thighs pushing hard against hers, and she cleared her throat and looked away. He was furious with her and unfairly so. She had not caused the fire at Broodmore, she had not even suggested it to Pigeon— and yet he would not believe her if she told him the truth. Nor would she want his wrath aimed at the poor moonstruck girl.

What good would it do to blame Pigeon? For all Tara knew, the girl might be already dead. Tara's heart lay heavy at the thought of lives lost, for though Rhys's companions were cutthroats and thieves, a few seemed to be decent souls and, surprisingly, had endeared themselves to her. Johnny had been good to Dobbyn, and Leland had offered her shy, toothless smiles.

She rode onward, accepting her fate for the time being, but she knew that at the first opportunity she would again attempt to escape. The key to who she was, where she belonged, and what was her destiny lay with Father Simon at Twyll. Beyond meeting with him and discovering the truth, she knew not what she would do. She glanced again at Rhys. Bastard. Outlaw. Jailer. Lover. The words spun around in her head, chasing after each other like a pup who spies his tail and tries vainly to capture it in his teeth.

Rhys twisted in the saddle and looked back over his shoulder. Their eyes met. Locked. Tara's stomach did a slow, sensuous roll. Her fingers were suddenly clammy. His eyelids narrowed just a bit, and the stare he sent her brimmed with unspoken lust—a hot hunger that promised sensual delights and hinted at a deeper purpose, one that frightened her a bit and caused her lungs to constrict.

"Where . . . where are we going?" she asked, pretending that she had no interest in fleeing.

Moving with Gryffyn's gentle gait, he considered her question, his lower lip protruding thoughtfully. He didn't answer.

"Will I not know when we get there?"

He lifted a shoulder. "We ride to a village between Marwood and Twyll, where I am to meet Abelard."

So they wouldn't be far from her destination. Her heart began to beat more rapidly.

"While we are there, you will do as you are told," he added. "And you will give up the stone." His face was stern. " 'Tis little enough payment for what you have done."

"I did not start the fire!" she said again, but her words fell upon deaf ears. Rhys's skin tightened over his face, and his glare silently told her that she would never be able to convince him of her innocence. He would never trust. Never believe her. Never love her.

Like a bolt of lightning, the thought struck her hard. Of course he would never love her. Why would she want him to? 'Twasn't as if she was in love with him.

He was ruthless. A rogue. An outlaw set upon his own ends. Nay, she would never—*could* never—love a man like the Bastard Outlaw. And yet her stupid heart jolted every time he cast a look over his shoulder, and the thought of making love with him scorched through her mind.

Fool, she chided herself as the path led onto a well-worn road, a muddy expanse rutted by cart wheels and carved by hooves and boots. Farmhouses were visible, many cut into the hills with their few fallow acres flanking the sparse homes. Without pausing, Rhys turned toward the hills and, Tara assumed, the village where he was to meet Abelard.

Clouds roiled in the sky overhead, turning day to night. Somewhere far away thunder rumbled, and the first icy drops of rain began to fall.

His muscles tense, Tremayne drew back on his bow, narrowed his eyes, and aimed his arrow at the target, a mound of hay covered with a hide painted to look like a stag. He released. The arrow shot forward. Hissed through the air. _Thwack!_ Deep into the stag's chest. Tremayne smiled. In his mind's eye he saw the mighty beast stagger and fall to its knees. Good. His aim was true. With a sensation of pride he glanced down at his son.

Bareheaded, Quinn watched the display without much expression. As if anyone could do as well.

" 'Twas a good shot," Tremayne said and tried to ignore the feeling that this boy, his only son, was odd.

Quinn pursed his lips thoughtfully and reached into his own quiver. Sighting without much thought, his fingers bare, he positioned the arrow against his bow, pulled hard on the bowstring, and released. The deadly missile streaked through the air and buried itself deep in the target, not two inches from Tremayne's shot.

Tremayne felt more than a bit of irritation. Aye, he was proud of the boy, but 'twas Quinn's insolent attitude, his lack of interest in anything to do with Twyll, that burrowed like a nettle under Tremayne's skin. Someday Quinn would be baron—well, unless Cavan had his way.

"Your aim be true, Quinn, lad."

Quinn rolled bored eyes up at his father, and Tremayne was tempted to shake some sense into him. But 'twould do no good. He was young. In a few years the boy would realize his good fortune and take pride in someday becoming a baron in his own right, ruler of the keep.

Or so Tremayne hoped.

"Now let us try again." Despite the rain, Tremayne reached for a second arrow, intent on felling another imaginary beast and somehow impressing his brooding son. When he looked up, he spied Percival slogging through the outer bailey.

From the old man's expression, Tremayne could tell he wasn't bearing good news. But there hadn't been much lately. The bastard Rhys had not been found at Broodmore, nor had Abelard or the woman. They'd searched the grounds, then set the castle on fire, hoping to flush him out. It hadn't worked. Tremayne could only hope that he'd died in the ensuing blaze. But he had an unsettling feeling in his gut that the thief had gotten away. Gryffyn hadn't been on the grounds—a bad sign, for the bastard would never have given up the prized steed, the best stallion in all of Wales, Tremayne's most valuable possession.

His fingers clenched around the arrow, breaking the shaft. A tic began to jump beneath his eye. All this, plus that upstart, Cavan of Marwood, was soon to attack.

"What is it?" he asked as Percival hobbled close. The rain, as cold as ice, started in earnest, peppering the ground, creating puddles.

"Ah, m'lord," Percival said, as he stopped and drew a breath. "Sir Regan has questioned all of the men in Rhys's band." The old man was wheezing a bit from

his exertion. He sniffed, coughed, and leaned heavily
on his cane.

"And?"

"They know not where Rhys is."

"They lie." Tremayne spat on the ground. Lying
dogs, every one of them. Quinn was watching the exchange with wide blue eyes. "You, boy, go inside," he
said and saw a moment's defiance cross the lad's face.
"Now. We will practice again later, and next time . . .
next time I will take you hunting," he promised,
though he knew 'twas a lie. For the next few days he
would not be leaving the castle. Not until he'd dealt
with Cavan. "Run along."

One of Quinn's eyebrows raised in a look of disdain
and mild curiosity that Tremayne found unsettling, but
rather than say a word, the boy hitched his quiver
onto his back. As if making an inner decision, he tightened his fist around his bow and took off at a dead
run, his dark hair flying in the drenching rain. Tremayne wondered vaguely if the boy would search out
the silent old priest, for several times he'd caught
Quinn sneaking out of the north tower, where Father
Simon claimed a small room. Barren save for a pallet
and a cross mounted on the wall, the chamber seemed
to be the silent man of God's prison cell, a place
where he prayed upon his bony knees for forgiveness
of some ancient, unknown sin.

Ah, the old one was daft. Talked to no one. Smiled
rarely. A troubled soul. If God had any sense, He
would call him up to heaven soon. But then, God
didn't pass out many favors these days.

"Not one of the prisoners seems to have an idea
where your brother be," Percival said, once Quinn,
splashing swiftly and defiantly through puddles, had
disappeared around the potter's hut.

"Half brother," Tremayne reminded him. "Son of a whore."

"Aye." Percival tugged on the edge of his hood and shot an angry glance at the gray heavens. Rain dribbled down his nose and dripped onto the ground.

"The prisoners—can they not be bought? Would not coins loosen their tongues?"

Poking at the soft, muddy grass with his walking stick, Percival shook his head. "They be fiercely loyal." He blew on his hands for warmth.

"Fine, fine," Tremayne said, disgusted that he was coddling the traitors. "Then have them all flogged— in view of the others. One by one. Afterward they can take turns in the pillory. Mayhap then someone will remember where their leader has gone."

Percival sniffed loudly. "I doubt that will change their minds."

"Well, something will." Tremayne turned on his heel and glowered at the skeletal man who had once been his father's most trusted knight. Percival was now only a shell of that bold warrior. "Is there not someone who will speak? Take away food and water— make them starve or die from lack of a drink. Mayhap then their memories will return."

Hesitating, the older man focused on the target, his drooping eyelids pinching a bit as he thought.

"There is something you're not saying," Tremayne prodded, knowing the signs well enough.

"Aye." Percival sighed and scratched at his chin with a yellowed fingernail. "There is one in the group who does not fit. A girl—the big woman's daughter. She be an odd one, and she said something about a witch or a sorceress to Sir Regan."

"What does the witch have to do with Rhys?" Tremayne asked, but in his mind he was already putting this together with the information he'd heard before. That Rhys had been spotted with a woman.

"Only that the girl was certain this witch had cast a spell upon Rhys."

Tremayne's temper snapped. "A spell?" he sneered. "A spell? Bring her to me. In the great hall. Away from the others."

"She knows no more, I assure you."

"Mayhap not, but I mean to speak to her." He slid a wet arrow from his quiver, took sight, and let fly. The missile hissed through the air and struck just above the stag's head. A miss. Just the mention of the bastard's name caused his aim to falter.

As he walked through the outer bailey, past pens of bleating sheep and pigs rooting and grunting, their snouts buried in soft mud, Tremayne thought again of Broodmore, where victory over his half brother had been so close. For a fleeting second he'd felt the anticipation of a chance to give the criminal his due. But the sensation had been short-lived. When they rounded up the sorry group of criminals and misfits that had been inhabiting the decaying castle, they found a surly, weak lot, sickeningly loyal to the bastard, but nowhere was there any sign of Rhys or the other leader, Abelard, or the woman.

No, for all his trouble Tremayne had ended up only with a dozen or so new prisoners, including a woman and her daughter, and more mouths to feed—unless he let them starve. Unless Rhys was willing to bargain for their lives.

He passed the armorer's hut, where men were busy cleaning mail. Several suits at a time were dropped into a barrel and sprinkled with vinegar and sand. Then the barrel was rolled, which helped the rust to disappear. A couple of boys in tatters—orphans, if

Tremayne remembered correctly—polished helmets and shields with bran. They were working feverishly, knowing the equipment would be used soon. Against Cavan. Or Rhys.

"M'lord," the armorer said, bowing slightly as Tremayne passed.

The boys, too, mumbled and stared at the ground. Good. At least they knew their place.

Tremayne stepped in a puddle and cursed under his breath as cold water seeped through his boot. By the gods, would nothing ever go right?

He strode onward, past the farrier, who was busily shoeing horses to get them ready for battle. At the moment he held a destrier's leg between his knees and tapped nails into the animal's hooves with a small hammer.

Aye, the castle was preparing for a siege. Just this morning the steward, a nervous sort with a thin moustache, pale eyes, and, Tremayne was beginning to suspect, fingers that dug too easily into the stores of spices, had already mentioned that the supplies of sugarloaf and rice were low.

Tremayne couldn't be bothered.

He didn't expect a siege. No, Cavan of Marwood would be dealt with and dealt with swiftly. The whelp would learn the painful lesson of what it was to do battle with the baron of Twyll.

Dry leaves fluttered as a stiff breeze caused them to whirl and dance, but Tremayne barely noticed. Neither did he notice the huntsmen hauling in the few quail, rabbits, and squirrels nor pay any attention to the soldiers greasing the gears of the portcullis.

As he crossed the last stretch of the bailey he saw, out of the corner of his eye, the thatcher, a scrawny man with few teeth and a nasty sense of humor, box the ears of his eldest son for shirking his duties. The boy, red-faced, let out a pitiful wail that could be heard over the carpenter's hammer and the mason's chisel.

"Be not a crybaby, Paul," his father reprimanded. " 'Tis a man's job ye can do. Now, do na make me take a switch to ye." Sniffing loudly, Paul set his jaw and turning his back to his father, did as he was bid, continuing to bundle reeds, straw, and heather together.

Tremayne wondered how it was that he, baron of Twyll, had less luck in disciplining his own boy. 'Twas as if Quinn resented him.

As Tremayne reached the steps of the keep, he caught a glimpse of Father Simon—the odd, silent priest—walking around the perimeter of the inner bailey. Seeming not to notice the wind and sleet, he ambled, his lips moving in mute prayer, his fingers caressing the beads of a rosary. His robes, once fine, were worn, the hem dirty from other solitary treks, miles upon miles, around the bailey.

His mind was gone. Surely.

Bothered by the old priest, Tremayne hurried up the stone steps of the keep and shouldered open the door. The dogs bolted to their feet, muscles tense, then relaxed at the smell and sight of the lord. They settled back into the rushes, their jaws resting between their paws, their brown eyes following Tremayne's every movement.

Mangy, useless beasts.

Wiping the rain from his face with a gloved hand, he walked to the grate, where a fire roared, snapping and popping as flames devoured a massive chunk of oak—nearly the size of the Yule log that had burned for days during the Christmas Revels last year.

He flung his wet mantle over a bench, pulled off his gloves with his teeth, and with stiff, freezing fingers shoved the damp strands of his hair off his face. Slowly the heat from the blaze found its way to his bones, and the chilling worry that had been with him since Broodmore lessened a bit. He was home—in the great hall of Twyll, where he belonged. Despite rumors, ghosts, and bastard half brothers bent on doing him harm, Tremayne belonged here. He was destined to rule. To be the baron.

With a careful eye, he studied this cavernous room where he'd made so many decisions. Dozens of candles burned in sconces, their tiny flames giving off flickering light and illuminating the tapestries that decorated the walls. Blue, red, gold, and green, the woven pictures added life to the dingy, once white walls. Aye, this was home.

So why did it feel so empty, so lifeless—as if it were a crypt?

Because there is no woman.

Anna is gone . . . so long gone.

You need another one—a wife to warm your bed and your tired, weary heart.

As if anticipating his return, Mary, the kitchen wench who had spent fruitless hours in his chamber, poured him a mazer of wine. "Is there anything else, m'lord?" she asked, blushing and swiftly looking away.

He swirled the crimson liquid in his cup. "Nay, but mayhap I will think of something later."

"Oh." She swallowed, looked at the ground, and hurried away, her buttocks swaying beneath the folds of her dress and the strings of her apron. She was a pretty girl and eager to please, but 'twas to no avail. 'Twas Anna he longed for. Anna he dreamed of. Anna . . . sweet lying Jezebel. His fingers tightened over his cup, and he felt the same excruciating pain in his chest that he had for a decade. A decade. Would it never go away?

Regan appeared, and with him was a thin, pasty-skinned girl with mussy, wet hair and enormous eyes—the waif they'd found in Broodmore—so frightened she was trembling. Regan had to urge her forward with his hand. "This be Peony," he said, obviously vexed. "You wanted to see her?"

"Aye."

Tremayne walked to his chair and climbed easily into the carved wooden seat. From his raised position, he knew, he appeared even more intimidating.

"Now, child—er, Peony—tell me of the witch that was at Broodmore."

She gulped. Linked her fingers in front of her and stared down at the rushes.

"You mentioned her to Sir Regan, did you not?"

Regan opened his mouth to answer, but Tremayne lifted a hand, stilling him.

"Answer me."

"A-aye," was the barely audible reply.

"But she was not in the keep when we arrived."

Again silence.

"Listen, Peony," he said, barely able to hold on to his patience, "you must answer me. If you do not, the rest of them—the men who were taken prisoner with you and your mother . . ." She flinched, her head jerking back, and he caught a glimpse of her eyes as she sought his gaze for a moment, then stared at the floor again. "Surely you do not wish any harm to come to them."

"Nay." She shook her head vehemently and bit her lower lip. Her fingers twisted together.

"Good, good. Then you must help me." Cradling

his cup of wine, he propped one boot on the knee of his other leg. "Who is this witch?"

Peony's face crumpled upon itself. Her eyebrows drew together, her lips pursed, and small lines appeared over the bridge of her nose.

"Who?"

The girl drew in a long, shaky breath, and then, as if her tongue had finally been released, she said, "Her name is Tara. She comes from somewhere near Gaeaf, I think. So me mum says."

"Why think you she be a sorceress?"

"Oh, she is." Her eyes were suddenly round with conviction as they stared up at him. "She chants spells, she does, and . . . and . . . she draws runes in the mud—the work of the devil, me mum says."

"You think she has Rhys under some kind of spell?" he asked, not believing it for a moment.

"Oh, 'tis certain." She licked her lips and her fingers fluttered. "He is . . ." She thought for a moment and storm clouds gathered in her eyes. "Bewitched. Aye, there be no other explanation."

Tremayne swirled his drink and thought. "What is it about her that bewitches him?"

"A spell, of course," she said quickly, and for the first time Tremayne sensed another emotion running through the girl's words. Envy? Nay, more like jealousy. Why? He smiled inwardly because he knew he'd found a chink in this girl's armor.

"Of course," he said dryly, and something shifted in Peony's small face. "Is she beautiful?"

One scrawny shoulder lifted. "Some might say," she said grudgingly.

"Is she a lady?"

"Nay—the daughter of some old midwife."

This didn't make any sense. "Then why did she take

up with Rhys? And tell me not again of the spell she cast upon him. There must be another reason." Leaning back in his chair, he sipped his wine and observed the woman/child over the rim of his mazer. "Mayhap he is in love with her," he guessed.

She tensed. Her little nose wrinkled in disdain.

"Because she is so beautiful," he nudged, seeing Peony's girl's cheeks flush with color, her lips purse as if she'd just tasted something poisonous. "Is she not?"

" 'Tis because she is a witch," the girl maintained. "She . . . she cast a spell on him, and she has an . . . an amulet that has mystical powers."

Now she was making things up. "I think not."

"Oh, but 'tis true. I overheard Abelard talking about it when he thought I wasn't listening. He wants it."

"The amulet?" Tremayne asked, his interest piqued.

"Aye, 'tis a ring or . . . or a stone . . . I could not hear which, and me mum, she doesn't like me listenin' . . ." Her voice drifted off and she looked away, as if she realized she'd spoken too much.

But now Tremayne *was* interested. "So Rhys is chasing after a witch who has a magical stone?" His thoughts drifted to another time when he'd heard of such a ring . . . but . . . could it be? Nay! Yet at the thought his blood pounded through his veins.

Though Peony studied the rushes, he saw the movement of her eyes beneath her eyelids. She looked quickly from one side to the next, as if trying to come up with an answer. "I . . . I . . . don't really know what I heard. 'Twas in hushed voices they spoke," she admitted, her thumbs rubbing the insides of her fists. "Could be I be mistaken."

"But Rhys is in love?"

"Nay! He . . . he . . . is bewitched. That's what me mum says."

Tremayne had heard enough. He wouldn't get anything more from this scrawny girl with the wild hair. "Take her away," he ordered a guard, and as she was half dragged back to the dungeon he thought long and hard. Where was the bastard? Had he aligned with Cavan? What about the amulet or stone . . . the only jewel he knew of was the dark emerald of Twyll, and surely this witch-woman did not have it.

Or did she?

The headache that had been with him all day raged even stronger, pounding at his temples, echoing through his brain. Regan, who had been listening without saying a word, came forward. "Well?" Tremayne said. "What say you?"

"About?"

"The stone," he said. "The ring. Could this woman with Rhys have the dark emerald of Twyll?"

"There are many rings."

"But few that are magical." Regan's eyebrows lifted a fraction. "Do you think the stone exists?"

"Do you?" Regan countered.

At that moment Percival entered, and the dogs lounging by the fire lifted their heads from their paws and gave off disgruntled "woofs."

"Shh, you bloody mutts." Tremayne was in no mood for the hounds' ill temper.

"I could not help but overhear," the older man said, his eyes bright. "Is it possible? Does the dark emerald of Twyll exist?" His face was flushed, and he hurried toward the dais with hardly any help from his cane.

"If it does, why would the witch have it? Why not Cavan, if he be the true issue of Gilmore?" Tremayne pulled at the hint of a beard that darkened his chin.

"Mayhap he is not."

"Then old Innis lied."

" 'Tis possible he did not know. He was addled, they say." Percival hitched himself close to the fire, and the flames cast his bony features in shifting shades of amber. "But"—he raised a crooked finger as he thought—"if the ring exists, then the old tale is true." Turning, he pinned Tremayne in a gaze that was alight with anticipation. "And if the tale is to be believed then there really is a true heir to Gilmore."

Tremayne snorted. "But not Cavan of Marwood."

"Nay . . ." Percival scratched his hollow cheek, and the dogs, as if sensing a presence in the corridor, both lifted their heads and peered into the shadowy hall-way. One growled. The other sniffed, then thumped her tail. Tremayne's own gaze followed the animals' line of sight. That all-too-familiar feeling that he was being watched whispered across his skin. "Mayhap the witch herself," said Percival.

"The witch?" Tremayne snorted and drained his mazer of wine. "A *woman*?"

"A woman with magical powers."

"Bah." Getting quietly to his feet, Tremayne told himself he wouldn't believe it. " 'Tis all old women's wagging tongues and far-flung dreams."

"A woman with the dark emerald."

"If the child is to be believed." He didn't like the feeling that was stealing through his blood. He walked past the old man to the arch leading to the corridor. He heard the scrape of boots on stone and was certain he would find someone listening to his conversation with the old man, but as he stood near the rushlights, peering down the gloomy hallway, he saw no one.

But someone had been watching him. He was cer-tain of it, for the candles in the sconces at the far end of the corridor flickered, smoke trailing unevenly, as if someone had just hastened away.

His stomach curdled at the thought of treachery within his own keep. Who? Which of his men would play the role of Judas? Sweat prickled his scalp, and he touched the hilt of his dagger for reassurance.

"Send the spy to me," he said, as he strode to the fire and wished the flames would somehow chase away the chill in his soul.

"James?"

"Aye." He slid his dagger from its sheath and studied the fine, sharp blade in the shifting light. 'Twas a heavy weapon and deadly, honed to a fine edge that would slit a man's flesh easily. " 'Tis time the spy and I come to an understanding."

"Undress." Rhys's voice was firm. Uncompromising. He stood at the door in the tiny room of the inn, his shoulders pressed against the thick planks, his arms folded across his chest. His gaze was cold. Without a trace of warmth. "Do it. Now."

"Why?" Tara asked, knowing the answer before it passed his lips.

"I want the ring."

"But—"

"Either take the damned tunic off yourself or I will help you out of it." His mouth compressed into a hard line of determination; his eyebrows pulled together, becoming one dark line over eyes that gleamed a cold, inflexible gray. She knew him well enough to realize that he wouldn't back down. Not at all.

She had no choice as she stood near the narrow bed pushed under a small, solitary window. " 'Tis no gentleman you be, Rhys of—"

"Aye. So you've said. Get on with it." He pointed at her and moved his finger in a quick, tight circle. "Now."

"Bastard," she said in a whisper—just loud enough that he could hear over the pounding of rain on the roof and the sounds of laughter, conversation, and someone—a woman—singing that drifted through the floorboards from the alehouse on the floor below.

Turning so that her back was to him, she lifted her tunic over her head, did the same with her chemise, and realizing that her entire backside was exposed, felt a warm rush of color climb up her neck and spread over her face. " 'Tis a true blackheart, you be!"

He didn't argue.

Anger and shame burned through her. How could she ever have thought she loved this man? How? He was a beast. A cruel, hard-edged monster with a heart of stone. Outside, the wind was fierce, the sound of rain pebbling against the roof as if it never intended to stop.

"This is . . . this is robbery," she accused, fumbling with the cord that strapped the ring to her naked waist.

Again no answer.

"Do you hear me? Thievery!"

"But then, I be a thief. You know 'tis so."

But not from me, Rhys. I never thought you would steal from me! Tears of humiliation burned in her eyes, and she wished for just a second that she'd never seen the cursed ring, never been told the story of how she happened to be adopted by Lodema, never heard of Gilmore's missing baby. Swallowing against a lump in her throat, she worked the knot, but it had tightened, the cord having swollen with rainwater, sweat, and time.

"Trouble?" His voice was mocking.

She didn't answer, just worked harder and more

fruitlessly. *Damn!* But the knot wouldn't budge, refused to be unraveled.

"Come, come," he said and she sent him a glance over one shoulder filled with venom. Angry gazes locked and she quickly looked away, her hair falling around her face as she yanked and pulled at the cursed tangle.

She heard him step forward, closing the distance between them. She held her breath. Did he dare kiss her? Her skin tingled in anticipation. *Hissss.* His dagger was drawn swiftly from its sheath. Cold steel touched her back.

She flinched. "What—"

"Hold still."

"But—" *Ssst.* The cord tightened for a second, then parted as it was cut cleanly. It would have fallen to the floor had he not caught it, his big fingers finally capturing the stone in midair.

Scooping up her tunic and holding it over her breasts, she whipped around. "How could you?" she cried, distraught. Her heritage—the link to her parents—was being stuffed into a thief's pocket, hidden away in Rhys's tunic. He ignored her question. Rammed his dagger into its sheath. "Abelard waits downstairs."

Hurt—nay, *wounded*—by how easily he could make love to her one minute, then rob her blind the next, she wanted to argue. To rant. To rave. To scream at him and call him vile names, then pummel his chest with her fists.

" 'Tis a cruel man you be," she said, her chin trembling.

"So 'tis said." His eyes darkened.

Leveling a haughty glare at him that she hoped hid the hot tears lurking behind her eyelids and the pain ripping through her soul, she said, "I hope Abelard is satisfied."

"Oh, he will be." His smile held not a drop of warmth, not a glimmer of humor. "Wait for me."

She didn't answer.

"Tara." His voice was low. Firm. Again he crossed the short distance and glared down at her. "Stay in this room. Do not move. I will be back within minutes."

"Of course," she replied, sarcasm lacing each word. "Where would I go?"

"I hate to think. But there is a guard posted in the hallway, another outside below this window."

"And if I needs relieve myself?" she asked, her throat tight.

"Use the bucket." He motioned toward a pail near the door.

"Ah, yes. The bucket. You be so kind, *Sir* Rhys. A true gentleman."

His jaw tightened. His fists clenched, then slowly relaxed. For a second there was a hint of regret in his silvery gaze, and she thought that he would grab her, hold her tight, and kiss her until the breath was sucked from her lungs. "Stay." He turned on his heel and was out the door.

Bang! It slammed shut.

Tara started. Her skin was suddenly cold.

She heard his voice as he paused in the hallway to issue orders to whoever was standing guard. "Bastard. Curse you, Rhys of Twyll, curse and damn you." Warm tears tracked from her eyes, and her fists were so tight that her fingernails drew blood from her own palms. How had she trusted him? Why? Because he made love to her. But he was and would always be an outlaw.

His footsteps rang on the steep wooden steps. Fading away.

This was her chance. She knew that if she didn't take this opportunity to slip away from Rhys, she would have no other. And she had to leave him. Had to find out the truth. Had to run from him.

Because you love him, you pathetic fool. You've given your heart to the Bastard Outlaw.

"Nay!" she cried, refusing to believe the horrid words. She shoved them out of her mind. She had to get out. Away. Now. There was so little time. Yet the hallway was guarded. She climbed on the bed and opened the shutters to the night. A sudden rush of cold, wet air blew into the room.

Squinting into the blackness, she spied a guard, a big man huddled out of the slanting rain against a building on the far side of the narrow, rutted street. He bit a fingernail, spat, then moved on to the next finger. Every once in a while he hazarded a glance at the inn.

Though the rain afforded her some cover, Tara couldn't climb out the window without him spying her. She looked down and judged that the drop to the street wouldn't kill her. If she did dare make an attempt, the soft and muddy ground would provide a cushion when she landed.

Now! You must do it now! There is little time.

Her heart pounded and she felt a moment's hesitation, a stupid desire to stay with Rhys, to trust him.

But he's an outlaw. A thief. He stole from you, Tara. Took your stone without a moment's hesitation! Run! Now!

But it was too risky.

Or was it?

She licked her lips and her palms began to sweat.

A plan started to form in her mind, and she set to it. She didn't have much time; Rhys had said he planned to return soon. When he did, she wouldn't have the chance to leave again, nor, mayhap, she thought angrily, would she want to, for the outlaw truly did have a piece of her heart.

Fighting back tears and a painful sense of despair, she scooped up the empty pail, filled it with most of her treasures—the candle, the cord, and even her precious flint. The sparse room offered few things to add to the pail except for a bit of soap.

She blew out the single candle that burned upon a tiny table near the bed—the only furniture in the cramped space—and tossed it, as well as its holder, into the bucket. Her gaze lingered on the mattress for a second, and in her mind's eye she imagined that she and Rhys were sleeping together on it, and her throat went dry.

"Don't think it," she whispered under her breath, though the pain in her heart was a heavy stone. "Don't think it ever again. He's got what he wanted from you. The cursed ring is now in his pocket."

Angry all over again, she climbed onto the bed once more. Peeking over the windowsill she bit her lip. *Morrigu, be with me.*

Using all the strength she could muster, she pulled her arm back, then snapped it forward and flung the pail through the opening, sending it and the items inside hurtling through the night, as far from the inn as possible.

Bam!

The bucket hit.

Pop! Pop! Rattle! Clunk! Pop! Clatter!

The contents spewed everywhere, causing a wild racket as the pail rolled down the street.

"What the devil?" the guard growled and Tara

didn't waste any time. Praying that he'd gone to investigate, she hoisted herself onto the window ledge, lowered her feet on the outside of the building and as her hands slipped, let go, sliding down the wooden frame and tumbling to the ground. Her feet hit first. Her right ankle twisted. Pain blasted up her leg.

She gasped, then bit her tongue. She couldn't let anything, not even a broken leg, deter her. She had to keep moving. As soon as the guard figured out that she'd intentionally distracted him, he would sound the alarm.

Rain pounded the street, showering into puddles, offering a shifting curtain that was cold as death. It rattled against roofs and gurgled in the ruts of the road.

Tara straightened and tried to run, but her boot caught in the mud. Her heart thudding, she threw her weight forward, barreling along the front of the inn, ignoring the pain. She passed the door, then stole along the path at the side of the building. Around the corner she flew, out of sight of the guard or anyone else, as the village was sparse, with only a few buildings scattered around a road leading to the mill.

At the back of the inn she hobbled into a lean-to shed that sheltered the horses, a wooden building attached to the lower floor of the alehouse.

Her ankle throbbed. Water ran into her eyes, and she had trouble seeing. By now the guard had probably discovered the pail and its contents. In a matter of minutes he would inform Rhys that they'd been duped, and then—oh, then, there would be hell to pay.

The spit dried in her throat as she contemplated Rhys's ire. *Help me,* she prayed silently and didn't care what deity paid heed. The door to the shed was open, and light from a small window in the alehouse gave enough weak illumination that Tara was able to make out shapes. A stableboy was curled on the straw near his pitchfork, his legs blocking the entrance. Snoring softly, dead to the world, he lay only feet from the horses. Her heart beating a wild cadence, she stepped over his long legs and slipped inside, hardly daring breathe.

A horse snorted. Hooves rustled in straw. The overpowering scents of horseflesh, urine, and manure hit her nostrils. A few drops of rain found their way through a roof that leaked, but all in all, the stable was some protection from the wind and rain that raged outside.

Expecting the door to the inn to be thrown open at any second and Rhys's angry visage to be cast in stark relief, Tara fumbled her way along the wall, found a bridle hung on a nail, and creeping softly so as not to disturb the sleeping guard or unsettle the horses, took it and reached out for the first horse she came to.

Gryffyn!

Her heart was pounding wildly.

Fear surged through her blood.

At any second Rhys was sure to find her. *Do not think it. Just get out of here!*

The destrier was nervous. She could feel his hot breath on her hands, and he flung back his head and stomped a foot. She had to take this horse. Rhys's mount. The fleetest horse she'd ever seen.

Heart threatening to jump out of her chest, she slid the bridle over his nose and up over his flattened ears. Her fingers felt stiff and uncoordinated as she buckled the chin strap and then, praying that he would step over the snoozing guard, led him outside.

The horse's eyes were rimmed in white, his muscles quivered beneath his coat as she hobbled on her right ankle, gritting her teeth against the pain.

Come on, Gryffyn, you can do it!

Nervously he followed her out of the shed, stepping over the guard and out into the driving rain to a low fence. Nostrils distended, ears cocked, he neighed anxiously.

"Hey!" The door was flung open and light poured into the stables.

"What the—?" The boy stirred, and Tara stepped onto the lowest board of the fence, then the second.

"Halt!" Rhys's voice boomed through the shed.

No!

Horses neighed, Gryffyn sidestepped.

'Twas now or never.

Tara threw herself across Gryffyn's wet back.

Rhys sprang out of the shed. "For the love of God, woman, don't—"

"Hi*ya!*" She kicked Gryffyn hard in the flank. Rhys was already upon them, running swiftly, one hand reaching for the reins. "Run, you devil!" she cried. "Run, run, run!" The horse bolted. Hooves thundered, flinging mud and water.

"Tara!" Rhys yelled, but his voice faded as Gryffyn barreled into the night.

Through the rain, Tara chanced a glance over her shoulder and saw him, furious, hands on his hips, rain slashing over him. She felt a second's hesitation, a silly tug on her heartstrings, then turned her face forward, to the black, stormy night. To Twyll.

She didn't fool herself for a second. Leaning low, she urged the fleet stallion ever faster. In seconds, Rhys would be after her, and though whatever horse he chose would be slower than this destrier, he, an outlaw who had lived in the forests surrounding Twyll for ten years, would know the shorter, quicker path to the castle.

Nay, she was not safe.

But, then, she would never be. Not as long as the Bastard Outlaw chased her.

Chapter Eleven

" 'Tis . . . 'Tis . . . sorry I be," the stableboy apologized, his Adam's apple working up and down like a hungry chicken pecking at a nest of ants as Rhys, seething and wet, strode into the stable area. Licking his lips nervously, the boy stared at the straw-covered dirt and fiddled with the handle of his pitchfork. "I . . . I . . . believe that mayhap I fell asleep."

"You *believe*?" Rhys repeated, his temper snapping. Drenched, angry, and humiliated, he had watched Tara disappear around the bend in the road leading out of town. Every muscle in his body ached with tension, his hands were balled into tight, quivering fists and his jaw was clenched so tightly that his teeth ached. Damn the woman. "We ride now!" he declared.

"For what purpose?" Abelard stood near his horse, stroking the stallion's thick neck. He and the guard who had allowed Tara to escape had followed Rhys out the back door of the inn. The sentry had the grace to look embarrassed, but Abelard acted as if losing Tara was of no consequence.

"We ride to catch her, of course."

"Why?"

Was the man thick as blood pudding? He glanced

at the guard and the boy. "Leave us." Neither needed further encouragement; they were out the door like twin shots from a catapult. Hanging on to his temper by the merest of threads, Rhys wheeled on Abelard and crossed the short distance between them. " 'Tis for her safety," he said through clenched teeth. Each second that ticked by gave Tara a better chance of eluding him, of racing headlong into trouble. He grabbed a bridle from a nail and slid it quickly over the nose of Abelard's steed.

The other animals, Dobbyn and an aging cart horse, were restless, shifting nervously, nickering and snorting, sensing the tension that crackled between the two men.

"What do you think you're doing?" Abelard demanded as Rhys buckled the bridle into place, then with swift, sure motions found a blanket and saddle and slung them over the beast's broad back. "Just because the witch tricked you out of your mount is no reason to steal mine—"

Rhys whirled on the older man once again. "You were paid and paid well for the animal," he growled. "Have you not the stone?"

"Aye, but—"

"Leave me be, Abelard." He pulled on the cinch as rain pounded against the roof and a keening wind tore at the thatching.

"Let Tara go."

"To Twyll? To Tremayne?" Tightening the strap, he buckled it, then swung easily into the saddle. "I think not."

" 'Tis her choice."

"Is it? Like the choice she had of giving up the emerald?" Rhys bit out. He pulled on the reins, turning the beast in the small confines, and stared through the doorway into the black, wet night beyond.

"You be a fool."

"At the very least."

"Loving her will only cause you pain."

"I love her not!" With a kick, he urged the horse through the opening, then slapped the beast's rump with the reins.

The stallion launched down the muddy road, slipping and galloping wildly, as if spooked by some invisible, terrifying demon. Sleet sliced down from the dark heavens, cold as ice, a shimmering veil that hid and protected. Water as frigid as a winter sea poured down Rhys's face and blurred his vision, but he spurred the horse ever onward, ever faster.

The odds were against his locating Tara. She had enough of a head start on a swifter horse to make it to Twyll long before Abelard's slower mount could catch her, but Rhys was undaunted—a fool of a man who thrived on adversity.

He would find her. Swearing to himself, he vowed that he would catch up to her before she entered the gates of Twyll. And when he did overtake her and look into that beautiful, deceitful face again, he would extract his own personal kind of vengeance.

The witch would never forget the cost of defying him.

"What do you mean, 'he's missing'?" Tremayne demanded, his gaze riveted on the man who was his constable, a man in whom his faith was rapidly deteriorating. Tremayne had been leaning back in his chair, swirling wine in his cup, watching the embers of the fire glow red, and contemplating battle. Word had come that Cavan was only days away from marching, and Tremayne had been working out his battle plan, a surprise of his own for the upstart. He had considered ordering Mary or some other wench to his room to relieve his frustration. His only reluctance had been the thought that his manhood might fail him again— he didn't want to risk being fodder for women's ugly gossip and the sniggering of his men behind his back.

The lord of Twyll, limp as a dead chicken's neck.

The baron whose cock is as soft as doeskin.

Tremayne of Twyll, master of a barony, unable to rule his own bed.

He could just imagine the taunts and cackling comments.

But Regan had broken into his unhappy reverie. Now Tremayne was on his feet, his wine and his weak member quickly forgotten.

Regan braced himself, as if he expected to be struck. He stood rigid as oak, his mouth twisted into an unhappy frown. "As I said, the spy is missing."

Tremayne's brain clamored within his skull, his patience drawn thin as a butcher's blade and twice as sharp. "Did I not tell you to put James under lock and key?"

" 'Twas done. He was in one of the cells earlier, but no one has seen him since the criminals from Broodmore arrived. The bloody cur must have slipped away while the jailers were busy with the new prisoners—when the cell gate was open." Regan's blond eyebrows drew together in annoyance, and he chewed anxiously on the inside of his cheek.

"How did this happen?" Tremayne demanded. "Was no one watching him?"

"We know not. As I say, mayhap in the confusion—"

"The confusion? In the confusion?" Tremayne bellowed and threw his mazer onto the floor. It clanged and bounced, startling a cat that had been searching the rushes for mice and causing the dogs lying near the fire to scramble wildly to their feet. Hissing. Howling. Scratching, scurrying claws. Tremayne swore. God in heaven, he was cursed. "Find him," he snarled, his lip curling as if he, too, were a beast.

He stalked to the constable and grabbed Regan's tunic in one large hand. Crumpling the fabric, gathering a few chest hairs in the process, and pulling tight, he whispered, "Locate the spy. Bring him to me and let me deal with him. Say not a word. Hear me? I will handle this myself."

He felt the other man flinch beneath his grip, then slowly released him and continued, "If he be not found, Sir Regan, I will hold you personally responsible—do you understand? *Personally* responsible."

"Aye, m'lord." Was it his imagination or did the constable's voice actually quaver? His skin was white as thin milk, his eyes round. For the first time in nearly a week, Tremayne's manhood stirred. So there was life in the old rod yet. The lord of Twyll watched the miserable, useless, weak constable slink away, and he considered finding a woman. But he would wait. He had too much on his mind right now, too much to do.

Soon, when he found the right woman, he would haul her to his bed, strip her of her clothes, and make her do anything he wanted. *Anything!* He'd force her to please him, and she would be only too happy—or afraid not to do his bidding. He was, after all, the baron. His will was law. 'Twas time everyone understood this one simple, undeniable fact.

"By the saints," Tara whispered and hastily crossed herself as she stared at Twyll, dark and foreboding in the night. *This* sinister-looking behemoth of a castle was her heritage, her home? She told herself she was being silly, a ninny. Twyll was alive and vital, unlike Broodmore. 'Twas just the night that was causing her nerves to be strung tight, her mind to conjure up dark images. Clucking softly, she urged Gryffyn out of the cover of the forest. His nostrils quivered as the breeze lifted his mane, and she realized that he recognized his home. A sliver of fear pierced her heart.

Mounted high upon the crest of a hill, Tower Twyll rose cathedrallike toward the heavens, where but a slice of moon and a few brave stars winked behind a thin veil of clouds. The storm had passed, its fury abated, leaving only a cold, clear night where puddles reflected in the weak moonglow and the winter air did little to dry her soggy clothes.

Shivering, she patted the sleek horse on his neck. He'd been surefooted and swift, and though she'd expected Rhys to cut her off at every crossroad, to have somehow ridden ahead of her, he had never appeared.

She rubbed her arms, hoping to force the chill of winter away, and regarded the edifice where, if Lodema was right, she'd been born.

The castle was dark. Silent. Though she strained to hear any noise emanating from the tower, no sounds of laughter, no murmur of muted conversation, not even the bark of a hound permeated the thick stone walls of the keep.

Could this be her home? She felt an ungainly lump in her throat. Her heart thudded as she considered her plan to sneak into the castle sometime after dawn, joining the peasants, soldiers, peddlers, and villagers who came and went once the portcullis was lifted in the early-morning hours. With the gray mists of morn-

ing light as her cover, she intended to blend into the
throng that would pass through Twyll's gates.

*And what about Lord Tremayne—the baron who
had flogged Rhys and left him for dead? What if you
have to face him?* Her fingers gripped the reins more
tightly. He knew not who she was. As long as her
identity remained secret, she had naught to fear
from him.

She rode into the woods again and dismounted in a
dense thicket where she wound her cloak more tightly
around her body. She and Gryffyn were hidden. Exhaustion overcame her and she closed her eyes. She
would rest but a few minutes. Just long enough to
regain her strength, for she could not risk anyone discovering her, especially Rhys.

She hated to think what would happen if he found
her. Oh, she could not risk that. But as she drifted
off, she couldn't help imagining that he was lying beside her, holding her close, whispering that all would
be well. She could almost feel the scratch of beard
stubble against her cheek, smell the scents of leather,
horse, and man that clung to him, hear the steady
sound of his heartbeat, and look into eyes as hard as
newly forged steel.

Ah, outlaw, how you vex me, she thought. Aye, he
had taken her eagerly given virginity as well as her
unwilling gift of the ring, yet the feelings she held for
him were strong and the pull he had on her heart was
impossible to ignore. *'Tis a fool you are,* she told herself. Caring even a bit for him was insanity, pure and
simple, a stupid girlish whim, but right now she was
too tired to argue with herself. Once she was rested,
her mind would clear and all her romantic fantasies
would be chased away.

They had to be.

*   *   *

Lodema whispered a prayer over the shallow grave. 'Twas an omen, she thought, and felt a deep sadness for her Luna, who had been little more than a kitten when Tara had come to her. Though the cat had been old, had lived years longer than anyone could have hoped, Lodema would miss the comfort of her warm body curled beside her on the bed. There would be a new emptiness in the little hut.

Not only was her daughter gone, mayhap never to be seen again, but now the cat was gone as well. Fool that she be, she felt a warm tear in her eye as she walked through the first gray light of morning, the mists of Gaeaf rising in the forest to join the curling smoke from her fire.

She could get another cat to keep the mice and rats out of her stores of flour, but 'twould not be the same. Luna had been more than a mouser, she'd been a friend. Ah, well, 'twas the way of things.

As she hobbled down the path to her door, she felt the rush of wind—bitter-cold and from the north. The wind of death. Goose bumps rose on her flesh, for this was not about the cat. Nay, this gust was about Tara. She knew it deep in the farthest reaches of her soul.

Inside her little home several of the hens squawked, not knowing that they had been saved from the butcher's knife. She'd already killed an old black-and-white one that had given up laying, and before she prepared it for the stewpot, she picked up the carcass and spilled its entrails onto the table.

She'd had a feeling of death—an omen as cold as the waters of the North Sea had seeped into her blood. Waking up to find the cat dead was the beginning, but there was more, and it had to do with Tara. Lodema felt it deep in the marrow of her bones.

Frowning at her task, she strewed the guts in front of her and whispered a prayer to the Great Mother for Tara's safety. Surely she was wrong, just borrowing trouble. The movement of the smoke had been her old eyes playing tricks on her, nothing more, and the wax that had dripped in its ominous manner in her cup had been a mistake. Surely.

With a crooked, spotted finger she moved the heart and intestines, exposing the dead fowl's liver. "God's eyes," she whispered when she saw the reddish brown and slick mass, shining in the light from her candle. The hump of the organ was missing. Usually there was a projection, a piece of good luck, the larger the better. If the hump was cleaved, 'twas a sure sign of trouble, but this . . . this absence of it, was the gravest omen of all.

Morrigu, Earth mother, protect Tara, she prayed. Her heart thudded erratically. She had trouble breathing and leaned heavily on the table. She had to draw a rune and chant a spell . . . she would need mistletoe, Saint-John's-wort, fern, and snapdragon for the spell, then she would draw runes for protection. She only hoped she wasn't too late.

Rhys rode like a demon. He pushed his borrowed horse faster and faster, determined to catch his quarry before she reached Twyll. The stallion labored, but Rhys wouldn't let up. For if Tara ever found Tremayne, all would be for naught.

As the horse dashed through the forest, Rhys told himself that he could save Tara, that it wasn't too late, that he would somehow be able to keep her from whatever horrid fate Tremayne would mete out if he discovered who she was. 'Twas best that she no longer had the stone, he told himself, best that she was carrying no proof that she was the daughter of Gilmore.

If, in fact, she be his daughter.

The rain had stopped and dawn was fast approaching. Trees sped past and the stallion's coat was flecked with lather, bits of white foam surfacing on his wet, dark hide.

Still Rhys pushed the animal.

Tara's life was at stake.

At that thought, a hard pulse throbbed in his temples. His jaw clenched to the point of aching, and he felt an overwhelming sense of panic for a woman he had barely known for a fortnight, if that. A woman he didn't trust.

What was she?

A witch—one who believed in magic and the Earth Mother. A woman who chanted spells, drew runes, and yet prayed to the Christian God? What manner of sorceress was this?

Or was she truly the stolen babe, daughter of Lady Farren and Lord Gilmore, the true ruler of Twyll?

Did it matter? Nay. He was trapped in the web of her beauty, lost in the feel and touch of her. Never had he felt this way about any woman.

Not even Anna.

At that thought his heart jolted and he denied to himself that he cared for the witch, a harsh-tongued woman who was forever eluding him and making him appear a fool. By God, he couldn't think of the emotions she engendered in him. Not now. First he had to find her and somehow keep her safe.

The horse was wheezing, his legs slowing. "Come on, come on!" He stumbled a bit and Rhys realized he was finished. If he rode him any further, he would die. He thought about slapping him hard on the rump, but he couldn't. The damned beast had run bravely. Rhys slowed him to a walk. He felt guilty at abusing him but was still fired by the driving need to get to Twyll. The stallion would never make it.

But another horse would.

He smiled to himself. All he had to do was locate a fit animal and steal it.

As he had dozens of times in the past.

Clang!

Tara opened one eye at the noise. It took a second for her to realize that she'd slept on a bed of fir needles and leaves in the forest outside of Twyll. With a grinding of gears, the portcullis was being lifted. Soon, unless she was discovered, she would be within the walls of her home castle and searching out Father Simon. "Gods help me," she whispered, crossing herself.

She would leave Gryffyn here, ready for her escape, because once she had found the old priest and ascertained her true identity, she planned to locate Rhys. Aye, she needed to find out who she was, but now, after their loving, she also had a need to face him again.

As she waited, certain that Rhys would come upon her at any second, the sun rose in the heavens, giving the clouds a pearly glow and offering some warmth. Tara picked the twigs, leaves, and needles off her cloak, finger-combed her hair, and waited. Slowly they came. Carts pulled by oxen, wagons filled with casks of ale or bags of grain. Peddlers and foot soldiers, women carrying baskets of eggs and boys loaded with firewood. From within the towering walls of Twyll came the sounds of hammers clanging, voices shouting, even an occasional burst of laughter.

When the traffic was heaviest, Tara emerged from

the forest and joined the men, women, and children entering Twyll. No one should stop her. Aside from a few soldiers who may have caught a glimpse of her with Rhys on that fateful day when she'd met the rogue, no one would know her or question her.

They passed by a sentry who asked the carter his business, then paused to speak with a heavily pregnant woman carrying a basket of leeks while shepherding three children behind her. Then he glanced at Tara as she passed.

"Halt," he ordered, and she stopped. Small eyes appraised her. "What be your business?"

"I wish to speak to Father Simon."

"The old one?" The guard's forehead furrowed. "Why?"

" 'Tis greetings I am to bring him from me mother, who knew him as a girl. She is ill now, and she wanted the father to know."

The guard sniffed, wiped his nose, and frowned. "Who is your mother?"

"Lodema of Gaeaf."

"Let us pass," a grumpy wagon driver called out. "I've got spices to deliver here; the steward, he's waitin' on me."

"Aye!" another man, carting in a wagonload of straw, agreed.

The sentry snorted, stared for a long moment at Tara's face, then waved her in. "Go on about yer business."

She quickly moved along the muddy road through the outer bailey, where animals were penned—horses, sheep, cattle, and pigs—near the stables.

Everyone seemed in a hurry. In the inner bailey, men seemed edgy. Women, laden with candle wax, laundry, or pails of fish scurried toward the keep. Boys toted buckets of rocks and arrows to the highest towers, where carpenters were busily building hoardings, wooden extensions of the wall walk to protect the defenders in battle. The air was charged and tense. Faces were grim. Women barked orders at children to help stack firewood, make candles, spin wool, gather eggs, lug pails of water.

All about her Tara heard whispered conversations, talk of war.

"And jest 'ow long do ye think we could stand a siege?" one hefty woman asked as she tended a barrel of salt for preserving meat in a lean-to near the keep.

"Saints preserve us, I know not," her compatriot, an alewife from the look of her, answered, crossing her arms over her apron-covered bosom.

A carter was busily repairing a broken wheel, the armorer pounded out metal into swords, and the crier, standing on the keep steps and ringing a bell, announced that every able-bodied man was to take up arms against Cavan of Marwood.

Tara shivered. Who was this man who claimed to be the son of Gilmore? An impostor? A liar? Or was he really the babe born of Lady Farren?

Trying not to attract any attention to herself, Tara walked through the castle grounds, wondering as she saw the inner reaches of Twyll if this truly was her home. Her destiny. Where she belonged.

Aye, and what of Rhys?

What of him? she threw back at that cursed voice in her mind, refusing to think of him now or to acknowledge the tiny niggle of regret that had wormed its way into her consciousness. *Do not think it,* she told herself and made her way to the keep. A boy ran by chasing a cat and she grabbed his arm. "Where is the chapel?" she asked, and the lad, with a mop of red hair, freckles, and several spaces where teeth were missing in his mouth, stopped short.

"The chapel?"

"Yes, and Father Simon."

"Ye mean Father Alden, surely."

"Nay, his name be Simon." Tara managed a smile.

"But Father Alden, he be . . . oh." Large brown eyes rounded in understanding. "Ye mean the daft old one, don't ye?" Before she could answer he bobbed his head up and down rapidly. "Oh, he's not in the keep. He stays in the tower, there, up a floor or two, me mum says." He pointed a grubby finger at a square tower that rose above the battlements. "He don't talk, ye know."

"I—I've heard. Thank you."

She hurried across the bailey, past an herb garden and the atilliator's hut, where crossbows were stacked in readiness for war. Swallowing hard, she ducked around a hay cart and reached the door. From the kennels, the hounds set up a racket. Overhead, hides were being stretched to cover the wooden hoardings, making them impenetrable to flaming arrows.

The threat of war and death hung heavy in the air. She reached the door, yanked it open, and half ran up the winding stairs. Her heart pounding and her throat dry, she soon reached a floor where a door was open slightly. Through the crack, in the flickering light of a single candle, a priest, bareheaded, his face gaunt, knelt. His eyes were closed, his shoulders stooped, his lips moving without a sound.

This, she knew, was Father Simon, the only man who knew the truth of her past.

"M'lord, we found yer horse."

The soldier, a cocky boy named Jason, swaggered into the great hall.

"My horse?" Tremayne repeated.

"Aye, sire. Gryffyn. We was searchin' fer that no-good James and we comes acrost the beast. Big as life, 'e was."

Tremayne vaulted out of his chair and grabbed the insolent pup by the front of his tunic. "If this be a joke—"

"Nay . . ." the boy whined, his bravado slipping. He looked as if he might soil himself.

"Where?"

"In the woods outside of the castle. We brought him back to the stables. We thought ye might want to—"

"Fool!" Spittle exploded from Tremayne's mouth with his rage. "If the horse is here, then so is Rhys!" He let go of the boy's tunic and wished he could strangle his half brother. "Search the grounds, the castle . . . and . . ." His brain was pounding with an ache that burned the backs of his eyes. "Wait—take the horse back to where you found him."

"What?" Jason rubbed his chest.

"Yes, yes, the outlaw will be back. Leave the horse as he was, hide in the forest, and when Rhys returns, capture him!" He was striding through the keep, on his way to Regan's quarters. "Take the best men, twenty of them—and make no mistake"—he whirled as Jason ran to keep up with him—"if Rhys slips through your fingers again everyone in the castle will suffer, you worst of all!"

Could it be? Could his luck finally have turned? At the thought of his half brother stalking through the castle his stomach turned sour. But he would be caught. This time he would! "Search the castle, every inch of it. Flush him out. If we don't catch him here,

we'll pounce on him when he runs back to the horse."
He rubbed his hands together. Finally. Finally!

"But what of Lord Cavan of Marwood?" Jason
asked as they rounded a corner, the rushlights flickering as they passed. "Is not his army marching on
us?"

"There is still time," Tremayne insisted. "First we
capture the bastard, then we'll give Cavan of Marwood his due. Do not fear."

He threw open the door to Regan's quarters and
found the constable sharpening the blade of his sword.
" 'Tis time," he announced as Regan looked up. "The
bastard is within our grasp." His eyes held those of
the constable. "Catch him, Sir Regan, search him out
and bring him back to me." He sketched out his plan
as the constable stopped honing his blade.

". . . So he has the audacity to sneak into Twyll,"
Tremayne ended. "For that he will give his life." He
stared at Regan and curled a fist. "This time, constable, do not fail me."

Chapter Twelve

At the sound of the door opening, the priest's lips stopped moving. Still kneeling, his expression harsh and irritated, he twisted his neck and looked over one shoulder.

"Excuse me, Father," Tara said, suddenly tongue-tied. "I would like to have a word with you."

Slowly he straightened, pulling himself up to a standing position, as if the movement of uncurling his spine was painful. His eyes were sunken, haunted in their bleakness, his hair thin over an age-spotted pate, his body barely more than a tall skeleton. He nodded curtly, encouraging her to speak, his expression guarded. With one hand he beckoned her inside the small room.

"You are Father Simon?" she asked, stepping into the tiny, austere chamber with its cold stone floor and smooth, confining walls. No window allowed light in. Only the wavering flame from a slowly melting candle burning on a narrow table gave any illumination at all.

He nodded and studied her without a sound. Tara's skin crawled. The dark room and the silent, cadaverous man were in eerie contrast to the near-frantic activity elsewhere in the castle.

"I come to you from Lodema."

His breath whistled through his teeth. There was a

long, searching moment of hesitation. Thin, graying eyebrows quirked, and fear as dark and deep as a demon's soul blackened his eyes. He shook his head as if he'd never heard of her mother, but there was a glimmer of recognition he couldn't hide, a shadow of knowledge. With one hand he reached into his pocket and fingered the beads of his rosary.

"Aye, Father, I be Tara, Lodema's daughter, the babe you brought to her in a basket." His head was still shaking and now more vigorously. He held up his free hand to quiet her, but she had not come this far and endured all that she had just faced to be silenced. "My mother, Lodema . . . she . . . she . . . told me that I was not of her womb, that I was brought to her, by you, when you were a priest here at Twyll. She thought I be the daughter of Lord Gilmore and Lady Farren, and she showed me the ring—the emerald ring and the coins . . . and the faded old basket in which I was swaddled when you brought me to her."

"No," he mouthed, though he spoke not. He removed the other hand from his pocket and held both his palms toward her, moving them rapidly from side to side, causing the flame to dance wildly, the shadows on the wall to flutter and fade.

"Say you that I am not Gilmore's daughter?"

He blinked rapidly, as if startled and thinking hard.

"Did you not take me in a cart the very day I was born—the day my parents were slain by Merwynn?" she demanded, her throat growing tight with the horrid, tragic thought of it all. "You arrived with blood on your vestments, with a child and a ring." Her voice had risen with passion, and she thumped a finger on her chest. "That child was me," she whispered. "Was it not?"

Again the violent shaking of his head, and now Tara

thought she heard the sound of a footstep on the stairs.

Swiftly Father Simon snatched her hand, lifting her fingers toward the candle. His skin was cool and dry, rough as parchment, stretched tight over fleshless bones. Holding up her bare fingers, he frowned.

"I know, I know . . . I wear not the ring, nor do I have it any longer. It was taken from me." She swallowed hard and stared into wary eyes partially hidden by the sag of wrinkled eyelids. "But Lodema gave it to me, I swear. I am the girl she raised from a babe. But only you can tell me if I be the daughter of Twyll."

His skin lost what little color it had. He crossed himself swiftly and motioned that she should leave.

"Nay."

Anger flared in his gaze. His shoulders stiffened. He towered over her and would have frightened her were it not for the fear she saw in his eyes.

"Can you not break your vow of silence?" she asked.

"He's got no tongue," another voice whispered.

Tara nearly fell through the floor. Whirling, her heart clenched, she faced a boy who was standing in the doorway—a thin, sober-looking lad of about ten, who regarded her through suspicious eyes.

"What say you?"

"Cut it out, he did," the boy said, as he slipped into the room on quiet feet and shut the door softly behind him. Father Simon's expression turned to stone. "Himself."

Tara recoiled at the horrifying thought. "Nay," she said, disbelieving as she stared at the priest. "Nay—"

"Why do you think he speaks not?"

"A vow of silence, his own private communion with

God . . ." She swallowed back revulsion at the thought of the man actually mutilating himself. "This . . . this is true?" she whispered, her hand on her chest as she met the older man's gaze.

He lifted a weary shoulder, but there was a spark of defiance in his tormented eyes.

"But why?"

"To hide his secrets, of course," the boy said.

"And how do you know this?" she demanded, wondering at this youth's insolence. Pride angled his jaw, rebellion pulled at the corners of his mouth, and she realized he was far older than his years. Experience, she assumed, had been his teacher.

"I know."

"How?"

"I know everything."

Impudent pup. "Do you? And how do you accomplish that, by . . . by listening at doors and peeking through keyholes?'

"Sometimes," he said. He seemed to relish baiting her.

"As you listened just now."

"Aye."

"Who are you?"

"Quinn." He tossed his dark hair off his face and lifted his chin proudly, as if she should know from his answer that he was someone to be reckoned with. When she didn't respond properly, he had the audacity to raise an insolent eyebrow, reminding her for a minute of Rhys. Her heart ached for a second. "I will be baron someday." The last he said without a hint of pride, as if it were a simple fact, one that no one dared dispute.

This boy was Lord Tremayne's son? Then she understood his arrogance, for he thought—nay, he *knew*—he would someday rule Twyll. 'Twas his birthright, or so he believed.

"Who be you?" he demanded.

Father Simon's eyes grew wider, his lips twisted into a hard frown of disapproval, and Tara suddenly felt as if she were walking on a thin, crumbling bridge that spanned a dark, yawning abyss ready to swallow her if she stumbled.

"Tara . . . of Gaeaf. I be the daughter of an old friend of Father Simon's."

The boy glanced at the priest, as if for affirmation, and Father Simon gave a curt, irritated nod.

"He speaks to no one." The boy was adamant.

"Except you," she guessed. "But how, if he has no tongue?"

"There be other ways," the lad said with a mischievous smirk. "If ye be clever enough to find them."

"And you are?"

He didn't respond, and Tara had to remind herself that she was talking to no mere boy. No, this upstart was arrogant and wise beyond his age, a lad who knew far more than he would tell. He held up a hand, then pressed a finger to his lips. Footsteps sounded on the spiraling stone stairs outside this tiny chamber, and Quinn, like a shadow, slipped noiselessly out the door to disappear into the darkness.

She turned back to Father Simon, but he motioned her quickly to a space behind the door. As if he'd done it a thousand times, he pretended not to hear the commotion on the stairway, dropped to his knees and took up his vigil again. Boots pounded up the stairs—loud, the sound of many feet. Tara's heart thudded. She put one hand in her pocket and fingered the hilt of her knife, her palms suddenly sweaty. Holding her breath, she melted against the wall as the sound of voices reached her.

"You, Jack—go up to the top of the watchtower, talk to the lookout, see if he's seen the outlaw," a deep voice ordered.

The outlaw? Surely they didn't mean Rhys! She strained to hear the conversation through the crack between the hinges of the door.

" 'E ain't 'ere, I'm tellin' ya. Someone woulda seen 'im."

"Just like they seen him stealing the lord's horse?" the first voice sneered.

"That be 'Enry's fault." A snort. "The stable master paid for 'is mistake if ye ask me. 'Ow could he let the Bastard Outlaw outwit 'im? Now git along with ye!"

Oh, God, Rhys was here. In Twyll. Probably looking for her. And Lord Tremayne already knew it and was searching for him. Regret tightened her lungs. Guilt hammered through her brain.

"All right, all right," the raspier voice finally agreed. "I'll go up, talk to the guard, but 'tis all for naught, I'm tellin' ye." The footsteps drew nearer. Tara's heart knocked wildly, fear pulsed through her blood. Father Simon, his back to the door, bowed his head and began to pray again. His lips moved soundlessly as he fingered the rosary hanging out of his pocket.

"Ahh, Father," the voice boomed, and Tara shrank as one soldier paused at the half open door. "If I could have a word with you—"

Father Simon held up a hand, effectively cutting the man off as he continued his prayer. Tara felt the sweat bead on her scalp. She heard a rustle of feet, as if the soldier were shifting his weight. Peering through the crack between the hinges, Tara could barely make out the guard. His features were indistinct in the shadowy light—but he was big, large enough to fill the doorway. He rubbed his jaw anxiously, waiting.

"Aye, well," he muttered, "I hate to be botherin' ye, seein' as yer prayin' and all, but—"

"Come along, Tim," another voice, from outside the door, instructed. "There be no one in the father's quarters."

Tim nodded, hesitated, then disappeared from the doorway. The footsteps faded and Tara let out her breath slowly.

Was it possible? Was Rhys in the keep? Oh, sweet Holy Mother, she hoped not. She bit her lip and waited until the old tower room was silent again. Slowly she peeled herself off the wall and stepped into the tiny circle of shifting light from the candle's flame.

"Please, Father Simon," she said, certain that this was her only chance to find out the truth. "Tell me, did you take the child from this castle and leave her with Lodema?" For long, excruciating minutes he continued in his prayer. She waited until she could stand it no longer. When she was just about to leave, certain that he would never answer her question, he slowly turned and stared up at her from his knees. Their eyes locked, held, and he raised his scraggly eyebrows and gave the barest hint of a nod. "Aye," he mouthed mutely, then turned back to his prayers.

Tara stood rooted to the spot. So it was true. She was the infant stolen at birth. Could she dare believe it? And what if it were true? Did it change anything? Nay. Nothing. "But how—"

He frowned, kept praying.

"Please, Father Simon, I needs know—"

With a slash of one hand, he impatiently waved her to the door without meeting her gaze again. His lips moved in pious conversation, and Tara realized she had no choice but to leave. Soon the soldiers would be back and she couldn't allow herself to be trapped in this stony room where there was no exit, nowhere to hide.

So what did it matter if she had been born here? Other than having her curiosity satisfied by the priest's confirmation, nothing had changed.

Except that with your own stubborn bullheadedness, you've endangered Rhys.

Any exhilaration she might have felt about learning that she was indeed Lord Gilmore and Lady Farren's daughter quickly vanished with the horrid realization that she'd led Rhys into certain danger. She had to find Rhys, to warn him.

He didn't have to follow you, Tara. 'Twas his decision.

But she couldn't absolve herself of the blame. Sick at the thought that he might be captured because of her, she started down the stairs, her feet moving swiftly. True, he'd held her prisoner and stolen the ring from her, but he'd also been worried about her safety and warned her not to ride to Twyll. At the door to the tower she paused, took a deep breath, then slipped through the opening into a cold, gray afternoon. The wind was harsh and brittle as it sent dry leaves, twigs, and feathers scattering across the bailey. It slapped her in the face and snatched at the hem of her mantle.

How could she find Rhys? Though she apparently had been born the daughter of Gilmore, this keep was strange to her. She knew not where one would hide, nor could she ask anyone without raising questions. Yet she had to find him, to help him to safety.

Too late, Tara. Far, far too late. Already soldiers were searching for him everywhere within the great

stone walls. They scoured the chambers, peered behind doors, and stuck swords into carts of grain and
hay, leaving no stone unturned in their quest.

Outlaw. Bastard. Beloved.

Her heart ached, and she realized she was hopelessly in love with the blackheart.

"Fool," she muttered under her breath. She kept
her hood over her hair and tried to blend in with the
peddlers and workers who hustled through the bailey.
Hurrying along a well-trod path near the slaughterhouse, where the butcher was busy salting pork, she
noticed men with swords, quivers, and crossbows,
striding along familiar paths that wound among the
huts and pens of the bailey. The restless energy she'd
felt earlier, the tension in the keep, crackled through
the bailey like the air before a thunderstorm. The
sounds of axes splitting lumber, saws grating through
beams, and hammers pounding were interspersed with
the bark of sharp orders, the cackle of nervous laughter, and the scream of a peacock. Stern-faced mothers
shepherded children as they lugged provisions to the
garrison.

Several women cast worried glances her way, and
she read the questions in their eyes but knew they
were too distracted to wonder much who she was or
what business she had in the keep.

So where could Rhys be in this maze of a castle?
Her gaze swept the bailey. The gong farmer was
mucking out the stables, and a girl was chasing geese
at the edge of the pond. Feathers flew and a particularly loud goose honked wildly as carts creaked and
rattled their way along the rutted, muddy alleys.
Somewhere a pig squealed, while the stern-faced soldiers continued their search through the huts, stopping

to ask questions, their eaglelike eyes penetrating to
the farthest reaches of the castle.

Rhys would never escape this.

'Twould be impossible.

"Hey!" she heard, and her heart stopped. "What
business d'ye have 'ere?" a huge male voice boomed.
She turned quickly, a half-baked explanation forming
on her lips, but then she realized that a soldier was
questioning a farmer with an empty wagon. She
ducked behind a hayrick and reached into the pocket
where her little knife was hidden. Thank the Holy
Mother she hadn't tossed it into the bucket with her
precious flint when she'd escaped the inn.

"Psst."

She froze.

"Lady—"

Glancing over her shoulder, she spied Quinn hiding
behind a post near the entrance to a dark hut. He
motioned her closer with one finger, then disappeared
through the small doorway. She hesitated, but told
herself that she had nothing to fear from the boy. He
was a child.

*Aye, but he's Baron Tremayne's son, he is, and as
he now knows your true identity, he is your sworn
enemy. Mayhap he's leading you into a trap, one his
father has set.*

Why then did he warn her at the tower?

"Well?" the guard demanded.

"Nay, I have seen the outlaw Rhys not." A thin-
voiced woman on the other side of the hayrick was
being interrogated.

"You be sure?" The guard was having none of it.

"Not even his shadow, I tell ye. He be a man a
woman doesn't forget quickly. If I'd seen him, Sir
Ewan, I would have remembered it."

"Humph." The soldier snorted, then spit. "So ye've seen nothing out of the ordinary?"

"I didna say that, Ewan," the woman replied, almost flirting with the soldier. "Ye be puttin' words into me mouth. I says I have na seen Rhys, but there was a strange woman in the keep this morn. I saw her, and me daughter Isabel here caught sight of her as well . . . didn't ye, dearie?"

"Aye," a small voice mumbled.

Tara's back stiffened.

"Black hair she had—dark as a raven's wing it was, and wild, curly." The woman sounded thoughtful, and Tara glanced hastily through the pens and huts, searching for a place to hide. "Her hair, it framed a fair face and big eyes—I can't be tellin' ye what color they were, though. She kept her hood up high, as if she was hidin' somethin'."

"A woman, ye say?"

"Aye! Aye! Be ye deaf, Ewan? I'm tellin' ye there is a strange woman in the keep—a beauty she is, but none I've seen before, and ye know me, Ewan, I know everyone."

"I know ye have a way of stretchin' the truth, Sylvie. You tell a good story as well as ye make yer candles fer the keep."

"Not this time. I swear it. She be actin' strangely, if ye know what I mean. Tryin' not to cause attention to herself, but she . . . she walked into the watchtower— there to the north. I seen her slip through the door, I did."

Tara's mouth turned to dust. New fear sizzled through her.

"Ain't that right, darlin'?" the woman continued and a small voice peeped her agreement.

"Yea. I seen her too, I did. In a black cape she was. A long one."

"Well, now, that's interestin'," the guard agreed. "A comely woman with black hair and a big cape?"

"Aye, and a small woman she be. Not much to her. But ye would remember her if ye saw her, I'm tellin' ya. Ye've got an eye for the lasses, don't ya now, Ewan?"

His laughter turned into a coughing fit. Tara glanced at the door where Quinn had disappeared. Could she risk following him? Once the soldier had cleared his throat, he said, "If this woman be a small thing, then she'll be no trouble. I'd best be checkin' the tower—"

"Oh, nay. She's not there no more. I seen her come out of the tower," the child said. "A bit ago."

Oh, dear God, Tara thought, her heart pounding more loudly than the carpenter's hammer. If she were questioned and 'twas found out that she was indeed the daughter of the slain baron and his wife, she would surely be imprisoned for treason—mayhap hanged. There was no end to what torture the baron could inflict upon her—and if she were locked in a dungeon she could not help Rhys. She was forced to trust the boy.

Whispering a prayer to the Earth Mother and fearing that she was stepping into a deadly, well-planned trap, she noiselessly slipped through the dark doorway after Quinn and paused but a second for her eyes to adjust to the lack of light.

"So this be it—the jewel that so many covet?" Cavan walked to a small window in the private quarters of his keep and held the ring toward the window, where a bit of light dared pierce the keep and now bounced off the facets of the emerald. Tapestries, rich and thick, with images of comely half-dressed maids in colorful gardens, hung over the whitewashed walls. Candles lit each corner of the chamber, and a fire crackled in the huge hearth. A large bed stacked with furs filled one corner, and a table with two chairs was placed near the grate. Down the hallway the music of a harp filtered through the sounds of conversation from the hallway.

"Aye, the dark emerald of Twyll."

"And it has magical powers?" Cavan asked, his voice tinged with skepticism. He frowned to himself, leaving Abelard to guess what was going through his greedy little mind.

"So 'tis said."

"But you have not witnessed any."

"Nay."

"Where did you get this?"

Abelard had anticipated the question. "Know you not that I am a thief?"

"Aye, and a rogue, and a thug, and an outlaw, a pickpocket, and mayhap even a murderer," Cavan said without emotion. "So I am to assume you stole it?" Cavan clutched the ring in his fist as if in tightening his grip on it, he could learn the mysteries it held.

"Aye."

"From whom?" The poignant notes of the harp stopped, yet other sounds of life in the castle—shouts, laughter, footsteps—still could be heard through the thick stone walls.

"Does it matter? If indeed you be the rightful heir of Twyll, now you have it. Many others may have owned it fleetingly, but now 'tis yours."

"For a price?" He tossed the ring into the air, watching it sparkle as it arced, then catching it again and testing its weight. "A small barony for you and your friend. Is that correct?"

"Seems fair," Abelard ventured.

"Where is this friend of yours now?" Cavan asked. "I thought he was to help us with the siege. We ride at dawn."

"He will be here," Abelard promised, and Cavan snapped his fingers, ordering wine from a page lurking near the doorway. "Two cups and some of the best in the cellar. Bring it to the great hall," he said to the nervous boy, who was but a few years younger than the ruler of Marwood. The page scurried out of the room, quick to fulfill his mission.

Cavan paused to throw on a deep crimson mantle and tie the laces. "Come," he finally said, clapping Abelard on the back, and the older man sensed that the young lord was about to try to fool him, that their bargain—now that Cavan was in possession of the ring—was not as solid as it had once been. "We will celebrate, though I must tell you, I be disappointed that your—what did you call it, army of thieves and outlaws?—is not with you. Were they not part of our original bargain?"

"Aye." Abelard was troubled. What had happened to Kent, Rosie, Leland, and the lot? Were they safe? What about the simpleton of a girl, Pigeon? Had some horror befallen her? At the thought his stomach soured and bile rose in his throat. "There was some trouble."

"There always is," Cavan said, with more wisdom than his years should have allowed. "There always is." Together they walked through the keep, down the stairs to the great hall, where not only the wine was waiting for them but trenchers of salty salmon and pike. And two women—beautiful maids who blushed and avoided Abelard's curious eyes as he settled onto a bench.

The page had been quick to anticipate his lord's needs.

"Ahh, Belinda and Kate," the lord of Marwood explained with a smile meant as introduction. "They will be with us until morn, when we ride and catch up with the garrison."

"They have already left?" Abelard asked, though he'd suspected as much, since the castle was quieter than the last time he'd visited. As he'd ridden into the bailey he'd noted that all the weapons and soldiers he'd seen on his last trip to Marwood had disappeared.

"They left at dawn. 'Twill be no trouble to catch up, for the catapult and ram are slow to move. By the time we reach them, they will be close to Twyll. Worry not," he added, waving off what he assumed were Abelard's concerns. "We will miss none of the attack." His smile dripped with pure evil, and Abelard yet again questioned his own judgment in joining forces with this overbearing whelp. "Take your pick. Either girl will do anything you ask." He popped a wedge of fish and some bread into his mouth. "Or, if you prefer, you can have them both." He lifted a shoulder draped in velvet. "There are others for me."

Abelard glanced from one blushing girl to the next, and his stomach curdled. He'd had his share of women, some as young and innocent as these, but as the years had slid away he no longer hungered for the lush young ones whose names he couldn't remember.

Cavan grinned. "But do not lose all your strength this night," he warned, wagging his greasy dagger in Abelard's direction. "Tomorrow you will need to be strong and cunning. Especially if we are to beat Tremayne of Twyll without your 'army' or the Bastard

Outlaw." He washed down a mouthful of fish and bread with a long swallow from his cup, then wiped the grease and wine from his lips with a blood-red sleeve. "Where do you suppose your friend Rhys is?" he asked. "Hmm?"

Abelard shook his head. "I know not," he admitted. "But he will appear and ride with us."

"Will he?" Cavan didn't seem to believe it for a second. He patted Kate—or was it Belinda—on the rump through her bliaut and sighed. "For all our sakes, let us hope that you are right, my friend," he said.

Abelard didn't answer, couldn't. Rhys was different these days. All because of the witch. By the gods, that woman had addled his friend's brain, and if he wasn't careful, she was certain to ruin everything.

"Halt!" A sharp, deep-timbred warning rang through the forest, bouncing off the surrounding trees.

Damn! Low in the saddle, Rhys kicked his mare, a white palfrey he'd stolen from a farmer when the stallion had turned up lame. The little horse shot forward, racing along the muddy path, kicking up clods, stretching her legs. Trees and sun-dappled glens flashed by. Cold winter wind slapped his face.

"Halt, I say!" The soldier who had spied him gave chase.

"Run, damn it!" Rhys growled, his fingers tight on the reins as he guided her around a stand of pine—and saw a fallen tree blocking the path a hundred yards ahead.

Birds flushed from the underbrush, flapped into the sky.

"You can do it," he urged, and the horse ran faster, legs flashing through the mossy-barked trees. He was so close to Twyll, so damned close! And now the sentry. Curse his luck!

With a glance over his shoulder, Rhys spied the rider, a big man wearing the colors of Twyll, astride a fleet bay destrier that was closing the distance between them with each long stride.

His white mare would never be able to outrun the faster steed.

"Halt! You!"

Never! "Come on, come on," he muttered.

Zzzt! An arrow zipped through the air, narrowly missing his head. He kicked his horse harder, straight at the upturned oak.

Thunk! Another arrow buried itself in the thick bark of a gnarled pine tree.

"Bloody Christ," he growled, moving with the horse as the dead tree loomed ever nearer.

Quail scattered. A rabbit bounded into skeletal berry vines, rattling dry branches and leaves. The wind whistled and clouds blocked most of the sun as the dead oak loomed before them.

The horse gathered herself, then launched, flying over the desiccated log. As she landed, Rhys slapped her hard on the rump and let go. He rolled to the ground, his shoulder striking hard. Pain exploded in the joint. He gritted his teeth and slid backward, against the broken stump, hiding as the sound of hoofbeats echoed through the canyon. Searching the ground, he found a stone that fit in the palm of his hand and, breathing hard, ignoring the fire in his left shoulder, he hid, coiled, ready.

"Blast you!" the soldier growled, but still the horse galloped, shaking the ground. Rhys waited, listened hard, heard the change of gait, and saw the dark animal spring.

He unleashed the stone, throwing all his weight behind it. It hit the beast hard in the shoulder. With a startled squeal the animal stumbled. Its hooves grazed the tree and splinters flew.

"Hey—wha—?" Soldier and beast fell, tumbling to the ground in a mass of flailing legs and arms. Mind-chilling screams rang through the frigid winter air. "Oooooaaawwww—oh, Christ!" the man cried in agony. Pinned beneath the downed animal, his body crushed, he bellowed in a roar of pain.

Rhys shot forward as the frightened stallion scrambled to his feet. With pain burning in his own shoulder, he grabbed the soldier's flayed arm, stripped him of sword, quiver, and bow, and left him writhing in the dead leaves.

Rhys didn't wait to see if the man was alive or dead. As the wild-eyed destrier got his balance and started to run off, Rhys grabbed the flying reins, wrapped them around his good hand, and planted his feet. The horse shot forward, dragging him, but Rhys held fast. Dirt, mud, leaves, and twigs scratched at him, but he didn't give up his grip, and when the horse slowed he found his feet and painfully hoisted himself into the saddle.

"Bloody hell. Ye can't leave me 'ere, ye bastard!" the wounded warrior yelled, desperation in his voice.

Rhys didn't listen. His new mount's strides were strong, swift. Though the animal was still panicked and running wildly through the trees, he was unharmed. Rhys felt a small niggle of guilt for the downed man, but he remembered that if the man had had the chance or if his aim had been a little more true, he would gladly have killed the Bastard Outlaw and collected whatever reward Tremayne had placed upon his half brother's head.

Now, with quiver, bow, and a second sword, Rhys was ready. He would storm the gates of Twyll if need be. For he intended to find Tara by the time the sun set. And no one—not Abelard and his greed, Lord Tremayne and his hatred, or Satan himself—could stop him.

As God was his witness, he would find her.

Within seconds he was closer to Twyll, and he felt a thrill of anticipation steal through him. Through the copses of pine and oak, he spied the behemoth of a castle, stretched like a spiny-backed dragon atop the hill. A bright standard, mounted from the highest watchtower, snapped in the breeze, and smoke from the ovens and fires within the thick walls curled upward toward the shifting clouds that covered a weak winter sun.

Somewhere deep inside that monster of a keep was Tara. He knew it.

Newfound fear gnawed at him. What if she had already been discovered by Tremayne? What if she'd become Tremayne's captive? Rhys remembered the dungeons beneath the towers, the dank, rotting smell, the desperation of those imprisoned, the painful sting of a flogging.

Not Tara, please, not Tara. He remembered the smooth lines of her back, her flawless skin.

For the first time in years the bastard sent up a prayer to a God he didn't trust.

At the edge of the woods, he slowed his steed's strides and guided the big bay around the perimeter of the castle, through the brush and trees, careful to avoid the main roads, searching for a place to hide his horse while he found a way to enter the massive stone fortress. He'd done it often enough and knew those inside who would help him, but he suspected that because of the impending war with Cavan, the guards, who were usually an easily distracted lot, would be doubly cautious. He would have to tread carefully.

He rounded a bend, and his horse's ears pricked up. The steed snorted, and his muscles quivered in anticipation.

Through a curtain of ash, Rhys saw another stallion. Tethered to a sapling, one back foot cocked lazily, his sleek coat spattered with mud, Gryffyn lifted his huge head. A breeze ruffled his mane. He let out a soft nicker.

Rhys's heart soared.

Mayhap Tara was nearby.

There was a chance he'd caught her before she'd been foolish enough to enter the castle.

He started to dismount. Surely Tara was nearby or planned to return to the horse . . .

A prickle of dread slid down his spine as he considered that this might be a trap. A twig snapped.

Tara?

Was she safe after all? Hope surging through his blood, he glanced toward a shady open space where the barest bits of sunlight played in gloomy shadows.

Every muscle in his body froze and hope dissolved into dread.

Muscles coiling, ready to strike, he reached for his sword.

Too late.

Twenty soldiers stepped from behind trees and out of brush. Each and every man wore the colors of Twyll.

Bloody hell.

How had he been so damned blind?

Gritting his teeth, he held his tongue. He refused

to demand information about Tara. Mayhap they knew not of her.

The archers were all at the ready, their bows fitted tight to their shoulders, twenty arrows aimed directly at his heart.

"If you've got a brain in that sorry head of yours, you will not move," a tall man, the leader, said. Rhys recognized him as Regan, Tremayne's constable. With blond hair and cold, lizardlike eyes that squinted in an impassive face, he kept Rhys in the sights of his deadly crossbow. "Now, get off your stolen horse, outlaw, and be quick about it. The baron, he wants a word with you."

Chapter Thirteen

Tara squinted at the inside of the room she'd entered. It was dark as a tomb and smelled of hay and grain. Dusty. Dry. No light came in, but the sound of scurrying paws convinced her that the castle rats nested here.

"This way," Quinn said, and she felt his fingers lace through hers. With her free hand she touched the rough weave of sacks of grain that were stacked in this storage chamber. Quinn walked unerringly through the piled sacks and around wooden casks. She smelled onions and apples, stored for the winter along with the grain. Once in a while she felt a post, and a couple of times her fingers brushed the rough wattle and daub of a wall.

Quinn moved quickly, his course changing direction often through a maze of stored provisions. Stumbling blindly, Tara followed him as he made his way to some unknown destination. Through passageways and doors, around support columns and crates, she allowed him to lead her.

Drawing a breath was difficult, for the air was thick and unmoving—stale as death.

"Wait here," he finally ordered, and he released her hand for a moment, placing her fingers against the splintery side of a post. "I'll be back."

"Nay—"

But he was gone, his quick, nearly silent footsteps fading away. She coughed and tried not to let fear sink into her bones. If he left her she would never find her way out of this inky tomb—never again see the light of day.

Of course you will, Tara. Fear not. Think of Rhys.

She heard a grunt, then something heavy—mayhap a sack of grain or a cask—slid or was forced across the floor. There was a rattle of chain and the scrape of metal against metal. "Bloody damn," Quinn muttered under his breath. Another scrape, and then the distinctive click of a lock and the creak of old, rusted hinges.

Within seconds he was beside her again, taking her hand. "Where are we going?" she asked.

"To a safe place."

She wasn't so certain as he took hold of her wrist and pulled her forward again. "Now, follow me," he said. "Down the ladder."

He knelt and, with his hand guiding hers, let her touch a hole carved into the floor.

" 'Tis an old entrance to the dungeons," he explained.

"And you have the key?" she asked.

"Aye. I too be a thief."

"I'm not—"

"I speak not of you." He let go of her hand again.

"Does anyone else have a key?" she asked.

"Follow me." Without answering her question, he slipped through the hole, his boots softly scraping on metal. "Close the door."

She hesitated but a moment. The boy knew his way around the castle, and she couldn't take the chance of being found. Not before she discovered if Rhys had been taken prisoner . . . or worse. She gulped, set her teeth, and descended through the opening.

The rungs of the ladder were rusted, the metal rough against her fingers. She heard the drip of water and smelled dank earth. "Careful," the boy whispered as she pulled on a rotting rope handle and the door closed over her head with a soft but distinctive thud. If anyone set a sack of grain or a cask of wine over it, neither she nor Quinn would be able to force it open again. If there were no other exit to this tunnel, they would be trapped.

Don't panic. The boy seems to know what he's doing. Aye, but he's just a lad.

Refusing to let the fear within her take command of her heart and head, she descended. When her feet touched down again, she realized that the floor was no longer stone but packed dirt. The walls were stone but crumbling. "Hurry," he said, taking her hand again. She followed him, though he could be leading her into certain death. And her only defenses were her wits, her quick tongue, and the knife tucked inside her boot.

They were beneath the castle, in a tunnel that split, veering off in two directions. They reached a set of stairs, this time made of boards. "There be thirteen of these," Quinn said, leading the way. She nearly fell but counted the steep steps until she reached solid ground again.

"Where are we?" she whispered.

"An old part of the castle," he said, and she believed him. The underground corridor was thick with dust that caught in her nostrils while cobwebs brushed her face and hair. She heard the sound of scraping claws and imagined rats scurrying out of their way. Her boots crunched on pebbles and debris. "Come on, make haste," Quinn urged. She followed this strange boy, wondering if she was being led to freedom or to certain death.

"Where is this safe place?" The air was thick, dusty, and heavy to breathe.

"Where there is someone we must meet."

"Who?" She nearly stopped, but his hand, now beginning to sweat, pulled insistently on hers.

"You'll see."

The tunnel traveled downward, and other corridors angled one way or another. Tara, one hand along the wall, wondered where each branch of this maze led as they passed openings with air that was cooler, fresher.

She was beginning to think she would have been better off staying in the bailey in the light of day and avoiding the soldiers on her own. Why should she trust this boy? He was, after all, the baron's son.

Yet that was odd. Why was he not a page at another castle, learning the duties of a knight? Why was he leading her through this labyrinth beneath the keep? The tunnel jogged to the right and they began to climb steadily, without the aid of stairs.

Finally, when Tara thought she could breathe the stale air not a moment longer, he reached another door, pushed it open, and walked into a room lit by three small candles. There, sitting on a pallet of old sacks, surrounded by stacks of weapons—crossbows, longbows, arrows, bolts, and piles of rocks, was a man she'd never seen before.

"Who is this?" he demanded, jumping to his feet and eyeing her suspiciously. He wasn't a large man, but in the wee light of the musty room he looked as tough as tanned leather, and his gaze was rock-steady. Confident. The barest breath of a breeze filtered through the cracks of mortar in the walls.

"She is called Tara. 'Tis said she be a witch. She was with Father Simon, and the soldiers were looking for her and the outlaw."

"You were with Rhys?" the man asked.

"Nay," she said, not trusting him for a minute. She heard the steady drip of water running down one wall. "I came alone."

"But the soldiers are seeking him," the boy insisted. "Found the horse he stole from the keep."

"Then something's amiss." Hand on the hilt of his sword, the man paced from one end of the small cell to the other.

Relief washed over Tara. "Then they will find Rhys not. I rode Gryffyn here."

"Tremayne's horse? The one Rhys stole?"

"Aye." She nodded and felt as if a weight had been dragged off her heart.

"And how did you wrest him from the outlaw?"

"I—I tricked him," she admitted, wondering how much she could reveal to this man who had befriended the odd son of Lord Tremayne.

"Did ye? 'Tis not an easy task." So he didn't believe her. Not that it mattered. "And how do ye know Rhys so well?"

"I was his prisoner."

"And ye managed to escape?"

"I told you. She's a witch!" Quinn said proudly.

"If she be a witch and has all these powers she can use—powers that helped her to elude Rhys, why be she here with you and me, Quinn-lad, eh? Why does she not call up the spirits and cast herself away from this place?"

"Mayhap she wants to be here." The lad was unmoved by the older man's argument.

Tara had no time to waste. "Who be you?" she

demanded. "And why are you here, underground, hiding like a field mouse?"

"I, lady," he said, his white teeth flashing as he turned to face her, "am a spy."

Her muscles tensed. The knife pressed against her leg. "A spy? For whom?"

One side of his mouth lifted in a cocky grin. "Whoever pays the most."

"A mercenary." She spat out the word in disgust. She had no use for men who sold their souls for a few coins, warriors who had no cause, no faith, soldiers who would fight to the death but had no heart.

"It could be said."

"Have you no name?"

"James."

Had she heard Rhys mention this man? The name seemed familiar, as if she might have heard Rhys and Abelard discussing him. But James was a common name—shared by many. She could be mistaken. "What are you doing here?"

"Waiting."

"For?"

"Rhys, Aberlard, and Cavan's army." He rubbed his hands together and resumed his pacing. "I fear something's gone wrong." Turning on a worn boot heel, he looked her up and down and frowned in distaste, as if he didn't like what he saw. "What brings you here?" he asked, his brow knitting in thought. " 'Tis known there will be war and yet you come to talk with the priest who does not speak."

"I thought mayhap he would give up his vow of silence for my request," she admitted, knowing she was saying too much but unable to keep the words from tumbling out. She was worried for Rhys's life.

She needed an ally, and this man—this spy—was the only one she had. Well, unless she counted the boy.

"His vow of silence?" The spy shook his head. "Never will he be able to."

She rubbed her arms from the cold—she knew what he was about to say. "He cannot speak, you know." With a shake of his head he added, "Father Simon cut out his tongue . . . oh, about ten years back."

"Quinn told me." She glanced at the boy, as the candlelight played upon his features. He was young but had endured much pain, she thought.

"Yes. By his own hand, Simon silenced himself."

Again bile rose in her throat. "But . . . why?"

"No one knows. Only Simon, but now he'll never tell. Most people think that he speaks not because of some holy pact with God. The truth is, lady, that he keeps his silence because of some secrets he knows. Secrets he shares only with the devil."

Tara nodded tightly and felt an unwarranted sense of guilt, for she knew at least one of the secrets he meant—that she was the daughter of Lady Farren and Lord Gilmore. Simon had saved her life, stolen her away as a babe.

But if this were his darkest secret, why wait nine or ten years to cut out his tongue? She shuddered and closed her mind to the thought.

"Why did you wish to speak to Simon?" James asked.

"He knew my mother."

James studied her in the flickering light. "If you were just speaking with Simon, why did you follow Quinn into the catacombs?"

"She thinks she is the daughter of Lord Gilmore," Quinn blurted out.

"You heard that?" Tara asked, surprised. The boy

had given her no indication that he knew she thought she was the rightful heir to a castle his father now ruled.

Quinn raised his chin a notch and set his jaw with pride.

"Is this true?" James demanded.

"Aye." No reason to lie. Not now.

In the flickering light James's eyes narrowed. "Then you have the stone? The dark emerald of Twyll?"

"It was taken from me," she said bitterly, though her heart had softened a bit where Rhys was concerned.

"Then what of Caven? Why thinks he that he be the son of Gilmore?"

"Lord Innis told him so," Quinn said. "I heard it discussed."

"Christ Jesus, have you ears within the walls?" James asked, and the boy's expression turned dark.

"Mayhap I be a better spy than you, Sir James," he said indignantly. "At least I be not hiding underground like a scared rabbit."

"Nor will I. Not much longer," James assured him.

Tara didn't understand the bond that held these two unlikely allies together. "Are you not loyal to your father?" she asked Quinn.

The boy's face was grim. "I be very loyal to him," he said fervently and James laughed.

"You see, m'lady—daughter of Lord Gilmore—his father is not the baron of Twyll."

"But—"

"Why think you Father Simon cut out his tongue?" James taunted. "Because of you—if you really be who you think you are—or because of something else, something mayhap a little more dangerous?"

She was beginning to understand.

"Aye, Quinn here, he be Rhys's son."

She didn't know what to say, for a pain, an unlikely ache that had no bond with sense, attacked her. The thought that Rhys had fathered a child, any child, with another woman burned through her soul.

"What do you think would happen to the boy if Lord Tremayne found out, eh?" James asked.

"He would be killed," she whispered, thinking of Tremayne's cruel reputation while staring into the eyes of a child—Rhys's child. The boy at the center of all this. The person in most peril.

"At the very least. Now, m'lady, we have a job to do. Somehow we must save Quinn's hide, warn Rhys that he is about to be ambushed— for if the sentries have found his horse they will lie in wait for him. Then we must release the prisoners from the dungeons—the ones who were taken from Broodmore."

"Broodmore?" she whispered. "You mean . . ." Her voice faded as she understood.

"All of the men who had bound themselves to Rhys and Abelard are now in these very prisons."

"And the women?"

James nodded darkly. "No one escaped. Except me. With Quinn's help I was able to sneak off in the confusion of locking up so many."

"And now you feel an obligation to free them?" she asked.

"Nay. 'Tis part of the job. I help them, we save Rhys, open the gates of Twyll for Cavan, and I accept payment. You have provided it, you see, for I think for all my service I should be given the dark stone."

Tara was tired of the gem and the stories of magic and inheritance that surrounded it. As far as she was concerned, the ring was cursed. Whoever had it fought to keep it; whoever wanted it was willing to shed

blood to obtain it. The dark emerald of Twyll was
only good for causing heartache, jealousy, and greed.
"If you can get it from whoever now holds it, so be
it," she whispered. "But let us not get the cart before
the horse. First we must save Rhys and the prisoners."

"Aye." He reached into his pile of weapons and
handed her a sword. "As soon as darkness falls, we
will strike and release the prisoners."

"And Rhys?"

"Let us hope he has his wits about him and isn't
foolish enough to follow you here. Now, there be one
more question, m'lady. If you be the daughter of Gilmore, then who is Cavan of Marwood?"

"An impostor," Quinn said, reaching for a dagger.

James grinned wickedly, his smile evil in the golden
shadows. "As are we all, lad. As are we all."

The sky threatened rain again. Clouds gathered,
blocking the sun, and the wind swept across the bailey
in sharp gusts that tugged at skirts and tore off hoods
as the women and men hurried through their tasks.

Livid, Tremayne tried to rein in his anger, but it
proved impossible. He'd spoken to the damned atilliator, Albert, a miserable ever grumbling man who for
a healthy price constructed crossbows, and the baron
was disgusted with how few new weapons were being
made. Albert, a wiry man with pock-marked skin and
no lips, had been adamant that it took time and skill
to create a true and reliable weapon and that he was
certain someone was stealing from him, though he
couldn't say who. Tremayne suspected the old man
was just plain lazy. As were most of the workers in
Twyll. He glanced at the top of the wall walk and
towers and saw that the wooden hoarding was nearly
in place. And not a minute too soon. Cavan's army

was on the march, according to Red, if the lackluster spy was to be believed. Tremayne eyed the work, watched animal hides being stretched over the slats. Soon they would be drenched with water in case that son of a dog Cavan had the audacity to shoot fire-burning tar pots over the wall.

"Bloody hell," he grumbled, kicking at a cat that was slinking around the wheel of a manure cart and had the nerve to cross his path. "Out of the way." With a hiss, the insufferable tabby arched its back, streaked across the mashed grass of the bailey, and slipped through a crack in the wall near the shed where the oxen were housed.

Would nothing go right?

"Is something troubling you, m'lord?" 'Twas the irritatingly pious and calm voice of Father Alden, who was hurrying along a stone path leading from the chapel. His robes, as fine as any king's, billowed behind him and his face was round, his expression so serene Tremayne wanted to shake him. Did he not know that the castle was threatened? That the Bastard Outlaw was plotting against them all? There were spies within the keep and talk of the dark emerald of Twyll's magical powers, and Cavan's army was intent on destroying everything Tremayne held dear. Father Alden hiked his vestments closer to his neck. "You seem vexed."

"Do I?" Tremayne sneered as the first drops of rain fell from the dark heavens.

Again the patient, condescending smile that Tremayne wanted to wipe off the man's face. "Mayhap a quiet moment in the chapel— "

"The soldiers have returned!" a sentry crowed from the tower near the main gate, and the portcullis, which

had been lowered pending Cavan's attack, rattled as
it was winched upward.

Tremayne whirled, ignoring the priest. Hooves clat-
tering, earth shaking, horses and riders flew into the
bailey. Leading the charge was Regan, triumph in his
eyes. With one hand he held fast to the reins of a
following steed. Atop that familiar animal was a prisoner, hands bound behind him, lower jaw covered
with a gag, eyes flashing rebellious fire. His breeches
were torn. Blood and mud covered his tunic. His face
was scratched and swollen, and the scar that cleaved
his eyebrow seemed to pulsate.

Rhys! At last!

Tremayne's smile slowly stretched from one side of
his mouth to the other as he recognized his bastard
of a half brother. Finally! Oh, by the saints, he wanted
to fall down on his knees and pray to God, Mary,
Jesus, and any other deity who would listen.

Near the eel pond Regan yanked on his horse's
reins and the destrier slid to a stop. The horse behind
nearly ran into the first. Rhys almost toppled off the
beast. Almost.

"M'lord!" Victorious at last, Regan threw a leg over
his mount's back and hopped lithely to the ground.
"We caught the prisoner in the forest. He was just
where you thought he'd be, with your horse." Regan
tossed his reins to a page who had appeared. The
stable master, Henry, was on his heels, ready and willing to take charge of the horses.

Tremayne's eyes left Rhys for a second to appraise
Gryffyn, whose reins were held by another of the soldiers. The beast was none the worse for wear, proud
and soaked in sweat, dirt flecking his coat, eyes as
bright as ever. Dark ears pricked forward and he shot

out a stream of breath, pulling at his bridle with the fiery spirit that so many of the horses at Twyll lacked.

Some of the work in the castle stopped. Tremayne felt curious eyes turn toward the warriors. A few men wandered closer. Children peeked out from behind their mothers' skirts as the laundresses and alewives paused in their duties, inching toward the center of the bailey.

"Bring the outlaw to me," Tremayne commanded.

Regan, along with two other soldiers who had dismounted, dragged Rhys off his horse and pushed him forward.

"Remove the gag."

One man untied the rag covering Rhys's beard-stubbled jaw.

Hammers stopped banging, the potter's wheel no longer creaked or hummed, conversation at the dye vats was muted, and even the geese and chickens ceased to honk and cackle. Only the mill's sweeps turned in the wind, the gears groaning a bit, the sails shushing. Somewhere near the kennels a dog gave off a solitary bark.

Stiff-spined, arrogance radiating from him, far from broken, Rhys stood before Tremayne and held his gaze though one of his eyes was bruised and nearly swollen shut. Rain drizzled down his nose and clung to his hair.

"So, Bastard, your luck has finally run out," Tremayne said, glaring at the man he'd hated for nearly all his life. Son of his father's whore, Rhys had not only stolen Merwynn's attention from Tremayne but he was a constant reminder of his father's lack of faith to his mother. And if that weren't enough to stoke the fires of rage in Tremayne's soul, there was always Anna—sweet, beautiful, lying bitch of a wife.

Rhys didn't answer. Just managed a half smile, as if he were amused at the situation. *Amused!*

Tremayne's blood boiled. His fists clenched. "Do you not understand that you are my prisoner? That your life is in my hands?"

Rhys's lips twitched. The wind snatched at his hair. His eyes glittered irreverently. "Never."

"You have always been a fool," Tremayne growled.

Again silence. A horse's bridle jangled and a pair of ducks landed on the eel pond with a slight splash, but the crowd that had gathered, the peasants and freeman who had been so furiously laboring before the return of the search party, had stopped their tasks. The gong farmer leaned upon his shovel, the farrier had stepped out of his hut, the carpenters on the hoardings had stilled their hammers and were looking down on the bailey from their precarious perch. Boys lugging firewood or strings of fish paused on their way to the kitchens, and girls tossing oyster shells and grain to the chickens forgot their tasks.

Tremayne felt the dozens of pairs of eyes upon him and knew everyone was wondering what he would do. Asking, now that the traitor was captured, what would happen. Rhys had once cuckholded Tremayne, gained a reputation as an outlaw and thief, spurned any kind of legality and, as Tremayne's half brother, the son of a whore, had defied the baron at every turn. 'Twas time for justice.

His fingers itched to grab Rhys's thick throat and shake the life from him, but 'twas important now, when the castle was about to be attacked, when there were spies within the very walls of Twyll, when loyalty was needed, that Tremayne appear to be fair and just, a ruler all could depend upon.

"Toss him into the dungeon," he ordered the constable and wiped at the moisture that had collected on his face.

"With the others?"

"Nay—alone. Separate from the rest of the thugs and thieves in his band."

Rhys's shoulders flexed, his back snapped to attention, and for a second there were questions in his eyes. "Ah, brother, did you not know?" Tremayne asked, satisfaction melting like warm butter in an empty stomach. "Those you left to fend for themselves at Broodmore are now my prisoners."

Rhys's smile disappeared from his face. White brackets pinched the corners of his mouth.

"Ah, well, I see you didn't. They, too, will be brought before me and tried as the traitors they are. Their lives are on your conscience, brother." Seeing that he'd finally hit a nerve, Tremayne couldn't resist adding, "And their fates will be determined long before yours so that you will be able to hear their punishments and watch as they are meted out." Warming to his subject, he clasped his hands behind his back and paced in front of the band of soldiers who stood near their mounts. " 'Twill be interesting, will it not? For you are the reason they are here, the cause for their incarceration." Rhys's muscles bunched. His eyes flashed fire as the wind picked up and the storm advanced.

Oh, 'twas worth the wait! "Yes, bastard, were it not for you, all of the men and women—oh, you know there is a woman and her daughter, along with the men who banded with you? Yes, I see you do. Anyway, were it not for you, they would all go free. I would not have had cause to chase them down. As it is, I have no choice but to punish them. Each and every one. Including the girl."

A vein throbbed near Rhys's temple.

Tremayne motioned toward the tower above the dungeon "Take him away."

"Excuse me, m'lord," Regan interjected.

"What?" Tremayne shot back. Could not one man obey him without question?

" 'Tis true we found this one at a clearing where Gryffyn was tethered, but there was a second horse as well. Sir Giles's steed. We came upon Sir Giles in the forest, wounded, and yet another horse, a white palfrey"—he pointed at a dirty mare held by a bearded soldier—"running free."

Tremayne scowled.

"Three horses. Two riders," Regan said.

Tremayne felt the prick of apprehension and glanced at Rhys, whose face had turned to stone, as if he'd suddenly willed that no expression would cross his features.

"There may be an intruder in the keep—someone other than this one," Regan ventured.

"Another one?" Tremayne muttered, his fears beginning to gel. Hadn't he felt as if someone was following him throughout the castle? Hadn't he sensed a presence looking over his shoulder at odd times? Hadn't he heard footsteps scurrying off more often than not? "Who?"

"Mayhap Sir James. He has not yet been found," Regan offered, though he didn't seem convinced.

"Or the woman," another soldier with a blade-thin nose and a fringe of graying hair that nearly covered his eyes offered.

"Woman?"

"Aye, the candlemaker, she and 'er daughter spied a woman with black hair in the bailey this morning— a woman Sylvie knew not."

Was it his imagination or did Rhys pale a bit? No longer was there a cocksure grin on the prisoner's lips. "A dark-haired woman? A stranger?" He remembered the discussion when Rhys had eluded his soldiers in the mist-shrouded canyon soon after he'd stolen Gryffyn. There was talk that he had been seen embracing a woman with black hair. The same woman the girl prisoner claimed carried a mystic ring? "Know you whom we speak of?" he asked, enjoying the moment once again.

The son of a whore's gaze was rock-steady. "I know many women."

"But this one, she was with you before, methinks. At the creek in the canyon near Gaeaf when you eluded my soldiers?"

Rhys didn't answer.

"My men saw her. And you. Embracing, they claimed. She has a ring with her, does she not? And it may have a dark stone not unlike the dark emerald of Twyll."

" 'Tis only a myth." Rhys never faltered. He didn't so much as blink, just stared, like a hawk focusing on its prey. He didn't seem to notice the rain that had collected on his skin and eyelashes, drops he could not wipe away since his hands were bound.

"But the child—what was her name?" Tremayne asked, knowing full well as he snapped his fingers. "Peony. That was it. She talked of this woman but called her a witch, said she'd heard about a ring with a dark stone that you and your friend Abelard discussed. This girl, she was certain that you were bewitched by this woman."

Again the prisoner didn't flinch. "She is a child, her mind is filled with fantasies. She sees what she wants to see."

"She thinks you are in love with the witch."

Did Rhys's jaw tighten ever so slightly? "Then she is mistaken."

"So you have no cause to worry, do you?" Tremayne didn't believe this traitor for a second. He glanced at the soldiers who were still astride their horses. "Find her," he ordered. "Bring her and the damned ring to me." The vein was throbbing madly at Rhys's temple again and the scar running down his face was as pale as winter snow. Tremayne nearly grinned. Ah, revenge was so, so sweet. He would savor it long this time. His gaze skated over each of his soldiers. "Do not fail me."

Regan had the nerve to clear his throat. "What of Cavan?" he asked. "Red returned with the news that his army moves ever closer. They come well equipped, with a trebouchet large enough to hurl boulders or dead hogs over the castle walls, a battering ram to force open the portcullis, and mantlets for their archers and miners to hide behind as they lay siege to the castle."

"I have not forgotten Cavan!" Tremayne snapped, the taste of revenge souring on his tongue. "But what better way to take the wind from his regal sails than by proving he is not the son of Gilmore?" As he paused, he heard the whisper of conversation between some of the freemen and serfs who had lived long enough to hear of and believe in the stone and the lost heir of Gilmore. "If we find the woman with the ring, his claim of being the ruler of Twyll will be for naught. I have a plan to stop him. Now—" He looked at the men and women who had gathered in a wide circle around him. His gaze moved slowly from face to face and he wondered who among them were traitors. "All of you! Back to work. We have not much time." His voice rang with authority and everyone scattered to his task. Within seconds the bellows was whooshing again in the armorer's hut, the wheelwright's hammer pinged, and the soldiers dismounted, leaving Henry and several stableboys to tend to the horses. Carts rolled, wagons creaked forward, and conversation buzzed.

"May I have a word, m'lord?" 'Twas Henry, the stable master, a man whom Tremayne loathed. Were it not for Henry's uncanny way of making even the most temperamental steed take bridle and saddle, Tremayne would have dismissed him years ago. But he was the best horseman in all of Twyll, mayhap Wales. "I would like to speak with the prisoner—just a word."

Eyes narrowing suspiciously, Tremayne nodded and watched Henry hand the reins of the horses he was holding to a witless page; then he rolled up his sleeves and approached Rhys with determined steps. Hatred burned bright in the burly man's eyes.

Two soldiers still held the prisoner. Henry stopped three feet from Rhys, held out an arm, showing off a new brand upon his palm, one Tremayne had ordered put upon him. "This is the thanks I got fer losin' the baron's horse to ye," he growled.

Rhys didn't move.

"A bastard ye're called and a bastard ye be!" Henry hauled back and spat. Spittle flew through the air, landing on Rhys's neck, and dripped down.

Rhys's temper unleashed at the insult. Swearing roundly, he lunged. The two guards holding him lost their grip. "Go to hell!" Rhys screamed. He threw his body at Henry, knocking him back.

"Ooof!" *Thud!* They fell to the ground. Grappled.

Men shouted. Women screamed. Henry smashed his curled fist against Rhys's jaw.

Crack! Rhys's head snapped back. His hands were useless tied behind his back, but he kicked with a vengeance and the two men rolled in the mud, swinging, kicking, muscles straining. The soldiers watched and hooted, incensed by the sight and smell of blood.

"Give 'im 'ell, 'Enry! The bastard deserves it!"

"That's it! Hit him again!"

"Watch his feet! Christ, look at him kick!"

One group of farmers fell back as the two men struggled, rolling on the ground, gasping, blood flowing from noses and cuts. Sweat and rain poured off them. Mud covered their clothes. Given enough time, Tremayne thought, with a grain of satisfaction as the bastard was being beaten senseless, the men would start betting and Rhys would die. Tough as he was, he was losing this one and badly.

"Enough!" Tremayne ordered.

"Break it up, you two." A guard reluctantly reached down and pulled Henry off Rhys. But the prisoner lunged again, and another man, one Tremayne couldn't quite place, pulled him back. Both men finally stood, heaving, eyeing each other with hatred, their lips curled, their nostrils flared.

"Take him away!" Tremayne ordered, waving to the guards to haul Rhys to the dungeon.

Two burly knights half dragged Rhys toward the square-faced north tower that spired above the curtain wall and hid the dungeon at its base.

Tremayne blinked against the icy rain that slanted from the sky. The black clouds were not an omen—sleet was to be expected in winter—but the few seconds' jubilation and satisfaction he'd felt at Rhys's capture had quickly evaporated.

There was much to do.

The first was to find the woman—or was she a witch?

Tremayne reminded himself that he didn't believe in witchcraft and the dark arts. Though he had no fear of immortals, ghosts, or creatures of the night, a tiny niggle of concern wormed its way into his brain, and a strange sensation of icy desolation froze his soul.

Even now, standing in the bailey surrounded by men and women who had pledged to be loyal to him, he sensed unseen eyes upon him, a plot forming against him, a fear that he could trust no one. Who were the traitors? Regan, his constable? The old cook, who regularly boxed the ears of his own son? Red, who had returned only with the news that Cavan was approaching? Grumpy Albert, who couldn't seem to make enough crossbows? Henry, the stable master, who had been fast asleep when Gryffyn had been stolen from under his very nose and now just almost beat the life out of the bastard? Old Percival, who leaned on his cane only when he thought 'twould gain him sympathy? Mary the kitchen maid, who tried and failed to please him in his very own bed? Who? *Who?*

As if the floodgates of heaven had suddenly been opened, the rain became a torrent. Icy drops peppered the ground and puddles grew deeper as Rhys, held fast by two of the strongest men in the keep, disappeared into the tower.

He would have to be tortured, of course, for how else could his tongue he loosened and those who were in league with him flushed out?

But Rhys had already once survived being flogged nearly to death. He'd endured the harshest of physical torments that Tremayne had inflicted upon him, and never had his will been broken.

No, the lord of Twyll decided as his mantle soaked up the rain, the only way to make Rhys talk was to threaten physical harm to those he cared about. If Tremayne suggested that some of his men be hanged or flogged or that the woman, Rose, and that odd daughter of hers be either branded or thrown to the soldiers and used as whores, Rhys might break his silence. Tremayne's lip curled at the thought, for Peony was young. But this was not the time to be weak of stomach. His entire barony was at stake.

"M'lord." Percival's thin voice brought him out of his reverie. "Let us go inside, for 'tis time for you to make a plan. Cavan's army approaches."

The old man clutched his hood with bony fingers and though the sodden fabric covered most of his bald head, raindrops ran down his nose and dripped from its tip.

"Aye. 'Tis well past time, old man," Tremayne grumbled and started walking toward the keep. His boots sank in the mud, but he barely noticed as he thought aloud. "The men who were to go out and ambush Cavan's army will remain in the castle a while longer."

"If you wish, m'lord."

"I do. First we find the witch. I want every soldier to search this keep until she is discovered."

They walked up the steps to the great hall. "And what if she isn't found?"

"She will be."

"She is but a woman—a nuisance, nothing more."

"Nay, Percival, this is where you are wrong." Ignoring a greeting from a guard at the door, Tremayne strode to the fire and threw off his mantle, letting it fall onto a bench where it dripped onto the rushes. Wondering whether his old friend could be trusted or was a Judas like so many others, he said, "Finding this woman is the key to defeating the bastard and uncovering those traitors who had joined with him." He held up a finger as he thought. "When Rhys knows we have her and her life is threatened, he will offer up his spies to save her."

Percival let out a long, low sigh and tossed off his hood. His face was ruddy from the cold, his lips a color akin to that of a mussel's shell. "I think not. He is loyal to those men. He would not give up so many lives for one."

"But a woman changes a man's thinking." He thought of Rhys's betrayal, how the bastard had accepted any kind of punishment in order to save Anna years before. "Rhys would die himself, turn traitor to all those who trust in him, give up any treasure or friend, to save the woman he loved."

"And ye think he loves this one?"

"No, Percival, I do not think it," he said, wondering why the fire's hot breath could heat his skin but wasn't able to chase the winter from his soul. "Nay," he admitted with a sigh, "I know it."

Spying a page, he snapped his fingers and ordered wine for himself and the old man. 'Twas true. He knew that Rhys loved this woman, and that disturbing thought brought him the only hint of joy he'd felt since seeing the bastard in chains.

"Do we know why the woman dared come here?" he thought aloud, then shook his head for he couldn't answer the question himself. Did she have the magical stone, the dark emerald of Twyll? Was she the daughter of Lord Gilmore and Lady Farren? If 'twas true, where had she been all these years and why would she appear now, just as Cavan was making his claim?

The page returned with two mazers, offered one to

Tremayne, then handed the other to the older man.
Percival took a long swallow and let out a loud
"aahh," as the wine slid down his throat. "And she
has the stone to prove that she is daughter of
Gilmore?"

"According to the girl," Tremayne said.

"So is she here to cause trouble?"

"Why else?" Tremayne paced in front of the fire,
disturbing the dogs, who thumped their tails in the
rushes and stared up at him lazily. Worthless spotted
beasts.

"To seek the truth?"

"Mayhap."

"From whom?"

Tremayne's fingers drummed around the base of his
cup as he thought. "She was seen by the watchtower
that old Father Simon calls home, was she not?"

"Coming out of it, according to Sylvie, the butcher's
wife. She and her daughter, little Isabel, spied the
woman. Now, Sylvie, she's been known to spin a tale
of two, but this time, it seems, she be tellin' the truth
about a beautiful strange woman that had been in the
north tower."

"So this woman—the stranger—must've been going
to meet someone or to visit the old priest," Tremayne
thought aloud. "No one else is in that tower."

"Aside from the watchman. And Quinn."

"Quinn?" Tremayne froze. Images of the lad skulking around in the shadows slid through his mind and
danced in forbidden, deceitful territory.

"Aye, the lad is known to spend time with the old
priest."

That much was true. A knot tightened in Tremayne's stomach. Surely his own son would not . . . nay,
he would not think it. Never!

"So the woman seeks out the old priest. Why?" Tremayne frowned darkly and wondered at this twist, and a new thought, warm and sweet as honey in the sun, came to him, chasing away his worst fears. Rhys would have to be killed.

There was no choice but to hang the traitor, but 'twas too simple, too quick and painless for a criminal who had caused him so much pain. He needed to suffer and feel the pain of humiliation that Tremayne had endured, not only when the bastard had been born to a whore but later when he'd had the audacity to rape Anna, the woman that was to be Tremayne's bride.

Would it not be sweet justice to bed the one woman Rhys loved—this witch? "You think this woman be beautiful?" he asked, gazing up at the high ceiling, now darkened with smoke and cobwebs.

"The few who saw her all agreed."

For the first time in a long while Tremayne's manhood stirred. The thought of mounting this particular comely woman—the bastard's witch—one with enough courage to sneak into his castle, brought a tightening to his gut. Unexpectedly, his cock hardened a bit.

Mayhap this wench was the one who could bring his old member back to life. Ah, 'twould be sweet, sweet vengeance.

"Call for the watchman, Father Simon, and anyone else who was in the tower today. I'll speak with each of them."

"And Quinn?"

He hesitated. Then nodded. "Aye, the lad as well." Did he hear a swift intake of breath in the hallway or was it his overzealous imagination again? No matter. Other, more pleasant ideas kept him occupied. "Would it not be a bitter turn for Rhys if I were not only to bed his woman but marry her as well?" he asked suddenly, as soon as the thought struck him.

"Marry her?"

"You have always said I need a wife."

"But . . . but . . . you know this woman not!" Percival sputtered. "She . . . she could practice the dark arts or call up the spirits or—"

"She has the dark emerald, does she not?" Tremayne cut in. "What if she be the true daughter of Lady Farren and Lord Gilmore?" He took a long swallow of wine and finally felt his blood begin to warm. "Would it not be wise to meld the two houses—to rule with mine enemy, as opposed to fighting her?"

"But you know not that she is the real heir, nor that she would agree."

"Oh, she would agree," Tremayne was certain. "There are ways to ensure her submission."

"I do not think—"

"Send for the guard and the priest and the rest of the lot who were in the tower today." As Tremayne warmed to his plan, he became impatient. This would be perfect. "We must find the woman. Now!"

"Father Simon—"

"I know, I know. He speaks not, but today will be different."

"What about your son?"

Tremayne scowled into the blood-red depths of his wine. What was it about his boy that made him chase after the old silent man of God? 'Twas odd. But then, everything about Quinn was. Older than his years, he often stared at Tremayne with troubled, haunted eyes.

"Aye, find him as well." Mayhap the boy had seen something. Tremayne tossed back his wine, smelled the mingled scents of dogs, smoke, and wet wool as his mantle started to dry, and heard the barest scrape of a boot move off down the hall.

Was someone watching him?

A man he trusted?

A spy? For Cavan of Marwood?

One of Rhys's informants?

A gossiping wench?

Who?

"Be off with you," he ordered. He dropped his mazer onto the table. "And check with Regan. Find out why we haven't found the woman. God's teeth, how hard can it be to locate her?"

"Mayhap she be a witch and has cast a spell upon the castle."

"Aye," Tremayne sneered. "And mayhap I be Llywelyn ap Gruffydd, the last true prince of Wales."

Chapter Fourteen

"They caught him." Quinn was breathing rapidly as he flew into the dark chamber that had been Tara's prison for what seemed hours. Gasping, he nearly tripped over the stack of six crossbows and tumbled against the wall.

"Who?" she demanded, but she knew the answer. Her heart nearly stopped and her knees sagged. *No! No! No!*

"Rhys. The outlaw. My . . . my father . . ." He stumbled over the last word.

"Nay, oh . . . Rhys," she said, not wanting to believe a word that the boy spoke. Her heart tore and she tried to think. They had to save him. Somehow. Some way.

"Go on." James was more practical as he stacked the weapons that he and the boy had stolen with the help of some unnamed friends.

"He is to be taken to the dungeon and they—the soldiers—they be looking for you." He was nodding wildly as he stared at Tara.

"For me?" she replied.

"That makes the two of us. They search for me as well." In the shifting light, James stuffed arrows into quivers.

"Nay, three. Tremayne ordered me found as well,

and Father Simon and the guards and anyone who was in the tower today."

"Dear Lord." Tara was beside herself. Why had she been such a fool? So interested in her own destiny? What had it mattered? The thought of Rhys imprisoned brought her painful despair.

This is your fault, Tara. Yours. He followed you here, that horrid, nagging voice reminded her. She'd been stacking bolts for the pilfered crossbows, but now she stopped, dropped the short, heavy, barbed missiles, and concentrated on the boy.

"Where is Rhys now?" she asked him.

"In the dungeon, under the north tower."

"With the rest?" James asked.

"Aye." Quinn nodded so vigorously that a candle flame flickered and threatened to fail. "But he is to be put in a separate cell."

"Good."

"Good?" Tara demanded. "There is no good in this." Unable to stand another minute of being cooped up, she began walking the length of the small room. There had to be a way to free Rhys. There had to be.

"We will make it so," James said. "But we will have to work fast. As soon as darkness falls, we must leave this place with the weapons and disburse them to those who are our allies."

"Have you many?" she asked, hardly daring to hope. Hiding in this dank crypt, knowing that she was doing nothing while the candles burned low and the walls dripped, added to her case of nerves.

"A few." James's smile twisted at the irony.

"Who are they?"

"Only I know," he said with a finality that warned her he would never divulge his secrets. "Why are the soldiers looking for the lady?" he asked the boy.

" 'Tis said she is a witch. The girl—Peony—she told Tremayne that Tara has a magic ring that she used to bewitch Rhys." He said Tremayne's name with a snarl, and Tara wondered about this odd boy, a lad who would turn against the man who had raised him, a child who embraced the notion that he was sired by a rogue outlaw. In his own way, Quinn was as odd as was Peony, the lovestruck girl who seemed so adoring of Rhys that she would do anything to champion her cause, to win his heart.

"Is this true?" James asked, and Tara shook her head. "Have you this ring?"

"Nay, but I did," she admitted, feeling the fool. "It . . . it was taken from me."

"Stolen?"

"By Rhys."

"The master thief." James, who was squatting, rocked back on his heels and ignored the stack of longbows he'd been counting. "So now Tremayne has the ring."

She hesitated. "Rhys planned to give it to Abelard. I know not if he did."

James sighed. "But Tremayne believes you have it still?"

"I know not."

"There is more," Quinn insisted. "I overheard Tremayne telling Percival that 'twould be sweet justice if he were to . . . to . . . be with the lady as some kind of repayment for Rhys and . . . my mother. He . . . he even talked of marriage."

"Marriage," Tara whispered, appalled and stunned. Her stomach roiled at the thought.

"Aye, because he was married to my mother and she loved Rhys and . . . and 'twould be only fair . . ." Quinn's voice broke a bit and his jaw trembled for only a second before he regained control, but in that second, Tara caught a glimpse of the real boy who tried so hard to be a man.

"Think not of it," she said softly and resisted the urge to reach forward and rumple his hair or to pull his young body close and reassure him. Fearless and smart as he was, Quinn was but a boy.

A boy who took chances with his life by spying on the man who thought he'd sired him. And now he brought news of Rhys. Guilt wrapped around her heart and squeezed so painfully she knew her face had turned ashen. "Mayhap I should bargain with the lord."

"You?" James stopped short from gathering long-bows. "Why?"

"He might release Rhys and the others . . ."

"And why is that? Have you the stone?"

"Nay. But . . . if what Quinn says is true—"

Quinn was nodding furiously. "It is. I swear it on me poor mum's grave."

"I know, I know. It's not you I doubt," Tara reassured him.

" 'Twould do no good for you to give yourself up. Without the stone you have no bargaining power. Unless you want to agree to marry him."

The thought brought bile to her throat. She'd not met Tremayne of Twyll but had heard of his cruelty, not only from Rhys but from others as well. Had not her own mother warned her? *Oh, Lodema, I miss you.* She rubbed her arms and tried to think. There had to be a way to save Rhys. To save the others.

"If you were to approach Tremayne there would be yet another prisoner to help escape," said James. He motioned to the piles of weapons. "We will move these closer to the door to the bailey, in the stables. Then we will be ready."

"For what?" she asked, still not certain that she could trust this man who admitted to being a mercenary.

"For the end of Tremayne." His eyes glittered in the shadowy room. "Now, come. There is no time to tarry. Gather as many weapons as you can and follow me. Quinn, you as well."

Tara grabbed several longbows, James lugged two of the six or seven crossbows that he'd managed to steal, and Quinn slipped two quivers filled with arrows upon his back.

Morrigu, help us. Help us all, Tara silently prayed as she pretended to go along with James's plan.

But she wasn't convinced that throwing in their lot with Lord Cavan was the answer. The new lord of Marwood was an impostor to the barony of Twyll, a warrior interested only in his own selfish gains.

Should James's plan fail, Tara would have to barter herself for Rhys's release. 'Twas she who had dragged him into this war, and she would not let him give up his life for her. Again she sent up a prayer and hoped that God was listening.

Rhys stumbled down the stairs. The stench of the dungeon permeated the air.

Every bone in his body ached. His head throbbed. His muscles felt as if they'd been turned to mush. But the fight had been worth every bruise and cut he'd suffered. Each blow he'd taken to his chin and even the spittle that had run down his face was a humiliation he would have gladly gone through again, for now, hidden in his fingers, he had a weapon.

"In with ye!" The fat jailer opened a cell door,

pushed him inside, then unlocked the chain that bound his hands behind him. Rhys clutched the barbed arrowhead hidden in his fist so tightly that it drew blood.

"The lord 'e's gonna want ta 'ave a word with ye, so clean up from the bucket there and make yerself presentable."

Rhys didn't respond but held fast to his tiny blade. The dungeon with its smells of rot and waste, smoke-blackened walls, and sense of despair ebbing from souls without any hope brought back memories he'd kept locked away for years. Jaw clenched tight, he remembered waiting in this very cell and listening for Tremayne's boots as he stormed down the stone steps, knowing what fate held for him. The posts where he'd been strapped and flogged were still in place, ready for the next victim his half brother wanted to whip into submission.

The little bit of metal Henry had passed to him during the fight would be his way out of this dungeon. His freedom. And the freedom of those men and women who were here because of him. A simple arrowhead would give him an advantage, so that he could find Tara and save her from . . .

"Sir Rhys!" A girl's voice. He glanced over his shoulder to the next cell and spied Pigeon, her face white as death, her hair matted and tangled. She stared at him with round, fearful eyes. "What happened?" Small feet flying, she nearly tripped over the old bones and filthy straw lying upon the cell floor, then flung herself against the rusting bars. Her tiny, dirty hands gripped the cold metal and, sliding to her knees, she pressed her body as close to his as possible. "How did they catch you?" she whispered, her small face drawn into a knot of worry.

"Shh, lass." Rosie waddled over, only to sigh. Crossing her heavy breasts with swift, practiced fingers, she whispered, "Saints be with us." She shook her head in despair as she studied Rhys. "I believed, I truly did, that with ye still free we had a chance, but now—"

"Hey! He left us! Threw us to the bloody wolves, he did!" A voice Rhys recognized as belonging to Leland echoed throughout the dark chamber. Rushlights burned low and gave off only the barest light. Smoke crawled across the blackened ceilings, permeating the cells, clinging to the walls, tinging the stale air of this suffocating cage.

"Hush!" Kent this time. "We be with you, Rhys!"

Another voice, this one belonging to Benjamin, agreed, "Aye, Rhys, ye can count on me."

"And me!"

"Hmph."

"Shut up, all of ye! Prisoners ye be." The jailer spat on the floor in front of Rhys's cell. "Ye can claim yer allegiance from now until forever, but it matters not. Half of ye will be dead in a week, the rest will rot a while longer, then die as well." He rubbed the stubble that covered the thick folds of flesh that had once been his chin. "Speak no more or I'll see that ye do na eat fer a day or two."

"The slop ye feed us here isn't fit for the castle hogs," Rosie chimed in. "Now, if the lord could see his way to allowin' me to help in his kitchen—"

"And have ye poison him?" The guard laughed.

"And ye as well," Rosie said sassily, as if she were flirting with the obnoxious animal who held the keys.

"Well, ye've got spunk, woman, I'll give ye that. Careful or I might come in and have me way with ye."

"Oh, would ye now?" Rosie said with a laugh. Rhys couldn't believe his ears. Rose was not a woman who gave away her charms. Many men had tried over the years, but she'd rebuffed each and every one, saying that no man could ever replace her poor, dear dead husband.

"Aye, and that lass of yers too."

"Nay!" There wasn't a hint of flirting or laughter in her voice now. "If 'tis me ye want, we'll see if ye be man enough to handle me, but touch my daughter and I'll rip off yer privates and stuff 'em down yer throat with me own hands."

The guard sidled up to Rosie's cell. "Or with yer mouth and throat, woman?"

"Mayhap."

Bile climbed Rhys's throat. He opened his mouth to speak, but the glance Rose shot him stilled his tongue.

Adjusting her scarf, she let a tendril of graying red hair escape. "Ye never know what a woman might do for the right man."

The jailer thought for a moment, and the cells were deathly quiet. Pigeon stared at her mother in petrified horror.

"Don't be thinkin' ye be pullin' some trickery on me," the guard warned as his gaze swept the interior. "Rosie, here, would only give herself to me if she thought she might find a way to escape."

"Nay!" Rose said swiftly. " 'Tis not my freedom I'd bargain for, but I would give meself to ya if my daughter could be spared. That be me promise."

"Mum, no—" Pigeon cried.

"Hush!" The jailer's eyes narrowed, and Rhys, through his pain and swollen eyes, envisioned the battle being waged in the fat man's head. Could he trust a woman who was the baron's prisoner—nay. But would she offer herself up for her daughter's life? 'Twas hard not to believe that a mother would do anything to spare her child.

Rhys didn't know the answer, but just the thought made his blood turn to lava and his fist tighten over the sharp metal barb that was his way out.

He would gather his strength and then strike.

Soon.

Before Rose did anything foolish.

And before Tara was discovered.

"Twyll is just over that rise." Cavan, astride a sorrel steed with crooked white blaze and stockings, pointed to a wooded hill as the last of his army rounded a bend not far ahead. 'Twas close to nightfall and the sky was dark with swollen clouds that poured rain.

"I've been there, many times," Abelard remarked and couldn't quell the feeling that he'd cast his lot with the wrong side. Aye, he hated Tremayne, and his stub of an index finger was only part of his anger, but in the time he'd been with Cavan he'd found the young ruler to have no interests other than his own.

Not unlike yourself, especially as a younger man, he thought as the two men advanced upon the troops.

Were you foolish to trust him with the ring? What if he betrays you? Or what if he loses? You gave up a fortune for a chance to destroy Tremayne.

Aye, and 'twould be worth it.

Long had Abelard waited for this battle, and now he smelled it, simmering in the air—the scent of war yet to be waged, the heightened tension in the men, the crackle that surged through strained, nervous conversations, each man wondering if it would be his last yet each believing himself to be immortal and anxious for the chance to prove it.

As they rounded a bend, Abelard caught his first glimpse of the size of the army. Hundreds of foot soldiers, dozens of knights on horseback, and wagons filled with supplies. The wheels of the carts turned slowly in the mud, the oxen and horses strained at their yokes, and the heavy battering ram, dragged on small, mud-caked wheels, seemed to inch along.

" 'Twill take forever," Cavan grumbled, his handsome face twisted in irritation. Abelard had seen the like—young cubs eager for their first battle and taste of blood, with no patience for the execution of a well-thought-out strategy.

Cavan rode his nervous horse to the wagon master, who was urging the team of oxen dragging the battering ram. "Move these beasts faster!"

"They're laborin' as it is, m'lord. There be nothing more I can do."

Abelard agreed. He watched as the two beasts threw their combined weight against the yoke. Huge muscles straining, heads and horns low, drool and tongues hanging from their mouths as rain pelted their tawny hides, they slogged through the mud.

"Then get some men to help push and keep the wheels clean!" Cavan's steed, an anxious animal, pranced and minced as he attempted to hold it in check, not letting it gallop ahead. "You and you—yes, you!" he ordered, pointing at some foot soldiers who were lagging behind. "Help this man out. We have little time!"

Wheels creaked as they slowly turned, the hoofprints of hundreds of horses mashed the road along with the wheel ruts that carved deep grooves into the earth. Piles of manure were trampled and Cavan's army, large and ready for battle, moved forward.

To Twyll.

To Tremayne.

To a final stand.

Abelard's fingers, deep in his gloves, sweated with

anticipation while cold winter rain slithered down his
nose and cheeks. Blinking against the icy drops, he
embraced the storm, for he considered early darkness
a good omen.

Lightning forked in the sky and thunder boomed
across the land, causing the horses to jump.

Aye, a very good sign.

By this time tomorrow, Tremayne of Twyll would
be defeated or Abelard would be dead.

Either way, the battle that had burned bright in his
soul for a large part of his life would finally be over.

Calming his prancing horse, he turned slightly,
heard a movement over the rush of rain, and twisted
in the saddle.

Zzzttt.

His body jerked. Pain burned through his chest.
Hot. Wet. Something was wrong. He looked down and
saw the shaft of an arrow above his right breast and
blood, his own blood, weeping from the wound.

"Ah!"

"God!"

A man's howl of pain.

A horse's scream.

Suddenly the mantle of darkness turned against
them. Soldiers fell as arrows hissed from the cover of
the trees.

Abelard reached for his sword, but the world swam
before his eyes. He bit his lip so hard he tasted blood.
He dragged the heavy sword from its sheath, then
swayed. His horse buckled beneath him, seemed to
sink down, squealed in terror. The blackness behind
his eyes closed in on him, and he looked down to see
not one but two arrows buried in his body. The metal-
lic taste of blood filled his throat and he pitched forward, knowing he would surely die.

* * *

" 'Tis time!" James pushed open the trapdoor of the stables and slipped into the darkness. Tara was right behind him, with Quinn at her heels. They passed the weapons up through the small hole, and though she heard no voices, saw no one, she felt the presence of several men.

When there was but one crossbow left, Henry reached down for it, but Quinn refused. " 'Tis mine."

"Don't be silly, ye be only a lad."

" 'Tis mine," he insisted again.

"Now, lad—"

"Did I not help steal all the weapons? Crossbows, longbows, swords and knives?"

"Yea, but—"

"Did I not listen to the baron, let you know his plans?"

"You be just a boy." But as he said the words this time, James seemed to change his mind. "Just be careful. 'Tis a heavy weapon."

"Aye."

"Now, you know your positions," James said to the others, and there was the muted sound of boots making their way through straw. "You two stay with me," he ordered. For once Tara didn't argue. Any plan was better than none, and just the thought that they were doing something, *any*thing, to help Rhys sent her into motion. She helped Quinn through the opening, and then they closed the door and covered it with straw. In the darkness she could see little, but she heard the sound of horses, the whisper of straw moving as the animals shifted, the snorts of curiosity at having been disturbed. Familiar odors of horses, dung, and musty straw laced the cool, fresh scent of rain-washed air.

She and Quinn followed after James, keeping close

to him through the quiet keep. Only a few fires glowed from huts in the bailey, and the sheeting rain, though cold as death, provided a shifting veil that hid their movements.

She knew there were sentries posted in the towers, guards walking the curtain wall, knights searching the darkness for any sign of trouble. Yet she followed James. Fingers curled around the hilt of her little knife, she crept through the wet shadows toward the north tower.

Her heart banged against her ribs, her breathing sounded loud enough to wake the dead, and she tried to keep her wits—though 'twas difficult. The thought that Rhys was a prisoner in the dungeon and that soon she would see him again, free him, touch him, propelled her ever faster over the sodden grass to the tower.

Please God, keep him safe.

At the door James met another man, and they spoke softly for a few moments. The man nodded. James pulled Tara into the shadows at a corner behind the pillory. "Wait here," he whispered in her ear.

"Nay—"

"Aye, you must warn us if others approach."

Rather than linger to hear her arguments, he and the other man disappeared down the stairs. Quinn started after him, but Tara reached forward, her fingers twining in the wet wool of his mantle. "We must be patient," she reminded him.

"But 'tis my father's life." He wiped the rain from his face with one hand. The other held fast to his heavy weapon.

"Aye, I know. We aid him best by watching the door."

"Not both of us," he argued.

"Nay, James has a plan—"

"He is but a mercenary," Quinn said. "He said so himself."

"But you must wait—"

In the darkness the boy glared at her for a second, until she relaxed her grip. As soon as she did, he yanked his arm away and was off, running through the darkness toward the tower.

She started to yell but snapped her mouth shut and took off after him through the rain, her boots sliding, her fingers icy as they clutched the handle of her knife. Curse the boy! She'd nearly caught him when she saw the movement and her heart pounded in her throat. A dark shape, the looming figure of a soldier, appeared.

"Halt!" the man ordered.

Fear tore at Tara's soul.

"Who goes there? Oh . . . it be ye, lad."

Tara flattened herself against the wall of the tower and prayed that she hadn't been seen. Mayhap Quinn could talk his way out of this, but doubts still nagged at her. Slowly she edged closer, her back pressed so hard against the stones that she was certain they would make impressions upon her flesh.

"What're you doing about at this time of night?" the guard asked Quinn, but before there was an answer, he added, "Say, what's this? A crossbow? Why do you—no, wait! Do not aim that weapon—"

Thunk.

"Awwwww!" The man's horrid cry rang through the bailey.

"Who goes there!" This from a sentry on the curtain. Doors creaked open. The man was screaming, writhing, intent on raising the castle. Quinn shot forward, running ever faster through the blackness toward the tower, but 'twas too late.

Peasants poured out of their huts. The door to the great hall opened wide, and soldiers, backlit by the fires within and torches held aloft, filled the doorway. Swords gleamed malevolently.

Tara's heart leaped to her throat. They'd been found out. All would be lost.

With a snap of his fingers a tall man, presumably Tremayne, ordered his men out of the castle. They ran through the bailey, torches sizzling in the rain, heading toward the soldier who was yowling. "Down there," one of the sentries said, "in the bailey. Someone wounded Randall! The criminal's there, near the north tower. Grab him!"

No!

A dozen soldiers headed toward them, and Tara ran for Quinn, snatching at his cloak. "Come," she ordered, grabbing his arm and racing toward the stables. They could hide away again in the hut where the grain was stored and the tunnel opened. 'Twas only a few paces. Then, when things quieted, they would return to the dungeon and—

Lightning flashed, illuminating the grounds in a blue-white blink.

"Halt!" A huge man leaped down from a cart, landing in front of Tara. With a sizzling torch in one hand and a sword gleaming silver in the other, he blocked their path. "What the bloody hell?" he said as he recognized the boy in the weak circle of light from his torch. "Master Quinn? And who be you?" His eyes narrowed for an instant, and then, as if the doors of memory opened in his brain, allowing a shaft of understanding to pierce through, he roared, "Over here! 'Tis Master Quinn and the witch! She be taking him hostage!"

Nay! Tara's mind screamed. *Nay! Nay! Nay!* Her

legs were trembling, but she couldn't give up. She pulled Quinn in another direction. She wasn't stealing the boy. Never. Boots slipping on the wet grass, she ran, but at every turn a soldier appeared, blocking her way and giving chase.

Think, Tara, think! Use your wits! She was pulling Quinn toward the chapel when she felt a hand on her shoulder. Hard fingers dug into her flesh. *Nay!*

"Come with me, witch," a thin man ordered as he dragged her to a stop. Another soldier blocked their path. Quinn's legs skidded, and he nearly toppled over. Dogs barked from the kennels.

Tara whirled upon the man who held her. "Let me be," she ordered, her eyes locking with the soldier's. "Aye, I am a witch and if you don't leave me be, I'll level a curse on you that will swell your tongue and shrink your manhood."

"Nay—"

"By Morrigu, I will," she insisted, throwing off his hand and watching the doubts fill his eyes in the weak, reddish light.

" 'Tis nonsense." But his voice quivered slightly.

"Is it? So ye be willing to take a chance?" Closing her eyes and lifting an arm to the heavens, she whispered loudly enough for him to hear, "By earth and water, air and fire, save me now and cast mine enemy into the brine that swells the tongue and makes his cock—"

"Stop!" an authoritative voice commanded, and her eyes flew open. "So you would steal my son," said a tall man with lips that flattened over his teeth. She shivered, for this was not a man to be bullied. Pure hatred poured from him. "You be the bastard's witch," he said, and she realized with a feeling of horrid desperation that she was staring into the cold, hate-filled eyes of the baron of Twyll. Lord Tremayne. Her sworn enemy. "Leave my son be."

"I be not your son!" Quinn insisted, puffing out his chest.

Oh, God, no. Not now. "Nay, do not—" Tara warned, fearing that the wrath of hell was about to explode.

" 'Tis true. I . . . I be sired by Rhys."

Tremayne whirled on the boy and cuffed him with the back of his hand. "Never," he warned. "Never again say such heresy!"

Blood spurted and crawled down the corner of Quinn's mouth. Rebellion flared in his eyes, and he spat at the feet of the man who had raised him. " 'Tis true," he said. "If ye believe me not, talk to Father Simon."

"The silent priest?"

" 'Tis why he cut out his tongue. When me mum confessed to him."

"Nay," Tremayne whispered, but his voice was low, his color pale as a waning moon. He spied the crossbow still in the boy's hands. "What be this?"

"He wounded Sir Randall with it," one of the soldiers said as they gathered around, their swords gleaming red in the dying light of their torches.

"Simon cannot speak."

"But I can read," Quinn insisted. "And Father Simon . . . he writes in secret journals that he thought would not be discovered until his death. He told me as much when he found me with the books he'd hidden in the hole in the castle walls. 'Twas his way of holding on to the truth."

For a few seconds no one said a word. Rain pummeled the ground. Tremayne stared at the boy, and his expression changed from disbelief, to acceptance,

and finally to seething rage. His gaze swung to Tara.
Anger burned in his eyes and his fists clenched. Icy
rain dripped from his nose. "Bring the bastard to me,"
he ordered to the men surrounding them. "Into the
great hall. And," he pointed a damning finger at Tara,
"bring her and the boy as well. 'Tis time the truth be
known." As if another thought struck him, he added
through lips that barely moved, "And you, woman.
Show me the stone. The dark emerald of Twyll."

"But I have it not—"

"Then you'd better find it quickly. The fate of this
pathetic excuse of a boy," he grabbed Quinn by the
scruff of his neck, "your precious Rhys—oh, yes, I
know of you and him—and your own life depends
upon the damned stone."

"Halt! Hey!" The sentry's cry rang through the
bailey.

"What now?" Tremayne grumbled, but over his
voice there could be heard shouts and horses' hooves
and creaking wheels on the other side of the castle's
great walls.

"Halt! Who goes there? I say—bloody hell!"

Whistling over the wall, a huge boulder flew into
the bailey, landing with a jarring thud only a few feet
from the lord.

"Cavan," Tremayne growled, his expression turning
vexed. To one of his guards, he said, "Did not Regan
lead a garrison of troops to ambush the upstart?"

"Aye. Hours ago."

"Mayhap they were found out. Or defeated."

"Curse the fates!" Tremayne shook a fist at the sky.
"But 'tis nightfall. Only a fool would strike at night."

"Or a man anxious for battle who knows we would
be taken by surprise without the light of day on our
side," another man offered.

"Get the tar pots! Order everyone to his station!"

Tara knew this was her chance. She grabbed Quinn's hand, and while the soldiers were still staring at the boulder that signified the start of war, she yanked him toward the stables. But 'twas too late. One quick-footed soldier caught her and wrapped his huge arms around her waist. Her fingers coiled over the hilt of her knife. She drew back and plunged the blade into his arm.

With a yelp he let her go, but another man, larger and smelling foul, grabbed hold of her, taking her wrists in one large hand and shaking the weapon out of her hands.

Tremayne lunged and held fast to the boy he'd thought was his son.

Bam! The castle walls rocked.

"What the devil . . ." Horror washed over Tremayne's face.

Bam! Again.

The very ground shook.

" 'Tis the ram," Tremayne shouted. "As I said, all men to your stations! Now! And you," he glared at Tara again. "Oh, bloody Christ, haul them both into the keep," he ordered his guards as he motioned to Quinn and Tara.

Men and women flew out of their huts. Soldiers streamed through the open doors of the great hall and the barracks. Children cried and curses flew in the ensuing chaos.

Rain lashed from the heavens.

Lightning forked through the sky.

Horses screamed.

Dogs howled and thunder clapped loudly, in sharp report against the horrifying thud of the battering ram.

As Tara and Quinn were dragged toward the great

hall, all the men of Twyll became soldiers. Donning quivers, carrying longbows and hauling buckets of rocks, farmers, merchants, freemen, and serfs climbed up the tower stairs to the wall walks and the hoardings while the battering ram continued to crash against the main gate.

"Move!" The meaty-armed guard pushed her toward the keep. "Come on, you!" Her thoughts were with Rhys as she stumbled to the great hall. Was he locked away? Had James saved him? *Dear God, help him. Help us all.*

Rhys feigned sleep, though in truth he was tense, every muscle rigid, his ears straining as Rosie seduced the heavy guard. The man, taken by his own sense of manhood, had locked himself into the cell with her and was mauling her in front of all the prisoners.

Pigeon was curled in a corner of the stinking cell, her arms wrapped around her knees, her tiny body rocking against the horror that had befallen them all.

And all the while Rhys thought of Tara. Was she alive? Hidden away? Would he ever see her again? *Oh, sweet, sweet woman. I would give my life for yours.* His body ached, aye, but 'twas nothing to the pain in his heart when he thought she might already be dead or held by Tremayne. Silently he vowed to escape and find her, tell her he loved her, save her from whatever dire fate was now hers.

"A fine lass ye be, Rosie girl," the guard was saying as he kissed her neck and fondled her breasts through her coarse gown.

Rhys's teeth were sore. He held fast to his tiny weapon and waited; for he and Rose had exchanged glances, and in the split second when their gazes met, they had passed a silent message.

Now, with her skirts bunched and the obese jailer having his way with her, she moaned as if in ecstasy, clung to the man, and ever so slowly inched backward, toward the bars that separated her cell from Rhys's. "Ahh . . . William . . . ahhh . . ." she moaned as her rump pressed against the metal.

The jailer reached beneath her skirts and his face was mottled and red. He fumbled with his breeches and Rosie sighed low as if in great want. 'Twas sickening. "Oh, yes," she breathed. "Now . . . now . . . do it now!"

Rhys sprang. Like a snake striking, his arm shot between the bars past Rose's head, and he jabbed hard, his arrowhead burrowing deep into the fleshy neck of the jailer. Blood spurted and sprayed. The man roared in disbelief and grabbed his wound, only to have blood pulse between his fingers. Rosie snagged his knife, drew it swiftly from its sheath, and with all her strength thrust it deep into the dying man's chest. With more dexterity than Rhys would have thought her capable of, she untied the ring of keys from the jailer's belt and tossed them to Rhys.

There were footsteps on the stairs. Damn! Rhys unlocked his cell, tossed the keys to the men in another cage, then searched for a weapon.

Too late. Two men burst down the stairs. Rhys sprang, only to realize that he was attacking James. Keys jangled, cell doors creaked open, and all the prisoners were free.

"By the gods, don't you know me?" James asked once Rhys had realized his mistake and let him go. "Christ, it stinks in here."

Rhys had no time for small talk. "Where is Tara?"

"Waiting at the pillory with your son."

"My son?" What was James saying? For a second
Rhys didn't move. There was some mistake . . .

"Ah, I see you do not know. Well, there is no time
to explain it all. I only learned of it recently, but
Quinn, who has been raised by Tremayne, is not of
his seed at all. It seems, Bastard, that Anna was carrying your child when she married Tremayne.
Come . . . now . . . 'twill all be told later."

Bam!

Mortar crumbled.

The walls shook.

" 'Tis the ram!" James said. "Cavan has reached us.
Just as we planned." He handed Rhys a crossbow.
"There are more men above. Let us be off!"

Rhys needed no further encouragement. He flew up
the stairs, two steps at a time. Men followed behind
him, and his head pounded with the thought that Tara
was safe and he . . . he had a son. Anna's boy. Could
it be true? Was Quinn safe? At the top of the stairs
he shouldered open the door and with his small army
of weaponless thugs behind him exploded into the
melee of the terror-riddled bailey. Rain poured. Thunder cracked. Men shouted and children ran. A few
torches sizzled and soldiers manned the curtain.

On wobbling legs, he ran to the pillory, yelling her
name. "Tara! Tara!" No one hid at the pillory, nor
were there more weapons. He slapped angrily at the
water running through his hair and down his face. His
gaze swept the bailey. Where was she?

Then with desperate certainty he knew. His gaze
fell on the great hall.

Rhys's heart stopped for a minute. The ram banged
hard against the main gate. Metal crunched. Timbers
cracked. 'Twould not be long.

"I'll go to the murder hole above the main gate."

James said. "I'll kill the guard, let down a rope, and bring in more troops once the portcullis is destroyed. Then," he vowed, " 'twill be the end of Tremayne."

Rhys didn't stop to listen. He stripped James of his sword and with a weapon in each hand ran straight for the keep. Suddenly, after years of plotting, it mattered not if Tremayne was the ruler of Twyll, it made no difference to him if his half brother lived to a hundred and was the baron. Now all that mattered was the lives of the woman he loved and the boy who just might be his son.

Tara stood in front of the lord of Twyll. Three guards were at her back, swords drawn, razor-sharp blades ready to slay not only her but Quinn as well.

"So you have no stone," Tremayne accused, his eyes appraising every inch of her. He was seated in a thronelike chair on the dais, drumming his fingers on one arm. "Where is it?"

" 'Twas taken from me."

"Convenient."

"My father has it!" Quinn piped up, as if he gained pleasure in goading the man who had raised him.

Tremayne's furious gaze landed full force upon the boy. "Your *father*," he sneered. "Your father." His lips trembled in rage. "I raised you as my own flesh and blood. Cared for you. Loved you as my son. And how do you repay me? By turning on me!"

"You beat me!" Blood crusted at the corner of Quinn's mouth. "My back has scars."

As does Rhys's.

"Because I was trying to turn you into a man. Oh, why should I explain myself to you? Percival!" he yelled, and an elderly man with a walking stick appeared. "Where are the others? Father Simon and—"

Bam! Crack!

"Mayhap we should surrender, sire," the old man said, his eyes moving from Tara to the boy and back again.

"Never." Leaning forward, resting his hands on his knees, Tremayne looked directly into Tara's eyes, and she saw more than simple greed there. Hunger lurked as well. She could barely swallow, wanted to shrink away, but she held her head high.

"I need that stone," Tremayne explained slowly, his gaze lowering to her breasts. "To prove that Cavan isn't the heir of Gilmore."

"I have it not."

"Where is it?"

She shrugged. "I know not."

"You had it once."

"I had a ring. It was stolen from me."

"By whom?"

"I know not."

"By me." Rhys's voice boomed through the keep and Tara's heart soared. She turned, saw him appear from behind a curtain, a crossbow aimed directly at Tremayne's heart, a sword in his other hand.

"So, brother, you are here to kill me." Amazingly calm, Tremayne leaned back in his chair, but there was animosity between the two, and the smell of hatred vied with the scent of burning wood as the fire crackled and popped. Dogs growled and every soldier in the keep eyed the intruder. The Bastard. Half brother to the lord. Outlaw and criminal.

"Do not even think of being a hero, any of you," Rhys warned, as if reading their minds, "or your ruler is dead."

"You would not kill me." Tremayne seemed certain. In an instant he lunged like a cat, pulling Tara in front of him as a shield, and stood facing his half brother.

There was the splinter of wood. The castle shuddered. Tara struggled. The crossbow was pointed straight at her heart. "Go ahead," Tremayne encouraged. "Kill us both."

"No!" Quinn flung himself at the man who had raised him and the soldiers, weapons drawn, lunged forward.

Thunder clapped loudly.

Again the ram pounded, and suddenly footsteps thudded up the stairs and into the castle. Men stormed through, the guards were taken aback.

A soldier grabbed the boy and lifted him off his feet.

Tara shuddered at the smell of Tremayne, so close.

The door burst open. A guard starting to protest was rewarded with a sword through his heart.

"Surrender!" A man in wet, muddy finery ordered as he entered with an army of thugs. He was young, his hair raven-black, his green eyes flashing fire. "Murdering brute, if you value your life, you will kneel down to me."

"Cavan," Tremayne spat.

"Lord Cavan," the regal one replied.

"This be my keep."

"Stolen from my father." In one hand Cavan wielded a sword with a jeweled hilt, in the other a fine dagger, and on his finger he wore the ring. The dark emerald of Twyll winked in the firelight.

"Nay!"

" 'Tis true. Give up the woman and surrender," Cavan ordered. In the moment of hesitation, Tremayne's grip loosened. Tara rammed her elbow hard against his ribs, kicked his shin, and as he tried to cling to her, catapulted away from him.

Tremayne drew his sword and swung at her, but before the arc was completed, Rhys fired.

Sst. The bolt shot through the air, burying deep in Tremayne's chest. He fell back, dropped to the cold stones of the floor, and with an agonized groan gave up his life.

"Nay!" Percival cried. "Nay, nay, nay!" He fell onto Tremayne's body and wept bitter tears.

" 'Tis finished," Cavan said with a smile of satisfaction.

"Not quite." Rhys advanced upon the baron. "Ye be not the true issue of Gilmore. The ring was bought."

"Was it?" Cavan's eyes glittered with an evil fire. "Does it matter?"

"Tara be the true ruler."

"She has no proof. I have the stone. Twyll is mine." He walked toward the dais, intent on taking the lord's chair.

"Where is Abelard?"

Cavan frowned. "Dead. We were ambushed. He gave up his life."

"Nay!" Rhys's lips pulled back hard against his teeth.

" 'Tis true." Cavan's eyes met Rhys's grief-stricken gaze. "A pity. But not a tragedy."

Rhys looked as if his soul was scraped raw, but the new baron of Twyll didn't notice. "Clean up this mess," he ordered his men. "Put those who will not pledge their fealty to me in the dungeon. We will kill them, one a day, until the rest understand. And you." He glared at Tara with hatred. "You, witch, will be first."

"No, Cavan, I will be," Rhys said, raising his sword.

Cavan smiled at the thought of battle with the infamous outlaw. "So be it." He lifted his own elegant weapon and the crowd in the great hall hushed. No one dared breathe.

Cavan lunged, but not before Percival struck. With a small dagger hidden in his hand, he leaped upward, threw his body on that of the younger man and shoved his blade into Cavan's neck.

"Die, bastard," he hissed.

"By the saints, *nay!*" Cavan hit the floor, clutching his neck, blood covering the ring on his fingers, but from his pocket rolled another piece of jewelry, another ring identical to the one on his finger.

Tara couldn't move.

As Cavan gave up his last rattling breath, his clouded eyes found Tara's and he whispered, "Sister . . . twin."

Tara froze. Her body and mind seemed separated. She didn't believe a word of it, though she felt Rhys's strong arms surround her, knew 'twas he who was kissing her neck and whispering that all would be well.

A brother? A *twin* brother? Nay, it couldn't be true . . . and yet he was here with the rings . . . dead at her feet.

" 'Tis true," Henry, the stable master said. "I was there, driving the cart when Father Simon took the boy to Lord Innis of Marwood, then dropped off his twin sister with the old crone in the forest."

"Lodema," Tara whispered.

The great hall was filling with soldiers and peasants and laborers. Father Simon stood at the back of the room, and when Tara looked at him, he nodded and crossed himself, his job finished.

"Come, lad," Rhys said to Quinn, and he kissed Tara full on the lips. "You, lady, need rest. The boy needs to sleep."

"I will tend to him." Rosie insisted, and from the corner of her eye Tara saw the big woman take Quinn's hand.

"Come—" Rhys smoothed the hair from her cheek.

"Nay . . . I . . ." Stunned, she began to cry. Tears fell from her cheeks and Rhys kissed each one. Lifting her from her feet, he carried her up the stairs. "You are home, Tara."

"And what of you?"

Through her tears, she saw him smile. "I'm home, as well. With you, love, and with my son. Come now, lady of Twyll."

"No . . . wait . . . I cannot stay here. Not without you. I'll not be lady unless you be lord."

She heard laughter behind them and saw James at the door.

"Are you proposing to me, witch?" Rhys asked as they reached the second story of the keep. The rush-lights had burned low, 'twas nearly dark in the hallway.

"Nay, 'tis not a proposition," she said with the hint of a smile. " 'Tis a command."

He laughed then, held her close and whispered into her ear. "You have one night to convince me that I should be your husband."

"Only one?"

"Need you more?"

"I think not, outlaw," she admitted with a wicked little grin. "I think not."

Epilogue

The baby cried loudly, his little lungs straining.

" 'Tis your son," Tara said to her husband.

"Not yours?" Rhys turned over and looked down at his wife. Her breasts were full, her waist still thick from giving birth to their child two weeks earlier, but she was the loveliest woman he'd ever seen.

Never before had he felt such peace. As the lord of Twyll. *What great irony,* he thought, as the door to their chamber opened and Lodema, carrying the swaddled babe, entered.

"Abelard, he be hungry again," she said, and Tara tossed her black curls from her face.

"He always be hungry."

"Like his brother," Rhys said, for it seemed there was not enough food in all of Twyll and Gaeaf put together to keep Quinn's hunger at bay.

Lodema chuckled as she handed her grandson to his mother. "I never thought I'd see the day," she admitted and walked to the window to look out. From his position on the bed Rhys saw Father Simon walk along the edge of the bailey, as he always did. A secretive smile crossed the older woman's lips, and she clucked softly. From the doorway a mottled kitten emerged, dashing playfully through the rushes to rub against the old woman's leg.

"Ah, Luna, ye be not as smart as the first, but you're a sweet thing," she said as she picked up the kitten and stroked its soft back. "I had a vision last night," she said as she edged toward the door.

"Did you?" Tara was bent over her child as the babe pulled at her nipple and gurgled contentedly.

"Aye."

"What of?" Tara seemed not too interested as she brushed her son's downy head.

"Children. For you. Two sets of twins. Daughters they be."

"Nay," Tara said, lifting her eyes to look at her mother, but the old woman wasn't joking. "Six children shall ye have, Tara, the two boys now and two sets of daughters." With a wink, she added, "May they give you the gray hairs that ye gave me, daughter."

With that she was out the door.

"She knows not of what she speaks," Tara said, though she didn't seem certain. Rhys laughed and linked his hand through hers, the twin emeralds of their rings winking in the morning light.

"I would like to have a daughter someday."

"But only one."

"Four is a good number."

"Then you carry and bear them," she teased, and when he looked at her, their gazes caught, and as always when he stared at her, his breath was lost in his throat.

" 'Tis not possible."

"Unless I cast a spell upon you," she teased, lifting a sassy eyebrow.

"You have already, witch." he admitted and kissed her long on her lips. "You have already."

Dear Reader,

Dark Emerald is one of my favorite medieval romance novels. Set in thirteenth-century Wales, this book has all my favorite things: a touch of magic, a little of the paranormal, and a whole lot of adventure! (How fun is that?)

I admit it. I love Tara and Rhys's story: the lies, the secrets, the fear, and, of course, the love. From the first time Rhys sets eyes on Tara in the forest, when he spies her wearing nothing but a chain with a ring upon it, the dark emerald winking in the fading light, he's intrigued. From that moment on, he can't forget her and has to have her. (Even if he does think she's a witch!)

Dark Emerald is actually the second book in my Dark Jewels trilogy. The first book is *Dark Ruby*, the story of Lady Gwynn and her seduction of Trevin, a thief, in order to save her life. Then of course, *Dark Emerald* followed with Tara and Rhys's story. The third book is *Dark Sapphire*, where Lady Sheena, accused of a horrendous crime, sneaks aboard Captain Keegan's ship and becomes a stowaway fated to fall for the sardonic captain. Both *Dark Ruby* and *Dark Sapphire* are available as e-books, as is *Dark Emerald*.

I hope you love reading them as much as I did writing them.

If you want more information on any of my books, please visit my Web site, www.lisajackson.com, or become a fan on Facebook, where we have some lively discussions.

I'm so glad you picked up a copy of *Dark Emerald*! "'Tis my great pleasure!"

Enjoy!

—Lisa Jackson

The Dark Jewels Trilogy continues with
two sexy historical romances by Lisa Jackson. . . .

Dark Ruby

Glimmering in the dying firelight, the jewels in the ring winked a deep bloodred. Beckoning. Seducing. Begging to be taken by trained fingers.

From his hiding spot behind the velvet curtains, Trevin wet his dry lips, rubbed the tips of his fingers together, and tried to quiet his thundering pulse. At fifteen he was a thief and a good one, an orphaned waif who stole to survive. Never had he attempted to snatch anything so valuable as the ring left carelessly on the window ledge. But he was desperate and the jewels and gold would fetch a good price, mayhap enough to buy a decent horse since his efforts at stealing one had gone awry. Painful welts on his back, the result of the farmer lashing him with a whip, still cut into his skin and burned like the very fires of hell to remind him that he'd failed.

But not this time.

Now he would have the means to escape Rhydd and his sins forever.

He listened but the lord's chamber was quiet. Aside from the occasional tread of footsteps in the hallway, the rustle of mice in the fragrant rushes tossed over the stone floor of the castle, or the hiss of flames in the grate, there was no sound but the pounding of his heart.

Noiselessly he slipped between the drapes and stole across the rushes to the window, where he plucked his prize and stuffed it swiftly into the small pocket sewn into the sleeve of his tunic for just such spoils as this. Holding his breath, he started for the door, only to hear a breathless woman's voice coming from the hallway.

"In here, Idelle. Quickly."

Trevin's knees nearly gave way as he realized the lord's wife was on the other side of the oaken door. He had no choice but to duck back behind the curtain and hide himself in the alcove, where Baron Roderick's clothes were tucked. Help me, he silently prayed to a God who rarely seemed to listen.

The door swung open and a rush of air caused the fire to glow more brightly. Golden shadows danced upon the whitewashed walls.

Trevin dared peek through the heavy velvet and watched as Lady Gwynn yanked her tunic over her head, then tossed it carelessly onto the floor. With a bored sigh, she, now clad only in her underdress, dropped onto the bed.

Trevin's groin tightened at the sight of the lacy chemise against Gwynn's skin. Idelle, the old midwife and a woman many proclaimed to be a witch, shuffled into the room and closed the door behind her. Half blind and a bit crippled, Idelle held some kind of special power, and even though her ancient eyes were clouded a milky white, she seemed to see more than most people within these castle walls. 'Twas said that she had the uncanny gift of searching out a man's soul.

"'Tis the time," she said in a voice not unlike that of a toad. Carefully she set her basket of herbs and candles on a small table. She laid each wick upon a red-hot coal

from the fire until all the beeswax tapers were lit. Once
the flames were strong and flickering in the breeze,
Idelle reached into a pouch in her basket and dropped a
handful of pungent herbs over the table. Some sparked
in the candles' flames, and the scents of rose and myrtle
blended over the odor of burning oak.

"Then let's get it done." Squirming upon the coverlet,
Lady Gwynn lifted her chemise over her legs and hips.
Trevin was suddenly much too hot. Higher and higher
the chemise was raised until the sheer fabric was wad-
ded beneath her breasts.

Though he knew it was a sin, he could not drag his
eyes away from her near-naked body. White and supple in the quivering firelight, she rolled toward the old
woman.

Trevin clamped his jaw tight. He couldn't resist eyeing her flat white abdomen, the slight indentations between her ribs, and the nest of red-brown curls that
seemed to sparkle in the juncture of her legs.

His throat turned to dust. So this was what a noblewoman looked like beneath her velvet and furs. Oh,
what he wouldn't give to run one of his callused fingers
over that soft, irresistible skin.

"There ye be, lass. Now, let me see what ye've got."
Idelle knelt at the side of the bed, and her fingers, knotted with age, moved gently over the younger woman's
smooth belly. Groping and prodding, she murmured
something in the old language—a spell, mayhap—as it
was common knowledge that she prayed and offered
sacrifices to the pagan gods of the elders, just as the man
who had raised him, the sorcerer Muir, had. "By the
gods, 'tis no use." With a sigh, she shook her graying
head. Sorrow added years to a face that was barely a
skull with skin stretched over old bleached bones. "'Tis
barren ye be, lass. There is no babe."

"Nay!" Gwynn cried, but lacked conviction.

Sadly, Idelle clucked her tongue. "'Tis sorry I be and ye know it."

"And wrong you be! Oh, please, Idelle, tell me I am with child," she insisted desperately.

"Nay, I—"

"Hush! There is a child. There must be!" Stubborn pride flashed in the lady's eyes as if by sheer will a baby would grow within her womb. "Oh, dear God, you must be mistaken!" she whispered, though her chin wobbled indecisively.

Try as he might, Trevin couldn't draw his gaze away from her. She pushed her chemise upward to the juncture of her arms, and for the first time in his life, he saw a noblewoman, a beautiful lady, naked. He'd caught glimpses of serving wenches and whores, of course, but never before had he seen the wife of a baron. His mouth drew no spit as he looked upon the sweet roundness of her breasts. Her nipples were small and pink, reminding him of rosebuds. His damned manhood, always at the ready, became stiff.

"Touch me again. Try harder to feel the babe," Gwynn pleaded, though she seemed resigned, as if she understood her fate.

Regret drew Idelle's old lips into a knot. She laid the flat of her hand beneath Lady Gwynn's navel, closed her sightless eyes, and whispered a chant. Upon the bed, the naked woman lay perfectly still.

With a sigh, Idelle removed her spotted fingers. "There's nothing."

"What will I do?" Gwynn asked, swallowing hard.

"I know not."

Dark Sapphire

*B*am! Bam! Bam!

"What the bloody hell?" Keegan growled from his bunk.

"Captain, I hates to disturb ye, and ye know it, but there's trouble afoot. May I have a word with ye?"

Keegan opened a bleary eye. His cabin, lit only by a single flickering candle mounted in a lantern hung near his bed, swayed with the roll of the sea.

"Captain! Can ye hear me? 'Tis Hollis and I hate to wake ye, but I needs to speak with ye."

"Trouble?" Keegan repeated, his head feeling as if it might split wide-open.

"Aye!"

"Pirates?" God's eye, Hollis was always conjuring up the devil, certain there was a horrid looming disaster afoot. The old man seemed certain the *Dark Sapphire* was cursed to her very keel.

'Twas enough to try a man's patience. But then, he'd saved Keegan's life. Hollis was, and always had been, loyal and true. But a pain in the backside.

"Nay, Captain, there be no pirates," Hollis yelled.

"Are we taking on water? Is the ship sinking?"

"Nay, but—"

"Are the men planning a mutiny?"

"Nay, nay, not that I'm aware of, Captain, but—"

"Then, go away." Keegan rolled over in his small bunk and jammed his eyes shut.

"Nay—"

"Leave me be!" He was cross and had no time for the old man's pointless worries.

There was a pause; then Hollis's nasal whine yet again. He wasn't a man to give up. "If ye'd please jest let me have a word with ye, Captain Keegan. . . ."

"Bloody Christ." Snarling at the intrusion, his head thundering from too much ale and too little sleep, Keegan tossed back the fur covers and, without bothering with his dressing gown, threw open the door.

There was a gasp—for a second Keegan thought it sounded like a women's—from the dark stairwell. But that was impossible. There were no women aboard, and they'd set sail three days earlier. A gust of bracing wind cut through his skin. "What is it, Hollis?" he demanded as his eyes adjusted to the darkness. "And whatever it is, it had better be good."

"Oh, sweet Jesus, Captain, if ye'd be so kind as to cover up—" Hollis's round face was illuminated by a lantern he'd hung on a hook near the door. Above his scraggly beard, one cheek bore four red welts that had been scratched deep into his skin, his sparse hair stuck out at all angles, and one of his eyes was nearly swollen shut.

"What the devil happened to you?" Keegan asked as he noticed the rope, a thick coil that wrapped around Hollis's hands and trailed behind him and ended with a knot over the bound wrists of a captive.

A woman.

A dirty, bedraggled mess of a woman, but a woman nonetheless. Jesus Holy Christ, where did she come from?

"Tell your man to untie me," she ordered, tossing off the hood that had covered her head. Wild red hair caught in the candle glow as it framed a smudged face with high, prideful cheekbones and fierce blue eyes that cut him to the quick. Perfect teeth flashed white against her filthy skin. For a heartbeat he thought he knew her. There was something about her that instantly triggered a dark, forgotten memory that refused to spark. Nay, 'twas impossible. "I am not a slave! Nor will I be treated as one!"

"Who the hell are you?" He ignored the unlikely thought that he'd met her before.

"She's a stowaway—that's what she is."

"I asked her." Irritated, Keegan leaned a scarred shoulder against the doorframe and folded his arms over his chest. "What's your name?"

Aside from the howl of the wind and the roar of the sea, there was only silence. The bit of a woman had the audacity to hold his stare, and there was something in her eyes that gave him pause—something that tugged at the corners of his memory yet again. Had he seen her somewhere? Defiantly she raised that pointed little chin of hers.

"She ain't sayin', Captain," Hollis finally offered. "I found her in the hold, hiding behind the ale casks." He cleared his throat and shifted so that his shadow fell across Keegan's bare loins.

Keegan didn't give a damn what the woman did or didn't see. "What were you doing in the hold?" he demanded of the scruffy, prideful wench. "For that matter, what in God's name are you doing on my ship in the middle of the night?"

"Hidin'—that's what she was. And up to no good, let me tell you," Hollis answered in his raspy voice. "Nearly tore me apart, she did. Clawed and hissed and spat like a damned she-cat. This one's the spawn of Lucifer, I tell ye. She's cursed this ship, to be sure."

"Have you, now?" Keegan asked.

She didn't bat an eye, just met his gaze with the angry fire of her own. The barest trace of a smile slid across her lips. "Oh, yes, Captain," she confided in a husky voice. "As surely as the moon rises behind the clouds and the wind screams over the sea." She took a step toward him without a trace of fear. "I be a witch sure and true. I've sent many a fine ship to the depths of a watery hell, and if you do not set me free at the next port, all of the wrath of Morrigu will be upon you."

"Morrigu?" Hollis whispered, horrified, his eyes rounding above his beak of a nose, his skin ghostly pale. His throat worked. "The goddess of death," he whispered.

"Oh, she is much more than that," the woman taunted, turning to stare down the man who had the audacity to leash her. "Fate and war ride on her wings. Destiny is her companion." Despite her bonds, the she-devil advanced upon her captor, and though much smaller than Hollis, she seemed to tower above him as he cowered in fear. "Morrigu's vengeance will be swift and harsh. Trust me. She will have no mercy on you, you pathetic insect of a man, or you, Captain Keegan." Whirling suddenly, she faced him. Fierce eyes, dark with the night, bored into him. Wild red hair caught in the wind. "This ship and all those aboard will be doomed to the most painful and vile of fates if I but say so. Death will be a blessing."

New York Times bestselling author

Lisa Jackson

SORCERESS

THE WATCHER: He smells her. Feels her. Knows she is
coming. Chosen by the Fates, she is the one. Only she can lift
the curse of darkness. But he will stop her—and he will
sacrifice her.

THE WOMAN: Flame-haired and green-eyed, Bryanna looks
enchanted but has always felt cursed, plagued by mysterious
visions and voices. Bound by destiny to save an innocent life,
Bryanna follows her path alone—until she meets a stranger
deep in the woods.

THE WARRIOR: Gavyn is a wanted man, as dark and
dangerous as the wolf that shadows his footsteps. But his touch
is electric, and he has much to teach—if Bryanna is
willing to learn...

**Available wherever books are sold or at
penguin.com**

S0324

Penguin Group (USA) Online

What will you be reading tomorrow?

Tom Clancy, Patricia Cornwell, W.E.B. Griffin,
Nora Roberts, William Gibson, Catherine Coulter,
Stephen King, Dean Koontz, Ken Follett,
Nick Hornby, Khaled Hosseini, Kathryn Stockett,
Clive Cussler, John Sandford, Terry McMillan,
Sue Monk Kidd, Amy Tan, J. R. Ward,
Laurell K. Hamilton, Charlaine Harris,
Christine Feehan...

You'll find them all at
penguin.com
facebook.com/PenguinGroupUSA

*Read excerpts and newsletters, find tour schedules
and reading group guides, and enter contests.*

Subscribe to Penguin Group (USA) newsletters
and get an exclusive inside look
at exciting new titles and the authors you love
long before everyone else does.

PENGUIN GROUP (USA)
us.penguingroup.com